SHON'JIR
THE SONG OF PASSINGS

From Dark beginning
To Dark at ending—
Between them a Sun,
But after comes Dark,
One ending.

From Dark to Dark
Is one voyage.
From Dark to Dark
Is our voyage.
And after the Dark,
O brothers, o sisters,
Come we home.

C.J. CHERRYH

THE FADED SUN: SHON'JIR

Book Two

DAW BOOKS, INC.
DONALD A. WOLLHEIM, PUBLISHER

375 Hudson Street, New York, NY 10014

FIRST DAW PRINTING, APRIL 1979

6 7 8 9 10 11 12 13

DAW TRADEMARK REGISTERED
U.S. PAT. OFF. AND FOREIGN COUNTRIES
—MARCA REGISTRADA,
HECHO EN U.S.A.

PRINTED IN THE U.S.A.

To Elsie Wollheim . . .
for being Elsie

Chapter One

THE MRI was still sedated. They kept him that way constantly, dazed and bewildered at this place that echoed of human voices and strange machinery.

Sten Duncan came to stand at the mri's bedside as he did twice each day, under the eye of the security officer who stood just outside the windowed partition. He came to see Niun, permitted to do so because he was the only one of all at Kesrith base that knew him. Today there was a hazy awareness in the golden, large-irised eyes. Duncan fancied the look there to be one of reproach.

Niun had lost weight. His golden skin was marked in many places with healing wounds, stark and angry. He had fought and won a battle for life which, fully conscious, he would surely have refused to win; but Niun remained ignorant of the humans who came and went about him, the scientists who, in concert with his physicians, robbed him of dignity.

They were enemies of mankind, the mri. Forty years of war, of ruined worlds and dead numbered by the millions— and yet most humans had never seen the enemy. Fewer still had looked upon a mri's living and unveiled face.

They were a beautiful people, tall and slim and golden beneath their black robes: golden manes streaked with bronze, delicate, humanoid features, long, slender hands; their ears had a little tuft of pale down at the tips, and their eyes were brilliant amber, with a nictitating membrane that protected them from dust and glare. The mri were at once humanlike and disturbingly alien. Such also were their minds, that could grasp outsiders' ways and yet steadfastly refused to compromise with them.

5

In the next room, similarly treated, lay Melein, called she'pan, leader of the mri: a young woman—and while Niun was angular and gaunt, a warrior of his kind, Melein was delicate and fine. On their faces both mri were scarred, three fine lines of blue stain slanting across each cheek, from the inner corner of the eye to the outer edge of the cheekbone, marks of meaning no human knew. On Melein's sleeping face, the fine blue lines lent exotic beauty to her bronze-lashed eyes; she seemed too fragile to partake of mri ferocity, or to bear the weight of mri crimes. Those that handled the mri treated her gently, even hushed their voices when they were in the room with her, touched her as little as possible, and that carefully. She seemed less a captive enemy than a lovely, sad child.

It was Niun they chose for their investigations—Niun, unquestionably the enemy, who had exacted a heavy price for his taking. He had been stronger from the beginning, his wounds more easily treated; and for all that, it was not officially expected that Niun survive. They called their examinations medical treatments, and entered them so in the records, but in the name of those treatments, Niun had been holographed, scanned inside and out, had yielded tissue samples and sera—whatever the investigators desired—and more than once Duncan had seen him handled with unfeeling roughness, or left on the table too near waking while humans delayed about their business with him.

Duncan closed his eyes to it, fearing that any protest he made would see him barred from the mri's vicinity entirely. The mri had been kept alive, despite their extensive injuries; they survived; they healed; and Duncan found that of the greatest concern. The mri's personal ethic rejected outsiders, abhorred medicine, refused the pity of their enemy; but in nothing had these two mri been given a choice. They belonged to the scientists that had found the means to prolong their lives. They were not allowed to wake—and that too was for the purpose of keeping them alive.

"Niun," Duncan said softly, for the guard outside was momentarily staring elsewhere. He touched the back of Niun's long-fingered hand, below the webbing of the restraint; they kept the mri carefully restrained at all times, for Niun would tear at the wound if he once found the chance: so it was feared. Other captive mri had done so, killing themselves. None had ever been kept alive.

"Niun," he said again, persistent in what had become a twice-daily ritual —to let the mri know, if nothing more, that someone remained who could speak his name; to make the mri think, in whatever far place his consciousness wandered; to make some contact with the mri's numbed mind.

Niun's eyes briefly seemed to track and gave it up again, hazing as the membrane went over them.

"It's Duncan," he persisted, and closed his hand forcefully on the mri's. "Niun, it's Duncan."

The membrane retreated; the eyes cleared; the slim fingers jerked, almost closed. Niun stared at him, and Duncan's heart leaped in hope, for it was the first indication the mri had made that he was aware, proof that the mind, the man he knew, was undamaged. Duncan saw the mri's eyes wander through the room, linger at the door, where the guard was visible.

"You are still on Kesrith," Duncan said softly, lest the guard hear and notice them. "You're aboard probe ship *Flower*, just outside the city. Pay no attention to the man. That is nothing, Niun. It's all right."

Possibly Niun understood; but the amber eyes hazed and closed, and he slipped back into the grip of the drugs, free of pain, free of understanding, free of remembering.

They were the last of their kind, Niun and Melein—the last mri, not alone on Kesrith, but anywhere. It was the reason that the scientists would not let them go: it was a chance at the mri enigma that might never, after them, be repeated. The mri had died here on Kesrith, in one night of fire and treachery—all, all save these two, who survived as a sad curiosity in the hands of their enemies.

And they had been put there by Duncan, whom they had trusted.

Duncan pressed Niun's unfeeling shoulder and turned away, paused to look through the dark glass partition into the room where Melein lay sleeping. He no longer visited her, not since she had grown stronger. Among mri she would have been holy, untouchable: an outsider did not speak to her directly, but through others. Whatever she endured of loneliness and terror among her enemies was not worse than humiliation. Her enemies she might hate and ignore, slipping into unconsciousness and forgetting; but before him, whose name she knew, who had known her when she was free, she might feel deep shame.

She rested peacefully. Duncan watched the gentle rise and fall of her breathing for a moment, assuring himself that she was well and comfortable, then turned away and opened the door, murmured absent-minded thanks to the guard, who let him out of the restricted section and into the outer corridor.

Duncan ascended to the main level of the crowded probe ship, dodging white-uniformed science techs and blue-uniformed staff, a man out of place in *Flower*. His own khaki brown was the uniform of the SurTac, Surface Tactical Force. Like the scientific personnel of *Flower*, he was an expert; his skills, however, were no longer needed on Kesrith or elsewhere. The war was over.

He had become like the mri, obsolete.

He checked out of *Flower*, a clerical formality. Security knew him well enough, as all humans on Kesrith knew him—the human who had lived among mri. He walked out onto the ramp and down, onto the mesh causeway humans flung across the powdery earth of Kesrith.

Nothing grew on the white plain outside, as far as the eye could see. Life was everywhere scant on Kesrith, with its alkali flats, its dead ranges, its few and shallow seas. The world was lit by a red sun named Arain, and by two moons. It was one of six planets in the system, the only one even marginally habitable. The air was thin, cold in shadow and burning hot in the direct rays of Arain; and rains that passed through it left the skin burning and dry. Powdery, caustic dust crept into everything, even the tightest seals, making men miserable and eventually destroying machinery. In most places Kesrith was uninhabitable by humans, save here in the lowland basin about Kesrith's sole city, on the shore of a poisonous sea: one small area where moisture was plentiful, amid geysers and steaming pools, and crusted earth that would not bear a man's weight.

No men were indigenous to Kesrith. The world had first belonged to the dusei, great brown quadrupeds, vaguely ursine in appearance, velvet-skinned and slow-moving, massively clawed. Then had come the mri, whose towers had once stood over toward the high hills, where now only a heap of stone remained, a tomb for those that had died within.

And then had come the regul, hungry for minerals and wealth and territory, who had hired the mri to fight against humankind.

It was the regul city that humanity had inherited, humans

the latest heirs to Kesrith: a squat agglomerate of ugly buildings, the tallest only two stories, and those stories lower than human standard. The city was laid out in a rectangle: the Nom, the sole two-storied building, was outermost, with other buildings arranged in the outline of the square before it. All streets followed that bow about the Nom square—narrow streets that were designed for regul transport, not human vehicles, streets crossed by the fingers of white sand that intruded everywhere on Kesrith, constantly seeking entry. At the left of the city was the Alkaline Sea, that received the runoff of Kesrith's mineral flats. Volcanic fires smouldered and bubbled under the surface of that sea as they did below that of the whole valley, that had once been a delicate land of thin crusts and mineral spires—a land pitted and ruined now by scars of combat.

There was a water-recovery plant, its towers extending out into the sea. Repairs were underway there, trying to release the city from its severe rationing. There had been a spaceport too, on the opposite side of the city, but that was now in complete ruin, an area of scorched earth and a remnant of twisted metal that had once been a regul and a mri ship.

Of ships onworld now, there was only *Flower*, an outworlds probe designed for portless landings, squatting on a knoll of hard rock that rose on the water-plant road. Beside her, an airfield had been improvised by mesh and by fill and hardening of the unstable surface—work that would quickly yield to the caustic rains. Nothing was lasting on Kesrith. Endure it might, so long as it received constant attention and repair; but the weather and the dust would take it in the end. The whole surface of Kesrith seemed to melt and flow under the torrential rains, the whole storm pattern of the continent channeled by mountain barriers toward this basin, making it live, but making life within it difficult.

It was an environment in which only the dusei and the mri had ever thrived without the protections of artificial environments; and the mri had done so by reliance on the dusei.

To such an inheritance had humanity come, intruders lately at war with the mri and now at war with their world, almost scoured off its face by storms, harassed by the wild dusei, befriended only by the regul, who had killed off the mri for them, an act of genocide to please their human conquerors.

Duncan traversed the causeway at his own slow pace, savoring the acrid air. His bare face and hands were painfully assaulted by Arain's fierce radiation even in this comparatively short walk. It was noon. Little stirred in the wild during the hours of Arain's zenith; but humans, safe within their filtered and air-conditioned environments, ignored the sun. Human authority imposed a human schedule on Kesrith's day, segmenting it into slightly lengthened seconds, minutes, hours, for the convenience of those who dwelled in the city, where daylight was visible and meaningful, but those were few. Universal Standard was still the yardstick for the scientific community of *Flower*, and for the warship that orbited overhead.

Duncan walked with eyes open to the land, saw the camouflaged body of a leathery jo, one of the flying creatures of Kesrith, poised to last out the heat in the shadow of a large rock—saw also the trail of a sandsnake that had lately crossed the ground beside the causeway, seeking the nether side of some rock to protect itself from the sun and from predators. The jo waited, patiently, for its appointed prey. Such things Niun had taught Duncan to see.

Across the mineral flats, in the wreckage wrought by the fighting, a geyser plumed, a common sight. The world was repairing its damage, patiently setting about more aeons of building; but hereafter would come humans in greater and greater numbers, to search out a way to undo it and make Kesrith their own.

The mesh gave way to concrete at the city's edge, a border partially overcome by drifting sand. Duncan walked onto solid ground, past the observation deck of the Nom, where a surveillance system had been mounted to watch the causeway, and up to the rear door that had become main entry for human personnel, leading as it did toward *Flower* and the airfield and shuttle landing.

The door hissed open and shut. Nom air came as a shock, scented as it was with its own filtered human-regul taint, humidified and sweeter than the air outside, that sunlight-over-cold heat that burned and chilled at once. Here were gardens, kept marginally watered during rationing, botanical specimens from regul worlds, and therefore important: a liver-spotted white vine that had shed its lavender blooms under stress; a sad-looking tree with sparse silver leaves; a hardy gray-green moss. And the regul-built halls—high in the center, at least by regul standards—gave a tall human a feeling of confinement. The corridors were rounded and recessed along one side, where gleaming rails afforded regul sleds a faster, hazard-free movement along the side without doors. As Duncan turned for the ramp, one whisked past almost too fast to distinguish, whipped round the corner and was gone. At that pace it would be a supply sled, carrying cargo but no personnel.

Regul tended much to automation. They moved slowly, ponderously, their short legs incapable of bearing their own weight for any distance. The regul who did move about afoot were younglings, sexless and still mobile, not yet having acquired their adult bulk. The elders, the muscles of their legs atrophied, hardly stirred at all, save in the prosthetic comfort of their sleds.

And, alien in the corridors of the Nom, humans moved, tall, stalking shapes strangely rapid among the squat, slow forms of regul.

Duncan's own quarters were on the second level, a private room. It was luxury in one sense: solitude was a comfort he had not had in a very long time, for he had come to Kesrith as attendant to the governor; but he was keenly aware what the small, single room represented, a fall from intimacy with the important powers of Kesrith, specifically with Stavros, the Honorable George Stavros, governor of the new territories of human conquest. Duncan had found himself quietly preempted from his post by a military medical aide, one Evans, E.; he had come back from Kesrith's backlands and from sickbay to find that state of affairs, and although he had hoped, he had received no invitation to move back into his old quarters in the anteroom of Stavros' apartments—that post of regul protocol which, among their conquered hosts, humans yet observed meticulously in public. An elder of Stavros' high rank must have at least one youngling to attend his needs and fend off unwelcome visitors; and that duty now belonged to Evans. Duncan was kept at a distance; his contact with Stavros, once close, was suddenly formal: an occasional greeting as they passed in the hall, that was the limit of it. Even the debriefing after his mission had been handled by others and passed second-hand to Stavros, through the scientists, the medics and the military.

Duncan understood his disfavor now as permanent. It was Stavros' concession to the regul, who hated him and feared his influence. And what his position on Kesrith would be hereafter, he did not know.

It was, for his personal hopes, the end. He might have promoted himself to a colonial staff position by cultivating Stavros' favor. He was still due considerable pay for his five year enlistment in the hazardous stage of the Kesrithi mission—pay and transport to the world of his choice, or settlement on Kesrith itself, subject to the approval of the governor. He had been lured by such hopes once and briefly, half-believing them. He had taken the post because it was an offer, in an area and at a time when offers were scarce; and because he was nearing his statistical limit of survival on missions of greater hazard. It had seemed then a way to survive, marginally at least, as he had always survived.

He had survived again, had come back from Stavros' service scarred and sunburned and mentally shaken after a trek through the Kesrithi backlands which the lately arrived regulars would never have survived. He had learned Kesrith as no human would after him; and he had been among mri, and had come back alive, which no human had done before him.

And in his distress he had told Stavros the truth of what he had learned, directly and trustingly.

That had been his great mistake.

He passed the door that belonged to Stavros and Evans, and opened his own apartment, Spartan in its appointments and lacking the small anteroom that was essential to status in the Nom, among regul. He touched the switch to close the door, and at the same panel opened the storm shields. The windows afforded a view of the way that he had come, of *Flower* on her knoll, a squat half-ovoid on stilts; of a sky that, at least today, was cloudless, a rusty pink. There had not been a storm in days. Nature, like the various inhabitants of Kesrith, seemed to have spent its violence: there was an exhausted hush over the world.

Duncan stripped and sponged off with chemical conditioner, a practice that the caustic dust of Kesrith made advisable, that his physician still insisted upon, and changed into his lighter uniform. He was bound for the library, that building across the square from the Nom, accessible by a basement hallway: it was part of the regul university complex, which humans now held.

He spent his afternoons and evenings there; and anyone

who had known Sten Duncan back in humanity's home territory would have found that incredible. He was not a scholar. He had been well-trained in his profession: he knew the mechanics of ships and of weapons, knew a bit of geology and ecology, and the working of computers—all in areas necessary for efficiency in combat, in which he had been trained from a war-time youth, parentless, single-minded in the direction of his life. All his knowledge was practical, gathered at need, rammed into his head by instructors solely interested in his survival to kill the enemy.

That was before he had seen his war ended—before he had seen his enemy murdered by regul; or shared a camp with the survivors; or seen the proud mri on human charity.

Two thousand years of records and charts and tapes lay in the regul library, truths concealed in regul language and regul obscurities. Duncan studied. He searched out what the mri had been on Kesrith, what they had been elsewhere, with an interest infinitely more personal than that of *Flower*'s scientists.

Stavros disapproved. It flaunted attitudes and interests that regul feared and distrusted; and offending the regul ran counter to humanity's new policies. It embarrassed Stavros; it angered him, who had vast authority on Kesrith and in its new territories.

But the library still remained Duncan's choice on his hours of liberty, which were extensive in his useless existence. He had begun by making himself a nuisance among *Flower*'s personnel, who themselves were mining the library for what could be gained, duplicating tapes and records wholesale for later study back in the labs of Elag/Haven and Zoroaster. Duncan searched out those particular records that had to do with mri, and made himself helpful to certain of the *Flower* personnel who could be persuaded to share his interest. With his own stumbling command of the regul tongue, he could do little himself toward solving the tapes or interpreting the charts; but he talked with the scientists who could. He reasoned with them; he tried to make them understand, with all his insistence, that which he did not understand himself.

To learn what it was he had spent his life destroying, what he had seen—utterly—obliterated.

He gathered up his notes and his handmade dictionary and prepared to leave the room.

The light on the panel flashed.

"Kose Sten Duncan," a regul voice said, still giving him his old title as Stavros' assistant, which surprised him. "Kose Sten Duncan."

He pressed the button for reply, vaguely uneasy that anyone in the Nom chose to intervene with him, disturbing his obscurity. His earnest ambition now was simple: to be let alone, to take those assignments that might be given him through lower channels, and to be forgotten by the higher ones.

"I am here," he told the regul.

"The reverence bai Stavros sends you his order that you join him in his offices immediately."

Duncan hesitated, heart clenched at the foreknowledge that his period of grace was over. Somewhere in the labyrinth of *Flower* papers must have been signed, declaring him fit for service; somewhere in the Nom papers were being prepared that would similarly mark him down in someone's employ. Nothing on colonial Kesrith could remain without some designated use.

"Tell the reverence," he said, "that I am coming now."

The regul returned some curt syllable, ending the communication; it lacked respect. Duncan flung his notes onto the table, opened the door and strode out into the corridor.

It was no accident that Stavros had summoned him at this hour. Duncan had become precise in his habits: from his treatment before noon, to his apartment at noon, and from his apartment to the library by a quarter til.

And concerning the library, he had received his warning.

He began, feverish in his anxiety, to anticipate the worst things that might await him: a reprimand, a direct order to abandon his visits to the library—or barring him from *Flower*, and from the mri. He had already defied Stavros' hinted displeasure; and did he receive and refuse a direct order he would find himself transferred permanently stationward, to *Saber*, Kesrith's military guard.

Where you belong, he could imagine Stavros saying. *Leave the mri to the scientists.*

He stalked through the corridor that wound down the ramp, shouldering aside a slow-moving regul youngling at the turn and not apologizing. Nor would the regul apologize to him, a human it needed not fear. A hiss of anger followed him, and other younglings paused to glare at him.

Stavros' offices, again a matter of status within a regul

community, were on the ground floor of the stairless Nom, beyond broad doors that afforded easy access to the regul sleds.

The office doors were open. The secretary at Stavros' reception office was human, another of *Saber*'s personnel, a ComTech whose specialized linguistic skills were wasted at this post; but at least Stavros considered security, and did not install a regul youngling at this most sensitive post, where too much might be overheard—and, by a regul, memorized verbatim at the hearing. The tech stirred from his boredom, recognized Duncan with an expression of sudden reserve. A SurTac, Duncan was outside the regular military, but he was due a ComTech's respect.

"The governor says go on in," the tech said; and with a flicker of a glance to the closed inner door and back again: "The bai is in there, sir."

Hulagh.

Elder of the regul on Kesrith.

"Thank you," Duncan said, jaw set.

"Sir," the ComTech said. "With apologies: the governor advises you to walk in softly. His words, sir."

"Yes," Duncan said, and restrained his temper with a visible effort for the ComTech's benefit. He knew how he was reputed at Kesrith base—for rashness marked with official disfavor. He also knew his way among the diplomats better than any deskbound tech.

It was not the moment for temper. His transfer to *Saber* would be complete victory for the regul bai. He could throw away every remaining influence he had on the behalf of the mri, with a few ill-chosen words between himself and Stavros or between himself and the bai, and he was resolved to keep them unspoken. The regul would not understand any difference of opinion between elder and youngling; any intimation of dissent would reflect on Stavros, and Stavros would not ignore that, not on a personal basis, not on an official one.

The secretary opened the door by remote and Duncan entered with a meek and quiet step, with a bow and a proper deference to the two rulers of Kesrith.

"Duncan," said Stavros aloud, and not unkindly. Both human and regul bai were encased in shining metal, alike until the eye rested on the flesh contained in the center of the sled-assembly. Stavros was exceedingly advanced in years, partially paralyzed, his affliction—which he had suffered on

Kesrith—still hindering his speech to such an extent that he used the sled's communication screen to converse with regul, in their difficult language; but to humans he had begun to use speech again. The stricken limbs had regained some strength, but Stavros still kept to the sled, regul-made, the prestige of a regul elder. Speed, power, instant access to any circuitry in the Nom: Duncan understood the practical considerations in which Stavros refused to give up the machine, but he hated the policy which it represented—human accommodation with the regul, human imitation of regul ways.

"Sir," Duncan said quietly, acknowledging the greeting; and he faced bai Hulagh in the next breath, serenely courteous and trembling inside with anger, smiling as he met the small dark eyes of the regul elder. Great hulking monster in silver-edged gossamer, his flesh fold over fold of fat in which muscle had almost completely atrophied, particularly in the lower limbs: Duncan loathed the sight of him. The regul's face was bony plate, dark as the rest of his hide, and smooth, unlike the rest of his hide. The composite of facial features, their symmetry, gave an illusion of humanity; but taken individually, no feature was human. The eyes were brown and round, sunk in pits of wrinkled skin. The nose was reduced to slits that could flare or close completely. The lips were inverted, a mere tight-pressed slash at the moment, edged in bony plate. Hulagh's nostrils were tightly compressed now, save for quick puffs of expelled air, a signal of displeasure in the meeting as ominous as a human scowl.

Hulagh turned his sled abruptly aside, a pointed rebuff to a presumptuous youngling, and smiled at Stavros, a relaxing of the eyes and nostrils, a slight opening of the mouth. It was uncertain whether such a gesture was native to the regul or an attempt at a human one.

"It is good," said Hulagh in his rumbling Basic, "that the youngling Duncan has recovered."

"Yes," said Stavros aloud, in the regul tongue. The com screen on the sled angled toward Duncan and flashed to Basic mode, human symbols and alphabet. *Be seated. Wait.*

Duncan found a chair against the wall and sat down and listened, wondering why he had been called to this conference, why Stavros had chosen to put him on what surely was display for Hulagh's benefit. Duncan's inferior command of the regul language made it impossible for him to pick up much of what the regul bai said, and he could gather nothing

at all of what Stavros answered, for though he could see the
com screen at this angle, he could read but few words of the
intricate written language, which the eidetic regul almost
never used themselves.

One hearing of anything, however complex, and the regul
never forgot. They needed no notes. Their records were oral,
taped, reduced to writing only when deemed of some lasting
importance.

Duncan's ears pricked when he heard his own name and
the phrase *released from duty*. He sat still, hands tightening
on the edge of the thick regul chair while the two diplomats
traded endless pleasantries, until at last Hulagh prepared to
take his leave.

The bai's sled faced about. This time Hulagh turned that
false smile on him. "Good day, youngling Duncan," he said.

Duncan had the presence of mind to rise and bow, which
was the courteous and proper response for a youngling to an
elder; and the sled whisked out the opened door as he stood,
fists clenched, and looked down at Stavros.

"Sit down," Stavros said.

The door closed. Duncan came and took the chair nearest
Stavros' sled. The windows blackened, shutting out the outside world. They were entirely on room lights.

"My congratulations," Stavros said. "Well played, if obviously insincere."

"Am I being transferred?" Duncan asked directly, an
abruptness that brought a flicker of displeasure to Stavros'
eyes. Duncan regretted it at once—further proof, Stavros
might read it, that he was unstable. Above all else, he had
wished to avoid that impression.

"Patience," Stavros counseled him. Then he spoke to the
ComTech outside, gave an order for incoming calls to be further delayed, and relaxed with a sigh, still watching Duncan
intently. "Hulagh," said Stavros, "has been persuaded not to
have your head. I told him that your hardship in the desert
had unhinged your mind. Hulagh seems to accept that possibility as an excuse that will save his pride. He has decided to
accept your presence in his sight again; but he doesn't like
it."

"That regul," Duncan said, doggedly reiterating the statement that had ruined him, "committed genocide. If he didn't
push the button himself, he ordered the one that did. I gave

you my statement on what happened out there that night. You know that I'm telling the truth. You know it."

"Officially," said Stavros, "I don't. Duncan, I will try to reason with you. Matters are not as simple as you would wish. Hulagh himself suffered in that action: he lost his ship, his younglings, his total wealth and his prestige and the prestige of his doch. A regul doch may fall, one important to mankind. Do you comprehend what I'm telling you? Hulagh's doch is the peace party. If it falls, it will be dangerous for all of us, and not only for those of us on Kesrith. We're talking about the peace, do you understand that?"

They were back on old ground. Arguments began from here, leading to known positions. Duncan opened his mouth to speak, persistently to restate what Stavros knew, what he had told his interrogators times beyond counting. Stavros cut him off with an impatient gesture, saving him the effort that he knew already was futile. Duncan found himself tired, exhausted of hope and belief in the powers that ruled Kesrith, most of all in this man that he had once served.

"Listen," said Stavros sharply. "Human men died, too—at Haven."

"I was there," Duncan returned, bitter in the memory. He did not add what was also true, that Stavros had not been. Many a SurTac had left his unburied corpse on Elag/Haven, and ten other worlds of that zone, while the diplomats were safe behind the lines.

"Human men died," Stavros continued, intent on making his point, "there and here, at the hands of mri. Humans would have died in the future—will die, if the peace should collapse, if somewhere the regul that want war find political power—and more such mercenaries as the mri. Or does that fail to matter in your reckoning?"

"It matters."

Stavros was silent a time. He moved his sled to reach for a cup of soi abandoned on the edge of a table. He drank, and stared at Duncan over the rim of the cup, set it down again. "I know it matters," he said at last. "Duncan, I regretted having to replace you."

It was the first time Stavros had said so. "Yes, sir," Duncan said. "I know it was necessary."

"There were several reasons," Stavros said. "First, because you offended bai Hulagh to his face, and you know you're lucky to have come off alive from that. Second, you were put

into sickbay with an indefinite prognosis, and I need help——"
He gestured at his own body, encased in metal. "You're no
medic. You didn't sign on for this. Evans is useful in that regard. Your skills are valuable elsewhere."

Duncan listened, painfully aware that he was being played,
prepared for something. One did not maneuver George
Stavros; Stavros maneuvered others. Stavros was a profes-
sional at it; and the mind in that fettered shell had very few
human dependencies, an aged man who had dealt with crises
involving worlds for more years than SurTacs tended to live,
who had thrown aside family and a comfortable retirement to
seize a governorship on a frontier like Kesrith. For a brief
time Duncan had felt there had been some attachment between himself and Stavros; he had given Stavros unstintingly
of effort and loyalty—had even believed in him enough to offer him truth. But to manage others with subtlety, even with
ruthlessness, that was the skill for which Stavros had won his
appointment; Duncan determined neither to believe him nor
to be angry that he had been used—and he knew that even
so, Stavros had the skill to lie to him again.

"I have excused your actions," Stavros said, "and covered
them as far as I can; but you have lost your usefulness to me
in the capacity in which you signed on. Hulagh can be persuaded to tolerate your presence; but the suspicion that you
have moved back into some position of direct influence
would be more than he could bear, and it might endanger
your life. I don't want that kind of trouble, Duncan, or the
complications your murder might create. Regul are simply
not prepared to believe the killing of a youngling is of equal
seriousness with the killing of an elder."

"I don't want to be sent offworld."

"You don't."

"No, sir. I don't."

Stavros stared at him. "You have this personal attachment
to those two mri. Attachment—obsession. You're no longer a
rational man on the subject, Duncan. Think. Explain to me.
What do you hope to do or to find? What's the point of this
sudden—scholarship of yours, these hours in the library, in
full view of the regul? What are you looking for?"

"I don't know, sir."

"You don't know. But it involves every mri record you can
find."

Duncan clenched his jaw, leaned back and made himself

draw an even breath. Stavros left the silence, waiting for him.
"I want to know," Duncan said finally, "what they were. I
saw them die. I saw a whole species die out there. I want to
know what it was I saw destroyed."

"That doesn't make sense."

"I was there. You weren't." Duncan's mind filled again
with the night, the dark, the blinding light of the destruction.
A mri body pressed against him, two men equally trembling
in the forces that had destroyed a species.

Stavros gazed at him a long time. His face grew sober,
even pitying, and this was unaccustomed for Stavros. "What
do you think? That it might have been you that drew the attack to them? Is that what's eating at you—that you might be
responsible, as much as Hulagh?"

It hit near enough the mark. Duncan sat still, knowing that
he was not going to be able to talk rationally about it.
Stavros let the silence hang there a moment.

"Perhaps," said Stavros finally, "it would be better if you
would go up to *Saber* for a time, into an environment more
familiar to you, where you can sort out your thinking."

"No, sir. It would not be better. You took me off assignment with you. I accept that. But give me something else: I
waive my transfer home, and my discharge. Give me another
assignment, here on Kesrith."

"That is a request, I take it."

"Yes, sir. That is a request."

"Everything you do, since you were attached to me, is observed and taken for omen by the regul. You've persisted in
aggravating the situation. You came here to assist, SurTac
Duncan, not to formulate policy."

Duncan did not answer. It was not expected. Stavros'
mouth worked in the effort prolonged speech cost him; he
drew a difficult breath, and Duncan grew concerned, remembering that Stavros was a sick man, that he was trying, amid
all other pressures, to remember something of personal debts.
He put a curb on his temper.

"You took it on yourself," Stavros said at last, "to accuse
bai Hulagh of murder. You created an incident that nearly
shipwrecked the whole Kesrithi diplomatic effort. Maybe you
think you were justified. Let us suppose—" Stavros' harsh,
strained voice acquired a marginally gentler tone. "Let us
suppose for the sake of argument that you were absolutely
justified. But you do not make decisions like that, SurTac

Duncan, and you must know that, somewhere at the bottom of your righteousness."

"Yes, sir," he said very quietly.

"As it happens," said Stavros, "I don't doubt you. And I'm positive the bai tried to kill you in spite of all my efforts to reassure him. When he found you among mri, that was too much for him. I think you know that. I think you're bothered by that possibility, and I wish that I could set your mind at ease and say that it wasn't so. I can't. Hulagh probably did exactly what you charge he did. But charges like that aren't profitable for me to pursue right now. I recovered you alive. That was the best that I could do, with all else that was going on. I recovered your mri too, quite incidentally."

"What remains of them. The medics—"

"Yes. What remains of them. But you can't undo that. You can't do a thing about it."

"Yes, sir."

"The medics tell me you've healed."

"Yes, sir." Duncan drew a deep breath and decided finally that Stavros was trying to put him at ease. He watched as the governor tried awkwardly to manipulate a clean cup into the dispenser—rose and took over that task, filling the cup the governor was going to offer him. Stavros favored him with a one-sided smile.

"Still not what I was," Stavros said ruefully. "The medics don't make extravagant promises, but the exercises are helping. Makes the metal beast easier to manage, at least. Here, give my cup a warm-up, will you?"

Duncan did as requested, put it in Stavros' hand, settled again with his own cup cradled in his palms. After a moment he took his first sip, savoring the pleasant warmth. Soi was a mild stimulant. He found himself drinking more of it than was likely good for him these last few days, but his taste for food had been off since his sojourn in the desert. He sipped at the hot liquid and relaxed, knew that he was being swept into Stavros' talented manipulations, set at ease, moved, directed; but he was also being heard, for what it was worth. He believed, if nothing else, that Stavros began to listen—and cultivated the regul for reasons that did not involve naïveté.

"It was a mistake, my speaking out," Duncan admitted, which he had never admitted, not to his several interrogators or in any of the written reports he had filed. "It wasn't that I didn't know what I was saying; I did. But I shouldn't have said it in front of the regul."

"You were in a state of collapse. I understood that."

Duncan's mouth twisted. He set the cup aside. "Security got a sedative into me to shut me up and you know it. I did not collapse."

"You talked about a holy place," Stavros said. "But you never would talk about it in debriefing, not even to direct questions. Was that where you found the artifact you brought back?"

Duncan's eyes went unfocused, his heart speeding. His hands shook. He attempted to disguise the fact by reaching for the plastic cup and clenching it tightly in both hands.

"Duncan?"

Dark and fire, a gleaming metal ovoid cradled in Niun's arms, precious to the mri, more than their lives, who were the last of their kind. *Do nothing*, Melein had bidden him while he stood in that place holy to the mri, *touch nothing, see nothing*. He had violated that trust, delivering the wounded mri into human care, to save their lives, by putting that metal ovoid into human hands, itself to be probed by human science. He had spoken in delirium. He looked at Stavros, helpless to shrug it off; he did not know how much he had said, or with what detail. There was the artifact itself, in *Flower*'s labs, to make lies of any denial.

"I had better write the reports over," Duncan said. He did not know what else to say. A colonial governor had dictatorial powers in that stage before there were parliaments and laws. He himself was not a civ, and unprotected in any instance. There was very little that Stavros could not do—even including execution, certainly including shipping him to some station elsewhere, away from the mri, away from all hope of access to them and to Kesrith, forever.

"Your account was not accurate, then."

Duncan cast everything into the balance. "I was shaken. I wasn't sure, after I was silenced the first time, how much was really wanted on record."

"Don't give me that nonsense."

"I was not rational at the time. To be honest—to be honest, sir, I had the feeling that you wanted to bury everything about the mri, everything that happened. I wasn't sure I might not be put off Kesrith because I knew too much. I'm still not sure that it won't happen."

"You know the seriousness of what you're charging?"

"This is a frontier," Duncan said. "I know that you can do what you want to do. Even to having me shot. I don't know the limit of what I know—or how important it is. If an entire species can be wiped off the board and forgotten—what am I?"

Stavros frowned, sipped at his drink, made a face and set it aside again. "Duncan, the regul are living; their victims aren't. So we deal with the regul, who are a force still dangerous—and the mri—" He moved the sled, turned it, looked at him at closer range. "You have your opinions on the mri, very obviously. What would you do with them?"

"Turn them loose. They won't live in captivity."

"That simple? But it's not quite that simple afterwards. What of the regul?"

"The mri won't fight for the regul any longer—and there are only two of them. Only two—"

"Caring nothing for their lives, even two mri are considerable; and they have a considerable grudge against bai Hulagh—who heads the regul peace party, SurTac Duncan."

"I know these two mri," Duncan said. "They did nothing to anyone on this world except to defend themselves. They only tried to get to safety, and we wouldn't let them. Let them go now, and they'd leave. That's all they want."

"For now."

"There is no tomorrow for them," Duncan said, and then Stavros looked at him quizzically. "There will be no more generations. There's a taboo between those two. Besides, even if there weren't—ten, even twenty generations wouldn't make a vast threat out of them."

Stavros frowned, backed the sled, opened the door. "Walk with me," he said, "upstairs. You're going nowhere else, I trust."

"Yes, sir," Duncan agreed. Stavros undoubtedly meant to put him off his balance, and he had done so. He was asked to accompany Stavros in public, before regul. It was a demonstration of something, a restoration of confidence: he was not sure what. Perhaps he was being bribed, in subtle fashion, offered status—and the alternative was transfer to *Saber*. Stavros made it very difficult to continue the debate.

The sled eased its way through the office door, past the ComTech; it passed the outer doors, into the corridor. Duncan overtook it as Stavros waited for him. Stavros did

not lock into the tracks that could have shot him along at a
rate no man afoot could match, but trundled along beside
him at a very leisurely pace.

"First thing," said Stavros, "no more library." And when
Duncan opened his mouth at once to protest: "You have to
walk among regul over there, and I'd rather not have that.
Flower staff can find what you need, if you describe it. Do
you understand me?"

"No, sir."

They walked some distance in silence, until a knot of regul
had passed them, and they turned the corner into the upward
corridor. "I want you," said Stavros, "to spend your time on
Flower as much as possible. Stay clear of the regul entirely.
Work at your private obsession through channels, and write
me a decent report—a full one, this time."

Duncan stopped on the ramp. "I still don't understand
you."

Stavros angled his sled to look up at him, a sidewise motion of the eyes. "Yes, you do. I want you to apply your tal-
ents and prepare me a full report on the mri. Use any
authority you want that doesn't involve actually touching the
mri themselves."

"What value is that?" Duncan asked. "I'm no scientist."

"Your practical experience," Stavros said, "makes such a
report valuable: not for the researchers, but for me."

"I'll need clearance over there."

Stavros scowled. "I'll tell you something, Duncan, and you
listen to me. I don't share your enthusiasm for preserving the
mri. They were a plague in the universe, a blight, at best an
anachronism among species that have learned their lessons of
civilization to better advantage. They are probably the most
efficient killers in all creation; but we didn't bring them to ex-
tinction, nor did the regul—nor did you. They are dying because they have no interest in comprehending any other way
of life. No quarter, no prisoners, no negotiation or compromise: everything is black and white in their eyes, nothing
gray. I don't blame them for it; but their way of life was
destruction, and they're dying now by the same standard they
applied to others: nature's bias, if you like, not mine. Convince me otherwise if you can. And be careful with them. If
you don't respect them for what they are, instead of what
your delirium remembers, then those two mri will end up kill-

ing someone: themselves certainly; you, likely; others, very possibly."

"Then I will be allowed access to them."

"Maybe."

"Give me that now, and I can talk with them as the staff can't. Keep the medics and their drugs away from them while they have minds left."

"Duncan—" Stavros started moving again, slowly, turning the corner at the top of the ramp. "You were the one exception to their no-prisoner rule, the one exception in forty years. You are aware, of course, that there may have been a certain irrational sense of dependency generated there, in the desert, in their environment, in your unexpected survival. They gave you food and water, kept you alive, contrary to your own natural expectations; you received every necessity of life from their hands. When you expect ill and receive good instead, it has certain emotional effects, even when you really know nothing about the motives of the people involved. Do you know what I'm talking about?"

"Yes, sir. I'm aware of that possibility. It may be valid."

"And that's what you want to find out, is it?"

"That, among other things."

They reached the door of Stavros' apartments. Stavros opened it by remote, slipped in and whipped the sled about, facing him in the doorway. Evans stood across the room, seeming surprised at them: a young man, Evans—Duncan looked at him, who had been the focus of his bitter jealousy, and found a quiet, not particularly personable youth.

"Take the afternoon off," Stavros said to Duncan. "Stay in the Nom. I'll prepare an order transferring you to *Flower* and salving feelings among the civs over there. I'll send you a copy of it. And I expect you realize I don't want any feelings ruffled over there among the scientific staff; they don't like the military much. Use tact. You'll get more out of them."

"Yes, sir." Duncan was almost trembling with anxiety, for almost all that he wanted was in his hands, everything. "And access to the mri themselves—"

"No. Not yet. Not yet. Go on. Give me time."

Duncan tried to make a gesture of some sort, a courtesy; it was never easy at the best of times between himself and Stavros. In the end he murmured something inarticulate and left, awkward in the leaving.

"Sir?"

Stavros turned the sled about, remembered that he had ordered lunch when he returned. He accepted the offered mug of soup and scowled at Evans' attempt to help him with it, took it into his own hands. Returning function in his afflicted limbs made him arrogant in his regained independence. He analyzed his irritation as impatience with his own unresponding muscles and Evans merely as a convenient focus. He murmured a surly thanks.

"Files on the mri," he ordered Evans. "And on Sten Duncan."

Evans moved to obey. Stavros settled and drank the soup, savoring something prepared entirely by humans, seasoned with human understanding of spices. It was too new a luxury after the long stay in regul care to take entirely for granted; but after a moment the cup rested neglected in his hand.

The fact was that he missed Duncan.

He missed him sorely, and still reckoned him better spent as he had just disposed of him. The SurTac had entered service with him as a bodyguard disguised as a servant, drawn out of combat at war's end to dance attendance on a diplomat. Duncan was a young man, if any man who had seen action at Elag/Haven could ever again be called young. He was remarkable in his intelligence, according to records which Duncan had probably never seen—another of the young men that the war had snatched up and swallowed whole before they had ever known what they might have been. Duncan had learned to take orders, but SurTac-style: loners, the men of his service, unaccustomed to close direction. They were usually given only an objective, limited in scope, and told to accomplish it: the rest was up to the SurTac, a specialist in alien environment, survival, and warfare behind the enemy's lines.

Stavros himself had sent the SurTac out to learn Kesrith.

And Kesrith had nearly killed Duncan. Even the look of him was changed, reshaped by the forge of the Kesrithi desert. Something was gone, that had been there before Duncan had gone out into that wilderness—his youth, perhaps; his humanity, possibly. He bore scars of it, face half-tanned from wearing mri veils in the searing sunlight, frown lines burned into the edges of his eyes, making them hard and different. He had come back with lungs racked and his breathing impaired from the thin air and caustic dust, with his body weight down by a considerable measure, and a strange, fragile tread, as if he mistrusted the very flooring. Days in sickbay had taken care of the physical injuries, restored him with all the array of advanced equipment available on the probe ship; but there was damage that would never be reached, that had stamped the look of the fanatic on the young SurTac.

The regul bai was correct when he perceived Sten Duncan as an enemy. The regul as a species had no more deadly enemy than this, save the mri themselves. Duncan hated, and Duncan knew the regul better than any human living save Stavros himself, for they two had come alone among regul, the first humans to breach the barriers to contact between regul and humanity, here on Kesrith.

And most particularly Duncan hated bai Hulagh Alagn-ni: Hulagh, who had done precisely what Duncan accused him of doing, killing the mri who had served regulkind as mercenaries, obliterating a sapient species. Hulagh had done it for desperate fear, and for greed, which were intertwined. But bai Hulagh was moved now by fear of disgrace among his own kind and by dawning hope of gain from humans; he had become stranded on the world he had hoped to plunder, among humans whom he had hoped to cheat and disgrace. And bai Hulagh thus became vulnerable and valuable.

The fact was that one could not, as Duncan tried to do, say *regul*, and comprehend in that word the reasons and actions of a given member of regulkind. A quasi-nation of merchants and scholars, the regul; but their docha, their associations of birth and trade, were each as independent as separate nations in most dealings. Hulagh was of doch Alagn, and Alagn, a new force in regul politics, had stopped the war. The employers of the mri mercenaries who had wrought such destruction in human space were doch Holn, the great rivals and enemies of Alagn.

Doch Holn had ceded Kesrith at war's end, compelled by the treaty; and in the passing of Kesrith to human control, Holn had fallen to Alagn. But Holn had had its revenge: it had cast Hulagh Alagn-ni into command of Kesrith ignorant of mri and of the nature of Kesrith. The weather had turned: Alagn had been faced with the collapse of their effort of evacuation and plunder of Kesrith; and confronted with incoming humans, Hulagh had panicked. In that panic, seeking to avert human wrath, Hulagh had done murder.

It was possible that by that act of murder, that annihilation of the mri, bai Hulagh had saved the lives of those incoming humans, all the personnel of *Saber* and *Flower*, *Fox* and *Hannibal*. It was possible that humanity guiltily owed bai Hulagh a debt of gratitude, for a sweeping action that human policy could never have taken.

Duncan, who believed in absolute justice, could not accept such a thought; but the truth was that doch Alagn and its ruler, Hulagh, were in every respect useful to Kesrith, most particularly in their reliance on humans and in their burning hatred for doch Holn, who had maneuvered them into this unhappy circumstance. For Duncan, as for the mri, there was only black and white, right and wrong. It was impossible to explain to Duncan that Alagn must be cultivated, strengthened, and aimed at Holn, a process too long-range and too little honest for the SurTac.

The mri, moreover, were Holn-hired and Holn-managed throughout their history—and it was above all else necessary that what Hulagh had done on Kesrith be final: that the mri species be in fact obliterated, and that Holn not maintain in some secret place another force of the breed, those most efficient and skilled killers, for whom Duncan found such tender sympathy. The regul without the mri were incapable of war, constitutionally and physically incapable. With the mri, the regul were capable to any extent. If any mri survived, they could bear no love to doch Alagn for what Hulagh had done to their kind; and personal involvement of the mri in a war, for their own motives and not for hire, was a specter that hung over both Alagn and humanity.

The soup turned sour in Stavros' mouth while he contemplated what measures might eventually prove necessary with the remaining two mri: Duncan's mri. Duncan was a man of single sight and direct action, innocent in his way; and it was something that Stavros had no wish to do—to destroy in the SurTac that which had made him at once a valued adviser and a reliable agent.

He loved Duncan as a son.

For one of his sons, he would have felt less remorse.

Chapter Two

——◦◉◦——

THE ORDER went out in the evening. Duncan read and re-read the photocopy over a solitary supper in his quarters in the Nom, at a table littered with other notes, his handmade and carefully gathered materials.

Special liaison: that was the title that Stavros had chosen to ease his transfer into *Flower*'s tight community. The order linked him to the governor's essentially civilian wing, and not to the military presence that orbited in conjunction with the station, and Duncan appreciated that distinction, that would find more grace with *Flower*'s personnel. He was given certain authorities—to investigate, but not to dispose of artifacts or records or persons: he could actually direct what lines investigations of others were to take: *fullest cooperation in pursuing his research . . .* that portion of the order began. He read that final section again and again, finding no exception in it, and he was amazed that Stavros had said it.

He began to wonder why, and found no answer.

Within the hour arrived a packet of documents—not on film, and therefore not something meant to be fed into the Nom receptors, where regul might have access to it: it came hand-delivered. Duncan signed for it and settled with the several folders in his lap—extensive files that seemed to comprise everything known and done in regard to the mri prisoners. Duncan read them, again and again, absorbing everything he could remotely comprehend.

Then followed messages, from one and another department within *Flower* —from security, from biology, from Dr. Luiz, the white-haired chief of surgery who had cared for him during his own stay aboard *Flower.* Luiz' message was warm: it

29

was Luiz who had tacitly given him leave to conduct his daily
visits aboard *Flower*, when his own treatments could as easily
have been given in the Nom, far from the mri. It was Luiz
who had kept the treatment of the mri as decent as it was,
who had kept them alive when it was reckoned impossible;
and this man Duncan trusted. From others there were more
formal acknowledgments, coldness couched in courtesies.

The governor's appointee, bringing power to alter things
dear to certain hearts: he began to reckon how the scientists
saw him, an intruder who knew nothing about the researches
and operations for which these civs had come so far to a
frontier world. He did not find it surprising that he was
resented. He wished that he had been given authority to alter
the condition of the mri, and less authority to threaten other
projects. The one he earnestly desired; the other he distrusted
because it was excessive and unreasonable; and he did not
know Stavros for an excessive man, and certainly not as a
man who acted without reasons.

He was being aimed at someone or something: he began to
fear that this was so. He had become convenient again for
Stavros, a weapon to be used once more, in a new kind of
warfare against some one of Stavros' enemies—be it the
regul, be it some contest of authority between civs and the
governor's office, or designs yet more complex, involving all
of them.

He was out of Stavros' reach now, and able to think—outside that aura of confidentiality that so readily swept a man
into Stavros' hands—and still he found himself willing to sus-
pend all his suspicions and take the lure, for it was all that he
wanted, all that mattered to him.

Obsession, Stavros had called it.

He acknowledged that, and went.

At *Flower*'s duty desk in the morning, more messages
waited, each from a department head waiting to see him.
Duncan began to find himself uneasy. He postponed dealing
with them, and descended first to the medical section, intent
most of all on the mri, on assuring himself as he did daily,
that they were well and as comfortable as possible under the
circumstances—most of all now, that no over-eager investiga-
tor had decided to be beforehand with them, to finish or initi-
ate some research before it could be forbidden.

But before he had more than passed the door into that section, Dr. Luiz hailed him; and he found himself diverted from the mri and hastened into an assembling conference of the various departments of *Flower*.

Being involved in the meeting irked him: he hated all such procedures. He was formally introduced to them, who had known him better as a specimen like the mri, himself the object of some of their researches when he had been dragged in off the desert half-alive, from where no human ought to have survived. He forced a smile to his face, and acknowledged the introductions, then leaned back in his chair and prepared himself for the tedium to come, long exchanges of data and quibblings over objectives and items of supply. He thought it deliberate, a petty administrative revenge that he be drawn into such proceedings, in which he had no knowledge and less interest. He sat surreptitiously studying the manners and faces of the other participants, listening to the petty debates and mentally marking down to be remembered the indications of jealousies and friendships that might be useful.

But the central matter did suddenly touch his interest: the news from the military wing that there were arrivals at the station. It troubled him, this piece of news, increasingly so as he listened. Probe ship *Fox*, along with the warship *Hannibal* and the rider *Santiago*, had returned from Gurgain, a world of the star Lyltagh, neighboring Arain, a mining colony of airless moons and rich deposits, only scantly developed by regul. New information was coming in, particularly of interest to the geologists: *Flower* was sending a crew up to *Fox*. Personnel were being shifted about, reallotted on new priorities; the mri project was losing some key personnel. Duncan, beginning to perceive the reorganization, felt uneasily that his authority might be sufficient to affect the transfers: he thought that he ought to say something, that he might be expected to do something, to be well-informed in questions of staff and policies and Stavros' wishes. He was not.

He sat frowning while matters were arranged to the satisfaction of the existing powers of *Flower*, realizing miserably that he was inadequate for the position he had been given: that at the least he should have been taking notes for Stavros' benefit—and he had done nothing, not aware until late what had happened, that a major portion of the directorates had dissolved about him, ill-content, it might be, with the governor's intervention in their researches: forces wishing to assert their independence of Stavros were aiming this at him, while other departments looked in vain for his support.

Academics and politics: he was not fit for either. He was conscious of the figure he cut among them, khaki amid their blue and white, a rough-handed soldier out of his element, a hated and ridiculous presence. They concluded their business in his angry silence and adjourned. A few lingered for perfunctory courtesies with him; those bound for *Fox* pointedly ignored such amenities and walked out without acknowledging his presence. He accepted what courtesies he was offered, still not knowing friend from enemy, bitter in his ignorance. He was pleasant, having learned from Stavros to smile without meaning it.

But afterward, as he tried to leave, he found Luiz' hand on his shoulder, and Dr. Boaz of xenology smiling up at him with more than casual interest, Boaz a portly woman with the accent of Haven in her speech, her head crowned with gray-blonde braids.

"Stavros," said Boaz, "recalled you mentioned a mri shrine."

He looked at them, this pair that already held the mri's existence in their hands, the medical chief of staff and this smallish plump woman whose department held all the mri's possessions. Boaz' interest was naked in her eyes, scholarly lust. Her small department had survived the dissolution virtually intact and capable of function, while Luiz' bio-medical staff had lost key personnel to the shift, angry medical personnel choosing the more comfortable existence of the station, under the guise of setting up systems for further probe missions.

Boaz and Luiz remained with *Flower*, and had come into positions of seniority in *Flower*'s depleted staff.

And Luiz approved her. Duncan searched the surgeon's face, looked again at Boaz.

"I was at such a place," he admitted carefully. "I don't know whether it would be possible to find it again."

"Let's talk in my office," said Boaz.

"SurTac Duncan," the page said for the second time. "You are wanted at the lock."

The aircraft was waiting. It could wait. Duncan pressed a

com button at a panel and leaned toward it. "Duncan here. Advise them I'm coming in a few minutes."

He walked then, as he had been granted Luiz' free permission to do, into the guarded section of the infirmary, no longer there by a bending of regulations, but bearing a red badge that passed him to all areas of the ship but those on voicelock. It was satisfying to see the difference in security's reaction to him, the quickness with which doors were opened to him.

And when he had come into Niun's room, the guard outside turned his back, a privacy which he had not often enjoyed.

He touched the mri, bent and called his name, wishing for the latest time he had had other options. He had obtained a position of some power again; had recovered favor where it mattered; had fought with every deviousness he knew; but when he looked at the mri's thin, naked face, it felt not at all like triumph.

He wished that they would allow Niun covering for his face; the mri lived behind veils, a modest, proud people. After some days with him, Niun had finally felt easy enough in his presence to show him his face, and to speak to him directly, as a man to a man of like calling.

There is no other way for us, Niun had told him, refusing offered help, at a time when the mri had had the power to choose for himself. *We either survive as we were, or we have failed to survive. We are mri; and that is more than the name of a species, Duncan. It is an old, old way. It is our way. And we will not change.*

There were fewer and fewer options for them.

Only a friend, Duncan thought bitterly, could betray them with such thoroughness. He had determined they would survive: their freedom would cost something else again; and that, too, he prepared to buy, another betrayal . . . things that the mri regarded as holy. In such coin he bought the co-operation of the likes of Boaz and Luiz; and wondered finally for whose sake he acted, whether Niun could even comprehend his reasoning, or whether it was only selfishness that drove him.

"Niun," he urged him, wishing for some touch of recognition, some reassurance for what he was doing. But Niun was far under this noon: there was no reaction to his name or to the touch on his arm.

He could not delay longer. He drew back, still hoping.
There was nothing.

He had not expected a pilot: he had looked to fly himself.
But when he climbed aboard he found the controls occupied
by a sandy-haired man who bore *Saber*'s designation of his
sleeve. *GALEY*, the pocket patch said, *LT*.

"Sorry about the delay," Duncan said, for the air was hot,
noon-heated. "Didn't know I wasn't solo on this one."

Galey fired up, shrugged as the engines throbbed into life.
"No matter. It's hot here, hot down there at the water plant
on repair detail, too. I'd rather the ship, thanks."

Duncan settled into the copilot's place, adjusted his gear,
the equipment that Boaz had provided, into the space between his feet, and fastened the belts.

The ship lifted at an angle, swung off into an immediate
sharp turn toward the hills. Cold air flooded them now that
they were airborne, delicious luxury after the oven-heat of
the aircraft on the ground.

"Do you know where we're going?" he asked of Galey.

"I know the route. I flew you out of there."

Duncan gave him a second look, trying to remember him,
and could not. It had been dark, a time too full of other
concerns. He blinked, realizing Galey had said something else
to him, that he had been drifting.

"Sorry," he said. "You asked something?"

Galey shrugged again. "No matter. No matter. How'd the
kel'ein make out? Still alive, I hear."

"Alive, yes."

"This place we're going have something to do with them?"

"Yes."

"Dangerous?"

"I don't know," he said, considering that for the first time.
"Maybe."

Galey absorbed that thought in several kilometers of
silence, the white desert slipping beneath them, jagged with
rocks. Duncan looked out, saw black dots below.

"Dusei," he said. Galey rocked over and looked.

"Filthy beasts," Galey said.

Duncan did not answer him or argue. Most of humankind
would say the same, would wish the remaining mri dead, with
just cause. He watched the desert slip under the airship's
nose, and the land roughen into highlands over which he had

traveled at great cost, in great pain—dreamlike, such speed, looking down on a world where time moved more slowly, where realities were different and immediate and he had learned for a time to live.

They circled out over Sil'athen, the long T-shaped valley remote in the highlands, a slash into the high plateau, much eroded, a canyon full of strange shapes carved by caustic rains and the constant winds that swept its length. There was wreckage there of ships not yet lifted back for salvage, aircraft that Niun had made the price of his taking; and wreckage too of nature, many an aeons-old formation of sandstone blasted into fragments.

When they landed at the crossing of the high valley and stepped out into that place, into the full heat of Arain's red light, the silence came suddenly on them both, a weight that took the breath away. Duncan felt the air at once, a violent change from the pressurized and filtered air in the ship, and began coughing so painfully that he had at once to have recourse to the canteen. Filter masks and tinted goggles were part of the gear; he put his on, and adjusted the hood of his uniform to shield his head from the sun, while Galey did the same. The mask did not overcome the need to cough; he took another small sip of water.

"You all right?" Galey's voice was altered by the mask. Duncan looked into the broad, freckled face and felt better for the company of someone in such silence; but Galey did not belong, he in no wise belonged. Duncan slung his canteen over his shoulder, gathered up the gear, and tried not to listen to the silence.

"I'm all right," Duncan said. "Listen, it's a long ways down the canyon and up into those rocks. You don't have to come."

"My orders say otherwise."

"Am I not trusted with this?" Duncan at once regretted the outburst, seeing how Galey looked at him, shocked and taken aback. "Come on," he said then. "Watch your step."

Duncan walked, at the slow pace necessary in the thin air, Galey walking heavy-footed beside him. The mri were right in the dress they adopted: to have any skin exposed in this sun was not wise; but when Galey began to drift toward the inviting shade of the cliffs, Duncan did not, and Galey returned to him.

"Don't walk the shade," Duncan said. "There are things

you can miss there, that may not miss you. It's dark enough where we'll have to be walking, without taking unnecessary chances."

Galey looked at him uneasily, but asked no questions. The wind sang strangely through the sandstone spires.

It was a place of ghosts: Sil'athen, burial place of the mri. Duncan listened to the wind and looked about him as they walked, at the high cliffs and caves that held their secrets.

A dead people, a dead world. Graves of great age surrounded them here, those on the east with weathered pillars to mark them, those on the west with none. There were writings, many already beyond reading, outworn by the sands, and many a pillar overthrown and destroyed in the fighting that had raged up and down Sil'athen.

And in the sand they found the picked bones of a great dus.

Sadness struck Duncan when he saw that, for the beasts were companions of the mri, and dangerous as they could be, they could also be gentle: sad-faced, slow-moving protectors of their masters.

This, too, was added to the destruction of a way of life.

Galey kicked at the skull. "Fast-working scavengers," he said.

"Leave it alone," Duncan said sharply. Galey blinked, straightened, and took a more formal attitude with him.

It was a true observation nonetheless, that there were scavengers in great numbers in the seemingly lifeless wastelands: nothing dropped to the sand but that something made use of it; nothing faltered or erred but that some predator was waiting for that error. The mri themselves did not walk the desert at night without the dusei to guide them. Even by day it was necessary to watch where one stepped, and to keep an eye to rocks that might hide ambush. Duncan knew the small depression that identified a burrower's lair, and how to keep the sun between himself and rocks to avoid the poisonous strands of windflowers. He knew too how to find water when he must, or how to conceal himself—the latter an easy task in Sil'athen, where the constant winds erased the tracks of any passage, smoothing the tablet of the sands almost as soon as the foot left the ground. Skirling eddies of dust ran like a mist above the ground, occasionally stirring up in great whistling gusts that drove the sand in clouds.

Such a trackless, isolated place the mri had chosen . . .

such an end Niun had chosen, as if even in passing they
wished to obliterate all trace that they had been.

They had been here, he had learned in his long studies, his
cajoling of translators, for many centuries, serving regul.
Here and hereabouts they had fought—against each other
. . . for regul in the beginning had hired them against the
mercenaries of other regul, mercenaries who also chanced to
be mri. The conflicts were listed endlessly in regul records,
only the names changing: *The mri (singular) of doch Holn
defeated the mri (dual) of doch Horag; Horag (indecipherable) fled from the territory (indecipherable).*

So it had begun here—until Holn flung the mri not against
mri, but against humanity. Solitary, strange fighters: humans
had known a single mri to taunt a human outpost, to provoke
a reaction that sometimes ended with more casualties in his
killing than humans were willing to suffer. Wise commanders,
knowing the suicidal fury of these mri berserkers, held their
men from answering, no matter how flagrant the provocation,
until the mri, in splendid arrogance, had passed back to his
own territory.

A challenge, perhaps, to a reciprocal act?

Niun was capable of such a rash thing.

Niun, whose weapons, worn on two belts at chest and hip,
ranged from a laser to a thin, curved sword, an anachronism
in the war he fought.

An old, old way, Niun had called it.

All that was left of it was here.

The place had a feeling of menace in its deeper shadows,
where the sandstone cliffs began to fold them closer, a sense
of holinesses and history, of dead that had never known of
humankind. And there were deeper places, utterly alien,
where mri sentinels had watched and died, faithful to a duty
known only to themselves, and where the rocks hid things
more threatening than the dead.

He had looked on such.

It lay there, distant above the cliffs where the canyon
ended, where heaps of rock had tumbled in massive ruin.

"How far are we going?" Galey asked, with a nervous eye
to the cliffs that confronted them. "We going to climb that?"

"Yes," Duncan said.

Galey looked at him, fell silent again, and trod carefully
behind him as he began to seek that way he knew, up among
the rocks, a dus-trail and little more.

It was there, as he remembered, the way up, concealed in dangerous shadow. He marked his way carefully with his eye, and began it, slowly.

Often in the climb he found himself obliged to pause, coughing, and to drink a little and wait, for the air was thinner still on the upper levels, and he suffered despite the mask. Galey too began to cough, and drank overmuch of their water. Duncan considered letting Galey, who had not come as he had, from a stay in sick-bay, carry more of the equipment; but Galey, from *Saber*'s sterile, automated environment, was laboring painfully.

They made the crest at last, and came into sunlight, among tall spires of rock, a maze that bore no track, no enduring sign to indicate that mri had walked here: in this place, as in Sil'athen, the wind scoured the sand.

Duncan stood, considering the sinking of red Arain beyond the spires, breathed the air cautiously, felt the place with all his senses. He had land-sense, cultivated in a score of trackless environments, and it drew at him, subtle and under the threshold of reason. Galey started to say something; Duncan curtly ordered silence, stood for a time, and listened. The omnipresent wind pulled at them, frolicked, singing among the spires. He turned left.

"Follow me," he said. "Don't talk to me. I last walked this in the dark, and things look different."

Galey murmured agreement, still breathing hard. He was silent thereafter, and Duncan was able to forget his presence as they walked. He would gladly have left Galey: he was not used to company on a mission, was not used to schedules or reports or being concerned for a night spent in the open— and SurTac that he was, he had little respect for the regulars when they were stripped of their protective ships and their contact with superiors.

It occurred to him that *Flower* staff had no authority to order a regular from *Saber* to accompany him.

Stavros did.

Dark overtook them on the plateau, as Duncan had known it would, in a place where the spires were few and a vast stretch of sand lay between them and the farther cliffs.

"We might keep going," Galey volunteered, though his voice seemed strained already.

Duncan shook his head, selected a safe spot, and settled to stay until the dawn, wrapped in a thermal sheet and far more comfortable than in his previous night in this place. They removed the masks and ate, though Galey had small appetite; then they replaced them to sleep, turn and turn about.

A jo flew, briefly airborne, a shadow against the night sky. Once Duncan woke to Galey's whispered insistence that he had heard something moving in the rocks. He sat watch then, while Galey slept or pretended to sleep, and far across the sands he saw the dark shadow of a hunting dus that moved into the deeper shadow of the spires and was gone.

He listened to the wind, and looked at the stars, and knew his way now beyond doubt.

At the first touch of color to the land, they folded up the blankets and set out again, shivering in the early dawn, Galey stiff and limping from his exertion of the day before.

The spires closed about them once more, stained by the ruddy sun, and still the sense of familiarity persisted. They were on the right track; there remained no vestige of doubt in Duncan's mind, but he savored the silence, and did not break it with conversation.

And eventually there lay before him that gap in the rocks, inconspicuous, like a dozen others thereabouts, save for the identifying shelf of rock that slanted down at the left, and the depth of the shadow that lay within.

Duncan paused; it occurred to him that even yet there was time to repent what he was doing, that he could lead Galey in circles until they ran out of supplies, and convince them all that he could not remember, that the place was lost to him. It would need great and skilled effort by Boaz' small staff to locate it without him. It might go unlocated for generations of humans on Kesrith.

But relics did not serve a dead people. That everything they had been should perish, that an intelligent species should vanish from the universe, leaving nothing—there was no rightness in that.

"Here," he said, and led Galey by the way that he well remembered, that he had seen thereafter in his nightmares, that long, close passage between sandstone cliffs that leaned together and shut out the sky. The passage wound, and seemed to spiral, down into dark and cold. Duncan used his penlight, and its tiny beam showed serpentine writings on the walls, turn after turn into the depths.

Daylight broke, blinding and blurring as they arrived at the cul-de-sac that ended their descent. They stood in a deep well of living stone, open to the sky. The walls here too were written over with symbols, and blackened with the traces of fire, both the stone and the metal door that stood open at the far side of the pit.

Galey swore: the sound of the human irreverence grated on Duncan's ears, and he looked to his left, where Galey stared. A huddled mass of bones and burned tatters of black cloth rested in a niche within the stone. It was the guardian of the shrine. Niun had paid him respect; Duncan felt moved to do so and did not know how.

"Don't touch anything," he said, and immediately recalled Melein's similar words to him, a chilling echo in the deep well.

He tried to put his mind to other things—knelt on the sand in the sunlight and opened up the gear that he had carried, photographic equipment, and most of all a signal device. He activated it, and knew from that moment that human presence in this place was inevitable. Searching aircraft would eventually find it.

Then with the camera he rose and recorded all that was about them, the writings, the guardian, the doorway with its broken seal, the marks of destroying fire.

And last of all he ventured into the dark, into the shrine that not even Niun had presumed to enter—only Melein, with Niun to guard the door. Galey started to follow him, stepped within.

"Stay back," Duncan ordered; his voice echoed terribly in the metal chamber, and Galey halted, uncertain, in the doorway—retreated when Duncan stared at him. Duncan drew a careful breath then and activated the camera and its light, by that surveying the ruin about him.

Shrine: it was rather a place of fire-stained steel, ruined panels, banks of lifeless machinery, stark and unlovely. He had known what he would find here, had heard the sound of it, the working of machinery the night the place had died, destroyed by the mri.

And yet the mri, who well understood machines, revered it—revered the artifact they had borne away from it.

Mistrust recurred in him, human mistrust, the remembrance that the mri had never offered assurances to him: they had only held their hand from him.

Banks of machinery, no trace of holiness. The thing that Niun had so lovingly carried hence, that now rested in *Flower*'s belly, suddenly seemed sinister and threatening . . . a weapon, perhaps, that could be triggered by probing. The mri penchant for taking enemies with them in their self-destruction made it entirely possible, made Niun's treasuring of it still comprehensible. Yet Boaz and security evidently had some confidence that it was no weapon.

It had its origin here—*here*, cradled in that rest, perhaps, that now was stripped and vacant. Duncan lifted the camera, completed his work among the dead, burned banks, explored recesses where the light pierced deep shadows, where yet the wind had not swept away the ash. Boaz' people would come here next; some of the computer specialists would try the wreckage of the banks, with little hope. Melein had been thorough, protecting this place from humanity, whatever it once might have been.

He had all he needed, all he could obtain. He returned to the entry, and delayed yet again, taking in the place with a last glance, as if that could fix it all in his mind and pierce through the heart of what was mri.

"Sir?" Galey said from the well.

Duncan turned abruptly, joined Galey in the daylight, moved aside the breathing mask that suddenly seemed to restrict his oxygen—glad to draw a breath of acrid, daylit air, wind-clean. Galey's broad, anxious face seemed suddenly of another, a more welcome world.

"Let's go," he said then to Galey. "Let's get out of here."

The lower canyon was already deep in shadow when they reached the edge of the plateau, that path among the rocks that led down into Sil'athen. It was late afternoon where they stood, and twilight down in the canyon beneath them.

"Dark's going to be on us again before we reach the ship," Duncan said.

"We going to go all the way anyway?" Galey asked.

Duncan shook his head. "No. At dusk we sit down wherever we are."

Galey did not look pleased. Likely whoever had given him

C. J. Cherryh

his orders had not well prepared him for the possibilities of nights spent in the open. Duncan's nose had started bleeding again on the return walk, irritated by the thin, dry air; Galey's cough had worsened, and if they must spend another night in the open, Galey would be suffering the like.

The regular attacked the descent first, scattering pebbles, slipping somewhat in his determination to make haste. And suddenly he stopped.

Duncan heard the aircraft at the same instant, a distant hum that grew louder, passed overhead and circled off again. He looked at Galey, and Galey likewise looked disturbed.

"Maybe it's weather moving in on us," Galey said, "or maybe it's something urgent at the port."

Duncan had the communicator; he fingered it nervously, reckoning that if either had been the case, then there should have been a call from the aircraft. There was silence.

"Move," he said to Galey.

There was no sign of the aircraft while they worked their way down the dangerous descent. They rested hardly at all; Duncan found blood choking him, stripped off the mask and wiped his face, smearing a red streak across his hand—dizziness blurred the rocks. He felt his way after Galey, stumbled to the valley floor, the soft and difficult sand.

"You're just out of sickbay," Galey said, offering with a touch on the straps to take the load that he carried. "Trust me with the gear at least. You'll be done up again."

"No," he answered, blindly stubborn. He gathered his feet under him and started walking, overwhelmed with anxiety, Galey struggling to stay with him.

Another kilometer up the canyon: this much ground Duncan made before he found his limit with the load he carried, coughing painfully; he surrendered the gear to Galey, who labored along with him, himself suffering from the cold air, rawly gasping after each breath. It was a naked, terribly isolate feeling, walking these shadowed depths among the tombs, carrying a record that did not belong to humanity, that others desired.

And there came a regul vehicle lumbering down the canyon, slow and ponderous. Galey swore. Duncan simply watched it come.

There was nothing to do, nowhere to go, no longer even any place to conceal the equipment. They were far from the rocks, in the center of the sandy expanse and under observation from the regul.

The sled rumbled up to them and stopped. The windscreen rolled back. A regul youngling smiled a regul smile at them both, a mere opening of the mouth that showed the ridge of dentition within.

"*Kose* Sten Duncan," said the regul. "We grew concerned. All right? All right?"

"Entirely," he said. "Go away. We do not need help."

The smile stayed. The round brown eyes flicked over his face, his hand, the equipage they carried. "Thin air. Heavy to carry, perhaps? Sit on the back, favor. I will carry you. Many bad things are here, evening coming. I am *koj* Suth Horag-gi. Bai Hulagh sent me. The reverence has profound concern— would not wish, *kose* Sten Duncan, accident to a human party here in the desert. We will take you back."

It was a small vehicle, a sled with a flatbed for cargo, where it was possible to sit without being confined: it was not imminently threatening, and it was pointless pride to refuse and keep walking, when the sled could easily match their best pace.

But Duncan did not believe the words he had been told— mistrusted the regul presence entirely. Galey was not moving without him, stood waiting his cue; and with great misgivings Duncan climbed aboard the flatbed of the little vehicle. He made room for Galey, who joined him, holding the gear carefully on his lap. The vehicle jolted into a slow turn on the sand.

"They must have landed down by our ship," Galey shouted into his ear. Duncan understood his meaning: regul all over their ship, that they had not secured because there was no living enemy against whom they reasonably ought to have secured it. He cursed himself for that overconfidence.

They two were armed. The regul were insane if they hoped to outmatch human reflexes in a direct confrontation; but the fact was that regul could expend younglings such as these with little regret.

And the reverence bai Hulagh had sent them—Hulagh, whose fear of the mri was obsessive and sufficient for murder.

Duncan touched Galey's arm, used the system of handsignals used in emergencies in space. *Careful. Hostiles.*

Friendlies, Galey signed back, hopeful contradiction. There was, to be sure, a treaty in effect, the utmost in courteous cooperation all over Kesrith base. Galey was confused. Humans did not like the regul, but hostiles was not a term used any longer.

Trouble, Duncan answered. *Possible. Watch.*

Shoot? Galey queried.

Possible, he replied.

The landsled lumbered on at a fair clip, enough that keeping their place on the flatbed was not an easy matter. But what would have been a long and man-killing walk in Kesrith's atmosphere—and likely an overnight camp—became a comparatively short and comfortable ride. Duncan tried inwardly to reason away his anxieties, trying to think it possible that in the intricacies of regul motives, these regul were trying to protect them, fearing Stavros' displeasure if they were lost.

He could not convince himself. They were alone with the regul, far from help.

They rounded the bend, and saw indeed that there was a regul ship on the ground near their own. They were headed directly for it. Duncan tugged at the straps in Galey's hands, took the equipment to himself, all of it, then with a nod to Galey rolled off and landed afoot on the sand, in a maneuver the heavy regul could not have performed.

They had covered a considerable distance toward the safety of their own ship before the regul driver reacted, bringing the sled back about to block their path; and other younglings began to come down the ramp out of the regul ship.

"Are you all right? You fell?" asked the regul driver.

"No," said Duncan. "No problem. We are going back to base now. Thank you."

It did not work. The other younglings walked heavily about them, surrounding them, smiling with gaping friendliness and at the same time blocking their way.

"Ah," said Suth Horag-gi, dismounting from the sled. "You take pictures. Mri treasures?"

"Property of Stavros," Duncan said in a clipped tone, and with the dispatch he had learned was humanity's advantage over the slow-moving regul, he shouldered a youngling, broke the circle, and walked rapidly for the ramp of their own ship, disregarding a youngling that tried to head them off.

"Good fortune," said that one with the proper youngling

obsequiousness. "Good fortune you are back safe, *kose* Sten Duncan."

"Yes, thank you for your concern. My regards to the reverence bai Hulagh."

He spoke in the regul tongue, as the regul had spoken in the human. He shouldered the heavy, awkward youngling with brutal force that to a regul was hardly painful. The push flung it slightly off balance, and he passed it. Galey overtook him on the ramp, almost running. They boarded, found another youngling in the aircraft.

"Out," Duncan ordered. "Please return to your own ship. We are about to go now."

It looked doubtful, and finally, easing past them, performed the suck of air considered polite among regul, smiled that gaping smile and waddled with stately lack of haste down the ramp.

Duncan set the gear down on the flooring and hit the switch to lift the ramp the moment the youngling was clear, and Galey shut the door and spun the wheel to seal it.

Duncan found himself shaking. He thought that Galey was too.

"What did they want?" Galey asked, his voice a note too high.

"Check out the ship before we lift," Duncan said. "Check out everything that could be sabotaged." And Galey stripped off the breathing mask and the visor and swore softly, staring at him, then flung them aside and set to work, began examining the panels and their inner workings with great care.

There was nothing, in the most careful examination, wrong. "Wish we could find something," Galey said, and Duncan agreed to that, fervently. The regul still waited outside.

Galey started the engines and slowly, testing out controls, turned the aircraft and hovered a few feet off the ground, running a course that vengefully dusted the regul craft, passing close enough to send the regul who were outside scrambling and stumbling ponderously toward cover.

Senior officer, Duncan should have rebuked that. He did not. He settled into the cushion while the aircraft lifted, his jaw clenched, his hand gripping the cushion with such force that when he realized it, long after they were at altitude enough that they had options if something went wrong, his fingers were numb and there were deep impressions in the cushion.

"Game of nerves," he said to Galey. "Game of nerves—or whatever they were going to do, they didn't have time."

Galey looked at him. There were the patches of half a dozen worlds on Galey's sleeve, young as he was. But Galey was scared, and it was a tale that would make the rounds of the regular military of *Saber*, this encounter with regul.

"This is Stavros' business," Duncan told him, for Galey's sake, not for the regul, not even for Stavros. "The less noise made, the better. Take my example."

His reputation was, he knew, widespread among the regulars: the SurTac who had lost his head, who had gone hysterical and accused a high-ranking ally of murder. Doubtless it would stay on his record forever, barring Stavros' intervention, barring a promotion on Kesrith so high that the record could no longer harm him—and that was at present unlikely.

Galey seemed to understand him, and to be embarrassed by it. "Yes, sir," he said quietly. "Yes, sir."

The lights of Kesrith base came finally into view. They circled the area for the landing nearest *Flower*, and settled, signalling security with the emergency code. Duncan unstrapped and gathered the photographic equipment from its cushioned ride in the floor locker. Galey opened the hatch and lowered the ramp, and Duncan walked down into the escort of armed human security with a relief so great his knees were weak.

Across the field he saw another aircraft come in, close to the Nom side of the airfield, where the regul might be closest to their own authority.

A security agent tried to take the equipment from Duncan's hand. "No," he said sharply, and for once security deferred.

He lost Galey somewhere, missed him in the press and was sorry he had not given some courtesy to the regular who had done so competently; but *Flower*'s ramp was ahead, the open hatch aglow with lights in the surrounding night. He walked among the security men, into the ship, down the corridors, and to the science section.

Boaz waited, white-smocked, anxious. He did not deliver the gear to her directly, for it was heavy, but laid it on a counter.

There was nothing for him to do with it thereafter. He had

completed his task for the human powers of Kesrith, and sold what the mri counted most valuable in all the world. The knowledge of it, like that of the ovoid that rested here behind voice-locked doors, was in human hands and not in those of regul, and that was, within the circumstances, the best that he could do.

Chapter Three

————◦◉◦————

THE MAJORITY of *Flower* personnel were in for the night after the initial excitement of receiving the records. The labs were shut down again, the skeleton night crew on duty. The ship had a different quality by night, a ghostly hush but for the whisper of machinery and ventilation, far different from the frenetic activity in its narrow corridors by day.

Duncan found the prospect of a bed, a quiet night in his own safe quarters, a bath (even the chemical scrub allowable under rationing) utterly, utterly attractive, after a three-hour debriefing. It was 0100 by the local clock, which was the time on which he lived.

The lateness of the hour did not stop him from descending to the medical section and pausing in Niun's room. There was neither day nor night for the mri, who lay, slack and deteriorating despite the therapy applied to his limbs, in the influence of sedation. Luiz had promised to consider a lessening of sedation; Duncan had argued heatedly with Luiz on this point.

There was no response now when he spoke to the mri. He touched Niun's shoulder, shook at him gently, hating to feel how thin the mri was becoming.

Tension returned to the muscles. The mri drew a deeper breath, moved against the restraints that stayed on him constantly, and his golden eyes opened, half-covered by the membrane. The membrane withdrew, but not entirely. The fixation of the eyes was wild and confused.

"Niun," Duncan whispered, then aloud: "Niun!"

The struggle continued, and yet the mri seemed only slightly aware of his presence, despite the grip of his hand. It

48

was another thing, something inward, that occupied Niun, and the wide, golden eyes were dilated, terrified.

"Niun, stop it. It's Duncan. It's Duncan with you. Be still and look at me."

"Duncan?" The mri was suddenly without strength, chest heaving from exertion, as if he had run from some impossibly far place. "The dusei are lost."

Such raving was pitiable. Niun was a man of keen mind, of quick reflexes. He looked utterly confused now. Duncan held his arm, and, knowing the mri's pride, drew a corner of the sheet across the mri's lower face, a concealment behind which the mri would feel more secure.

Slowly, slowly, the sense came back to that alien gaze. "Let me go, Duncan."

"I can't," he said miserably. "I can't, Niun."

The eyes began to lose their focus again, to slip aside. The muscles in the arm began to loosen. "Melein," Niun said.

"She is all right." Duncan clenched his hand until surely it hurt, trying to hold him to hear that. But the mri was back in his own dream. His breathing was rapid. His head turned from side to side in delirium.

And finally he grew quiet again.

Duncan withdrew his hand from Niun's arm and left, walking slowly at first, then more rapidly. The episode distressed him in the strangeness of it; but Niun was fighting the sedation, was coming out of it more and more strongly, had known him, spoken to him. Perhaps it was alien metabolism, perhaps, the thought occurred to him, Luiz had adjusted the level of sedation, more reasonable than he had shown himself in argument on the subject.

He went to the main lock, to the guard post that watched the coming and going of all that entered and left the ship. He signed the log and handed the stylus back.

"Hard session, sir?" the night guard asked, sympathy, not inquisitiveness. Tereci knew him.

"Somewhat, somewhat," he said, blinked at Tereci from eyes he knew were red, felt of his chin, that was rough. "Message for Luiz when he wakes: I want to talk with him at the earliest."

"Recorded, sir," said Tereci, scratching it into the message sheet.

Duncan started through the lock, expecting it to open for him under Tereci's hand. It did.

"Sir," Tereci said. "You're not armed. Regulations."

Duncan swore, exhausted, remembering the standing order for personnel out at night. "Can you check me out sidearms?"

"Sign again," Tereci said, opened a locker and gave him a pistol, waiting while he put his name to another form. "I'm sorry," Tereci said. "But we've had some action around here at night. Regulations aside, it's better to carry something."

"Regul?" he asked, alarmed at that news, which he had not read in the reports. Regul was all that immediately occurred to him, and had he not been so tired, he would not have been so impolitic.

"Animals. Prowling the limits of the guard beams. They never get inside them, but I wouldn't go out there unarmed. You want an escort, sir? I could get one of the night security—"

"No need," he said wearily. "No need." He had come in from the open, and though armed then, he had never thought in terms of weapons. He had walked the land in company with mri. He regarded no warnings of these men that were bound to the safety of *Flower* and the Nom, who had never seen the land they had come to occupy.

They could stand in the midst of Sil'athen and never see it, men of Galey's breed—solid men, decent.

Unwondering.

He belted on the gun, a heavy weight, an offense to a weary back, and smiled a tired thanks at Tereci, went out into the chill, acrid air. A geyser had blown out irreverently close to *Flower*. The steam made the air moist and clouded. He inhaled it deeply, not minding the flavor of it, found it grateful to walk the track by himself, in silence, without Galey. His head ached. He had not realized it before this. He took his time, and found nothing but pleasure in the night, under the larger of Kesrith's moons, with the air chill and the stars glittering, and far, far across the flats, lights illumined the geysers that spouted almost constantly. The land had become a boiling and impassable barrier, guarding the approaches to the ruins of the mri towers, that only the most intrepid of Boaz' researchers had scanned from the air.

Steel rang under his boots, the gratings that made firm the surface of the causeway. It was the only sound. He stopped, only to have complete silence for a moment, and scanned the whole of the horizon, the glittering waters of the Alkaline

Sea, the lights of the city, the steaming geysers, the ridges beyond *Flower*.

Rock scuffed, rattled. The sound seized his heart and held it constricted. He heard it again, spun toward the sound, saw a shadow shamble four-footed down a ridge.

It hit the guard beams and shied back, whuffing in alarm. Then it reared up against the sky, twice the height of a tall man, a great, long-clawed beast.

The dusei are lost, Niun had said.

Duncan stood still, heart pounding. He reckoned the danger posed by these great omnivores, these natives of Kesrith. venom-clawed and powerful enough to rip a man to shreds. This one tried the beam again, again, disliking the sensation, but single-minded in its attempt.

A second beast showed on the crest of the slope, coming down-hill. *Flower*'s spotlights came on, adding to confusion, her hatch open, men pouring out.

"Stop!" Duncan shouted. "No farther! Don't shoot!"

The dus tried the beam again, heaved his bulk forward, and this time energies of the defense system played along his great sides, useless. He broke through, reared up and screamed, a moaning, hollow cry that echoed off the walls of Kesrith's Nom.

A rifle beam cut the dark.

"Stop shooting!" Duncan shouted.

The second beast broke through, a sparkle of light against its sides, a stench of singed fur. They huddled together, the two invaders, backed rump to rump, and kept shifting nervously.

Niun's beasts.

Duncan saw them head for the ramp, toward the open door, where the men were—saw shots fired. The beasts shied off.

"No!" he cried, and the beasts backed, turned and came toward him, snuffing the air. Back at the hatchway, men shouted at him. They could not fire; he was too close to the beasts. Lights played on them, blinding. The dusei, locked into their inquisitive obstinacy, paid no heed. They came, long-clawed feet turned in, claws rattling on the mesh, heads lowered, ursine monsters—slope-shouldered, almost comic in their distracted manner.

The larger dus nosed at him, sniffed noisily from its pug nose. Duncan stood still, heart pounding so that the blood raced in his veins. The beast nudged him, nothing gentle, and he did not fall; it nosed his hand, investigated it with the mobile center of the lip.

And they circled one before him and then the other, shifting position in a strange ballet, constantly between him and the men with the rifles, uttering low, moaning cries. He took his life in pawn and moved, found that they moved with him. He stopped and they stopped.

They were surely Niun's beasts, that had come a long, hard journey from Sil'athen—far longer a trek for them than for men's machines. And with uncanny accuracy they had found Niun, across a hundred miles of desert, and singled out the place that confined him.

He had seen dusei and mri work, had watched the beasts react, so sensitive to the voice, the gestures of the mri. He had seen the mri glance at the beast, and the beast react as if some unspoken agreement were between them.

He felt them against him, touching, giving him the heat of their vast, velvet-furred bodies. Nearly impossible to kill, the dusei, immune to the poisons of Kesrith's predators, vastly powerful, gentle and comic in their preoccupied approach to difficulties. He felt himself for a moment dizzy, the closeness of the beasts, their warmth, his exhaustion too much: he was for an instant afraid of the men with their guns, of the lights.

He thought of Niun, and there was another blurring, a desire, overwhelmingly strong, warm, determined.

The men, the lights, the guns.

Terror/desire/terror.

He blinked, caught himself with a hand against one warm back, found himself trembling uncontrollably. He began to walk, slowly, toward the open doorway, toward the security crew, who had their guns levelled, guns that could do little to a dus' massive, slow body, much to his.

He felt the savor of blood. Of heat.

"No!" he said to the dusei. They grew calm.

He stopped within easy hailing of the security personnel.

"Get out of there," one called to him. "Get out of there!"

"Go back inside," he said, "and seal all the corridors except the ones that go down to the holds. Give me a way to a safe compartment for them. Make it quick."

They did not stay to argue. Two went inside, to consult with authority, doubtless. Duncan stayed with the dusei, a hand on either broad back, calming them. They sensed Niun and Melein. They knew. They knew.

He was safe with them. It was the men with the guns that were to be feared. "Go away from the door," he wished the remaining security men. "They are no danger to me. They belong to the mri."

"Duncan?" That was Boaz' female voice, high-pitched and anxious. "Duncan, confound it, what's going on?"

"They've come for Niun. They're his. These creatures—are halfway sapient, maybe more than halfway. I want clearance to bring them inside before someone sets them off."

There was a flurry of consultations. Duncan waited, stroking the two massive backs. The dusei had settled down, sitting like dogs. They, too, waited.

"Come ahead," Boaz shouted. "Number one bow hold, equipment bay: it's empty."

Duncan made to the dusei the low sound he had heard Niun make, started forward. The dusei heaved themselves to their feet and came, casually, as if entering human ships were an ordinary thing. But no human stayed to meet them: even Boaz fled, prudence overcoming curiosity, and nothing greeted them but sealed doors and empty corridors.

They walked, the three of them, a long, long descent without lifts, down ways awkward for the big dusei—passed with a slow, measured clicking of claws on flooring. Duncan was not afraid. It was impossible to be afraid, with the like of them for companionship. They had searched him and had no fear of him: though at the back of his mind reason kept trying to urge him that he had been right to be afraid of the beasts, he began to be certain that the beasts were utterly at ease with what he was doing.

He came down into the hold, and caressed the offered noses, the thrusting massive heads that, less gentle, could stave in ribs or break his back; and again came that blurred feeling, that surety that he had given them something that pleased them.

He withdrew and sealed the doors, and trembled afterward, thinking what he had done. Food, water, other needs they had none, not at the moment. They wanted in. They had gained that, through him.

He fled, fear flooding him. He was panting as he ran the final distance to the medical wing. He saw the door that he wanted—closed, like all other doors during the emergency. He opened it manually, closed it again.

"Sir?" the sentry on duty asked.

"Are they awake?" Duncan asked, with harsh intensity. The sentry looked confused.

"No, sir. I don't think so."

Duncan shouldered past him, opened the door and looked at Niun. The mri's eyes were open, staring at the ceiling. Duncan went to the bedside and seized Niun's arm, hard.

"Niun. The dusei. The dusei. They have come."

There was a fine sweat on the mri's brow. The golden eyes stared into infinity.

"They are here," Duncan almost shouted at him. Niun blinked.

"Yes," said Niun. "I feel them."

And thereafter Niun answered nothing, reacted to nothing, and his eyes closed, and he slept, with a relaxed and tranquil expression.

"Sir?" the sentry asked, invading the room contrary to standing orders. "Do you want someone called?"

"No," Duncan said harshly. He edged past the man, walked out into the corridor, and started for the upper levels of the ship. The intercom came on, the whole ship waking to the emergency just past. He heard that Boaz was paging him, urgently.

He did not remember the walk upstairs, the whole of it a blank in his mind when he reached the area of the lock and found Boaz anxiously waiting. He dreaded such lapses, remembering the dizzy blurring of senses that had assailed him before.

"They're domestic?" Boaz asked him.

"They—seem to be. They are, for the mri. They're—I don't know. I don't know."

Boaz looked at him critically. "You're through for the day," she said. "No more questions. If they're bedded down and secure, no questions."

"No one goes down there. They're dangerous."

"No one is going to go near them."

"They're halfway sapient," he said. "They found the mri. Across all that desert and out of all these buildings, they found them."

He was shaking. She touched his arm, blonde, plump Boaz, and at that moment she was the most beautiful and kindly

creature in all Kesrith. "Sten, go home," she said. "Get to
your own quarters; get some rest. One of the security officers
will walk you. Get out of here."

He nodded, measured his strength against the distance to
the Nom, and concluded that he had enough left in him to
make it to his room without staggering. He turned, blindly,
without a word of thanks to Boaz, remembered nothing until
he was out the door and halfway down the ramp with a security man at his side, rifle over one arm.

The mental gaps terrified him. Fatigue, perhaps. He wished
to believe so.

But he had not consciously decided to enter *Flower* with
the dusei.

He had not decided.

He tore his mind away, far away from the dusei, fighting a
giddy return to the warmth that was their touch.

Yes, Niun had said, *I feel them.*

I feel them.

He talked to the security man, something to drown the
silence, talked of banal things, of nonsensical things with slur-
ring speech and no recall later of what he said.

It was only necessary, until he was within the brightly
lighted safety of the Nom, in its echoing halls that smelled of
regul and humans, that there not be silence.

The security guard left him at the door, pressed a plastic
vial into his hand. "Dr. Luiz advised it," he said.

Duncan did not question what the red capsules were. They
killed the dreams, numbed his senses, made it possible for
him to rest without remembering anything.

He woke the next morning and found he had not turned
off the lights.

Chapter Four

———————•◦•———————

STAVROS, SEATED outside his sled-console, in the privacy of his own quarters, looked like a man who had not slept. There was a thick folder of papers on the desk in front of him, rumpled and read: the labor of days to produce, of a night to read.

Duncan saw, and knew that there was some issue of his work, of the hours that he had spent writing and rewriting what he was sure only one man would ever see, reports that did not go to Boaz or Luiz, or even to security: that would never enter the records, if they ran counter to Stavros' purposes.

"Sit down," Stavros said.

Duncan did so, subject to the scrutiny of Stavros' pale eyes on a level with his own. He had no sense of accomplishment, rather that he had done all that was in him to do, and that it had probably failed, as all other things had failed to make any difference with Stavros. He had labored more over that report than over any mission prep he had ever done; and even while he worked he had feared desperately that it was all for nothing, that it was only something asked of him as a sop to his protests, and that Stavros would discard it half-read.

"This mri so-called shrine," said Stavros. "You know that the regul are disturbed about it. They're frightened. They connect all this mri business in their thinking: the shrine, the artifact, the fact that we've taken trouble to keep two mri alive—and your influence, that not least. The whole thing forms a design they don't like. Do you know the regul claim they rescued you and Galey?"

Duncan almost swore, smothered it. "Not true."

"Remember that to a regul your situation out there may have looked desperate. A regul could not have walked that distance. Night was coming on, and they have a terror of the dark in the open wilderness. They claim they spotted the grounded aircraft and grew concerned for your safety—that they have been trying to watch over our crews in their explorations, for fear of some incident happening which might be blamed on them."

"Do you really believe that, sir?"

"No," said Stavros flatly. "I rather put it down to curiosity. To Hulagh's curiosity in particular. He is mortally afraid of what the mri might do, afraid of anything that has their hand in it. I think he's quite obsessed with the fear that some may survive and locate him. I am being frank with you. This is not for conversation outside this room. Now tell me this: was there any touching, any overt threat from the regul you encountered?"

"No hand laid on us. But our property—"

"I read that."

"Yes, sir."

"You handled it well enough," said Stavros, a slight frown on his face. "I think, though, that it does indicate that there is a certain interest in you personally, as well as in the mri relics. I think it was your presence drew them out there. And if I hadn't put Galey out there with you, you could have met with an accident. You neglected precautions."

"Yes, sir."

"They'll kill you if they can. I can deal with it after it happens, but I can't prevent it, not so long as you're within convenient reach of them. And why this shrine, Duncan? Why this artifact?"

"Sir?"

"Why do you reckon it was so important? Why did the mri risk their lives to go to that place and fetch it?"

Duncan gestured vaguely to the report that lay on the desk. "Religion. I explained—"

"You've been inside that so-called shrine. I've seen the pictures you brought out. Do you really believe that it's a place of worship?"

"It's important to them." He was helpless to say anything else. Other conclusions lay there in the photographs: computer banks, weaponry, communications—all such possibilities as regul would dread, as allies of the regul would have to fear.

"You're right: it's important to them. Boaz has cracked your egg, Duncan. Three days ago. The artifact is open."

It shook him. He had thought it unlikely—that if it were to be opened, it would need mri help, cooperation, that might be negotiated. But Boaz' plump hands, that worked with pinpoint probe and brush, with all the resources of *Flower's* techs at her command—they had succeeded, and now the mri had nothing left that was their own.

"I hadn't thought it would be possible that soon," Duncan said. "Does the report say what it was?"

"Is. What it *is*. Boaz says it was designed for opening, no matter of difficulty to someone with the right technique, and some assurance that it was not a weapon, which I understand your pictures provided. It's some sort of recording device. The linguistic part of it is obscure—some sort of written record is there; and there's no one fluent in the mri language to be able to crack the script. For obvious reasons we don't want to consult with the regul. But there's numerical data there too, in symbols designed to be easily deciphered by anyone: there was even a key provided in graphics. Your holy object, Duncan, and this so-named shrine, are some kind of records-storage, and they wanted it badly, wanted it more than they wanted to survive. What kind of record would be that important?"

"I don't know."

"Numerical records. Series of numerical records. What sort of recording device does that suggest to you?"

Duncan sat silent a moment. In his limited experience only one thing suggested itself. "Navigational records," he said at last, because Stavros waited, determined to have such an answer.

"Yes. And is that not a curious thing for them to want, when they had no ship?"

Duncan sat and considered the several possibilities, few of them pleasant to contemplate.

"It knocks out another idea," Stavros said, "—that the mri were given all their technology by the regul: that they weren't literate or technologically sophisticated on their own." He picked up a photo that lay face-down on the desk, pushed it across, awkward in the extension of his arm. "From the artifact, ten times actual size."

Duncan studied it. It showed a gold plate, engraved with symbols, detail very complex. It would have been delicate work had the original been as large as the picture.

"Plate after plate," said Stavros. "Valuable for the metal alone. Boaz theorizes that it was not all done by one hand, and that the first of that series is very old. Techniques of great sophistication or of great patience, one or the other, and meant to last. I'm told the mathematics are intricate; they've gone to computer to try to duplicate the series to navigational tape, and to try to match it out with some reference point. Even so it seems beyond our capabilities to do a thorough analysis on it. We may have to resort to the labs at Haven, and that's going to take time. A great deal of time. But you maintain you had no idea what it was you had."

"No, sir." He met Stavros' eyes without flinching, the only defense he could make. "I didn't know then and I'm not even sure now that the mri knew; maybe they were sent by their own authorities, and had no idea why. But I'll agree it's highly likely that they knew."

"Can you get it out of them?"

"No. No. I don't think so."

"They seem to have expected a ship—if this tape is what it appears to be."

"I don't think they did. They wanted offworld, yes, but they expected nothing. That's an emotional judgment, based on the general tone of things they said and did, but I believe it."

"Possibly a very valid judgment. But they may not commit your error, Duncan, of seeing all regul as alike. The mri dealt specifically with doch Holn; Alagn is Holn's rival; and Holn ...does have ships."

Cold settled from brain to stomach. The argument was plausible. "Yes, sir," Duncan said softly. "But it would be a matter of contacting them."

"The so-called shrine—is a possibility."

"No."

"Another emotional judgment?"

"The same judgment. The mri are finished. They knew it."

"So says Alagn; so, perhaps, said your mri. Perhaps neither is lying. But regul sometimes do not say all they know. Perhaps mri don't, either. Perhaps we haven't asked the right questions." Hand trembling, Stavros lifted a cup and drank, set it down again. "The mri are mercenaries. Are yours for hire?"

The question set him aback. "Maybe. I don't know."

"I think the regul as a whole fear that. I think that is one of several things Hulagh desperately fears, that having lost possession of the mri, he might find humankind possessing them. And using them. What is their usual price, do you know?"

"I don't know." He looked at Stavros, found that curious, half-mocking manner between him and the truth. He laid the picture down on the desk. "What are you proposing?"

"I'm not. I'm just wondering how well you profess to know them."

"It wasn't a thing we discussed."

"According to your records, you're a skilled pilot."

He looked at Stavros blankly.

"True?" Stavros asked.

"If the record says so."

"Elag/Haven operations required some interstellar navigation."

"I had a ship automated to the hilt. I can handle in-system navigation; but everything in transit operations was taped."

"That is rather well what we're dealing with here, isn't it?"

Duncan found nothing to say for several moments.

"Does all this come together somehow?" he asked finally. "What is it you're really asking?"

"Take the mri in charge. Take the artifact, the egg. You say that you can handle the mri. Or is that so, after all?"

Duncan leaned back in his chair, put distance between himself and the old man, drew several slow breaths. He knew Stavros, but not, he thought suddenly, well enough.

"You have doubts?" Stavros asked.

"Any sane man would have doubts. Take the mri and do what? What is this about navigation?"

"I'm asking you whether you really think you can handle the mri."

"In what regard?"

"Whether you can find out more than that report of yours tells me. Whether you can find some assurance for Kesrith that the mri are not going to be trouble, or that Holn does not have its hands on more of them."

Duncan leaned forward again and rested his arms on the front of Stavros' desk, knowing full well that there was deception involved. He looked Stavros in the eyes and was sure of it, bland and innocent as Stavros' expression was. "You're not influenced by my advice. You're going to send me off blind, and there's something else going on. Can I know what that is? Or do I guess at it?"

They had lived close, had shared, he and the old man; he leaned on that fact desperately, saw offense and a slow yielding in Stavros' expression. "Between us," Stavros said.

"Between us."

Stavros frowned, a tremor of strain in his lips. "I want the mri off Kesrith, immediately. I'm sending *Flower* up to station, where it can proceed about its work unhindered. The regul are getting nervous about the mri since your visit to Sil'athen. And a regul ship incoming is not an impossibility in the near future. Hulagh says his doch will be getting anxious because he's failed his schedule with a ship that was entrusted to him by their central organization: its loss is going to be a heavy blow to Alagn. And he's worried. He constantly frets on the topic of misunderstandings, demands a way offworld to meet his ships. If we have regul ships incoming, I don't want any of ours caught on the ground. I think moving *Flower* aloft will minimize any chance of an incident. *Saber* and *Hannibal* together have shields sufficient to protect the station and the probe ships if there should be a problem. But with the mri anywhere accessible to the regul, there could easily be a problem. The regul have a panic reaction where it concerns mri."

"I've seen it at work," Duncan said bitterly.

"Yes," said Stavros. "The bai has asked repeatedly about the artifact. I daresay the bai does not sleep easily. If you had at your disposal a ship, the mri, and the egg, Duncan, do you think you could find out the nature of that record?"

Duncan let out his breath slowly. "Alone?"

"You would have the original artifact. The mri would doubtless insist on it; and we have duplicated the object in holos—so we wouldn't be risking more than the museum value of the object, considerable though that may be. Under the circumstances it's a reasonable risk." Stavros took a long drink, rested the cup on the desk with a betraying rattle of pottery. His breath came hard. "Well?"

"Tell me plainly," Duncan said, "what the object of this is. How far. Where. What options?"

"No certainties. No clear promises. If the mri go for Holn

assistance, you'll lose the ship, your life—whatever. I'm willing to gamble on your conviction they won't. You can find out what that tape is and maybe—*maybe*—deal with the mri. You tell me. If you think it's impossible, say so. But going the route of the computers at Haven will take months, a year—with the regul-mri question hanging over us here at Kesrith, and ourselves with no idea what we're facing. We need to know."

"And if I refused?"

"Your mri would die. No threat: you know the way of it. We can't let them go; they'd get the regul or the regul would get them. If we keep them as they are, they'll die. They always have."

It was, of course, the truth.

"More than that," said Stavros, "all of us are sitting on the line here at Kesrith. And there's the matter of the treaty, that involves rather more than Kesrith. You appreciate that, I'm sure. You say you can reason with them. You've said that all along. I'm giving you your chance."

"This wasn't in the contract. I didn't agree to any offworld assignments."

Stavros remained unmoved. Duncan looked into his eyes, fully aware what the contract was worth in colonial territory—that in fact his consent was only a formality.

"It is a SurTac's operation," said Stavros finally. "But back out if you don't think you can do it."

"A ship," Duncan said.

"There's probe *Fox*. Unarmed. Tight quarters too, if there should be trouble aboard. But one man could handle her."

"Yes, sir. I know her class."

"*Boaz* is finishing up on the holos now. *Flower* is going up to the station this afternoon, whatever you decide. If you have to have time to think about it, a shuttle can run you up to the station later, but don't plan to take too long about a decision."

"I'll go."

Stavros nodded slowly, released a long breath. "Good," he said, and that was all.

Duncan arose, walked across the room to the door, looking back once. Stavros said nothing, and Duncan exited with resentment and regret equally mixed.

There was a matter of gear to pack, that only. He had

lived all his life under those conditions. It would take about five minutes.

Regul stared at him as he walked the hall to his room, were still interested when he walked back with his dunnage slung over his shoulder—carrying a burden, which neither regul nor mri would do: the regul not without a machine, and the mri—never.

They flatly gaped, which in regul could be smiles, and, he thought, they were smiles of pleasure to realize that he was leaving.

The mri's human, he had heard them call him, and mri was spoken as a curse.

"Good-bye, human," one called at him. He ignored it, knowing it was not for friendliness that they wished him farewell.

There was a moment of sadness, walking the causeway outside. He paused to look toward the hills, with the premonition that it was for the last time.

A man could not wholly love Kesrith: only the dusei might do that. But hereafter there was only the chill, sterile environment of ships, where there was no tainted wind, no earth underfoot, and Arain was a near and therefore dangerous star.

He heaved his baggage again to his shoulder, walked the ringing mesh to the lowered ramp. They expected him. He signed aboard as personnel this time, a feeling unfamiliar only because there was not the imminent prospect of combat. Old anxieties seized on him. Ordinarily his first move would be for whatever rider vessel he had drawn, to begin checking it out, preparing for a drop into whatever Command had decreed for him.

"Compartment 245," the duty officer told him, giving him his admitted-personnel tag: silly formality, he had always thought, where personnel were few enough to be known by sight to everyone on *Flower*. But they were headed for station, for a wider world, where two great warships, two probes, and an in-system rider mingled crews. He attached the tag, reckoning numbers. He was assigned near the mri. He was well satisfied with that, at least.

He went there, to ride through lift with them.

Chapter Five

———◦◉◦———

THE STATION was a different world indeed—regul-built, a maze of the spiraling tunnels favored by the sled-traveling regul. Everything was automated.

And strangest of all, there were no regul.

To walk among humans only, to hear their talk, to breathe the air breathed by humans, and never to be startled by the appearance of an alien face—in all this vast space: it was like being cast across light years; and yet Kesrith's rusty surface was only a shuttle flight away: the screens showed it, a red crescent.

The screens likewise showed the ships that clustered about the station—*Saber* foremost, a kilometer-long structure that was mostly power, instrumentation, and weaponry—and surprisingly scant of crew, only two hundred to tend that monster vessel. Shields made her strong enough to resist attack, but she would never land onworld. *Flower* and *Fox* had ridden in attached to *Saber*'s sides, as *Santiago* had ridden the warship *Hannibal*, like diminutive parasites on the flanks of the warships, although *Flower* and *Fox* were independently star-capable. Presently the probe ships were docked almost unnoticed in the black shadow of *Saber*. *Flower* had snugged into the curve to berth directly under the long ship, and from her ports and scanners there was very little visible but *Saber* and the station itself.

And the station, vast, complexly spiral, rolled its way about Kesrith, a curious dance that dizzied the mind to consider, as one walked the turning interior.

Most personnel made use of the sleds. The distances inside the station were considerable, the sleds novel and frighteningly rapid, whirling round the turns with reckless precision, avoiding collisions by careful routing at hairbreadth intervals.

Duncan walked, what of a walk was possible in the less than normal *g* of the station that was planned for regul comfort. The giddy feeling combined with the alien character of the corridors and the sight of Kesrith out of reach below, and fed his depression.

"That's the one that came in off the desert," he heard someone say behind his back. It finished any impulse he had toward mingling with these men, that even here he was a curiosity, more out of place than he was ever wont to be among regulars. He was conscious of the mask of tan that was the visible mark of the kel'en's veil, worn in the burning light of Arain; he felt his face strangely naked in their sight, and felt their stares on him, a man who had lived with humanity's enemy, and spoke for them.

On the first evening there was leisure for *Flower* personnel to have liberty, he wandered into the station mess . . . found Galey, whose face split into a broad and friendly grin at the sight of him; but Galey, of *Saber*, was with some of *Saber*'s officers, his own friends, and Duncan found no place with them, a SurTac's peculiar rank less than comfortable in dealing with officers of the regular forces. He ate alone, from the automated bar, and walked alone back to *Flower*.

He had done his tour of the station. It was enough. He had no interest even in seeking out the curiosities of the regul architecture, that the men of the warships seemed to enjoy on their hours of liberty.

He went into *Flower*'s lock, into familiarity, in among men he knew, and breathed a sigh of relief.

"Worth seeing, sir?" the duty officer asked him, envious: his own liberty had been deferred. Duncan shrugged, managed a smile; his own mood was not worth shedding on the regulars of *Flower*. "A bit like the Nom," he answered. "A curiosity. Very regul."

And he received from the man's hand a folded message of the kind that passed back and forth frequently at the desk.

He started back toward the level of his own quarters, unfolding the message as he walked.

It was Boaz' hand. *Urgent I talk with you. Lab #2.B.*

Duncan crumpled it in his hand and stuffed it into his pocket, lengthening his stride: the mri program and an urgency; if running would have put him there appreciably faster he would have run.

Number two lab contained Boaz' office. She was there, seated at her desk, surrounded by paper and a clutter of instruments. She looked up at him as he entered. She was upset, blue eyes looking fury at the world. Her mouth trembled.

"Have a seat," she said, and before he could do so: "*Saber*'s troops moved in; snatched the mri, snatched the artifact, the mri's personal effects, everything."

He sank into the offered chair. "Are they all right?"

"I don't know. Yes. Yes—they *were* all right. They were set into automeds for the transfer. If they just leave them in them, they'll fare well enough for a while. Stavros' orders. Stavros' orders, they said." She picked up a sealed cylinder from the center of the littered desk and gave it to him with a misgiving stare. "For you. They left it."

He received the tube and broke the seal, eased out the paper it contained and read the message to himself. *Conditions as discussed apply. Contingency as discussed has occurred. Observe patience and discretion. Stand by. Destroy message. Stavros.*

Regul troubles: ship incoming. The mri were going out, off-station, and himself with them, soon enough. He looked sadly at Boaz, wadded the message in his hand, pocketed it; he would dispose of it later.

"Well?" asked Boaz, which she surely knew she should not ask; he stayed silent. She averted her eyes, pursed her lips, and laced her fingers under her plump chin. "I belong to a ship," she said, "which is—unfortunately—under the governor's authority in some degree, where it regards putting us offworld or seizing what pertains to declared hostiles. For now, in those regards, that authority is absolute. I personally am not under his orders, and neither is Luiz. I shouldn't say this freely; but I will tell you that if you are personally not satisfied with the treatment of the mri—there can be a protest filed at Haven."

Brave Boaz. Duncan looked at her with an impulse of guilt in his heart. There was no word from her of canceled programs, interrupted researches, the seizure of work on which she had labored with such care. The mri themselves occurred to her. This was something he had not foreseen; and yet it was like her.

"Boz," he said, the name the staff called her. "I think everything is all right with them."

She made a noncommittal sound, leaned back. She said nothing, but she looked a little relieved.

"They didn't take the dusei, did they?" he asked.

Boaz smiled suddenly, gave a fierce laugh. "No. The beasts wouldn't sedate. They tried. There was no way they would go down into that hold with them. They asked *Flower* staff to do it, got rather high-handed about it; and Luiz told them they could go down for themselves and throw a net over them. There were no volunteers."

"I don't doubt," Duncan said. "I'd better get down there and see about them."

"You can't tell me what this business is."

"No. I'm sorry."

She nodded, shrugged. "You can't tell me whether things are likely to reverse themselves."

"I don't think they will."

Again she nodded. "Well," she said sadly. That was all.

He took his leave of her and walked out, through the lab that was, he saw, in a disorder that had nothing to do with research, small items that had been on the shelves now gone, books missing.

Saber's men had been thorough.

But if they had taken the mri from the ship, then the dusei might pine and die, like one that he had seen grieving over a dead mri, a beast that would not leave for any urging.

He took that downward corridor that led him to the hold. His stomach was already knotting in dread, remembering what they could do in distress. He had been among them since that first night, brought them food and water, and they had reacted to that with content. But now they had been disturbed by strangers, attacked; and the fear of that feeling that had possessed him once was as strong as any fear of venomed claws.

The sensation did not recur. He entered the hold high on the catwalk, looked down at the brown shapes that huddled below, and cautiously descended to them, fearing them and determined not to yield to it. The regul avowed that the dusei thrived on synthetic protein, which was abundant enough in the station stores; that they would, in fact, eat anything they were offered, which presumably included humans and regul, as he had heard Luiz remark.

The air was remarkably fresh, a clean though occupied aroma to the hold, not so pronounced as with the fastidious regul. The beasts were very neat in their habits, and remarkably infrequent in their necessary functions, metabolizing fluids in such a fashion that Boaz and Luiz found exceedingly intriguing, with a digestion that exacted fluids and food value from anything available of vegetable or animal tissue, and gave off practically no waste compared to the bulk they had ingested—and that quite dry. Regul information on them was abundant, for regul ships had kept kel'ein and dusei for many years. Dusei seemed to go dormant during long confinement, once settled and content. In general dusei put less demand on a ship's life-support than humans, mri, or regul.

It was the awesome size of them that made them uncomfortable companions, the knowledge that there was absolutely nothing that could be done should one of them run amok.

Duncan stepped from the last tread of the stairs, saw both dusei rise with a keening moan that echoed throughout the deep hold. They stood shoulder to shoulder, nostrils working, smelling the stranger. Their small eyes, which were perhaps not overly keen, glittered in the light. The larger of them was a ragged, scarred beast: this one Duncan took for Niun's own; and he thought he also knew the smaller, sleek one for a one-time companion of theirs.

The big one shambled forward with his pigeon-toed gait, looked Duncan up and down and rumbled a deep purring that evinced pleasure in the meeting. The smaller one came, urgently thrusting with its broad nose at Duncan's leg.

He sat down on the last steps between them, and the big animals settled in an enormous mass about his feet, so that they touched. He stroked the velvet-furred hides—remarkably pleasant, that velvet-over-muscle. There was no sound at all but the rumbling of the dusei, a monotonous, peaceful sound.

They were content. They accepted him, accepted a human because of Niun, because they had known him in Niun's company, he thought, although they had disdained his touch while Niun was there. When once he had attempted escape, the dusei had hunted him, had cornered him, all the while pressing at him with such terror as he began to understand was a weapon of theirs.

I wonder that they did not kill you, Niun had said that night.

Duncan wondered now that they rested so calmly after

what had been done to them, after humans had tormented them, trying to sedate them; but the dusei's metabolism absorbed poisons, and perhaps absorbed the drug. There was no evidence of harm to them, not even any of disturbance in their manner.

Neither men nor fully animal, the dusei, but four-footed half-lings, shadow-creatures, that partook of the nature of both . . . that offered themselves to the mri, but were not taken: they were companions of the mri, and not property. He doubted that humanity could accept such a bargain. The regul could not.

He sat content, touching, being touched, and calm; he had not known that night whether admitting the dusei to the ship was right: now it seemed very right. He found himself suddenly full of warmth—he was receiving. He knew it all at once, knew the one that so touched him, the small one, the small one that was still more than three times the bulk of a big man. It purred with a steady, numbing rhythm, leached passion from him as water stole the salts of Kesrith from the soil and displaced them seaward.

It drowned them, overwhelmed them.

He drew back suddenly, panicked; and this the dusei did not like. They snorted and withdrew. He could not recover them. They stood and regarded him, apart, with small and glittering eyes.

Cold flooded into him, self-awareness.

They had come of their own accord, using him: they wanted—and he had given them access; and still he needed them, them and the mri, them and the mri. . . .

He gathered himself and scrambled up the narrow stairs, sweating and tense when he gained the safety of the catwalk. He looked down. One of them reared up, tall and reaching with its paws. Its voice shook the air as it cried out.

He hurled himself for the other side of the door and sealed and locked it, hands shaking. It was not rational, this fear. It was not rational. They used it. It was a weapon.

And they were where they wanted to be now: at a station orbiting Kesrith, and near the mri. He had done everything they wanted. He would do it again, because he needed them, needed the calming influence they might exert with the mri, who drew comfort from them, who relied on them. He began to suspect variables beyond his reckoning.

But he could not leave them.

The thoughts wound him in upon himself, panic-fear and the gut-deep certainty of something wrong. He realized that he had been greeted by a man in the corridor some ten paces back, and absently turned and tried to amend the discourtesy, but it was too late; the man had walked on. Duncan enfolded himself in his private turmoil and kept walking, hands in his pockets, wadding into smaller and smaller balls the messages he had thrust there, Boaz' and Stavros'.

Confound you, Niun, he thought violently, and wondered if he were sane for the mere suspicion he entertained. The dusei, whatever they were, could not touch his conscious thoughts; it was at some lower level they operated, something elemental and sensual and sensory—possible to reject if a man could master his fear of them and his need of them: that was surely the wedge they used for entry, fear and pleasure, either one or the other. It felt very good to please a dus; it was threatening to annoy one.

Yet the researchers had not picked it up. There was nothing of the kind reported in their observations of the beasts.

Perhaps the beasts had not spoken to them.

Duncan closed the door to his own small quarters, opposite the now-vacant compartments of the mri, and began packing, folding up the clothes that he had scarcely unpacked.

When he had done, he sat down in the chair by his desk and keyed in a call to *Saber* by way of *Flower*'s communications.

Transfer of dusei possible and necessary, he sent to *Saber*'s commander.

Stand by, the message came back to him. And a moment later: *Report personally Saber Command soonest.*

Chapter Six

———◦◉◦———

THERE WAS nothing remarkable about a SurTac boarding a
military ship; there should not have been, but the rumors
were flying among the crew. Duncan surmised that by the
looks that slid his way as he was escorted up to Command:
escorted, not allowed to range at will, to exchange words with
crewmen. Even the intercom was silent, an unusual hush on a
ship like *Saber*.

He was shown into the central staff offices, not a command
station, and directly into the presence of the ranking commander over military operations in the Kesrithi zones, R.A.
Koch. Duncan was uneasy in the meeting. SurTacs had paper
rank enough to assure obedience from the run of regulars,
and that circumstance was bitterly resented, the more so because the specials flaunted those privileges with utter disdain
for the protocols and dignity of regular officers: the gallows
bravado of their short-lived service. He did not expect courtesy; but Koch's frown seemed from thought, not hostility,
the ordinary expression of his seamed face.

"Pleased to make your acquaintance, SurTac Duncan."
The accent was Havener, like most that had come to Kesrith,
the fleet of lately threatened Elag/Haven.

"Sir," he said; he had not been invited to sit down.

"We're on short schedule," Koch said. "Regul have a ship
incoming, *Siggrav*. Fortunately it seems to be a doch Alagn
ship. Bai Hulagh's warning them to mind their manners; and
we're probably going to have them docking here. They're
skittish. Get yourself and your mri clear as quickly as possible. You're going to be given probe *Fox*. Probably your instructions are clearer than mine are at the moment." A

71

prickle of distrust there, resentment of Stavros: Duncan caught it clearly. "*Fox* is transferring crew at the moment: some upset there. *Siggrav* is still some distance out. Your end of this operation is a matter of go when ready."

"Sir," said Duncan. "I want the dusei. I can handle them; I'll see to transferring them to *Fox*. I also want the mri trade goods that are stocked on-station, whatever you can spare me help to load."

Koch frowned, and this time it was not in thought. "All right," he said after a moment. "I'll put a detail on it now." He looked long at Duncan, while Duncan became again conscious that his face was marked with half a tan, that the admiral saw a stranger in more than one sense. Here was a power equal to that of Stavros, adjunct, not under Stavros' authority save where it regarded political decisions: and the decision that took *Fox* from Koch's command and overmanned Koch's own ship with discontent, lately transferred crew and scientists did not sit well with Koch. He did not look like a man who was accustomed to accept such interference.

"I'll be ready, sir," Duncan said softly, "when called."

"Best you go over to *Fox* now and settle in," said Koch. "Getting her underway would relieve pressure here. You'll have your supplies; we'll provide what assistance we can with the dusei. All haste appreciated."

"Thank you, sir," Duncan said. Dismissed, he took his leave, picked up his escort again at the door.

Koch had spent forty years on the mri, Duncan reckoned; he looked old enough to have seen the war from its beginning, and he doubtless had no love for the species. No Havener, who had seen his world overrun by regul and recovered by humanity at great cost, could be looked upon to entertain any charity toward the regul or toward the mri kel'ein who had carried out their orders.

The same could be said, perhaps, of Kiluwans—like Stavros; but remote Kiluwa, on humanity's fringes, had produced a different breed, not fighters, but a stubborn people devoted to reason and science and analyzing—a little, it had to be suspected, like the regul themselves. Overrun, they dispersed, and might never seek return. The Haveners were easier to understand. They simply hated. It would be long before they stopped hating.

And from the war there were also men like himself, thousands like himself, who did not know what they were, or from what world: war-born, war-oriented. War was all his life; it had made him move again and again in retreating from it, a succession of refugee creches, of tired overworked women; and then toward it, in schools that prepared him not for trade and commerce but for the front lines. His own accent was unidentifiable, a mingling of all places he had lived. He had no place. He had for allegiance now nothing but his humanity.

And himself.

And, with considerable reservations, the Hon. G. Stavros.

He exited *Saber*'s ramp onto the broad dock, his escort left behind, paused to look about at the traffic of men and women busy about their own concerns.

Haveners.

Regulars.

In the command station of *Fox*, Duncan found himself among *Fox*'s entire body of officers, unhappy-looking men and women, who exchanged courtesies with dutiful propriety.

"Sealed orders," the departing captain told him. "Crewless mission. That's as much as we know."

"I'm sorry about this," Duncan offered, an awkward condolence.

The captain shrugged, far less, doubtless, than the unfortunate man was feeling, and offered his hand. "We're promised another probe, incoming. *Fox* is a good ship, in good maintenance—a little chancy in atmosphere, but a good ship, all the same. We're attached to *Saber*, and *Saber*'s due that replacement probe as soon as it's ferried in; so we'll get it, sure enough. So congratulations on your command, SurTac Duncan; or my condolences, whichever are more in order."

Duncan accepted the handshake, in his mind already wondering what was contained in the sealed courier delivery that had come back by shuttle and resided now in the hands of the departing captain of *Fox*—in his own possession, once the passing of authorities was complete. Duncan accepted the courtesies all about, the log was activated a last time to record the transfer of command; and then, which was usual on SurTac missions, the log files were stripped and given over into the hands of the departing captain. There would be none kept on his flight.

Another, last round of ceremonies: he watched the officers

and their small crew depart the ship, until there was no one left but the ever-present security detail at the hatch—four men, with live and deadly arms.

There was quiet. Duncan settled into the unfamiliar cushion and keyed in the command that played the once-only tape from Stavros: under security lock as it was, it was destroying itself as it played.

Such procedures assured that Authority would not have records coming back to haunt them: that had been the saying during the war, when SurTacs routinely expected the destruction of all records that dealt with them, records destroyed not alone for fear of the enemy, but, they bitterly suspected, destroyed to keep clear the names of men that sent them into the field, should a mission fail: losing commanders lost commands.

Stavros' face filled the screen.

"My apologies," Stavros said softly, "for what I am about to ask I will make my proposal; and after hearing it, if you wish, you can return command of *Fox*, and accept temporary assignment at the station, pending stabilization of the situation here.

"By now you are in command of *Fox*. You are authorized to take the mri aboard, along with all their possessions, and the artifact. The probe will be equipped according to your requirements. In your navigation storage is one tape, coded zero zero one. It comes from the artifact. Proceed out on a course farthest removed from incoming regul, and maintain secrecy as much as possible. You are to follow the tape to its end. There will be no choice once the tape is activated; the system will be locked in. Gather what data you can, both military and personal, on the mri: that is the essence of your mission. Deal with them if possible. We grow more and more certain that it is in our interests to understand that tape. In those interests we are prepared to take a considerable risk. You will gather data and establish what agreement is possible with the mri.

"If you have decided by now to withdraw, wait until the end of this tape and contact *Saber*. If you have, on the other hand, decided to continue, make all possible haste.

"You will in either case say nothing of the contents of this taped message. You will exercise extreme caution in making records during your flight. We want nothing coming home with you by accident. You will have an armed self-destruct, and you will operate under no-capture priorities. If to the best of your judgment you have entered a situation which would deliver your ship into hostile hands, destruct. This is imperative. Whatever choice you make, whether accepting or rejecting this mission, is a free choice. You may refuse without prejudice."

The tape ran out. Duncan still sat staring at the gray screen, knowing that he wanted to refuse, go back to Kesrith, make his peace with the authorities—find some safe life in the Kesrithi hills.

He did not know by what insanity he could not. Perhaps it was something as selfish and senseless as pride; perhaps it was because he could not envision a use for himself thereafter—except perhaps to open the backlands to human habitation. And the world would change.

He cut the screen off, gazed around at the little command station that would be his for what might be the rest of his life, with which he could live for a little time. It was enough.

He boarded *Flower* with no change of insignia, nothing visible to indicate the change in circumstances; but the officers of *Flower* had been informed, evidently, of the authorizations granted him, for there was no demur when he asked the transfer of his gear and for preparations on the dockside.

And when he had done so, he went to Luiz, and last of all to Boaz.

It was the hardest thing, to break to her the news that all her labors were without issue so far as security would ever let her know, that he was taking her charges from her permanently—he, who had assisted her, and now returned to the military wing that she hated.

"Reasons are classified," he said. "I'm sorry, Boaz. I wish I could explain."

Her broad face was touched with a frown. "I think I have an idea what's toward. And I think it's insane."

"I can't discuss it."

"Do you know what you've let yourself in for?"

"I can't discuss it."

"Are they going to be all right? Are you yourself content with arrangements for them?"

"Yes," he said, disturbed that she seemed to guess so accurately what was in progress: but then, Boaz had done the researches on the artifact. Doubtless many on *Flower* had an idea—and surmised after one fashion and another what the military would do with the information they had found. He suffered the scrutiny of her eyes for a moment, guilty as if he were betraying something; and he did not know what power had claimed him—whether friends or enemies of Boaz' principles—or what he himself served, whether she would understand that, either.

She smiled sadly, a mask that covered other feelings. "Well," she said, "hard for us, but there's nothing to be done for it. Sten, take care." The smile died. "Take care for yourself. I'm going to worry about you."

He was touched by this, for if he had a friend anywhere about Kesrith, it was Boaz, fortyish and the only ranking woman in the civ sector. He took her by the hands and on an impulse, by the shoulders, and kissed her on the side of the mouth.

"Boz, I'm going to miss you."

"I will have to get myself some new dusei," she said. Tears were very close to the surface. "I imagine you'll be taking them, too."

"Yes," he said. "Be careful of those beasts, Boz."

"Watch yourself," she urged him hoarsely. For a moment it seemed she might say something further. At last she glanced down and aside, and together they set about the necessary business of arranging the transfer of the dusei.

The whole section was closed to foot traffic and all movement down the rails was halted while the transfer was being made—the matter of sealed canisters of supplies and Duncan's own uninteresting baggage first; and then the mri, from *Saber*, in the sealed automeds used in evacuations of wounded—not a man on the docks that could not guess who was being moved under such extraordinary security; but the precautions were as much to protect the mri as to conceal their removal. Mri were bitterly hated, and the looks that followed those sealed units were in many cases murderous.

And lastly, the docks entirely cleared, came the dusei, for whom no such protective confinement was practical. Duncan had consulted much with Boaz on the question of their transfer, considered using freight canisters, and finally, all such possibilities discarded, simply directed everyone to clear the corridors, ordered the loading crews behind sealed doors, and had the hatches opened.

Then he went down to meet the dusei, and touched them and soothed them, disturbed by their disturbance, fighting his own fear—and he felt their eagerness too, when he opened the door that let them completely free.

They walked with him, a shambling, rolling gait, broad noses snuffing the strange air as they entered the dock. About them lay a great expanse of docking area, vast room for them to stray off, get out of hand, break into freedom that could only end in harm. Duncan tried to think only of the ship *Fox*, of the mri, of the dusei going—trying to make them understand, if understand they could.

They went, the big one slightly before him and the smaller so close at his side it constantly touched. Once the big one gave a cry that echoed all over the vast station dock, a sound to send chills down the back.

In that moment Duncan feared he was going to lose control of them; but after a moment's skittishness, they walked docilely up the ramp to *Fox*, and inside. Doors were open along the way that they must go, unwanted alternatives sealed. Duncan walked them down to the hold that was prepared for them there, and let them in, himself delaying in the doorway to be sure they settled. They were excited, fretting with activity, pacing and swaying their massive bodies in the anticipation that coursed through them. One began that rumbling pleasure sound, that numbed and drew at the senses.

Duncan fled it, closed doors, sealed them, retreated into the sane corridors and deathly quietude of the ship that was henceforth his.

"Clear," *Saber* control informed him. A visual on his screen showed clear space all about; a second screen showed a system mockup, with a red dot at the limit of it, which was regul, and trouble. A second dot appeared at the margin, likewise red, and flashed alarmingly.

"*Saber*," he queried the warship, "is your system mockup accurate?"

There was a long pause, someone checking for clearance to respond, no doubt. Duncan waited, pulse elevated, knowing already that the screen would have corrected itself by now if there had been any mistake.

"Affirmative," *Saber* informed him. "Further details not yet available. You have no lane restrictions, *Fox*. Officially there's no one out there but you. Clear to undock, take course of your choosing."

"Thank you, *Saber*," Duncan replied, noting the flash of data to his screen. "Stand by."

He began the checks, a few run-throughs, though the most important would check once he was clear. *Fox* was recently in from a run through nonsecure space and her sheet was impeccable.

He warned *Saber* and loosed the grapple to station, a queasy feeling as he slipped tiny *Fox* through the needle's eye of clearance between *Saber* and the station. *Hannibal* obstructed his view as he came over the crest, then fell away below.

Fox came under main systems now, aimed for the shortest run away from Kesrith and Arain's disruptive pull. He kept the world between himself and the incoming regul. He heard voices relayed from the station: the regul ship was in contact, voices harsh and dialectic. He heard the station and *Saber* respond. He made out that they were doch Alagn vessels, come for the reverence bai Hulagh Alagn-ni, for his rescue: this was a relief, to know at least that the incoming ships were not doch Holn. He was grateful that they had chosen to relay to him, a consideration that he would not have expected with his status.

He could draw a whole breath, reckoning humanity at Kesrith base safe for the moment, poised on the knife's edge of safety that Stavros had prepared, cultivating the reverence bai Hulagh.

And absenting the mri, who rested now, secretly, in the belly of a very vulnerable and very small outbound probe.

Remain invisible, he mentally read the wish that came with that relayed message, a communication they dared not send him in other terms now. He reckoned himself well-placed— reckoned with grudging admiration that Stavros might have done the right thing. If Stavros imperiled the peace by antagonizing the regul, there would be outcries at Haven, once it was known—demands for his recall, even if Kesrith remained safe. If Stavros lost the mri and *Fox*, in this present mad venture, there would be questions asked, but the whole incident would be passed off and forgotten. The mri were out of the affair at Kesrith. Accidents happened to probes: they were written off. The mri were only two prisoners; and no one had ever kept mri prisoners successfully. Mri artifacts were curiosities, obtainable wherever mri had died in numbers—meaningless curiosities now, for the species was dead: that news would have flashed back from Kesrith with all possible speed, joyous news for humankind, glory for Stavros, who had done nothing to obtain it, and who had kept his hands clean in the massacre. Reports coming from Kesrith were doubtless carefully worded, and would be in the future.

It only remained to see whether Stavros could deal with the regul. It was highly possible that he was going to succeed.

Phenomenal luck, phenomenal intelligence, a memory that missed nothing: there was nothing that escaped Stavros' notice, and his apparent gambles were less chance than calculated hazard. While extending one hand toward the regul, another directed *Fox*, covering that possibility also, trusting no one absolutely.

Duncan frowned, began to relax to the familiar sights and sounds of the ship—unaccustomed leisure, to know that he was not dropping down to combat, that Kesrith's ruddy crescent did not represent threat, but shelter. He settled into *Fox* as into his natural environment, at home in ships, in the dark worlds, in the jungle and deserts and barrenness of humanless worlds, in freefall and heavy *g* and every other place where survival was not reasonable. He had known from the time that he had been shunted into special services, in a wartime confusion of transports and destructing orders from faceless men of Stavros' kind, that he would end in some such place, light years removed from the safety of Stavros' king. Stavros at this distance became only one of a long succession.

No one special.

At this distance, from now on, there was only Sten Duncan.

On his scan he saw that something else had occurred, that there was another ship free of station. It was *Santiago*, an in-system rider, armed, but not star-capable.

He absorbed that knowledge calmly enough, a little resentful that he had not been asked whether such an escort was wanted; but with regul in the system, he did not object to it.

And he looked at the deck beside him, where in a padded support rode a silver ovoid, strangely unmarred after all the accidents that had befallen it. It did not look ever to have tumbled among the rocks at Sil'athen, ever to have been opened and examined. Its surface was unscratched.

But it was no longer unique. It had been duplicated in

holos—and might be duplicated in more tangible detail one day at Zoroaster's more elaborate facilities, a museum curiosity for humans. Duncan reached down and touched it with his fingers, feeling the smoothness and the chill of it, drew his hand back and took a last check of the screens, where *Santiago* seemed locked onto his track.

He ate, the ship proceeding under automatic, silent and safe from alarms. The scan took in *Santiago* at its now accustomed distance, and the machines recognized each other. There was no other within threatening range. There was leisure finally for human needs.

And there was leisure, too, for beginning to reckon with the mri, who rode, unconscious, in the ship's labs.

He walked the corridors of *Fox*, checking to be sure that everything was in order, that nothing had come adrift in the shift from station operations to free flight. Units had reoriented themselves; the transition had gone smoothly. The dusei had ridden through it without visible difficulty: he observed them by remote, unwilling to enter that place now, disturbed as he was, and tense. The mri too rested safely, in their separate quarters. The medics had not taken them from their automeds.

Duncan did so, first the delicate, slight she'pan of the mri, Melein, arranging her into a more comfortable rest on a lab cot. Her delicate limbs felt of bone and loose flesh, appallingly slight; her eyes were sunken and stained with shadow. She did not respond when he touched her thin face and smoothed her bronze mane into order, trying to make her beautiful again. He was afraid for her, watching her breathe, seeing how each breath seemed an effort for her. He began to fear that he was going to lose her.

And in desperation he adjusted the temperature in the compartment downward, marginally reduced the pressure to something approximating Kesrith. He was not sure—no one was—what conditions were natural for the mri. It was only certain that they had less discomfort in Kesrithi atmosphere than did humans or regul.

Melein's breathing became easier. After a long time of sitting in the compartment, watching, he dared leave her; and in another compartment he opened the unit to remove Niun.

Niun likewise was deeply sedated, and knew nothing of

being moved, settled into yet another bed, a helplessness that would have deeply shamed the mri.

There would be no more drugs. Duncan read carefully the instructions that were clipped to the automeds, and found that medics had provided for such drugs, that they were to be found in lab storage, *sufficient*, the instructions said, *for prolonged sedation.* There were other things, meant to assist him in maintaining the mri. With two regul ships in the system and the likelihood of trouble, surely, Duncan thought, it was irresponsible to ignore those precautions, at least before jump; but when he touched the mri and felt how thin and weak they had become, he could not bring himself to do it.

They were days from jump, days more of sedation, so that the mri could ride through that condition which flesh and living systems found terrifying, sealed in their automeds, limbs unexercised, muscles further deteriorating.

It was only common sense, those few days more of precaution; those who had set him in control of the mri had reckoned that these certain precautions would apply.

But those who had laid the plans did not know the mri, who, confined, would simply do what all mri captives had done, whether or not they knew their jailer—and die, killing if they could. Disabled, with their inherent loathing for medical help, they would surely make the same choice.

Duncan himself had understood from the beginning; it was on his conscience that he had never made it clear to Stavros or to others. He could not restrain the mri without killing them; and with the dusei aboard it was not likely that he could restrain them at all.

There was only one reason that would apply with the mri, amid all the powers, regul and human, that converged upon them, one thing with which the mri could not argue.

He made a final check of both mri, found them breathing easily now, and went topside, settling again into the command post.

He activated navigation storage and coded in a number: zero zero one.

Fox swung into a new orientation, her sensors locking on Arain, analyzing, comparing with data that flashed onto her screens. Lines of graphs converged, merged, flashed excited recognition.

Chapter Seven

———◦❖◦———

NIUN WAKENED, as at so many other wakings, a great lethargy on him. His eyes rested first upon Duncan, sitting as he had so often, patiently waiting by the side of his cot. Niun grew confused, disturbed at a vague memory.

"I thought," he said to Duncan, "that you had gone."

Duncan reached forth a hand, laid it on his arm. Niun tried simply to move his fingers, and that effort was beyond his strength. "Are you awake?" Duncan asked of him. "Niun, wake up."

He tried, earnestly, knowing that he was safe to do so if it were Duncan asking him; but the membrane half-closed over his eyes, hazing everything, making focus too difficult. The dark began to come back over him, and that was easier and more comfortable. He felt a touch on his mane, a mother's touch—none other would touch him so; but the fingers that touched his face then were calloused. It remained something to perplex him, and hold him close to waking.

"Drink," he was told, a voice that he trusted. He felt himself lifted—Duncan's arm: he remembered. A vessel's plastic rim touched his lips. He drank, found cool water, swallowed several times. It slid to his stomach and lay there uneasily.

Duncan took the vessel away, let him back on raised cushions that did not let him sink back into his former peace, and the elevation of his head dizzied him for a moment. Niun began to be sure that he was meant to wake in this terrible place, that there was no refuge. In his nostrils, unpleasant on the hot, heavy air, was the scent of food.

He could move his limbs. He found this a wonder. He

tried to do so, began to absorb sensation again, and past and present finally merged in his mind.

He remembered fire and dark and a regul who—he thought—had killed him.

He lay now on a bed like a woman of the Kath, face-naked, his body naked and wasted beneath light coverings, his limbs without strength.

He was in an alien place. To this he had no wish to wake.

But there was dimly in his mind a belief that he had something yet to do, that there was a duty yet undone.

Someone had told him this. He could not remember.

He tried to rise, succeeded in sitting up for an instant before his arms began to shake uncontrollably and he collapsed. Duncan's arms caught him, gentle and yielding him to the mattress.

Thereafter it was easier to drift back into the Dark, where there was no remembrance at all. But Duncan would not let him. A cold cloth bathed his face, shocked awareness back into him.

"Come on," Duncan kept saying to him—lifted his head once again and poured water between his unwilling lips. Then followed salt-laden meat broth, and Niun's stomach threatened rebellion.

"Water," he asked, after he had swallowed the mouthful; and receiving it, took one sip. It was all that he could bear.

He drifted away for a time then, and came back, found himself propped half-sitting. A comfortable rumbling sound filled his ears, numbed his mind for a time; he felt warmth upon his hand, a movement. He looked and saw to his confusion that a great dus had come to sit beside him. It pushed at the cot, making it shudder, then settled, soothing his mind with its contentment.

And Duncan returned upon the instant—in the dress of humans: he noticed this for the first time. Duncan had rejoined his own kind, as was proper. It was a human place. For the first time Niun began to take account of his presence not as delirium, most real and urgent of the images that peopled his wakings, but as a presence that had logical place among humans.

Whose reasons were doubtless human, and threatening.

Disturbed, the dus looked about at Duncan, then settled again, giving only a weary sigh. It tolerated the human; and this perplexed Niun—frightened him, that even the incorruptible dusei could be seduced. He had no protection left.

Dark crossed his mind, memory he did not want, towers falling, the she'pan's pale face in the darkness, eyes closed.

The dus lifted its head again, moaned and nosed at his hand.

"Melein," he asked, focusing on Duncan, on white walls and reality, for he had to ask. He remembered that he had trusted his human: hope surged up in him, that no guilt touched Duncan's face when he asked that question.

The human came and sat by him, touched the dus in doing so, as if he were utterly easy with the beast; but fear . . . fear was in him: Niun felt it. "She is here," Duncan told him. "She is well—as well as you are."

"That is not well at all," Niun said thickly, with a twist of his mouth; but it was true, then; it was true, and he had not dreamed it among the other dreams. He could not close his eyes, lest the tears flow from them, shaming him. He stared at Duncan, and fingered the velvet skin of the dus between them, a hot and comforting sleekness.

"You are free," Duncan explained carefully, distinctly, as one would talk to a child. "Both you and she. We are on a ship, headed out from Kesrith, and I am the only one besides you aboard. I've done this because I trust you. Do me the favor of trusting me for a little while."

This, incredible, mad as it was, had the simple sound of truth in it: there was no flinching in Duncan's gaze. Niun accepted, bewildered as he was, and began at once to think of escort ships, of themselves surrounded, proceeding toward some human captivity, of a myriad other treacheries; but there was Duncan.

There was Duncan, on whom all hopes rested, who alone of human enemies and regul had understood him with honor, whose heart was honorable, a kel'en of the human folk.

He flexed his hands, trying their strength, found the numbness that had blanked his mind and weakened his limbs so long now retreating. Drugs: he recognized the probability of it; but they were losing their grip on his senses, leaving them increasingly clear. Duncan gave him water to drink again, and he drank; and more of the horrid broth, and he drank that too, and clamped his jaws and fought his stomach to keep his meal down.

The she'pan was alive: his true sister Melein, Mother of

the People. She was his duty. He was kel'en, a warrior, and the sickness and the wound and the drugs had taken from him his strength and his quickness and his skill, which were all the possession he had ever owned, for the only purpose of his life, which was to serve the she'pan.

He did not let himself think of what had become of him, only of the necessity of standing on his feet, of finding again the strength to walk and go to her, wherever she was.

Until then he would bear with anything.

Duncan returned after a dark space; and in his hands he bore a black bundle of cloth, that he laid on the table by the bed.

"Your clothes," Duncan said. "If you will let me, I will help you."

And Duncan did so, carefully, gently, helping him to sit for a moment that his senses spun and went gray, then settled him back again, wrapped in the familiar comfort of a kel'en's inner robe, and propped on cushions.

Duncan sat beside him, waiting until he had his breath again. "The she'pan is doing well," he said. "She took food and demanded her belongings and told me to go away. I did."

Niun slipped a hand within his robe, where a scar crossed his ribs, and knew that he should have died: they both should have died. "Tsi'mri medicines," he objected, his voice trembling with outrage; and yet he knew that these same forbidden things had kept them both alive, and he was, guiltily, unwilling to die. He was twenty-six years old; he had expected to die before this: most kel'ein did, but most kel'ein had had honors in plenty by this time. Niun had gained nothing wherewith he was proud to go into the Dark. All that he had almost won, he had lost, being taken captive, allowing the she'pan to be taken. He should have died.

But not here, not like this.

"It was not your fault," Duncan said.

"I have lived too long," Niun answered him, which was the truth: both he and Melein had outlived their kind, outlived the People; and that was bitter fact. He did not know what she would choose to do when she found him again, or what she would bid him do. He looked on Duncan with regret. Duncan's eyes were, Niun saw, shadowed with weariness, his person unkept, as if he had slept little. At the moment he looked distraught.

"The regul would have taken you," Duncan said hoarsely. "I had the chance to put you among my people, and I took it. The she'pan did not object. She knew what I did."

The assertion shook at his confidence of things trustworthy. Niun stared at Duncan for a moment, and at last put down his pride, asked questions as he would of a brother of the Kel.

"Where are my weapons?"

"Everything you own is here," Duncan said. "I will bring you your weapons now if you insist; but you've been half asleep and you've been sick, and I thought you might not know where you are or understand what's going on. I'd hate to be shot in a misunderstanding."

This was at least sensible. Niun let go a carefully controlled breath, reminding himself that this human tended to tell the truth, contrary to the experience of the People with tsi'mri in general. "I am not sick anymore," he said.

"Do you want me to go and bring your weapons?"

Niun considered the matter, staring at Duncan's naked face; he had challenged . . . Duncan had answered with an offer, though his truth had been doubted, insulting him. "No," Niun said, making an effort to relax. "You go and come much; when you come again, you will bring them."

"I would prefer," said Duncan, "to wait until I am sure you are well. Then I will bring them."

Niun glanced aside unhappily: face-naked, he felt the helplessness of his wasted limbs and lay still, compelled to accept the situation. The dus stirred, uncomfortable in his distress. He moved his hand and comforted it.

"I have brought some food," Duncan said. "I want you to eat."

"Yes," Niun agreed. He thrust himself up against the cushions as Duncan went out into the corridor to fetch what he had brought; he took the moment to catch his breath, had steadied himself by the time Duncan returned, and determined to feed himself, though his hand shook when he picked up the bowl.

There was cold, offworld fruit, of which delicacies he had heard, but never eaten; there was a sort of bread, too soft for his liking, and thick, but it was easy to eat; and soi, for which he had a fondness. He took the bittersweet cup in both hands and drank it down to the bitter last, for it was the only familiar, Kesrithi thing, even if it were regul, and he knew that it was good for him. He had eaten a great deal for his abused stomach to absorb; he rested very still when he had eaten, reckoning that to remain very still was the only means of keeping it down.

"At that rate," said Duncan, taking the tray and setting it on the table, where immediately the dus began to investigate it, "you'll recover soon enough." He rescued the tray and took it out to the corridor, followed by the traitor dus, which trailed him with that mournful, head-lowered gait, hoping for charity.

Niun shut his eyes and rested, hearing activity down the hall and measuring the distance from him: there was the rattle of dishes; he could hear no voices, only the explosive whuff of a dus, that the beasts expressed for their own reasons.

Melein? he wondered desperately. He had asked once; he had been refused in the matter of his weapons. He would not expose his anxieties a second time. It was necessary to remember that Duncan was tsi'mri, and the enemy.

Duncan returned after a long time, in which the meal had somewhat settled and Niun felt his stomach the easier for it. Duncan showed him a panel within reach of his arm, how to dim the lights and how to call for help if he needed anything, where the sanitary facilities were, also; and with that instruction a strong admonition against attempting to walk alone.

Niun said nothing, only absorbed all the instructions he was offered, and lay staring at Duncan.

"Sleep awhile," Duncan wished him after a moment, evidently feeling the ill will. He walked to the door and looked back. "There's food whenever you want it. You only have to call me."

Niun gave no response, and Duncan left, leaving the door open, the lights dimmed, the illumination coming from the corridor outside.

And when somewhere a door closed and sealed, Niun began, methodically, to try to move, to work muscles long unaccustomed to move. He worked until he was exhausted, and when he had rested a time, and slept, he found the dus returned. He spoke to it, and it came, laying its massive head on the edge of the bed. He set his hand on its great back and used it to steady him so that he could stand. Then he walked a few steps, leaning on the beast that moved with him, and walked back again, legs trembling so that he fell across the bed. For a while he lay still, breathing hard, close to being ill; it was a few moments before he could even drag his strengthless legs into bed again and rest.

But when he had rested, he began to move again, and arose with the help of the dus and began again to essay those few possible steps.

A long sleep: a day passed, more or less, time meant nothing. It was measured only in the arrival of food and those periods when he was alone, that he could attempt to bring life back to his limbs.

Another sleep: on that day he wakened alone, with only the dus for company. His limbs hurt from the exercise he forced, and Duncan still had not found it convenient to return his weapons. For a moment he lay still, in the darkness, staring out into the lighted corridor.

Then he rose, without the dus this time, and walked stiffly to the bath, washed in water and carefully dressed to the fullest in the clothing that had lain folded on the table. Last of all he put on the *zaidhe*, the tasseled headcloth, visored against the light of unfriendly suns: but the visor he left raised; and with the *zaidhe* he put on the *mez*, the veil, which he fastened under his chin—modesty abandoned here, alone with Duncan, who knew his face. In the black robes of the Kel he felt himself almost whole again, and felt a pang when he touched the gold honors that were his: the heavy symbol of Edun Kesrithun, stamped with the mark of an open hand . . . on a chain, that *j'tal*, for it had come from the neck of Intel, the departed Mother; and there was a small ring laced to the honor-belt—memory flashed back at him, bitter and terrible—from the hand of the Mother of Elag; and—more memories, full of recent pain—a small gold luck *j'tal*, in the shape of a leaf that had never grown on barren Kesrith: this came from an elder brother of the Kel, and called back others to his memory, the masters who had taught him arms and the law of the Kel.

And he received them back from the hand of a human.

He rested a moment against the wall, the dus nervously pushing at his leg; when he had caught his breath he went to the door, looked out, and walked out into the corridor unhindered, the dus behind him.

The very look of the place was alien: narrow, rectangular corridors, when he was accustomed to the slanting walls of his own ruined home, or the curving walls of regul interiors. It was hard to breathe, the air heavy and pungent with unfamiliar chemical scents. In his confusion he caught at the wall as his own dus shouldered him aside, and ahead of him, far down the corridor, he saw another dus thrust its broad head forth from a doorway. His shambled ahead to meet it, quite cheerfully.

He had known; somewhere in the drug-dazed depth of him, he had sensed the other presence, calming and drawing at him. Two dusei, and one with Melein, who had been of the Kel, who still might touch one of the beasts.

It was a long walk, the longest that he had tried; he thrust himself from the wall and went to that door, leaned upon the door frame and looked inside.

Melein, she'pan.

She was in truth alive; she slept—fully dressed in her modesty, in her tattered yellow robes of Sen-caste, that she had outworn. So frail she had become, Niun thought with pain, so thin; it was one thing that a kel'en should be hurt and starved and kept numbed with drugs—but that they should have dealt so with her: rage swelled up in him so that for a moment he could not see, and the dusei moaned and drew back into the corner.

He left his place at the doorway, came and knelt on the floor at her bedside, where she slept upon her side, her head pillowed upon her arm. The dusei returned, and crowded close about him; and he touched the slim fingers of her open hand.

Her golden eyes opened, nictitated in surprise. She seemed dazed at first, and then put out her hand and touched his naked face, as if to see whether he were a dream or not.

"Niun," she whispered. "Niun."

"What shall I do?" he asked of her, almost trembling in dread of that question, for he was only kel'en, and could not decide: he was the Hand of the People, and she was its Mind and Heart.

If she would not live, then he would kill her and himself; but he saw the cold, clear look of her eyes, and this was not the look of defeat.

"I have waited for you," she told him.

Niun took the dusei with him. They walked before him, single-file, for they were too big to go abreast in the corridor. Claws clicked on hard flooring, slowly, slowly. They knew whom he sought, in that curious sense of theirs—knew also that this was not a hunt in the way of game, with a kill at the end; but they were disturbed, nonetheless, perhaps because they had walked with him they hunted.

And they met Duncan in the narrow hall just beyond the turning.

Duncan was perhaps coming as he came so faithfully to see to them. He was not armed; he never had been, Niun recalled with a sudden confusion in his anger. And perhaps Duncan had tempted them to this moment, had waited for it. He seemed to know how things lay between them; he stood still before the dusei, waiting for Niun to say or do what he would. Surely he knew that his life was in danger.

"There are no others aboard," Niun reminded him, challenging him with his own statement.

"No. I told you the truth."

Duncan was afraid. Dus-feelings were close and heavy; but he did not give way to his fear, that would have killed him.

"Yai!" Niun rebuked the dusei, attracting their attention out of that single-minded and dangerous fixation. They shifted nervously and the feeling lifted. They would not defy him. "Duncan," he said then, as directly as he would speak to a brother of the Kel, "what did you hope to do with us?"

Duncan shrugged, human-fashion, gave a faint, tired twist of the mouth. Naked-faced as he was, he looked like a man long without rest either of body or of spirit. He was naïve at times, this man Duncan, but he was capable of having guarded himself, and knew surely that he ought to have done so. Niun momentarily put aside his thoughts of violence.

"I meant," Duncan said, "to get you out of the hands of the regul."

"You simply asked your people, and they gave you this for your own pleasure. Are you so great among them that they are that eager to please you?"

Duncan did not rise to the sarcasm. His expression remained only tired, and again he shrugged. "I'm alone. And I don't plan to contest the control of the ship. You can take it. But I will point out that this is not a warship, we are not armed, and we are possibly doing already what you would wish us to do. I don't think you can take actual control; we are on taped navigation."

Niun frowned. This, in his inexperience, he had not taken into account. He stared at Duncan, knowing his own strength limited, even to go on standing. He could loose the dusei; he could take the ship; but the thing that Duncan said made Duncan's calm comprehensible, that neither of them could manage the ship.

"Where are we going?" Niun asked.

"I don't know," Duncan said. "I don't know. Come with me to controls, and I will show you what I mean."

The ovoid rested in a case lined with foam, a shining and beautiful object, unique, holy. Not a flaw was on its surface, although Niun knew that it had tumbled down rocks and withstood the gods knew what afterward to come here. He knelt down, heedless of Duncan's presence, and stretched out a reverent hand, touched that slick, cold surface as if it were the skin of a sentient being.

A piece of the mri soul, this object, this pan'en, this mystery, that he had carried until he could carry it no longer. He would have died to keep this from tsi'mri hands.

And from tsi'mri it had come to them, touched and profaned.

Duncan's doing. There was none other who could have found it.

Niun stood up, eyes blurring, the membrane betraying him for the instant; and before a stranger of the People, he would have veiled himself in anger, but Duncan was closer to him than many another of his own kind. He did not know what manner of grace or threat was intended by this gift. He felt a counter at his back, welcome; his legs were foundering under him. The dus came, great clumsy-seeming creature, careful in this place of delicate instruments and tight spaces. It lay down at his feet, its warmth and steadiness offered to him at need.

"You know the mri well enough," Niun said, "to know that you have been very reckless to touch this."

"It is yours. I got it back for you; would you rather it had been lost out there, left?"

Niun looked down again at the pan'en, up again at Duncan, still trying to reckon what lay behind that veilless face; and slowly, deliberately, he fastened the veil across his own face—a warning, did Duncan chance to have learned that mri gesture, that severed what was personal between them. "Humans are mad with curiosity. So my elders taught me, and I think that they were right. It will not have been in your hands without your scholars looking into it; and it is even possible that they will have learned what it is. Being only kel'en myself, I am not entitled to know that. Perhaps you know. I do not want to."

"You are right in your suspicions."

"Being human yourself, you knew that this would happen if you brought it to your people."

"I didn't know what it was. I didn't know that it would be more than a curiosity to them."

"But it is," Niun surmised; and when Duncan did not answer: "Is that why we are here? One thing the mri had left, one treasure we had, and here it rests, and here are you, alone, and suddenly we are given rewards, and our freedom—a ship for our leaving, at great cost. For what service to humanity is this a just reward, kel Duncan? For the forty years of war we waged with your kind, are we given gifts?"

"The war is finished," said Duncan. "Over. A dead matter."

"So are the mri," Niun said, forced himself to that bitterness, repudiating tsi'mri generosity and all its complicated demands. The weakness was on him again, a graying of senses, a shudder in muscles too long under tension. He clenched his hand on the counter, drew a deep breath and let it go, brought focus to his vision again. "I do not know why you are aboard alone," he said. "One of us does not understand the other, kel Duncan."

"Plainly put," said Duncan after taking in that fair warning. "Perhaps I am mistaken, but I thought that you would realize I tried to do well for you. You are free."

Niun cast a look about at the controls, at the alien confusion of a system unlike the regul controls that he knew only in theory. A thin trickle of sweat went down his left side, beneath the robes. "Are we escorted?" he asked.

"We are watched, so far," Duncan said. "My people aren't that trusting. And neither you nor I can do anything about that guidance system: we're on tape. Maybe you can tear us free of that, but if you do that, I don't doubt it will destruct itself, the whole ship."

This, at least, had the ring of sound reasoning. Niun thought it through, his hand absently soothing the head of the dus that sat up beside him.

"I will go present what you say to the she'pan," Niun said at last. He dismissed the dus ahead of him with a soft word and followed after it and its fellow, leaving Duncan in possession of controls. Duncan could kill them all; but Duncan could have done that long since if that had been his purpose. He could have put them in confinement, but it was possible that the entire ship was a prison, guarded from the outside. The question remained why Duncan chose to be in it with them. Niun suspected that it had to do with the human's own curious feelings of honor, which apparently existed, far different from those of a mri.

Or perhaps it had nothing to do with Duncan's bond to his own kind; perhaps it was that to him, that they were both kel'ein, and lived under similar law, under the directions of others, and one chose what he could, where he could. He could comprehend that a man might find fellowship with another kel'en, that he might one day have to face and destroy. It was sung that this had happened.

It was never well to form friendships outside one's own House; it was proverbial that such attachments were ill-fated, for duty would set House loyalties first, and the commands of the she'pan first of all.

Chapter Eight

———◆———

IT WAS done.

Duncan stood and watched the mri depart, and knew that soon the she'pan Melein must come, to assume nominal control of the ship, now that Niun had assured himself that there would be no resistance or offense to her.

That was the way with the mri, that the she'pan made the decisions when she was available to be consulted. It was something that Boaz could have told the military; it was something that he himself could have told those that had laid the plans for security on *Flower*, had they asked—that the mri kel'ein, the black-robes, that had made themselves a terror wherever they had gone, were not the authority that must be considered.

Niun had not understood the artifact he revered. That also did not surprise Duncan. Niun, competent as he was, refused to know certain things that he did not consider appropriate for him; he had to consult Melein before any act of policy, given the chance to do so. Upon this, Duncan had relied desperately. It had worked. He felt vindicated, freed of a weight that had been on him for days, now that he saw Niun whole and on his feet, and bound precisely where he had calculated he would go.

He found himself with a curious lack of fear for the thing that he had done. Fear, he felt lying awake at night, remembering the ruin in the heights, the nightmare of Sil'athen, the inferno that had come down on them; or smiling at the regul who had tried to kill him and killed a sentient species instead. Of the mri he had only a knowledgeable respect.

There was still a good chance that the mri would turn on

him and kill him; he had reckoned that from the beginning—but it was not the way that he had known them. If it would happen, it would proceed from the depth of some mri logic that these two mri had never shown him, even bitterly provoked.

It was long past time for regrets: there was little time left for anything he would do. He wiped the back of his hand across his blurring eyes—he had napped when he could these past four days, but he had not slept in a bed, had not dared to, not with matters aboard in a state of flux, with two regul ships loose in the system and a nervous human ship tagging him.

He settled in at the console, called forth data from the instruments that flashed their busy sequences, saw that they were prepared for transition, their guidance system locked upon its reference star and prepared to make the move as soon as *Fox*'s other systems informed the computer that they were far enough from the nearest sizable mass. It could be as much as a day: automatic tolerances were wider than they had to be. It would surely not be more.

This far out, Kesrith was lost in sunglare, and red Arain itself was assuming its proper insignificance on a stellar scale, a mere boundary beacon for men, marking as it did the edge of human territories, a star orbited by one scantly habitable world and several that were not.

And on the one screen was the mockup that still showed the regul further out than they should be after such a time: they were making a cautious approach. He did not concern himself with regul position: they were far across the system and no part of what occupied him.

On another screen appeared the tiny object that was *Saber*'s rider *Santiago*, his faithful shadow.

It was closer than it was wont to be.

He bit at his lip, his heart quickening, for he did not want to break silence or to start a dispute with his escort: the mri were at large; but the fact of the mri impelled him to rapid consultation with the computer, and he swore to himself and reached for the com switch.

"*Santiago*," he signaled it. "*Santiago*, this is *Fox*. Request you draw back a space. You're in my scan and your mass is registering on my instruments. You are preventing jump."

There was a long pause. "We copy," *Santiago* answered. and seemed to pause for consultation. "*Fox*," came a new voice, "Zahadi here. Advise you we have difficulties developing."

Santiago's captain. A chill of foreboding went through him. "Explain," he asked of Zahadi.

"Fox," the answer came back in due course, "advise you neither regul ship has been receptive to approach. Hulagh has shuttled up to station. Situation there is extremely tense. Hulagh has demanded boarding on regul vessel *Siggrav*, Stavros' latest message as follows: *Boarding will be granted. All conditions with probe mission are unchanged. Proceed. End message as received.*"

"*Santiago*, advise you we are prepared to jump. Situation elsewhere irrelevant. You are preventing jump. Please move out of scan."

"We copy," Zahadi replied.

There was a long silence. Duncan waited, watching the scan. There was no change. He repeated the message, irritably.

There was still no response. *Santiago* still hung within scan.

He flipped the contact again and this time swore at *Santiago* and all aboard her: a condemned man was allowed that liberty. "Get out of my scan," he repeated. "*Santiago*, get out of my way."

Again there was no answer. A chill sense of something utterly amiss was over him now; *Santiago* still remained, stubbornly using its mass to prevent him—he was sure of it now.

Stavros' orders, a leash on a ship Stavros could not fully trust, deliberate delay.

And the mri would come. He reckoned in his mind what would happen when Melein arrived down that corridor with the dusei to enforce her wishes. Niun might wait to search for his weapons; they both might wait a time, biding the return of their strength: Niun was hardly able to walk, and perhaps Melein could not. It was too much to hope that they would not intervene.

Stavros' intervention. Stavros knew him, had not trusted him let loose without restraint.

And in a sudden flash of apprehension he flicked the scan to maximum. A moving dot appeared at the limit of the field, moving in fast.

He cursed and put in a panicked call to *Santiago*, complaining of it.

"*Fox, Fox,*" came the reply at last, "this is *Saber* via *Santiago,* assigned escort. Request acknowledgment."

Duncan leaned forward, adjusted the pickup, his other hand clenched. "*Saber,* this is *Fox.* Advise you no escort was in my orders. Pull off. Pull off."

There was no acknowledgment in the expected time. Nothing.

Saber did not vary course.

"Request explanation," Duncan sent at them.

Nothing came in reply. *Saber* continued on intercept. In a very little time there would be no options at all.

Duncan swore at them. "*Saber,*" he urged. "*Saber,* relay the following message to *Santiago.* Pull out of my scan: repeat, pull out of my scan. This ship is ready to jump, and your mass is registering. Request following message to be officially logged: *Santiago,* you have ignored five prior warnings. I will jump this ship on manual override in fifteen minutes. If you do not take immediate evasive action, you will be caught in my field. Advise you pull out now. Fifteen minutes, mark, and counting."

The seconds ticked off. His hand sweated on the override. The dot that was *Santiago* began to move away, but *Saber* was still coming in fast.

"*Fox,*" he heard. "This is *Saber,* Koch speaking. Advise you this operation henceforth ours too. We are assigned to track. Orders of the Hon. G. Stavros, governor Kesrith territories."

It hit him at the pit of the stomach: *O God, out of this, out of this,* he wished, either them or him, he did not know. He was shaking with the strain of the long-held position.

A kilometer-long warship, with escort scout. He watched *Saber* moving in, not close enough for her great mass to register, but closing. They were coming in on *Santiago*'s track, and *Santiago,* not star-capable, would link and ride *Saber*'s ungainly structure into jump.

Warships, not a probe mission. He had been made a guide for warships.

No, no, no! he raged at them in his mind, and in an action both impulse and deliberate, slammed his hand forward and hit the manual override.

Jump.

He held onto the panel while the whole of his body told him lies at once, while walls flowed like water, while forms seemed to twist inside out and space was not; and was again; and the flow reversed itself, wrenching them back into normality.

The stars in the screens were different. Duncan shivered in disorientation, fighting out of it as a man must who had flown combat out of deep space.

He reached for controls to scan, finding vertigo in the tiniest imbalance of his body, the impression that interstices still existed into which he could fall, neither up nor down. If there was time in jump, the mind did not perceive it, drew nothing with it out of that abyss, only that terrible wrenching inward. He swept the scan.

There was nothing but star noise.

There was nothing.

He slumped in the cushion and fought against the emotional dissolution that often hit after transition; and this time it was more than physical. He had made a terrible, irrevocable mistake—not for the mri, not for them: he had at least bought them time, while Koch and Stavros sorted out the thing that he had done, consulted and reckoned what side he was playing, and what should be done with him.

The regul are living, Stavros had said: *their victims aren't. So we deal with the regul, who are a force still dangerous.*

Warships, not *Flower*, not the likes of Boaz and Luiz. The half of Stavros' military forces had prepared to follow in unarmed *Fox's* wake, even with regul threatening Kesrith: warships, and himself before them, with mri aboard, to probe the defenses—an unarmed ship, and then the others.

To seek and destroy mri bases, whatever contacts the tape could locate: to finish what the regul had begun.

He bowed his head into his arms and tried to take his breath again, muscles shaking with rage and reaction. For a moment he could do nothing else; and then, fingers still shaking convulsively, he sought after the ampoule he had carried for days in his belt, never knowing at what time jump might come. He broke it, almost dropped it, then inserted the needle and let the drug enter his bloodstream.

Warmth spread through him, a sense of tranquillity, ability to cope with the unnatural wrench of jump, ability to function until there should be leisure to rest. His mind cleared, but kept its distance from stresses.

He reckoned clearly what he had done: that *Saber* would

track them; they had identical records: everything had been duplicated. The warships would come. There would be court martial, if ever humanity recovered him; his direct defiance of Koch had made that a certainty. But the mri, when they learned what had been done, might themselves care for that matter, so that human justice was a very remote threat indeed.

He was calm in thinking of these things, whether the exhaustion of days without rest—he wondered distantly if that was to blame for what he had done, or whether the trigger had been pulled much earlier, much earlier, when he had sought the mri's freedom. He tried to draw information from the tape: it would tell him nothing, neither running time to go, nor number of jumps, nor any indication where they were. He looked at the star in scan. Mri base, possibly. In that case, his time could be measured in days.

He pushed himself away from controls, his senses still sending him frantic signals even through the calming effects of the drug. It was worse than he had ever felt it: fatigue made it so. He thought that if things would remain stable only for an hour, he would go to his quarters and wash and lie down, now that it was too late to worry about anything.

And a dus ambled in the door, and the second dus after him; and behind them came the mri.

He drew back. Melein came, unveiled as was her wont, her fingers laced with Niun's, who supported her. She entered the control room as Duncan stepped back, and her golden eyes swept the place, centered on the object that rested beside controls: on the artifact in its cradle. She went to it, ignoring all else, and touched the silver ovoid with her fingertips, bending with Niun to provide her balance, felt it as if to assure herself that it was real.

Then she straightened. Her amber eyes sought Duncan's, shadowed and piercingly direct.

"I will sit," she said, her voice a hoarse whisper; and Niun carefully settled her on the edge of the reclined comstation cushion as if it were a throne. She sat straight, her hand pressed to her ribs where she had been injured, and for a moment she was short of breath; but it seemed to pass, and the hand dropped. The two dusei came to crowd at her feet, giving her a living wall at her knees; and she held out her left hand to Niun, who settled on the deck beside her, elbow against the larger dus.

Duncan looked on them both: in his hazed senses he saw the modern control center become a hall for a priestess-queen, himself the stranger there. Melein gazed at him directly: behind her the starscreens showed a dust of light, and the colored telltales flashed in lazy sequence, hypnotically regular.

"Duncan," Melein said softly, "where is this ship going?"

He remembered that it was not always permitted to speak to her directly, though once he had been permitted: things were different now. He looked at Niun's veiled and uncommunicative face. "Tell the she'pan that *that* guides us," he answered, with a shrug toward the ovoid that rested beside them.

"I will speak to him," Melein said, and an anxious frown came over her face. "Explain. Explain, kel Duncan."

"Do you know," he asked her, "what it holds?"

"Do you?"

He shook his head. "No. Records. Navigational records. But not where we are going. Do you know?"

Her lovely face became like a mask, unreadable as Niun's, though unveiled. "Why are you alone with us? Might you not be wiser to have kept us apart from controls, kel Duncan?"

She trod the edges of questions with him. He fought his mind clear, gathered explanations, but she held out her hand to him, insisting, and there was nothing gracious but to take her long, slender fingers in his. The alien touch disturbed him, and he found himself against the dusei, a position of danger. "Sit, sit down," she bade him, for she must look up at him as he stood; and there was no place but the deck, against the bodies of the dusei, as Niun rested. "Are you too strange to us now?" she asked, taunting him.

He did as she asked, his knees finding the deck painful; he touched the dusei of necessity, and knew the trap, the contact with the beasts, the blurring flow of senses. He grew afraid, and the beasts knew it, stirring powerfully against him; he repressed the fear, and they settled.

"Once," said Melein to him, her voice distant and soft, "I said that we would find a ship and a way off Kesrith; I said that I must have the pan'en, and you were there to hear. Kel Duncan, are these things your gift, yours alone?"

Not naïve, this child-queen: she asked what she did not

believe. He sensed depths opening at his feet. "Policy," he said, "does not want you in regul hands. You are free. No, it is not my gift; I didn't have it to give. Others—arranged these things. If you linger in regul space or human—you are done; this ship is not armed. But we have no escort now, she'pan. We are alone; and we will follow this tape to its end."

She was silent a moment. Duncan looked at Niun, found nothing of comfort, was not sure that he was believed in either quarter. Melein spoke in her own language; Niun answered in a monosyllable, but he did not turn his face or vary his expression. *Tsi'mri,* he heard: the mri word for outsider; and he was afraid.

"Do your kind hate you?" asked Melein. "Why are you aboard alone, kel Duncan?"

"To tend you—and the machinery. Someone must. She'pan, from *that*—from the object—scientists made our guidance tapes. We're locked on it, and there's nothing you or I can do to stop it. I will tend the ship; I will deliver you to your destination, whatever it is. And when I have done that, I will take the ship and meet my people and tell them that the mri want no more part of regul or human politics, and that the war is over, forever. Finished. This is why I'm aboard."

A troubled frown grew upon Melein's face as she gazed into his eyes. "I cannot read truth in you," she confessed, "tsi'mri that you are; and your eyes are not right."

"Medicines," Niun said in a low voice, the first word he had spoken without invitation. "They use them during transition."

The mri had none, refused medicines, even that: Niun's *they* acquired demeaning force, and Duncan felt the sting of it, felt the danger of it at the same moment. For the first time panic settled round him; the dusei jerked in alarm, and Niun rebuked them, steadied them with his hands.

"You do not know," said Melein then, "what your superiors have done to you, kel Duncan. How long are you given to return?"

"I don't know," he said.

"So long, so long a voyage. You should not be here. You should not have done this thing, kel Duncan."

"It's a long walk home, she'pan. We're across jump."

"This is a mri ship now. And where we go, no tsi'mri can go."

The dusei stirred, heaved up: Duncan started to rise, but Niun's hand seized his wrist, a pressure without strength, a warning without threat. "No," Niun said. The eyes above the veil were no longer hard. "No. Be quiet, Duncan."

The dusei had retreated into the recess to Melein's left, making sounds of alarm, small puffs of breath. Their small eyes glittered dangerously, but after a moment they settled, sat, still watching.

And quietly, in his own language, Niun spoke to Melein—received an answer and spoke again, urgently, as if he pleaded against her opinion. Duncan listened tensely, able only to catch the words *mri, Kesrith,* and *tsi'mri*—tsi'mri: as mri meant simply *the People,* the word for any other species was *not-people.* It was their thinking; he had known it long since. There was no reasoning against it.

Finally, with a few words, Melein rose, veiled her face and turned away, deliberately turning her back.

It was a chilling gesture. Duncan gathered himself to his feet, apprehensive; and Niun arose, using the cushion to steady himself, standing between him and the dusei.

"She has said," said Niun, "that I must not permit any stranger in her sight again. You are kel'en; I will fight you when I am able, or you may choose to stay with us and live as mri. You may choose."

He stared helplessly at Niun, even this made distant by the drug. "I didn't risk my neck getting you free only to kill one of you. No."

"You would not kill me," Niun said.

It set him off-balance. "I am not your enemy," he protested.

"Do you want to take service with the she'pan?"

"Yes."

He said it quickly; it was the only sane answer. When things were quiet, at some later time, then it would be the moment to reason with them, to explain why he must be set free with the ship: it was their own protection they considered.

But Niun remained still a moment, staring at him as if he suspected a lie in that consent.

"Niun," said Melein, her back still turned; Niun went to her, and they spoke in low voices. For a moment then Niun was still; the dusei shifted restlessly: one moaned and nosed at Niun's hand. He caressed it absently to silence, then came back to the side of the room where Duncan stood.

"Kel Duncan," he said, "the she'pan says that we are going *home*. We are going home."

It did not register for a moment—came then with a dull, distant apprehension. "You called Kesrith home," Duncan said.

"And Nisren. Kel-truth. The she'pan knows. Duncan—" The eyes above the veil lost their impassivity. "Perhaps we are the last; perhaps there is nothing left; perhaps it will be too long a voyage. But we are going. And after this, I must forget; so must you. This is the she'pan's word, because nothing human can stay with us, not on such a voyage. The she'pan says that you have given the People a great gift; and for this service, you may keep your name, human though it is; but nothing more. We have gone from the sun into the Dark; and in the Dark, we forget, the whole of what we have been and seen and known, and we return to our ancestors. This is what you have entered, Duncan. If ever you stand on the homeworld of the People, you will be mri. Is this understood? Is this what you want?"

A dus crowded them, warm and urgent with emotion. Duncan felt a numbness; sensed, almost, Niun's anxiety. Violation of privacy, of self-control: he edged back and the dus shied off, then returned obstinately to its closeness. There was no lying to the dusei; none, eventually, to the mri. They would learn one day what humans meant to do to them, what he had aimed at their home: a second, deadlier gift. It was irony that they asked him to share it.

"It's what I want," he said, for he saw no other choice.

Niun frowned. "A mri," he said, "could not have chosen what you have chosen."

The distance that the drug lent was leaving, deserting him to cold reality. He heard what Niun said, and it twisted strangely, forebodingly in his mind. He looked at Melein's back, wondering whether she would now deign to notice him, since he had yielded to all their terms.

"Come," said Niun, gesturing to the door. "You have given up the ship. You do not belong here now."

"She cannot manage it," he protested, dismayed to think of Melein, desert-bred, regul-trained, setting hands on human-made machinery.

Niun's entire body stiffened; the frown reappeared. "Come," he said again. "Forget first how to question. You are only kel'en."

It was mad. It was, for the moment, necessary; Melein's ignorance could kill them, but she surely had sense enough to refrain from rashness. The ship could manage itself. It was a hazard less immediate than quarreling with Niun.

There were the dusei.

There was the plain fact that did he defeat the mri, he must kill him: and he had not broken with Stavros' orders, cut himself off from Kesrith, to finish the reguls' job for them. In time he could learn the mri enough to reason with them, wherever they were, mri world or regul.

He yielded, and with Niun, left the control center, the dusei in their wake. The door closed behind them, sealed: he heard the lock go into place.

Chapter *Nine*

———◆◦◆———

TWO WARSHIPS, six rider-vessels.

Bai Hulagh Alagn-ni saw with satisfaction the difference that power made in the deportment of the humanfolk. They waited on the front steps of the Nom, two hands of human younglings to meet the caravan from the shuttle landing; and a number of regul younglings bringing four bright silver sleds. Hulagh spoke a curt instruction to his driver to draw up there, among the regul: some of the new personnel coming later in the caravan were skittish of humans yet, and Hulagh, despite his rank and the discomfort entailed, meant to be beforehand disembarking and wait upon the others. He himself had no fear of humans, and meant that none of the others should disgrace Alagn before them.

The car drew to a smooth halt. The hatch opened, admitting the familiar, acrid air of Kesrith: Hulagh snorted in distaste as it burned his nostrils—but it held a certain savor now, nonetheless.

He ignored the humans who peered at him in their curiosity; some reached out tentative hands to assist. His driver, Suth Horag-gi, urged them aside and with expert and efficient organization had the sled eased into position; carefully, carefully, Suth eased Hulagh's great weight up to his atrophied legs and swiftly down again in the indoors sled, a smoothness and gentleness that Hulagh had come greatly to value. He had come more and more to prize this youngling of the tiny doch of Horag; its comportment had been faultless in the delicate days at the station. He did not, of course, express this to Suth: it would spoil the youngling, whom he meant to train to further responsibilities.

105

Attendant not only to the first elder of Alagn, but to the first elder of the prime doch of the prime three of the regul: Suth did not know the good fortune to come. Hulagh smiled to himself, a gesture the humans would hardly recognize, a tightening of the musculature of his lower eyelids, a relaxation of his nostrils despite the biting air.

His long, careful maneuvering had succeeded.

Eight ships had come, a quarter the strength of doch Alagn, and others were waiting. They had come to discover the fate of their elder, delayed on Kesrith among humans and mri and long overdue. Humans had not apparently expected Alagn to react in such strength—as if Alagn could reasonably have done otherwise. Stavros had apparently failed to understand how much Alagn had committed here, in the presence of a prototype ship that was entrusted them by the high assembly of regul docha—now lost, twisted metal in the ruined port: a pang of fear disturbed Hulagh's satisfaction—but there was, in these anxious humans, the means to cover that loss and better the position of Alagn despite it.

It was evident in the faces of these human younglings, in the whole attitude of humans at the station, in communications with Stavros, that the humans did not want to fight. Hulagh had long believed that, and naturally applauded that common sense in the humans. On Kesrith, elders were committed, human ones and now three more regul, lesser elders of Alagn, in the portion of the caravan that was now beginning to disembark; it did not make sense to fight. Hulagh earnestly displayed this attitude by committing the elders of his own doch, and believed that it was safe. The humans could have begun battle at the appearance of the warships, at the first intimation that they were carriers for riders; but the humans had instead settled to talk, despite that they might have won: humans were fierce fighters, as evidenced by the fact that they had been able to meet the mri—with the advantage of numbers, to be sure, but regul could not have withstood the mri, and Hulagh privately acknowledged that fact. No, the humans did not want further conflict. After those first anxious days, Hulagh began sincerely to rely on the directness of bai Stavros, who avowed humans wanted the peace not only continued, but expanded.

There were surely, contained within that truth, deeper truths beneficial to Stavros and his private interests: Stavros, with a wisdom regul could respect, if not love, did not commit himself to one ally, but pursued many attachments, probing them for advantage.

There was, notably, the matter of the mri, whom Stavros still found of interest, through the agency of the allegedly mad youngling Duncan: the very thought caused Hulagh's skin to tighten. Mad, perhaps, but if the youngling were thus defective, then Stavros was mad to have reinstated him—and Hulagh did not believe that Stavros was mad.

A probe had gone out-system; the largest of the human warships had escorted the ship to the edge of the system, and returned home after a furious coded exchange with the ship and finally with Stavros. Hulagh regretted much that neither he nor his aides could understand that exchange, after which the warship and its rider had meekly returned to station, while the ship *Hannibal* had moved out to run escort for regul ships in their approach.

The ship with the mri aboard had left Kesrith immediately upon Stavros' being informed that regul ships were due; Duncan, after briefing with Stavros, had been sent to that ship with his belongings, such as remained from his original transfer: a permanent stay, then, the last vestige of his occupancy removed from the Nom, although he had been virtually residing on the ship. When regul presence in the system had been announced, the probe had left the station: Hulagh had learned this from his fellow elders.

Duncan, supposedly on the station, was not available, not to his most urgent request for the youngling, and humans were evasive.

Duncan's madness revolved around the mri, who were also—supposedly—at the station.

It was a regul kind of game. Hulagh's hearts labored whenever he let himself dwell on the mri; doubtless the humans knew his anxiety. It only remained to find out the nature of the bargain Stavros wished to strike with Alagn—for it was surely equally clear to the humans that he now had resources with which to bargain. Hulagh trusted the humans as he had never been able to trust the mri: he trusted well a human like Stavros, who reckoned profit as regul did, in power, in territory, in resources of metals and biostuffs—and in the protection of what was his. Such persons as Stavros Hulagh found comfortingly close to his own mind; and therefore he sought an early conference.

The last of the elders disembarked. Hulagh eased his sled

about, awaiting them, a term in the acrid air for which he would pay throughout the day, with a dry throat and stinging nasal passages. Three elders with their attendant younglings: Sharn and Karag and Hurn, the latter a male; Sharn, female, fourth eldest of the doch; Karag, a recently sexed male and prone to the instabilities that the Change brought on young adults: Sharn's protégé, and probably current mate, Karag still had the smooth skin of a youngling and he had not yet acquired the bulk of Sharn or Hurn, certainly not Hulagh's prosperous dignity, but he still rated the use of a sled—the last settled by the attendant younglings. Hulagh watched, patient as the younglings fussed about the three adults and brought them on their way through the cluster of humans.

Hulagh was no longer alone, sole elder on Kesrith, surrounded only by younglings of limited experience and strange docha. His own were with him now, Alagn-ni, and his ships sat up at station, constantly manned, able by reason of proximity to the human craft and the station, to prove a greater threat than ever they could in combat. The humans had allowed this; and this was another reason that Hulagh felt confident of the peace. He smiled to himself and turned, aimed the sled up the slight incline, Suth walking beside him, the humans giving way to admit him. He entered the warm, filtered atmosphere of the Nom at the head of a procession that awed the local younglings who stood inside to see it, and thoroughly satisfied his long-aggrieved pride.

"Stavros," he heard a human youngling inform Suth, observing regul protocol, "will see the bai immediately as requested."

"To the reverence bai Stavros," Hulagh intoned, when Suth had ceremoniously turned to him. "Now."

The meeting was not, as all previous meetings had been, in Stavros' small office, but in the formal conference hall; and Stavros had surrounded himself with uniformed younglings and a great deal of that immobility of countenance that in humans was evidence of a pricklish if not hostile mood. Hulagh, backed now by his three elders and an entourage of Alagn's younglings, looked about him and smiled human-fashion, far from disturbed at the new balance of powers that had doubtless troubled the humans.

"May we," Hulagh suggested at once, before seatings could

become complicated, "dispense with superfluous younglings and speak in directness, reverence?"

Stavros turned his sled and directed: human younglings sorted themselves out by rank and some began to depart. Hulagh retained Suth, and each of the Alagn elders a personal attendant, the while the four humans who counted themselves adult arranged themselves in chairs surrounding Stavros' sled. Hulagh stared curiously at one of the four, on whom no trace of gray showed . . . this coloring he had thought indicative of human maturity, since other colorations did not seem to have bearing: he remained mildly suspicious that Stavros breached protocol, seating this one in the inner circle, but in his expansive mood, he did not find himself inclined to object. Elder he might be: Hulagh had never learned accurately to determine seniority among these beings, who sexed in infancy and varied chaotically in appearance on their way to maturity, and after. He anticipated questions from his elders, and to his embarrassment, he did not know the answers.

There was, by the younglings, the interminable serving of soi: necessary, for the journey had taxed the energies of everyone; there were the introductions: Hulagh absorbed the names and stations of the so-named elder humans and responded with the names of his own elders, who still seemed dazed by the rapidly shifting flood of alien sights and by exhaustion. But in the introductions, Hulagh found reason for exception, and fluttered his nostrils in a sigh of impatience.

"Bai Stavros," Hulagh said, "is there no representative from the bai of station?"

"It would be pointless," said Stavros, using the communications screen of the sled, for Hulagh had addressed him in regul language, and so Stavros responded. "Policy is determined here. It is carried out there. Bai Hulagh, if your elders are fluent, may we use human speech?"

Characteristic of the humans, whose learning resided not in their persons, but in written records, considerable time on Kesrith had not served to give these fluency in the regul tongue. They forgot. It had amused Hulagh that meetings were often recorded on tape, lest the humans forget what they had said and what had been told them: doubtless this one was likewise being recorded. After another fashion, it did not amuse him at all, to reckon that every promise, every statement made by these creatures, relied on such poor memories. To state an untruth was a terrible thing for a regul, for what was once said could not be unlearned; but doubtless humans could unlearn anything they pleased, and sometimes forget what the facts were.

"My elders are not yet fluent," Hulagh said, and kept all trace of humor from his face as he added: "it will be instructive to them if you speak in human language; I will provide simultaneous translation on my screen."

"Appreciated," said Stavros aloud. "A pleasure to welcome your elders personally."

"We are pleased to be welcome." Hulagh set aside his empty cup and leaned back in the cushions, manipulating the keyboard to do as he had promised Stavros. "And we are pleased that our human friends were willing to interrupt their business to provide these welcoming courtesies. But true intent becomes obscured in much formality. We are not disputing docha, in need of such. You have not attacked; we have not attacked. We are pleased with the situation."

Such directness seemed to disturb the attendant humans. Stavros himself smiled, a taut, wary smile. "Good," he said. "We assure you again that we are most pleased with the prospect of wider dealings with doch Alagn and all regulkind."

"We are likewise anxious for such agreement. The mri, however, the mri remain an item of concern."

"They need not be."

"Because they are no longer at Kesrith?"

Stavros' brow lifted. It seemed a smile, perhaps; Hulagh watched the reaction carefully, decided otherwise. "We are working," said Stavros carefully, "to be able to assure the regul that there is no possible danger from the mri."

"I have inquired about the youngling Duncan," said Hulagh. "He is not available. The mri are off Kesrith. A ship has left. All these circumstances—perhaps unrelated—still seem to assume a distressing importance."

There was a long pause. Stavros' mouth worked in an expression that Hulagh could not successfully read, no more than the other: perplexity, perhaps, or displeasure.

"We are," said Stavros at last, "attempting to trace the extent of the mri. We have found a record which is pertinent. Bai Hulagh, the extent of the record is entirely disquieting."

Hulagh drew in air, held his breath a moment. Truth: he knew Stavros well enough to rely on it.

"Part of it," Stavros said, "may lie within regul space, but only part."

"Abandoned worlds," Hulagh said. He had neglected to translate in his distress: he amended his omission, saw shock register on the faces of his other elders. "Nisren, Guragen—but it is true that they have ranged far. A mri record, is it so?"

"They do write," said Stavros.

"Yes," said Hulagh. "No literature, no art, no science, no commerce; but I have been in the old edun—there, on the slopes. I have seen myself what may have been writings. But I cannot provide you translation, not readily."

"Numerical records, in great part. We have understood them well enough to be concerned. We are pursuing the question. It may prove of great concern to all regul. We are concerned about the size of what those records may show us. And about possible overlapping of our researches with regul territory. Marginal intrusion. Not troublesome to Alagn; but others—"

"Holn."

"Yes," said Stavros. "We are concerned about the path of that probe. Yet it had to be done."

Breath fluttered from Hulagh's nostrils; his hearts beat in disturbing rhythm. He was utterly aware of the frightened eyes of his elders upon him, reliant on his experience, for they had none to offer. He became agonizingly aware that he was faced with something that would have repercussions all the way to Mab, and there was no way to delay the issue or seek consultations.

Alagn had power to speak for the docha, had done so in negotiations with the humans before. Hulagh gathered himself, called for another drink of soi, and the other elders likewise took refreshment. He sipped at his, deep in thought, paused for a look at Sharn, whose counsel was welcome, if not informed; Sharn gave him a look that appreciated his perplexity, agreed with him. He was gratified in that. The other elders looked merely bewildered, and Karag did not well hide his distress.

"Bai Stavros," Hulagh said at last, interrupting a quiet consultation among the humans, "your . . . intrusion could be somewhat dangerous in terms of relations with the docha. However, with Alagn support, such an expedition might be authorized from here. The record of which you speak, I understand, extends farther than regul territory."

"Our understanding of your extent in certain areas is vague, but we believe so."

"Surely—our interests are similar here. We are not a warlike species. Surely you judged this when you launched the probe—and perhaps the great warship would have followed. Surely—" A thought struck Hulagh: his nostrils relaxed in astonishment. "You prepared that probe as an excuse. You let it ahead deliberately, to claim right of pursuit, to excuse yourself—a rebel mri craft. Am I right?"

Stavros did not answer, but looked at him warily: the faces of the others defied reading.

"Yet you held the warships back," Hulagh said. His hearts slipped into discordant rhythm. "For our consultation, bai Stavros?"

"It seemed useful."

"Indeed. Beware a misjudgment, reverence bai Stavros. A regul in home territory is much different from a regul in distant colonies. When a doch's survival is at stake—attitudes are very hard."

"We do not wish any incident. But neither can we let the possibilities raised by that record go uninvestigated. A mri refuge among Holn is only one such."

"We have similar interests," said Hulagh softly. "I will sanction passage of that warship—in a joint mission, with sharing of all data."

"An alliance."

"An alliance," said Hulagh, "for our mutual protection."

Chapter Ten

—————◦◉◦—————

THE HUMAN slept.

Niun, warm against the bodies of the dusei, his mind filled with the animal's peace, watched Duncan in the half-light of the star-screen, content to wait. There was in Duncan's quarters a second bed; he refused it, preferring the carpeted floor, the nearness of the dusei, the things that he had known in the Kel. He had slept enough; he was no more than drowsy now in the long twilit waiting, and he fought the impulse to slip back into half-sleep, for the first time finding acute pleasure in waking to this new world. He had his weapons again; he had the dusei for his strength; and most of all Melein was safe, and in possession of the pan'en and the ship.

Their ship.

He suspected they owed much to this human, shamefully much; but he was glad that Melein elected to take it, and to live. It was a measure of Melein's own gratitude that she bent somewhat, that she left the times of things in Niun's own hands; *when you think him fit,* she had said, and even permitted the ship's schedule to be adjusted so that they might enter a premature night cycle, which they themselves did not need: but Duncan needed the sleep, which he had denied himself in caring for them.

Elsewhere Melein surely rested, or worked quietly. The ship proceeded, needing nothing from them. They had far, impossibly far to travel. The reference star that shone wan and distant in the center of the screen was not their destination. They had only entered the fringe of the system, and would skim outward again, into transit.

113

And stars after stars there would be: so Melein had said.

They had made a second transit during the night, a space in which they were, and were not, and were again, and substances flowed like water. Niun had not panicked, neither this time nor the first, even though Duncan himself, experienced in such things, had wakened with a wild outcry and was sick after, sweating profusely and scarcely able to walk to the lab where he found the drugs that calmed him: they had thrown him into sleep at last; that still continued. And this, troubling as it was, Niun had tried not to see: this once, he allotted to the human's distraught condition. It was possible, he thought, that mri had some natural advantage in this state; or perhaps it was shame that kept a mri from yielding to such weakness. He did not know. Other shames he had suffered, at the hands of humans and regul, inflicted upon him; but this was his own body, his own senses, and of them he had control.

Their ship, their voyage, and the pan'en to guide them: it was the only condition under which living was worthwhile, that they ruled themselves, much as the fact of it still dazed him. He had not expected it, not though Melein had foreseen, had told him it would be so. He had not believed: Melein, who had been only sen Melein, his true sister—that was all that he had trusted in her: poor, houseless she'pan, he had thought of her, lost and powerless, and he had done what he could to fend for her.

But she had seen.

The greatest she'panei were said to have been foresighted, the greatest and holiest that had ever guided the People; and a feeling of awe possessed him when he realized that such was Melein, of one blood with him. Such kinship frightened him, to reckon that her heredity was also his, that there rested within himself something he did not understand, over which he had no power.

She was guiding them *home*.

The very concept was foreign to him: home—*a'ai sa-mri*, the beginnings of the People. He knew, as surely all mri had always known, that once there must have been a world other than the several home-worlds-of-convenience—despite that it was sung that the People were born of the Sun. All his life he had looked up only at the red disc of Arain, and, in the discipline of the Kel, in the concerns of his former life, he had never let his curiosity stray beyond that barrier of his child-born belief. It was a Mystery; and it was not pertinent to his caste.

Born of the Sun. Golden-skinned, the mri, bronze-haired and golden-eyed: it had never before occurred to him that within that song lay the intimation of a sun of a different hue, and that it explained more than the custom of the Kel, who were spacefarers by preference, who cast their dead into the fires of stars, that no dark earth might possess them.

He stared at the star that lay before them, wondering where they were, whether within regul space still or elsewhere. It was a place known to generations before Kesrith, to hands that had set the record of it within the pan'en; and here too the People had seen service. Regul space or not, it must have been so: the Kel would have hired to fight, as it had always been—mercenaries, by whose gold the People lived. He could not imagine anything else.

Stars beyond stars.

And from each in turn the People would have departed: so it was, in the Darks; it was unthinkable that they would have fragmented. All, all would have gone—and what might move them was beyond his imagining, save only that the vision of a she'pan would have led them. They either moved to another and nearby world, or they had entered a Dark; and in the Dark, in that voyage, they would have forgotten all that pertained to that abandoned star, to that former service; they had come to the next Sun, and another service; and therafter returned to the Dark, and another forgetting, a cycle without end.

Until Kesrith, until they two began to come home, a voyage in which the era of service to regul, the two thousand years that he had believed for all of recorded time, became merely interlude.

> *From Dark beginning*
> *To Dark at ending,*

So the People sang, in the holiest of songs.

> *Between them a Sun,*
> *But after comes Dark,*
> *And in that Dark,*
> *One ending.*

Tens of times he had sung the ritual, the *Shon'jir*, the Song of Passings, chanted at births and deaths and beginnings and endings. To a kel'en, it had sung only of birth and death of individuals.

Understanding opened before him, dizzying in perspective. More stars awaited them, each considered by the kel-'ein of its age to be the Sun . . . each era considered the whole of recorded time . . . until they should come in their own backward voyaging—home, to the Sun itself.

To the beginning of the People.

To the hope, the faintest of hopes, that there others might remain: Niun took to him that hope, knowing that it would surely prove false—that after so many misfortunes that had befallen them, it was impossible that such good could remain: they two were the last children of the People, born to see the end of everything, *ath-ma'ai*, tomb-guardians not only to a she'pan, but to the species.

And yet they were free, and possessed a ship.

And perhaps—a religious feeling stirred in him, and a great fear—it was for something else that they had been born.

Niun caressed the dus' velvet-furred shoulder, gazing at the human whose face was touched by the white light of the screen. In drugged abandonment the man slept, after giving them the ship, and his life, and his person. Niun puzzled over this, troubled, reckoned all the words and acts that had ever passed between them, that he could have moved the human to such a desperate act. Against the wisdom of the People, he had taken a prisoner; and this was the result of it—that Duncan had become attached to them, stubborn as the dusei, who simply chose a mri and settled with him or died of grief.

Human instincts surely did not run in that direction. For forty years the People had struggled to deal with humans, and suffered murder for it, kel'ein butchered by this species that fought only in masses and with distance-weapons. Forty years—and at the last, in human victory—came Duncan, who, ill-treated, brought the whole machinery of human mercy down upon them, who cast himself and his freedom into their hands for good measure.

Tsi'mri stupidity, Niun raged in his mind, wishing that he could separate himself from tsi'mri altogether.

Yet he remembered a long and terrible dream, in which

Duncan had been a faithful presence—in which he had fought for his sanity along with his life, and Duncan had stayed by him.

Atonement?

Perhaps, Niun thought, what had possessed Duncan had seized on the rest of his kind; perhaps, after all, there was some strange tsi'mri sense of honor that could not abide what the regul had done—as if humans would not take a victory so ill-won; as if the ruin of the People made a diminution in the universe that even humans felt, and in fear for themselves they tried to make restitution.

Not for tsi'mri, such a voyage as they made: and yet if such ever had a claim on the mri, inextricably entangled with the affairs of the People, such was Duncan—from the time that he, himself, had held the human's life and missed the chance to take it.

Niun, he is tsi'mri, Melein had argued, *and whatever he has done, he does not belong, not in the Dark.*

Yet we take the dusei, he had said, *and they are of the Between, too; and shall we kill them, that trust us?*

Melein had frowned at that; the very thought was terrible, for the partnership between mri and dus was old as Kesrith. And at last she had turned her face away and yielded. *You cannot make a dus into a mri,* she had said last, *and I do not think you will succeed with a human either. You will only delay matters painfully; you will arm him against us and endanger us. But try, if your mind is set; make him mri, make him mri, or we must someday do a cruel and terrible thing.*

"Duncan," Niun said into the dark, saw Duncan's light-bathed face contract in reaction. "Duncan."

Eyes opened, wells of shadow in the dim light of the screen. Slowly, as if the drug still clouded his senses, the human sat up. He was naked to the waist, his strange furriness at odd contrast with his complexion. He bowed his head against his knee and ran his hand through his disordered hair, then looked at Niun.

"It is a reasonable hour," said Niun. "You do not look well, Duncan."

The human shrugged, by which Niun understood that his ill was of the heart as much as of the body; and this he could well understand. "There are things to be done," Niun said. "You have said that there are trade supplies aboard."

"Yes," Duncan said, a marginal lifting of his spirits, as if he had dreaded something more distasteful. "Food, clothing, metals, all that there was at the station, that was intended for mri trade. I figured it properly belonged to you."

"You most of all have need of clothing."

Duncan considered, and nodded in consent. He had been long enough with them to know that his naked face was an offense, and perhaps long enough to feel a decent shame. "I will see to it," he agreed.

"Do that first," said Niun. "Then bring food for the dusei, and for us both; but I will take the she'pan's to her."

"All right," Duncan said. Niun watched as the human gathered himself up and wrapped a robe about himself—blue, that was kath-color, and inappropriate for a man. Niun considered the incongruity of that—what vast and innocent differences lay between mri and human, and what a thing he had undertaken. He did not protest Duncan's dress, not now; there were other and more grievous matters.

Niun did not attempt to rise, not until Duncan had left the room, for he knew that it would be difficult, and shaming. With the dusei's help he managed it, and stood against the wall, hard-breathing, until his legs would bear him. He could not fight against the human and win, not yet; and Duncan knew it, knew and still declined to risk the dusei's anger, or to dispute against him, or to use his knowledge of the ship to trap them and regain control.

And he had undertaken to destroy the human.

When he has forgotten that he is human, Melein had said, *when he is mri, then I will see his face.*

Duncan had consented to it. Niun was dismayed by this, knew of a certainty that he himself would have died before accepting such conditions of humans. When other things had failed to kill him, this would have done so, from the heart outward.

And someday, when Duncan had become mri, then he would not be capable of bending again. This acquiescence of his was tsi'mri, and must be shed along with all the rest: the naive, childlike man who had attached himself to them would no longer exist.

Niun thought to himself that he would miss that man that they had known; and the very realization made him uneasy, that a tsi'mri should so have softened his mind and his heart.

The worst acts, he told himself, must surely proceed from ir-resolution, from half-measures. Melein had feared what he proposed, had spoken against it with what he desperately hoped was not foresight. She had not forbidden him.

He went gingerly, on exhausted legs, into the bath, and looked on what things were there that belonged to Duncan. These must go, the clothing, the personal items, everything: when he was no longer reminded of humans by the things that surrounded him, then neither would Duncan be remind-ed.

And if change was impossible to the human, then best to know it soon: it was one thing to reshape, and another to destroy and leave nothing in its place. Mri that he was, Niun had not learned of his masters to be cruel, only to be pitiless, and to desire no pity.

He gathered up what of Duncan's belongings he could find and bore them into the lab, where he knew there was a dis-posal chute: he thrust them in, and felt a pang of shame for what he did, but it seemed wrong to compel Duncan to do this himself, surrendering what he had prized, a lessening of the man—and that he would not do.

And when that was done, Niun looked about him at the lab, at the cabinet from which Duncan had obtained his med-icines, and resolved on other things.

The door would not yield to his hand: he drew his pistol and ruined the lock, and it yielded easily thereafter. Load af-ter load of tsi'mri medicines and equipage he carried to the chute, and cast it out, while the dusei sat and watched with grave and glittering eyes.

And suddenly the beasts arose in alarm—shied aside from Duncan's presence in the doorway.

Niun, his hands full of the last of the medicines, thrust them within the chute and only then faced Duncan's anger, that had the dusei distraught and bristling.

"There is no need of such things," he said to Duncan.

Duncan had attempted to robe himself as mri: the boots and the *e'esin* he had managed, the inner robe; but the *siga*, the outer, he wore loose; and the veil he carried in his hand—he had never found the arranging of it easy. Face-naked, he showed his anguish, a despair that wounded.

"You have killed me," he said in a thin voice, and Niun felt the sting of that—less than certain, in that moment, of the honesty of what he had done, trusting that the human would not challenge, could not. The dusei moaned, crowding into the corner. A container crashed from a table under their weight.

"If your life is those medicines," said Niun, "then you cannot survive with us. You will survive. We do not need such things; you do not."

Duncan cursed him. Niun stiffened, set his face against such tsi'mri rage, and refused to be provoked.

"Understand," said Niun, "that you agreed. This is a mri ship, kel Duncan. You will learn to be mri, as a child of the Kath learns. I do not know any other way, only to teach you as I was taught. If you will not, then I will fight you. But understand, as all mri understand who enter the Kel, that kel-law works from the elder to the lesser to the least. You will hurt before you are done; so, once did I. And if you have it in you to be kel'en, you will survive. That is what my masters in the Kel once said to me, when I was of an age to enter the Kel. I saw twelve of my Kel who did not survive, who never took the *seta'al*, the scars of caste. It is possible that you will not survive. It is possible that you cannot become what I am. If I were convinced that you cannot, then I would not do what I have done."

The human quieted; the dusei snuffed loudly and rocked, still uneasy. But Duncan's naked face assumed a calm, untroubled look that was more the man they knew. "All right," he said. "But, Niun, I needed those medicines. I needed them."

Fear. Niun still felt it in the room.

And he was troubled after Duncan had gone away, whether he had in fact done murder. He had thought as mri, forgetting that alien flesh might indeed be incapable of what mri found possible.

And was it then wrong that aliens needed what mri law forbade?

It was not a kel-thought, not right for his caste to think or to wonder. He dared not even bring it to Melein in secret, knowing the thought beyond him and disrespectful to a young and less than certain she'pan, even from her kel'anth, senior of the Kel—such of a Kel as she possessed.

He hoped desperately that he had not killed Duncan.

And in that thought he realized clearly that he wanted Duncan to live, not alone for rightness' sake, but because two were a desolate sort of House, and because the silence in kel-hall could become very deep and very long.

He called the dusei to him, soothed them with his hands and his voice, and went to find where Duncan had gone.

Chapter Eleven

FOUR DAYS.

Duncan held them as a blur in his mind, a moiled confusion out of which he remembered little of reason. He worked to fill his hours, exhausted himself deliberately to cast himself to sleep of nights without long thought, without dreams. Niun did nothing except to exercise, quietly and often: *I am not a bearer of burdens,* the mri had insisted stiffly, when Duncan suggested he might well exercise by assisting him; and the mri then compounded the affront by reminding him that the dusei wanted tending.

Neither am I, Duncan had retorted, and bit off the oaths that rose into his mouth: the mri were not tolerant; they would kill or die for small cause, and there was time later to reason with Niun, whose limbs' weakness doubtless fed his temper, and whose uncertainty about his total situation likely hardened his attitudes.

The dusei, in fact, did want tending; and after a suitable delay, Duncan went and saw to their wants—rewarded by their pleasure-impulse, he felt shame for having put them off in spite—and fled it, for he could not bear much of it.

It was not the last crossing of purposes with Niun; the mri asked things and insisted he should understand the mri language—understand he did, in some words, with gestures— and at times Niun affected not to understand until he used a mri expression, though the mri was fluent. *Starve, then,* he was tempted to say; and did not, for there was later for quarrels, and the dusei that hovered about were becoming unpleasant and upset, contributing to the situation. In the end, Niun had his way.

It made sense, Duncan thought late, upon his bed, while the mri chose the floor. Niun fought to keep what was his, a way and a language that had almost entirely perished. It was a quiet battle, waged against him, who had most helped them and now most threatened them. It was something against which guns and skill did not avail, but life and death, all the same. It was why they were here at all, why they had been unable to live among humans, why he had argued with Stavros to free them. There was no compromise possible for them. They could not bear with strangeness. A human could; a human could adapt, facile as the jo, who looked like sand or stone, and waited. He considered this, and considered the sleeping mri, who lay with his head against his dus, unveiled as he would not unveil to an enemy.

Jo-fashion, a human could change and change again; the mri would obstinately die: and therefore it was inevitable that Niun should have his way.

In the morning Duncan set about his routines, and utterly bit back objections with Niun, went so far as to ask what he would have done.

Niun's amber eyes swept the compartment; a long-fingered hand made an inclusive gesture. *"E'nai,"* he said, *"i."—Remove it all.* Duncan stared, drew a long breath, and considered the matter.

The ship grew cold in the passing days, the air gradually resembling Kesrith's dry chill. Duncan was glad of the warmth of the mri robes that he wore from the skin outward. He learned the veil and the manners of it; he learned words and courtesies and gestures, and abandoned his own.

Niun sensed, surely, how far he was pressed, the frustration that welled upward in him at times, and averted his face and resumed the veil when matters came too close to impasse. There would be silence for a time, and finally words again. Niun named the things of which he did not approve: comforts and furnishings of all sorts. Duncan acquiesced, yielded up such of his own belongings as still remained, for the attachment he had to them seemed distant in this place, faced with what misery lay ahead for him; and as for damage to the ship, that seemed insufficient revenge on those that had sent him here. He worked at it, bewildered at first by what Niun asked, then grimly pleased in it. He stripped the accessible compartments of all furnishings, disassembled the furniture and stored what parts were useful metals and materials,

and cast the rest out the destruct chute. After that went all
machinery the mri considered superfluous, medical and otherwise, and all goods in storage that were counted luxuries.

It was madness. Duncan abandoned himself to it, began in
his own frustration to seek out things to cast away, destroying
for the joy of it, making of the ship only a shell, in which he
did not have to remember Stavros, or humanity, or any other
thing that he had cast away to come here. The loss of everything dulled all sense of loss.

The labs were mostly stripped already, back at station: all
that had been reckoned unnecessary to the mission had already been taken, and all that he would desperately have
saved, Niun had already destroyed. Duncan finished the job,
down to the cleats that had held the furnishings, chem-
scrubbed the floors, the walls, rendering the place acceptable—for this largest compartment on the ship Niun had
chosen for their own.

Thereafter Duncan slept on a pallet no thicker than a
folded blanket, and wakened stiff and fell to coughing again
in the chill air, so that he began to brood over his health, and
thought desperately of the medicines that Niun had
destroyed, for that and for other purposes.

But Niun looked at him with some concern, and tacitly
forgot his objection to work, and took on himself that day
the preparation of meals and the care of the dusei. Niun
flourished in the chill, thin air—had lost that frail, tottering
movement in his step, and ceased to tire so quickly.

"You rest," Niun wished him when he persisted in trying
to keep his schedule; Duncan shrugged and avowed the
machinery would not run without him, which it would; but
he was panicked now at the thought of idleness, sitting endlessly in the shell that he had left of the labs, of the rest of
the ship, without books—Niun had cast out the reading and
the music tapes in his quarters—without any occupation for
hands or mind.

And when he was forced, he returned to the lab, that featureless white room, and settled in the corner, where at least
his pallet and Niun's and the joining of the walls gave him
some feeling of location. There, as he would do late at night
to fall asleep, he sat and added chains of figures, did complex
calculations of imaginary navigation, anything to fill the
hours—watched the unchanging starscreen that was the lab's
only feature. There was for sound only the whisper of air in

the ducts, the steady machine noise of the ship's inner workings.

And nothing.

Nothing.

Niun was long absent that day—with Melein, Duncan
reckoned, in that part of the ship that was barred to him;
even the dusei were gone, constantly attendant on Niun. In
idleness Duncan found a bit of metal and made a design on
the tiles next his pallet, and then, with a certain grim humor,
made marks for the days that had passed, ship-time, desperately reckoning that there could come a time he would lose
track of everything in this place.

Nine days, thus far. Even of this he was marginally uncertain.

He began a chain of figures, thrusting his mind away from
the lattice-gaps he had begun to have in his memory, trying
to lose himself in regularities.

Unlike the jo, he was not successfully camouflaging, he
reckoned; even the jo, cast into this sterile cubicle, given
nothing to pattern from, could not find a place. It would
blacken like a wretched specimen he had seen in Boaz' lab,
going through color change after color change until it settled
on the most conspicuous of all—a method of suicide, perhaps, death wish.

He thrust his thoughts away from that, too, but the image
kept returning, the black winged creature in the silver cage;
himself, from godlike perspective, sitting in the corner of a
white and featureless room.

Nine days.

The afternoon of the tenth, Niun came back earlier than
previously, banished the dusei to the far corner of the room,
and unveiled, settled crosslegged on the floor a little removed
from Duncan and facing him.

"You sit too much," Niun said.

"I am resting," Duncan said with an edge of bitterness.

Niun held up two metal rods, slender, and no more than a
hand's length. "You will learn a game," Niun said, not: *I will
teach you;* not: *Would it please you?* Duncan frowned, considered taking offense: but that the grim mri had entertain-
ments: this pricked his interest, promised comradeship, a
chance to talk with the kel'en as he had not been able to talk
with him since the desert.

And it promised something to fill the silence.

He bestirred himself on his pallet, assumed carefully the position that Niun held, crosslegged, hands on knees. Niun showed him the grip he had on the end of the rod in his right hand.

"You must catch," said Niun, and spun the rod toward him. Duncan caught it, startled, in his fist, not his fingers, and the butt of it stung his palm.

The second followed, from Niun's left hand. Duncan caught it and dropped it. Niun held up both hands empty.

"Both at once," Niun said.

It was difficult. It was exceedingly difficult. Duncan's work-sore hands were less quick than Niun's slender fingers, that never missed, that snatched the most awkward throws from midair, and returned them always at the same angle and speed, singly until Duncan could make the difficult catch, and then together.

"We call it *shon'ai*," said Niun. "*Shonau* is *pass*. In your language, then, the Passing game. It sings the People; each caste plays in its own way." He spoke, and the rods flew back and forth gently between them, Duncan's fingers growing more sure than they had been. "There are three castes of the People: Kath and Kel and Sen. We are of the Kel, we black-robes, we that fight; the Sen is the yellow-robes, the scholars; and the white, the she'pan; the Kath is the caste of women neither Kel nor Sen, the blue-robes, and the children—they are Kath until they take caste."

Duncan missed. The rod stung his knee, clattered to the floor. He rubbed the knee and then continued, back and forth, back and forth in turn with Niun. It was hard to listen and concentrate on the rods; in recklessness he tried to answer.

"Men," he said, "neither Kel nor Sen. What of them?"

The rhythm did not break. "They die," said Niun. "The ones without skill to be Sen, without skill to be Kel, the ones with no heart, die. Some die in the Game. We are playing as the Sen plays, with wands. The Kel plays with weapons." The throws became harder, faster. "Easy, with two players. More difficult with three. With larger circles, it grows most difficult. I played a circle of ten. If the circle becomes much larger, it becomes again a matter of accidents, of chance."

The rods flew hard this time. Duncan flung his hands up to catch them, deflected one that could have injured his face, but could not catch it. It fell. The other he held. The rhythm ceased, broken.

"You are weak in the left hand," said Niun. "But you have the heart. Good. You will learn the skill before I begin to show you the *yin'ein*, the old weapons. The *zahen'ein*, the modern, you know as well as I; I have nothing there to teach you. But the *yin'ein*, one begins with *shon'ai*. Throw."

Duncan threw. Niun held up his hand, easily received the separate rods cast back to him—with one hand, sweeping them effortlessly from the air. Duncan blinked, dismayed at the skill of the mri, and measured his own.

"There is a time to rest," said Niun then. "I would not see you miss." He tucked the rods back into his belt. "It is time," he said, "that we begin to talk. I will not speak often in your language; I am ordered to forget it, and so must you. You know a few words of the mu'ara, the common speech; and even those you must forget, and stay to the hal'ari, the High Speech. It is the law of the Darks, that all the Between be forgotten, and the mu'ara that grows in the Between must die, too. So do not be confused. Sometimes there are two words for a thing, one mu'ara, one hal'ari, and you must forget even a mri word."

"Niun," Duncan protested, holding up a hand for delay. "I haven't enough words."

"You will learn. There will be time."

Duncan frowned, looked at the mri from under his brows, carefully approached what had already been refused. "How much time?"

Niun shrugged.

"Does the she'pan know?" Duncan asked.

The membrance flicked across Niun's eyes. "Your heart is still tsi'mri."

It was a mri kind of answer, maddening. Duncan traced the design he had scratched on the flooring, considering what he could do to reason with the mri; of a sudden Niun's hand stopped his. He jerked it free, looked up in deep offense.

"Another matter," said Niun. "A kel'en neither reads nor writes."

"I do."

"Forget."

Duncan stared at him. Niun veiled himself and rose, an unbending upward that a few days ago he could not have

done, a grace natural to a man who had spent his life sitting
on the ground; but Duncan, in attempting to rise and face
him, was less graceful.

"Listen," he said.

And a siren sounded.

It was in Duncan's consciousness a subtle moment before
panic took over, raw fear. Transition was approaching: they
had made a jump point. The dusei had learned. Their feelings
washed about the room like a tide—fear, abhorrence.

"Yai!" Niun shouted at them, settling them. He walked to
the doorway and took hold of the handgrip there. Duncan
sought that on the other side of the room, feigning calm he
did not feel; his gut twisted in dread of what was coming—
and no drugs, nothing. It was Niun's cold, unmoved example
that kept him from sinking to the floor to await it.

The siren stopped. In a moment a bell signaled imminent
jump, automatic alarm triggered by the ship as the tape
played toward its destination. They had not yet learned
where they had been. The nameless yellow star still hung as
only one among others in the field of the screen. No ships
had come. Nothing.

Suddenly came that initial feeling of uncertainty, and
walls, floor, time, matter, rippled and shredded. The mind un-
derwent something irretrievable on the outflow, as the process
reversed itself; but there remained an impression of in-
conceivable depth, of senses over-stimulated. The walls
rippled back into solidity. Hands felt. Breath and sight returned.

But the bell was still going, still warning of jump imminent.

"Something's wrong!" Duncan cried. He saw the look on
Niun's face, fear, that was not accustomed there; and Niun
shouted something at him that had to do with Melein—and
ran.

The dus-feelings were flooding the room. The dissolution
began again, rippling, stomach-wrenching, like a fall to death.
Duncan clung where he was, wishing to lose consciousness,
unable to do so. The room dissolved.

Reshaped.

The bell kept on and on, and the warping began a third
time. Dus-flesh was about him, radiating terror. Duncan
screamed, lost his grip and fell down among them, one with
them, beast-mind, beast-sense, and the bells. Another time the

rippling began, and faded back; and another; and another; and another.

He felt solidity about him, touch and sensations of light that were alien after the abysses he had voyaged. He cried out, and felt the dusei warm against him, their solid comfort, the mad irrationalities of their uncomprehending minds.

They were his anchor. They had held him, one with him. He gave up his humanity and gave way to them for a time, arm flung over a massive neck, receiving their warmth and comfort until he clearly realized what he yielded them, and cursed, and pushed them; then they withdrew, and he became aware of himself again.

Human, who had laid down with them, no more than they.

He hurled himself up and staggered to the doorway. His legs folded under him as he grasped the handhold, his fingers too weak to keep it. His stomach tried to evert itself, as if underfoot were sideways, but he had not the strength to heave up its contents, and grayed out.

He fell, sprawled, and realized it, still wanted to be sick and could not. He lay still a time, heaving with his effort to breathe, and the dusei crouched in the far corner, separate from him, giving him nothing but their fear.

Niun returned—after how long a time he knew not—sank down, bowed his veiled head wearily against his folded arms. Duncan lay still on his side, unwilling to chance more than breathing.

"Melein is well," Niun said in his own tongue: that much Duncan could understand; and something further he said, but Duncan could not put it together.

"What happened?" Duncan demanded to know, an effort that cost him much in sickness; but Niun only shrugged. "Niun, where are we?"

But Niun said nothing, perhaps unable to answer, or simply, mri-stubborn, pretending not to understand human language any more.

Duncan cursed him, and the effort knotted his stomach and heaved up the sickness at last. He could not move, even to move aside. After a long time Niun bestirred himself in what was surely disgust, and brought wet towels and cleaned the place and washed his face. The touch, the lifting of his head brought more dry heaving, and Niun let him alone thereafter, settling on the opposite side of the room just within his field of vision.

Came one of the dusei at last, nosing at him, urging at him with warmth. Duncan moved his limp hand and struck it. It reared aside with a cry of startlement and outrage, radiated such horrid confusion that he cried aloud. Across the room Niun rose to his feet.

And came the siren again; and the bell.

Dissolution.

Duncan did not seek the security of the wall, the illusion that he had some anchor. He let go. When it was over, he lay on the floor and retched and sobbed for breath, fingers spread on the unyielding flooring.

The dusei came back, urging their warm feelings at him. He began to gasp, unable to breathe, until something leaned on his chest and forced the air in, until Niun's hand gripped his shoulder and shook at him with bruising force, that dazed him and made him lose contact with the room again. He stared at the mri in utter blankness and sobbed.

He was composed again the next morning, a hard-fought composure, muscles of his limbs and belly still tending to spasm from the tension he could not force from them. He remembered with acute shame his collapse, how he had rested the remainder of yesterday—or the day before— tucked up in a ball in the corner, remembered tears pouring hotly down his face without emotion, without cause, only that he could not stop them.

This morning Niun stared at him, veiled amber eyes frowning as he offered a cup of soi into his trembling hand, steadying him so that he could drink it. The hot, bittersweet liquid rolled like oil into Duncan's unwilling stomach and lay there, taking some of the chill away. The tears started again, causeless. He drank slowly, holding the cup child-fashion in both hands, with tears sliding down his face. He looked into the mri's eyes and met there a cold reserve that recognized no kinship between them.

"I will help you walk," Niun said.

"No," he said with such force that the mri let him alone, rose and walked away, looked back once, then left, immune to the weakness that assailed him.

In that day even the dusei radiated distrust of him: crossing the room they would shy away from him, hating his presence; and Niun when he returned sat far across the room, soothing the troubled dusei and long staring at him.

With ship's night about them, they jumped once more, and a second time, and Duncan clung to his corner, clamped his jaws against sickness, and afterward was dazed, with vast gaps in his memory. In the morning he found the strength to stagger from his cramped refuge—to bathe, driven by self-disgust—finally to take some food into his aching stomach. But for the better part of the day he could not remember clearly.

Niun regarded him, frowning, waiting, Duncan thought distractedly, for him to die or to shake off the weakness; and Duncan felt the contempt like a tangible force, and bowed his head against his arms and brooded desperately, how he would wrest control from the tape before the malfunction killed them all, how he would take them to some random, lost refuge, where humanity could not find them.

But this he had no skill to do, and in his saner moments acknowledged it. The mri could survive, so long as the ship did. He began to think obsessively of suicide, and brooded upon it, and then remembered in his terrified and circular thoughts that the drugs were gone.

"Tsi'mri," Niun said of him finally, after standing and staring at him for a time.

Contempt burned in the mri's voice. The mri walked away, and the outrage of it gave Duncan strength to rise and fight his blurring senses. He was sick again immediately; he made it to the lavatory this time, blinked the tears from his eyes and washed his face and tried to control the tremor that ran through his limbs.

And came back into the living quarters and tried to walk across the naked center of it—halfway across before his senses turned inside out and he reeled off balance. He hurled himself for the wall, reaching wildly, found it and collapsed against it.

Niun stood watching. He had not known. Niun looked him up and down, face veiled.

"You were kel'en," Niun said then. "Now what are you?"

Duncan fought for words, found none that would come out. Niun went to his own pallet and sat down there, and Duncan sat where he was on the hard floor, wanting to rise and walk and give the lie to the mri. He could not. Niun's contempt gnawed at him. He began to reckon time again, how many days he had lost in this fashion, mindless and disoriented.

"A question," Duncan said in the hal'ari. "How many days—how many gone?"

He did not expect Niun to answer, was inwardly prepared for silence or spite. "Four," said Niun quietly. "Four since your illness."

"Help me," Duncan asked, forcing the words between his teeth. "Help me up."

Silently the mri arose, and came to him and took his arm, drew him to his feet and helped him walk, providing him an anchor that made it possible to move. Duncan fought his senses into order, trying to lie to them—persuaded Niun to guide him about the routines of maintenance in their sector, tried to do what he had been accustomed to do.

He rested, as best he could, muscles still taut; and began the next morning, and the next, and the next, with the determination that the next jump would not undo him.

It came, days hence; and this time Duncan stood fast by the handhold, fighting the sickness. Within a little time he tried to go to the hall, managed to walk, and returned again to his pallet, exhausted.

He might, he thought in increasing bitterness, have let the mri die; he might have had comfort, and safety; he hated Niun's ability to endure the jumps, that set of mind that could endure the phasing in and out without unraveling.

And Niun, whether sensing his bitterness or not, deigned to speak to him again—sat near him, engaged in one-sided conversation in the hal'ari, as if it mattered. At times he spoke chants, and insisted Duncan repeat them, learn them: Duncan listlessly complied, to have peace, to be let alone eventually, endless chains of names and begettings and words that meant nothing to him. He cared little—pitied the mri, finally, who poured his history, his myths, into such a failing vessel. He felt himself on the downward side of a curve, the battle won too late. He could no longer keep food down; his limbs grew weak; he grew thin as the mri, and more fragile.

"I am dying," he confided to Niun finally, when he had learned hal'ari enough for such a thought. Niun looked at him soberly and unveiled, as he would when he wished to speak personally; but Duncan did not drop the veil, preferring its concealment.

"Do you wish to die?" Niun asked him, in a tone fully respectful of such a wish. For an instant Duncan was startled, apprehensive that the mri would help him to it on the spot: *Would you like a cup of water?* The tone would have been the same.

He searched up words with which to answer. "I want," he said, "to go with you. But I cannot eat. I cannot sleep. No, I do not want to die. But I am dying."

A frown furrowed Niun's brow. The eyes nictitated. He put out a slim, golden hand and touched Duncan's sleeve. It was a strange gesture, an act of pity, had he not better learned the mri.

"Do not die," Niun wished him earnestly.

Duncan almost wept, and managed not to.

"We shall play *shon'ai*," Niun said.

It was mad. Duncan would have refused, for his hands shook, and he knew that he would miss: it occurred to him that it was a way of granting him his death. But Niun's gentility promised otherwise, promised companionship, occupation for the long hours. One could not think of anything else, and play *shon'ai*.

By the side of a red star, for five days without a jump, they played at *shon'ai*, and spoke together, unveiled. There was a chant to the Game, and a rhythm of hands that made it yet more difficult to make the catch. Duncan learned it, and it ran through his brain even at the edge of sleep, numbing, possessing his whole mind; for the first time in uncounted nights he slept deeply, and in the morning he ate more than he had been able.

On the sixth day by that star, they played a more rapid game, and Duncan suffered a bone-bruise from a hit, and learned that Niun would not hold his hand with him any longer.

Twice more he was hit, once missing by nervousness and the second time by anger. Niun returned a cast with more skill than he could manage when he had thrown the mri a foul throw in temper for the first hit. Duncan absorbed the pain and learned that to lose concentration from fear or from anger was to suffer worse pain, and to lose the game. He cleared his mind, and played in earnest at *shon'ai*, still with wands, and not yet as the Kel played, with edged steel.

"Why," he asked Niun, when he had words enough to ask, "do you play to harm your brothers?"

"One plays *shon'ai*," said Niun, "to deserve to live, to feel the mind of the People. One throws. One receives. We play to deserve to live. We cast. Hands empty, we wait. And we learn to be strong."

There was a threshold of fear in the Game, the sure knowledge that there was a danger, that there was no mercy. One could be secure in it a time, while the pace stayed within the limits of one's skill, and then one realized that it was in earnest, and that the pace was increasing. Fear struck, and nerves failed, and the Game was lost, in pain.

Play, Niun advised him, *to deserve to live. Throw your life, kel'en, and catch it in your hands.*

He understood, and therein another understanding came to him, how the mri could take great joy in such a game.

And he understood for the first time the peculiar madness in which the mri could not only survive, but revel in the unnatural feel of the jumps, by which the ship hurled herself at apparent random from star to star.

Twice more they jumped, and Duncan stood still and waited as the bell rang and the dissolution began. He watched the mri, knew the mind of the kel'en who stood opposite him—knew how to let go and cast himself utterly to the rhythm of the Game, to go with the ship, and not to fear.

A wild laugh came to him on that second emergence, for the teaching of the Service had been *survive,* but that of the Game was something complexly alien, that careless madness that was the courage of the mri.

Kel'en.

He had shed something, something he once had valued; and as with the other possessions that he had cast into oblivion, the sense of loss was dim and distant.

Niun gazed at him, silently estimated, and he met that look directly, loss still nagging at him. One of the dusei, the lesser one, nosed his hand. He jerked it back, turned his face from Niun's critical stare, and went to the corner that was his—limbs steady, senses trying to deceive him and denied the power to do so.

He was not what Stavros had launched.

He sat on his pallet and stared at the scratched reckoning of days that he had begun, and that he had omitted to do. It was no longer the time that passed that mattered, but that which lay ahead, time enough that he could indeed forget.

Forget writing, forget human speech, forget Kesrith. There were gaps in his past, not alone in recent days, those fevered and terrible hours; there were others, that made strange and shifting patterns of all his memory, as if some things that he remembered were too strange to this ship, this long voyaging.

The Dark that Niun spoke of began to swallow such things up, as it lacked measure, and direction, and reason.

With the same edge of metal that had made the marks, he scratched through them, obliterating the record.

Chapter Twelve

———◆◉◆———

THE LOST days multiplied into months. Duncan passed them in careful observance of maintenance schedules, stripped down units that did not need it and reassembled the machinery, only to keep busy—played *shon'ai* what time Niun would consent; memorized the meaningless chants of names, and constantly rehearsed in his mind what words he had recently gathered of the hal'ari, the while his hands found occupation in the game of knots that Niun taught him, or in the galleys, or in whatever work he could devise for the moment.

He learned metalwork, which was a craft appropriate to the Kel; and carving—made in plastic a blockish figure of a dus, for which he found no practical use in its beginning; and then purpose did come to him. "Give it to the she'pan," he said, when he had done it as well as possible; and pushed it into Niun's hands.

The mri had looked greatly distressed. "I will try," he had said, with perplexing seriousness, and arose at once and went, as if it were a matter of moment instead of a casual thing.

It was late before he returned; and he settled cn the floor and set the little dus-figure between them on the mat. "She would not, kel Duncan."

No apology for the she'pan's hatefulness; it was impossible that Niun apologize for a decision of the she'pan. Understanding came, why Niun had hesitated even to try to take the gift to her, and after a moment heat began to rise to Duncan's face. He did not veil, but stared sullenly at the floor, at the unshapely and rejected little figure.

"So," he said with a shrug.

"It was bu'ina'anein—you invaded," Niun said.

"Presumptuous," Duncan translated, and the heat did not leave his face.

"It is not the time," said Niun.

"When will be?" Duncan asked sharply, heard the mri's soft intake of breath. Niun veiled himself in offense and rose.

Discarded, the little figure lay there for two days before Niun, in a mild tone of voice, and after fingering it for some little time, asked if he might have it.

Duncan shrugged. "Take it," he said, glad to have it gone.

It disappeared into the inner folds of Niun's robes. Niun rose and withdrew from the room. The dusei went, and returned, and went again, restless.

There was a line drawn in main-corridor, an invisible one. Duncan knew the places within the ship that he could go, and those that were barred to him, and he did not attempt the forbidden ones. It was not from the ship's workings that he was barred, so much as from Melein's presence; and Niun came and went there, but he could not.

Duncan went now, impelled by humanish obstinacy, curious where Niun had gone with the figure; and his steps grew less quick, and finally ceased at the corridor that he had not seen in uncounted days: around the bending of the passage as it was, he had not even infringed so far as to come this way—and the sight of it now cooled his anger and gave him pause.

The lights were out here, and faintly there was the reek of something musky that the filters had not entirely dispersed. A vast brown shape, and a second, sat in the shadows before an open doorway: the dusei—Niun's presence, he thought.

There was humanish stubbornness; and there was stubbornness mri-fashion, which he had also learned, which, in Niun, he respected.

There was the simple fact that, challenged, Niun would not back away.

But there were ways of pressing at the mri.

Silently, respectful of the barrier, Duncan gathered his robes between his knees and sank down crosslegged, there to wait. The dusei, shadows by the distant doorway, stood and snuffed the air nervously, pressing at him with their uncertainties. He would not be driven. He did not move. In time, the lesser dus came halfway and lay down facing him, head between its massive paws. When he stayed still it rose up again, and halved that distance, and finally, much against his will, came and nosed at his leg.

"Yai!" he rebuked it softly. It settled, not quite touching, sighed.

And from the doorway appeared a blacker shadow, that glittered here and there with metal.

Niun.

The mri stood still, waiting. Duncan gathered himself to his feet and stood still, carefully at the demarcation.

It was not necessary to say overmuch with Niun—the mri observed him now, and after deliberation, beckoned him to come.

Duncan walked ahead into that shadow, the dus at his heels, as Niun waited for him at the doorway; and human-wise he would have questioned Niun, what manner of thing was here, what impulse suddenly admitted him to this place. But still in silence Niun swept his hand to the left, directing his attention into the room from which he had come.

Part of the crew's living quarters had been here. The musky smell hung thick in this shadowy place, that was draped in black cloth. The only light within was live flame, and it glistened on the ovoid that rested at the far wall of the compartment, behind a shadowed steel grating. Two conduits rose at the doorway, serving as pillars, narrowing the entry so that only one at a time might pass.

"Go in," Niun's voice said softly at his back.

He felt the touch of Niun's hand between his shoulders, and went forward, not wishing to, feeling his skin contract at the shadow, the leaping flame so dangerous on the ship, the incense was thick here, cloying. He had noticed it before, adhering to the clothing of the mri, a scent he associated with them, thought even natural to them, though he had missed it in the sterile labs.

Behind them the dusei breathed, unable to enter because of the pillars.

And there was silence for some few moments.

"You have seen such a shrine before," Niun said in a low voice, so that the prickling of his skin became intense. Duncan looked half-about at the mri, heart pounding as he recalled Sil'athen, the betrayal he had done. For a terrible moment he thought Niun knew; and then he persuaded him-self that it was the first time he had come that the mri recalled to him, when he had come with permission, in their company.

"I remember," Duncan said thickly. "Is it for this you have kept me from this part of the ship? And why do you allow me here now?"

"Did I misunderstand? Did you not come seeking admittance?"

There was a stillness in Niun's voice that chilled, even yet. Duncan did not try to answer—looked away, where the pan'en rested behind its screen, at the flickering warm light, gold on silver.

Mri.

It had no echo now, this compartment, of the human voices that had once possessed it, no memory of the coarse jokes and warmer thoughts and impulses that had once governed here. It contained the pan'en. It was a mri place. It held *age*, and the memory of something he had done that he could not admit to them.

"In every edun of the People," Niun said, "has been a shrine, and the shrine is of the Pana. You see the screen. That is the place beyond which the Kel may not set foot. That which rests beyond is not for the Kel to question. It is a symbol, kel Duncan, of a truth. Understand, and remember."

"Why do you allow me here?"

"You are kel'en. Even the least kel'en has freedom of the outer shrine. But a kel'en who has touched the pan'en—who has crossed into the Sen-shrine—he is marked, kel Duncan. Do you remember the guardian of the shrine?"

Bones and black cloth, pitiful huddle of mortality within the shrine: memory came with a cold clarity.

"The lives of kel'ein," Niun said, "have been set to guard this; others that have carried it have died for that honor, holding secret its place, obeying the orders of a she'pan. But you did not know these things."

Duncan's heart sped. He looked warily at the mri. "No," he said, and wished himself out the door.

But Niun set his hand at his shoulder and moved him forward to the screen, there knelt, and Duncan sank down beside him. The screen was a darkness that cut the light and the shape of the pan'en into diamond fragments. Behind them the dusei fretted, barred from their presence.

There was silence. Duncan slowly let go his breath, understanding finally that there was no imminent threat. A long time Niun rested there, hands in his lap, facing the screen. Duncan did not dare turn his head to look at his face.

"Do you understand this place?" Niun asked of him finally, without moving.

"No," Duncan said. "And you have not taught me words enough to ask. What do you honor here?"

"First of Kel-caste was Sa'an."

" . . . *Giver of laws*," Duncan took up the chant in silence that Niun left, *"which was the service that he gave to Sarin the Mother. And the law of the Kel is one: to serve the she'pan . . ."*

"That is the *Kel'es-jir*," Niun said. "The high songs each have a body, that is first learned; then from each major word comes a limb, that is another song. In the *e'atren-a* of Sa'an are twenty-one major words, that lead to other songs. That is one answer to your question: here kel'ein learn the high songs. Here the three castes meet together, though they keep to their places. Here the dead are laid before the presence of the Pana. Here we speak to the presence of Sa'an and the others who have given to the People, and we remember that we are their children." There was a long silence. "Sa'an was not your father. But bend yourself to kel-law and you may come here and be welcome. The kel-law I can teach you. But the things of the Pana, I cannot. They are for the she'pan to teach, when she will. It is a law that each caste teaches only what it best knows. The Kel is the Hand of the People. We are the Face of the People that outsiders see, and therefore we veil. And we do not bear the high knowledge, and we do not read the writings: we are the Face that is Turned Outward, and we hold nothing by which outsiders could learn us."

It explained much.

"Are all outsiders enemies?" Duncan asked.

"That is beyond kel-knowledge. The lives of the Kel are the living of the People. We were hired by the regul. It is sung that we have served as mercenaries, and those songs are very old, from before the regul. That is all I know."

And Niun made a gesture of respect and rose. Duncan gathered himself up and followed him out into the outer corridor, where the dusei waited. Pleasure feelings came strongly from them. Duncan bore it, trying to keep his senses clear, aware—fearfully aware—that his defenses were down, with the mri and with the dusei.

In kel-hall they shared a cup of soi. Niun seemed in an un-usually communicative mood, and expressions played freely through his eyes, which could be dead as amber glass.

As if, Duncan thought, his seeking out the shrine had pleased Niun. It occurred to him that the long silences were lonely not only for himself, but perhaps for Niun too, who shared living space with a being more alien to him than the dusei, who could less understand him—and of whom Melein disapproved.

They talked, quietly, of what little was immediate, when they reckoned that jump might occur, and what was to be done on the morrow. There was a vast area of things they did not mention, that lay in past and future. There were things that Duncan, finding Niun inclined to talk, would have asked another human, things that he might have said—questions of the past, to know the man: *What was it—to live on Kesrith, when there were only regul and mri? Where did you come from? What women did you know? What did you want of life?* But Kesrith had to be forgotten; and so did the things that he himself remembered, human and forbidden to men-tion. The past was gone; the future was full of things that a kel'en must not ask, must not question, must not see, save in dim patterns—as beyond the screen.

Duncan finished his cup, set it aside, pushed at the dus that instantly sought to nose it.

"I will play you a round," said Niun.

Day after day, the Game, each day the same. The same-ness became maddening. And on this day, with the memory of the shrine fresh in his mind, Duncan bit at his lip and weighed his life and gave another answer.

"With weapons," he said.

Niun's eyes nictitated, startlement. He considered, then from his belt drew the *av-tlen*, the little-sword, two hands in length. He laid that before him; and his pistol, that he put to the left, and apart; and the weighted cords, the *ka'islai*, that depended from his belt and seemed more ornament than weapon. And from an inner pocket of his belt he drew the small, hafted blades of the *as-ei*, with which the Kel played at *shon'ai*. All these things he laid on the mat between them, pistol on the left, and the *yin'ein*, the ancient weapons, on the right.

"There is missing the *av-kel*," Niun said. "It is not neces-sary here."

The kel-sword: Duncan knew it, a blade three feet long and razor-edged; he had returned it to Niun, and it lay now wrapped in cloth, next Niun's pallet.

"You may touch them." Niun said; and as he gathered up the small blades of the *as-ei*: "Have a care of them. Of all these things, kel Duncan, have great care. *This*—" He gestured at the pistol. "With this I have no concern for you. But kel'ein who have played the Game from childhood—die. You are barely able to play the wands."

A chill, different fear crept over him in the handling of these small weapons, not panic-fear—he no longer entered the Game with that—but a cold reckoning that in all these arms was something alien, more personal and more demanding than he had yet calculated. He considered the skill of Niun, and mri reflexes, that quite simply seemed a deadly fraction quicker than human, and suddenly feared that he was not ready for such a contest, and that Niun waited for him to admit it.

"It seems," Duncan said, "that quite a few kel'ein might die in learning these."

"It is an honorable death."

He looked at the mri's naked face and sought some trace of humor there, found none.

"You are a kind," Niun said slowly, "that fights in groups. We are not. The guns, the *zahen'ein*, they are your way. You do not understand ours, I see that. And often, Duncan, often we tried to approach humankind; we thought that there might be honor in you. Perhaps there is. But you would not come alone to fight. Is this never done among humans? Or why is it, Duncan?"

Duncan found no answer, for there was a great sadness in the mri, so profound a sadness and bewilderment when he asked that—as if, had this one thing been understood, then so much else need not have happened.

"I am sorry," Duncan said, and found it pathetically little.

"What will you? Will you play?"

The grief still remained there. Of a sudden Duncan feared edged weapons with such feeling still in the air. He looked down at the small blades he held, cautiously attempted the proper grip on them nonetheless.

Niun's slender fingers reached, carefully adjusted his, then withdrew. The mri edged back to a proper interval.

"One blade at a time, Duncan."

He hesitated.

"That is no good," Niun said. "Throw."

The blade flew. Niun caught it. Gently it returned.

Duncan missed. It hit his chest and fell to his lap. He rubbed the sore spot over his heart and thought that it must be bleeding despite the robes.

He threw. Niun returned it. Awkwardly he caught the hilt, threw again; it came back, forth, back, forth, back—and his mind knew it for a weapon suddenly, and he froze, and a second time it caught him in the ribs. He gathered it from his lap and his hand was shaking. He cast.

Niun intercepted it, closed his hand on it and did not return it.

"I will keep playing," Duncan said.

"Later." Niun held up his hand for the other. Duncan returned it, and the mri slipped both back into his belt.

"I am not that badly hurt."

The mri's amber eyes regarded him soberly, reading him from shaking hands to his unveiled face. "Now you have realized that you will be hurt. So do we all, kel Duncan. Think on it a time. Your heart is good. Your desire is good. Your self-knowledge is at fault. We will play again, sometimes with wands, sometimes with the blades. I will show you all that I know. But it is not all to be learned today. Let me see the injuries. I judged my throws carefully, but I could make a mistake."

Duncan frowned, opened the robe, found two minute punctures, one over his heart, one over his ribs, neither bruised, neither deep. "I suppose that I am the one more likely to make a mistake," he admitted. Niun regarded him soberly.

"True. You do not know how to hold your strength. I still must hold mine with you when we play at wands."

He regarded the mri with resentment.

"Not much," Niun conceded. "But I know your limit, and you do not know mine."

Duncan's jaw knotted. "What is the hal'ari for *arrogant?*"

Niun smiled. *"Ka'ani-nla.* But I am not, kel Duncan. If I were arrogant, you would have more than two small cuts: to use an opponent badly, that is arrogant. To press the Game beyond your own limits: that is stupidity. And you are not a stupid man, kel Duncan."

It was several moments before Duncan even attempted to answer. The dusei shifted weight restlessly.

"If I can make you angry," Niun said when he opened his mouth to speak, "I have passed your guard again. If I can make you angry, I have given you something to think about besides the Game. So my masters would say to me—often, because I myself was prone to that fault. The scars I have gained of it are more than two."

Duncan considered the mri, found it strange that after so long a time he learned something of Niun as a person, and not as mri. He considered the amusement that lurked just behind the amber eyes, and reckoned that he was intended to share that humor, that Niun instead of bristling had simply hurled back the throw that he had cast, as a man would with a man not his enemy.

"Tomorrow," Duncan said, "I will try the *as-ei* again."

Niun's face went sober, but there was pleasure in his gesture of assent. "Good." He absently extended a hand to fend off the dus that intruded on them: the beasts could not seem to resist intervening in any quiet conversation, wanting to touch, to be as close as possible.

But the dus, the lesser one, snarled an objection and Niun snatched his hand back quickly. The beast pushed roughly past him, and settled between them. An instant later it moved again, heaved its bulk nearer and nearer Duncan.

"It does that sometimes," Duncan said, alarmed by its behavior. There was a brush at his senses, affecting his heartbeat. The massive head thrust at his knee, and with a sigh the beast worked its way heavily against him, warm, beginning the pleasure sound. He lost himself in it a moment, then shuddered, and it stopped. He focused clearly, saw Niun sitting with his arm about the shoulder of the other, the larger dus.

"That is a shameless dus," Niun said. "that prefers tsi'mri."

He was, Duncan thought, vexed that the dus had snarled at him. Duncan endured the touch a moment more, knowing the attachment of the mri to the beasts, fearing to offend either by his complaint; but the touch at his senses was too much. A sudden shiver took him. "Get it away from me," he said suddenly; he feared to move, not knowing what afflicted the beast.

Niun frowned, carefully separated himself from the larger dus, put out his hand to touch that which lay against

Duncan. It made a strange, plaintive sound, heaved the more closely against Duncan, hard-breathing. Niun, veilless already, took off the *zaidhe* that covered his mane—unwonted familiarity—leaned forward and shook hard at the animal. Duncan felt the strain of dus-feelings, of alienness. He tried to touch the beast himself with his hand, but it suddenly heaved away from him and shied off across the room, shaking its massive head and blowing puffs of air in irritation as it retreated.

"Tsi'mri," Niun judged, remaining kneeling where he was. "The dus feels something it cannot understand. It will not have me; it cannot have you. That is going to be a problem, Duncan. It is possible you cannot accept what it offers. But it can be dangerous if you will not accept it eventually. I cannot handle this one. There is a madness that comes on them if they cannot have what they want. They choose. We do not."

"I cannot touch that thing."

"You will have to."

"No."

Niun expelled a short breath, and rose and walked away, to stand staring at the starscreen, the dusty field that was all that changed in kel-hall. It was all there was to look at but a confused beast and a recalcitrant human. Duncan felt the accusation in that frozen black figure, total disappointment in him.

"Niun."

The mri turned, bare-faced, bare-headed, looked down on him.

"Do not call me tsi'mri," Duncan said.

"Do you say so?" Niun stiffened his back. "When the hal'ari comes easily from your mouth, when you play at the Game with weapons, when you can lie down to sleep and not fear the dusei, then I shall no longer call you tsi'mri. The beast will die, Duncan. And the other will be alone, if the madness does not infect it, too."

Duncan looked at it, where it crouched in the corner. To have peace with Niun, he rose and nerved himself to approach it. Perversely, it would have none of him, but shied off and snarled. The dark eyes glittered at him, desiring what it could not find.

"Careful."

Niun was behind him. Duncan gave back gratefully, felt

the mri's hand on his shoulder. The dus remained in its corner, and it did not seem the time to attempt anything with it.

"I will try," Duncan said.

"Slowly. Let it alone for now. Let be. There is no pressing
them."

"I do not understand why it comes at me. I have tried to
discourage it. Surely it understands I do not want it."

Niun shrugged. "I have felt its disturbance. I cannot answer
you. No one knows why a dus chooses. I could not hold them
both, that is all. It has no one else. And perhaps it feels in
you the nature of a kel'en."

Duncan glanced at the dus, that had ceased to radiate hostility, and again at Niun, wondering whether he understood
that in what the mri had said was an admission that he had
won something.

That night, as they were settling to sleep on their pallets,
Niun put away his weapons in the roll of cloth that contained
all his personal possessions, and there, along with a curious
knot of cord, was the ill-made figure of a dus, as if it were
valued.

It pleased Duncan. He looked into the shadows at the living model that lay some distance from him, eyes glittering in
the light of the starscreen, head between its paws, looking
wistfully at him.

He whistled at it softly, an appeal ancient and human.

A soft puff of air distended the beast's nostrils. The small
eyes wrinkled in what looked like anguished consideration.

But it stayed at a distance.

Chapter Thirteen

NO LONGER gold-robed, but white, Melein. She had made herself new robes, had made herself a home from the compartment nearest controls, plain and pleasant—one chair, hers, and mats for sitting, and upon the walls she had begun to write, great serpentines of gold and black and blue that filled the room she had taken for her own hall, that spread down the corridor outside in lively and strange contrast to the barren walls elsewhere. From her haven she had begun to take the ship, to make it home.

Out of her own mind she had resurrected the appearance of the lost edun, the House of the People. She had recalled the writings; and of her own skill and by her own labor she had done these things, this difficult and holy work.

Niun was awed when he saw it, each time that he came to attend her, and found her work advancing through the ship. He had not believed that she could have attained such knowledge. She was, before she was she'pan, youngest daughter of the House: Melein Zain-Abrin, Chosen of the she'pan Intel.

He had utterly lost the Melein he had known, his true sister, his comrade once of the Kel. The process had been a gradual one, advancing like the writings, act by act. He put from his mind the fact that they had been children of the Kath together, that they had played at being kel'ein in the high hills of Kesrith. Hers became the age and reverence of all she'panei. Her skills made her a stranger to him. Being merely kel'en, he could not read what she wrote, could not pierce the mysteries in which she suddenly spoke, and he knew to his confusion how vast the gulf was that had opened

147

between them in the six years since they had both been of the Kel. The blue *seta'al* were cut and stained into her face as well as his, the proud marks of a warrior; but the hands were forbidden weapons now, and her bearing was the quiet reserve of the Sen. She did not go veiled. A Mother of an edun almost never veiled, her face always accessible to her children. Only in the presence of the profaning and the unacknowledgeable did she turn her face aside. She was alone: the gold-robed Sen should have been her servants; experienced warriors of the Kel should have been her Husbands; the eldest of the Kath should have brought bright-eyed children for her delight. He felt the inadequacy of everything he could do for her, at times with painful force.

"Niun." She smiled and touched his offered hand. He knelt by her chair—knelt, for the Kel did not use the luxury of furniture, no more than the ascetic Sen. His dus was near him, warm and solid. The little one, visitor, crowded near the she'pan's feet, adoring, dus-wise. A Sen-caste mind was said to be too complex, too cold for the dusei's taste. Niun did not know if this were true: it was strange that even when Melein had been of the Kel, no dus had ever sought her, a source of grief to her, and bitter envy of other kel'ein. Now she had none, would have none. The dus adored, but it did not come close with its mind—preferring even a human to Melein s' Intel, to the calculating power of a she'pan.

He bowed his head beneath her touch, looked up again. "I have brought Duncan," he said. "I have told him how to bear himself; I have warned him."

Melein inclined her head. "If you judge it time," she said, stroking the back of the dus that sat by her. "Bring him."

Niun looked up at her, to make one final appeal to her patience—to speak to her that he had known as a child; but he could not find that closeness with her. The disturbance passed to the dusei. His shook its head. He rose, pushed at the beast to make it move.

Duncan waited. Niun found him standing where he had left him, against the door on the other side of the corridor. "Come," he told the human, "and do not veil. You are not in a strange hall."

Duncan refastened the *mez* just beneath his chin, and came inside with him, hesitated in the middle of the room until Melein herself held out her hand in invitation, and showed him where he should sit, at her left hand, where the lesser dus rested.

Duncan went, fearing the dus, mortally afraid of that beast. Niun opened his mouth to protest, but he thought that he would shame Duncan if he did so, and make question of his fitness to be here. Carefully Duncan settled where he was asked; and Niun sat down in his own place at Melein's right, within arm's reach of Duncan and the other animal. He touched the smaller dus with his fingertips, felt it settled and was relieved at what he felt.

"Duncan," Melein said softly. "Kel Duncan. Niun avows you are able to understand the hal'ari."

"I miss words, she'pan, but I understand."

"But then, you did understand somewhat of the mu'ara before you came into our company."

"Yes. A few words."

"You must have worked very hard," she said. "Do you know how long you have been aboard?"

"No. I do not count the time anymore."

"Are you content, Duncan?"

"Yes," he said, which Niun heard and he held his breath, for he did not believe it. Duncan lied: it was a human thing to do.

It was wrong thing to have done.

"You know," said Melein, "that we are going home."

"Niun has told me."

"Did your people surmise that?"

Duncan did not answer. The question disturbed him greatly: Niun felt it through the dusei, a shock of fear.

"Our outward journey," Melein continued softly, "was long ago, before such ships as this were available to us, no such swift passage, no; and we delayed along the way that brought us to you, sometimes a thousand years or two. Usually there is time that the People in truth do forget, that in the Dark between suns there are generations born that are not taught the Pana, the Forbidden, the Holy, the Mysteries—and they step out onto a new earth, ignorant of all they are not told. But this time, this time, kel Duncan, we carry our living past with us, in your person; and though this is against every law, every wisdom of she'panei before me, so is this voyage different from other voyages and this Dark from other Darks. I have permitted you to remain with us. Did your people surmise, Duncan, that we are going home?"

There was a forbidden game the children of the Kath
would play, the truth-game: touch the dus and try to lie.
When the Mothers knew it, they forbade it, though the great
beasts were tolerant of the children, and the children's innocent minds could not disturb the animals.

Find where I have hidden the stone.

Is it near? Is it far?

Touch the dus and try to lie.

But not among brothers, not within the Kel or the Sen.
"Melein," Niun protested. "He fears the beast."

"He fears," she echoed harshly. "Tell me, Duncan, what
they supposed of the record they put within this ship."

"That it might be—that it might be the location of mri
bases."

The feeling in the air was like that before a storm, thick
and close and unreal. The great dus shivered, lifted its head.
"Be still," Niun whispered in its blunt ear, tugging at it to
distract the beast.

"Ah," said Melein. "And humans have surely duplicated
this record. They will have taken this gift that was in the
pan'en, that rested within their hands. And to make us trust
it, they gave us you."

The dus cried out suddenly, moved, both of them. It hurled
Duncan aside, away—he rolled to the wall, sprawled at the
impact and both dusei were on their feet, their panic tangible.
"Yai!" Niun cried at his own, clapped his hands, struck it. It
reacted, threw its weight against its lesser companion, and
kept the confused dus at bay, constantly shifting to remain
between it and him; and Niun flung himself to Duncan's side,
forcing his dus to shield them both.

The panic crested, subsided. Duncan was on his knees,
holding his arm against his body, shuddering convulsively;
his face was white and beaded with sweat. Niun touched him,
dragged the arm outward and pushed up the sleeve, exposing
the ugly, swelling wound.

Dus-poison.

"You will not die of it," Niun told him, holding him, trying to ease the sickly shuddering that wracked the human. He
was not sure that Duncan could understand him. Melein
came, bent down, touched the wounded arm; but there was
no pity in her, only cold curiosity.

The dusei crept back. The little one, abused, hung back
and radiated distress, blood-feelings. The greater one nosed at

Duncan, snorted and drew back, and the human flinched and cried aloud.

"You have hurt them both," Niun said to Melein, thinking that she would feel remorse for one or the other, the dus or the man.

"He is still tsi'mri," she said. "And Niun, he has lied to us from the beginning; I have known it; you have seen it."

"You do not know what you have done," said Niun. "He feared the dusei, feared this one most especially. How could you expect to get truth from him? The dus is hurt, Melein; I do not know how far."

"You forget yourself."

"She'pan," he said, bowed his head, but it did not appease her. He took Duncan's good arm and helped him to stand, and flung his arm about him, holding him on his feet. The human was in utter, deep shock. When Niun began to move, the dus came, and slowly, slowly they left the presence of the she'pan.

Sometimes the human fought his way out of the fever, became for a moment lucid; at such times he seemed to know where he was, and his eyes wandered his surroundings, where he lay against the dus, in the corner of the kel-hall. But it did not last. He could not hold, and retreated again into his delirium. Niun did not speak to him, did not brighten the lights too much; it was best to keep both man and dus as free of sensation as possible.

Finally, when by night-cycle there was no improvement, Niun went to Duncan, and, as a kath'en might undress a child, took from him his *mez* and *zaidhe*, and his robes too, so that he might take warmth from the dus. He bedded him between his own dus and the afflicted one, and covered him with a doubled blanket.

The poison was strong in him; and a bond had been forced between two creatures that had not been able to bear each other. The wound was a deep puncture, and Duncan had taken more venom from the hollow dewclaw than was good even for a mri who was accustomed to it. But the old ways said (and being kel'en, Niun did not know whether this was truth or fable) that a dus knew its man by this thereafter, that once the substance had gone into a man and he had lived, then he would nevermore be in danger from the venom or the anger of that particular dus, which would never part from him in life. This was not entirely so, for a man who handled dusei frequently received small scratches from the dewclaw; and occasionally deeper ones, which might make him fevered. But it was also true that a man not accustomed to a particular dus might react very stongly, even fatally, to a bad wound from it.

Melein had known better than what she had done: kel-trained and sen-trained, she knew dusei, and she knew that she was provoking the beast dangerously, worrying at Duncan, drawing panic from him. But like the other she'pan that he had served, Melein had coldness for a heart.

And Duncan, his naked skin exposed to the heat and the secretions of the dus' hot hide, its venom flowing in his veins, would adapt to the dus and the dus to him—if he did not die; or if the beast did not go *miuk*, into that madness that sometimes came on stressed dusei, that turned them killer. That was what Melein had risked, and knew it.

If the beast went, Niun did not know now whether he could prevent the human from going with it. He had heard of it happening: a mri dragged into insanity by a *miuk'ko* dus; he had not, he thanked the gods, seen it.

The warning siren sounded.

Niun looked frantically at the starscreen, and cursed in anguish. It was the worst of all possible times that they should prepare to transit.

The bell sounded. The dusei roused, terrified, and Duncan for his part simply flung his arms about his beast's neck and bowed his head and held on, lost, lost in the dus-fears and the mind of the beast.

Perhaps it protected him. They jumped, emerged, jumped again within half a night. The man and the dus clung together, and radiated such fear that the other dus could not stay by them.

It was said of the dusei that they had no memory for events, only for persons. And perhaps it was that which drew the human in, and provided a haven from which he would not emerge.

"Duncan," Niun said the next morning, and without pleading with him, held a cup to his lips and gave him water, for he was not a dus, to go without. He bathed the human's face with his fingertips.

"Give me my robe," Duncan said then softly, startling him,

and he was glad, and drew the human away from the afflicted dus, helping him to stand. Duncan was very weak, the
arm hot and swollen still; he had to be helped into his clothing, and when he was given the headcloth and veil, he veiled
himself as if he earnestly wished its privacy.

"I will speak to the she'pan," Niun offered earnestly.
"Duncan, I will speak to her."

The human drew a great breath, let it go with a shudder,
and pushed away the dus that nosed at his leg. It nearly
threw him with its great strength. He caught himself with
Niun's offered hand, then pushed help aside a second time,
stubborn in his isolation.

"But you are wrong," Duncan said, "and she was right."
And when he had drawn another breath: "There are ships on
our trail. My people. Warships. I lied, Niun. It was no gift.
They have the same series of directions we do, and they will
come on our heels. What they will do then, I do not know. I
am not in their confidence. They put me aboard for the reason the she'pan guessed: to make you trust the gift, to learn
things the tapes cannot tell, to get me and the information
back if I could. I tore the ship out of their hands and ran.
Tell her that. It is all that I know. And you can do what you
like about it."

And he walked off, to the far side of the room, and curled
up in the corner. The dus padded over, head hanging, and
wearily flung its bulk down against him. Duncan put his arms
about its neck and laid his head against it, and rested. His
eyes were blank and weary, and held such a look of despair
as Niun had never seen on any face.

"Bring him," Melein told him when he had reported the
things Duncan had admitted.

"She'pan," he protested, "he has helped the People."

"Be silent," she answered. "Remember that you are kel'en,
and kel'anth; and that you owe me some loyalty."

Right was on her side, the rightness of the mri, the
rightness of their survival. He felt the impact of it, and
bowed his head against her head and acknowledged it—and
sat by in misery that evening while she began to question
Duncan, and to draw forth from him all that he could tell.

It was in the guise of a common-meal, the first that they
had held on the ship, a sad mockery. It lacked all fellowship,
and the food was bitter in the mouth. Duncan hardly ate at

all, but sat silent when he was not being directly questioned; the dusei were banished, and he had nothing, no one, not even—Niun thought wretchedly—his own companionship, for he must sit at the she'pan's right, taking her part.

There was a temptation to them all to over-indulge in the drink, the biting regul brew that filled the stores, *ashig*, fermented of the same source as soi. But at least, Niun thanked the gods, there was no *komal*, that had kept his last she'pan in thrall to drug-spawned dreams, illicit and shameful—dreams in which she had laid the plans that had launched them forth; dreams that were as guilty as ever Duncan was in ruining the People, in creating the danger they now knew followed them.

He saw again the arrogance of the she'pan who had no mercy for her own children.

But such a thing as that he dared not say to Melein, could not quarrel with her, whom he loved more than life and honor, over a tsi'mri who had tangled them in so much of evil. It was only when he looked at Duncan's face that it hurt, and the human's pain gnawed at him.

Each evening for four days they ate common-meal, and talked little, for most questions had been answered. There was during that time a chill in the she'pan's presence, and afterward a chill in kel-hall—weapons-practice cold and formal and careful, concerned more with rituals than with striking blows, with the traditions of combat rather than the actuality of it. At times there was such sickness in Duncan's eyes that Niun forbade him the *yin'ein*, and refused to practice with him at all.

Duncan had betrayed his own.

And there was no peace for such a man.

"Tsi'mri," Melein said of him in Duncan's absence, "and a traitor even to them, who shaped him blood and bone. How then should the People ever rely on him? This is a weak creature, Niun. You have proved that."

Niun considered him, and knew his own handiwork, and grieved for it.

The venom-fever left, but the misery did not: the dus, rejected by turns and grudgingly accepted, mourned and fretted; the man grew silent and inward, a sickness that could not be reached.

The ship departed that star, and jumped again and again.

Chapter Fourteen

THEY PASSED close, this time, to the worlds of the system, dangerously close. For many days their course had been taking them for the yellow star and its worlds, until now the largest of the inner planets loomed before them, dominating the field of the screen in kel-hall.

Home? Niun wondered at first, and held his hope private in Melein's silence: if she knew, he reckoned, she would have told him. But as days passed a worried look settled on Melein; and often now she looked on the screens with fear in her eyes. It ceased to look as though they were hurtling toward the world—rather that the world filled their sky and was falling down on them, a half-world first, that lent Niun some hope they would hurtle just past it—terrifying, but an escape, all the same: but the disc began to rise in the scanner.

They were caught, going earthward like a mote in a burrower's sandpit: the image came unwelcomely to Niun as he sat by Melein's side and stared at the starscreen she had set in her own hall, to look constantly on the danger. He felt his own helplessness, a kel'en whose knowledge of ships was all theory; all his knowledge told him now was that everything was wrong, and that Melein, who likewise had never set hands to ship's controls, knew little more than he.

Perhaps, he thought, she knew the name of the world into which they were falling: but it was not going to stop them.

And the outrage of it grew in him—that they should die by mischance. For a time he awaited a miracle, from Melein, from some source, certain that the gods could not have directed them so far—only to this.

155

He waited on Melein; and she said nothing.

"You have two kel'ein," he reminded her at last, on the day that there was hardly any darkness left in the starscreen.

Still she said nothing.

"Ask him, Melein."

Her lips made a taut line.

He knew the stubbornness in her: they were of one blood. He set his own face. "Then let us fall into the world," he said, staring elsewhere. "Surely there is nothing that I know to do, and your mind is set."

There was long silence between them. Neither moved.

"It would assure," she said at last, "that one danger did not reach our destination. I have thought of that. But it would not stop the other. And in us is the knowledge of it."

Such a thought shook at his confidence. He felt diminished, who had thought only of their own survival, who have been forward with her. "I spoke out of turn," he said. "Doubtless you have weighed what we ought to do."

"Go ask him," she said.

He sat still for a moment, finding her shifts of mind as unsettling as transit, and his nerves taut-strung at the thought that the matter did indeed come down to Duncan.

Then he gathered himself up, called softly to his dus, and went.

Duncan sat, beneath the screen that held the scanner image, eternally whetting away at the blade of an *av-tlen* that he had made out of scrap metal: it was laser-cut and of a balance that Niun privately judged would never be true, but it kept Duncan's hands busy, and perhaps his mind, whatever darkness hovered in it. The dus lay near him, head between paws, eyes following the sweep of Duncan's hands.

"Duncan," Niun said. The noise of the steel kept its rhythm. "Duncan."

It stopped. Duncan looked up at him with that bleak hardness that had grown there day by day.

"The she'pan is concerned," Niun said, "about our near approach to this world."

Duncan's eyes remained cold. "Well, you do not need me. Or if you do, then you can find some means to work around me, can you not?"

"I respect your quarrel with us." Niun sank down on his heels, opened his hands in a gesture of offering. "But surely you know that there is no quarreling with the world that is drawing us into it. We will die, and you will have no satisfaction in that. As for your cause with us, I do not want to quarrel at all on this small ship, with the dusei in the middle of it. Listen to me, Duncan. I have done everything I know to give you an honorable way to put aside this grievance with us. But if you threaten the she'pan, then I will not be patient. And you are doing that."

Duncan went back to his task, sweeping steel against steel. Niun fought with his temper, knowing the result if he laid hands on the tsi-mri: a dus that was already precariously balanced on the verge of *miuk*, and the ship plummeting toward impact with a world—with some things indeed there was no quarreling. It was likely that the human was no more rational than the dus, affected by the ailing beast. If the dus went over the brink, then so did the mind that held knowledge of the ship.

Melein's handiwork. Niun clenched his arms about his knees and sought something to say that would touch the man.

"We are out of time, Duncan."

"If you cannot deal with this," Duncan said suddenly, "then you certainly could not land safely when you reach your home. I do not think you ever intended to be rid of me. You two seem to need me, and I think the she'pan has always suspected that. That was why she let you have your way. It was only a means of making me less an inconvenience than I would have been, a way of getting past my guard and getting from me what she wanted. I am not angry with you, Niun. You believed her. So did I. She had what she wanted. Only now I am needed again, am I?" The ring of steel continued, measured and hard. "Become like you. Become one of you. I know you tried. You armed me—but you never reckoned on the beast. Now you cannot deal with me so easily. It and I . . . make something new on this ship."

"You are wrong from the beginning," Niun said, cold to the heart at such thoughts in him. "There is an autopilot to bring us in. And the she'pan never lied to you, or to me. She cannot."

Duncan's eyes lifted suddenly to his, cynically amazed, and his hands fell idle. "Rely on that? Maybe regul automation is better than ours, but this is a human ship, and I would not trust my life to that if there were a choice. You could come down anywhere. And would you know how to engage it in the first place? Perhaps the she'pan is simply naïve. You do need me, kel Niun. You tell her that."

It had the sound of truth. Niun had no answer for it, shaken in his own confidence. There were things Melein could not reasonably know, things involving machines not made by the regul and motives of those not born of the People. Yet she proceeded on her Sight; he wished earnestly to believe in that.

"Come," he pleaded with Duncan.

"No," said Duncan, and fell to work again.

Niun rested unmoving, panic stirring in him. The rhythm became louder, steel on steel, metal clenched in taut, white-edged fingers. Duncan would not look up. A body's-length away, the dus stirred, moaned.

Niun thrust himself to his feet and stalked out of kel-hall, through the corridors, until he came again to Melein.

"He says he will not," Niun told her, and remained veiled.

She said nothing, but sat quietly and stared at the screen. Niun settled by her side, swept off *mez* and *zaidhe* and wadded them into a knot in his lap, head bowed.

Melein had no word for him, nothing. She was, he thought, finally reckoning with what she had wrought, and that reckoning was too late.

And by the middle of the night there was no more darkness left in the screen. The world took on frightening detail, brown patched with cloud swirls.

Suddenly a siren began, different from any that had sounded before, and the screens flashed red, a pulse terrifying in its implications.

Niun gathered himself to his knees, cast an anguished look at Melein, whose calm now seemed thinly drawn.

"Go to Duncan," she bade him. "Ask again."

He rose and went, covered his head, but did not trouble this time to veil himself: he went to plead with their enemy, and shame seemed useless in such a gesture.

The lights in kel-hall had dimmed: the screen, pulsing between the red of alarm and the white glare of the world, provided all the light, and Duncan sat, veilless, before it. There sounded still the measured scrape of metal, as if he had never ceased. Beside him lay the mass of the two dusei, that stirred and moved aside as Niun came and knelt before Duncan.

"If you know anything to do at this point," Niun said, "it would be well to do it. I believe we are falling quite rapidly."

Duncan rasped the edge one long stroke, his lips clamped into a taut line. A moment he considered, then laid aside his work and wiped his hands on his knees, looked up at the world that loomed in the pulsing screen. "I can try," he said equably enough, "from controls."

Niun stood up, waited for Duncan, who rose stiffly, then walked in with him through the ship. The dusei started to trail them. Niun forbade them with a sharp word, sealed a section door between, and brought Duncan into that section that belonged to the she'pan.

Melein met them there, in the corridor.

"He will try," said Niun.

She opened controls to them, and came in after, stood gravely by as Duncan settled himself into the cushion at the main panel.

Duncan paid them no further heed. He studied the screens, and touched control after control. A flood of telemetry coursed one stable screen. One after another the screens ceased their flashing and took on images of the world in garish colors.

"You are playing pointless games," said Melein.

Duncan looked half-about, back again. "I am. I have watched this world for some few days. It is puzzling. And it is still possible that the ship's defenses may take over when we reach the absolute limit: there are choices left, but for some reason it is not observing the safety margin, and the world's mass has anchored us, so that jump is impossible. Here." He took the cover off a shielded area of controls and simply pushed a button. Lights ran crazily over the boards. Immediately there was a perceptible alteration in course, the screens shifting rapidly. Duncan calmly replaced the cover. "An old ship, this, and it has run hard. A system failed. It should have reset itself now. It will avoid, then pull us back on course. I think that will solve the problem. But if there is an error in the tape that caused it to happen, why, we are dead."

He offered that with a cynical tone, and slowly rose, still looking at the scanners. "That world is dead," he said then. "And that is strange, given other things I read in scanning."

"You are mistaken," said Melein harshly. "Read your instruments again, tsi'mri. That is a world called Nhequuy and the star is Syr, and it is a spacefaring race that lives there and all about these regions, called the etrau."

"Look at the infrared. Look at the surface. No plants. No life. It's a dead world, she'pan, whatever your records tell you. This is a dead system. A spacefaring people would have come to investigate an intrusion this close to their home-world. But none have. Not here, not anywhere we have been, have they? You could not have answered a challenge. You could not have reacted to their ships. You would have needed me for that, and you have not. World after world after world. And nothing. Why do you suppose, she'pan?"

Melein looked on him with shock in her unveiled face, a helpless anger. She did not answer, and Niun felt a chill creeping over his skin in her silence.

"The People are nomads," Duncan said, "mercenaries, hiring out whatever you have been. You have gone from star to star, seeking out wars, fighting for hire. And you have forgotten. You close each chamber after you, and forbid the Kel to remember. But what became of all your former employers, she'pan? Why is there no life where you have passed?"

Niun looked at the screens, at the deadness they displayed, at instruments he could not read—and looked to Melein, to hear her deny these things.

"Leave," she said. "Niun, take him back to kel-hall."

Duncan thrust back from the panel, swept a glance from her to Niun, and in the instant Niun hesitated, turned on his heel and walked out, striding rapidly down the corridor in the direction of kel-hall.

Niun stared at Melein. Her skin was pale, her eyes dilated: never had she looked so afraid, not even with regul and humans closing on them.

"She'pan?" he asked, still hoping.

"I do not know," she said. And she wept, for it was an admission a she'pan could not make. She sank down on the edge of a cushion and would not look at him.

He stayed, ventured finally to take her by the arms and draw her out of that place, back to her own hall, where the chatter of the machines could not accuse her. He settled her in her chair and knelt beside her, smoothed her golden mane as he had done when they were both only kath'dai'ein, and with his own black veil he dried her tears and saw her face restored to calm.

He knew that she was lost, that the machines were beyond her capacity; she knew that he knew; but he knelt at her knees and took her hands, and looked up at her clear-eyed, offering with all his heart.

"Rest," he urged her. "Rest. Even your mercies were well-guided. Is it not so that even the she'panei do not always know the Sight when it moves them? So I have heard, at least. You kept Duncan, and that was right to do. And be patient with him, for my sake be patient. I will deal with him."

"He sees what is plain to be seen. Niun, I do not know what we have done."

He thought of the dead worlds, and pushed the thought away. "We have done nothing. *We* have done nothing."

"We are heirs of the People."

"We do not know that his reckoning is right."

"Niun, Niun, he knows. Can you be so slow to understand what we have seen along the track of the People? Can there be so many worlds that have failed of themselves after we have passed?"

"I do not know," he said desperately. "I am only kel'en, Melein."

She touched his face, and he felt the comfort that she meant, apology for her words, and they did not speak for a time. Long ago—it seemed long ago, and impossibly far—he had sat by another she'pan, Intel of Edun Kesrithun, and leaned his head against the arm of her chair, and she had been content in her drugged dreams to touch, to know that he was there. So he did now, with Melein. Her hand restlessly stroked his mane, while she thought; and he sat still, unable to share, unable to imagine where her thoughts ran, save that they went into darkness, and into things of the Pana.

He heard her breath shudder at last between her teeth, and forebore to breathe, himself, fearful of her mood.

"Intel," she said at last, "still has her hand on us. The she'pan's kel'en: she held you by her until I wonder you did not go mad; and passed you to me—to see that her chosen successor succeeded not only to Edun Kesrithun, but to rule all the People. That Intel's choice survive. She would have waded to her aim through the blood of any that opposed her. She was *the* she'pan. Old—but age did not sanctify her, did not cleanse her of ambition or make her complacent. O gods, Niun, she was hard."

He could not answer. He remembered the scarred and

gentle-eyed Mother of Kesrith, whose hands were tender and whose mind was most times fogged with drugs; but he knew that other Intel too. His stomach tightened as he recalled old angers, old resentments—Intel's possessive, adamantine stubbornness. She was dead. It was not right to cherish resentments against the dead.

"She would have taken ship," Melein said in a hollow voice, "and gods know what she would have done in leaving Kesrith. We no longer served regul; we were freed of our oath. She sent me to safety; I think she tried to follow. I will never know. I will never know so many things she had no time to teach me. She talked of return, of striking against the enemies of the People—ravings under the *komal*-dreams, when I would sit by her alone. The enemy. The enemy. She would have destroyed them, and then she would have taken us home. That was her great and improbable dream, that the Dark would be the last Dark, to take us home, for we were few already; and she was, perhaps, mad."

Niun could not bear to look at her, for it was true, and it was painful to them both.

"What shall we do?" he asked. "May the Kel ask permission to ask? What shall we do for ourselves?"

"I have no power to stop this ship. Would that I did. Duncan says that he cannot. I think that it is true. And he—"

There was long silence. Niun did not invade it, knowing it could bring no good; and at last Melein sighed.

"Duncan," she said heavily.

"I will keep him from your sight."

"You have given him the means to harm us."

"I will deal with him, she'pan."

She shook her head again, and wiped her eyes with her fingers.

The dusei came: Niun was aware of them before they appeared, looked and saw his own great beast, and welcomed it. It drew close in the wistful, abstracted manner of dusei, and sank down at Melein's feet, offering its mindless solace.

Afterward, when Melein breathed easier, Niun felt another presence. Astonished, he saw the lesser dus standing in the doorway. It also came, and lay down by its fellow.

Melein touched it; it offered no hostility to the hand that had caused its hurt. But somewhere else in the ship there would be pain for that touching. Niun thought on Duncan, of his bitter isolation, and wondered that his dus could have been drawn here, by her whom Duncan hated.

Unless he had brutally driven it away—or unless his thoughts had turned the dus in this direction.

"Go see to Duncan," Melein said finally.

Niun received back his veil from her hands and flung it over his shoulder, not bothering to wear it. He rose, and when his own dus would have followed him he bade it stay, for he wanted it by Melein, for her comfort.

And he found Duncan, as he had thought he would, back in kel-hall.

Duncan sat still in the artificial dawning, hands loose in his lap. Niun settled on his knees before him, and still Duncan did not look up. The human had veiled himself; Niun did not, offering his feelings openly to him.

"You have hurt us," Niun said. "Kel Duncan, is it not enough?"

Duncan lifted his face and stared toward the screen, where the world that had been called Nhequuy was no longer in view.

"Duncan. What else will you have of us?"

Duncan's dus was with Melein, touched and touching; he was betrayed. When his eyes shifted toward Niun there was no defense there, nothing but pain.

"I argued," said Duncan, "with my superiors, for your sake. I fought for you. And for what? Did she have an answer? She knew the world's name. What happened to it?"

"We do not know."

"And to the other worlds?"

"We do not know, Duncan."

"Killers," he said, his eyes fixed elsewhere. "Killers by nature."

Niun clenched his hands, that had gone chill. "*You* are with us, kel Duncan."

"I have often wondered why." His dark eyes returned to Niun's. Of a sudden he pulled the veil away, swept off the tasseled headcloth, making evident his humanity. "Except that I am necessary."

"Yes. But I did not know that. We did not know it before."

It touched home, he thought; there was a small reaction of the eyes.

And then Duncan turned, a wild, distracted look on his face as he looked to the door.

Dus-feelings. Niun received them too, even before he heard the click of claws on tiling. Senses blurred. It was hard to remember what bitterness they had been about.

"*No!*" Duncan shouted as it came in. The beast shied and lifted a paw in threat, then dropped it and edged forward, head slightly averted. By degrees it came closer, settled, edged the final distance to Duncan's side. Duncan touched it, slid his arm about its neck. At the door appeared the other beast, that came quietly to Niun, lay down at his back. Niun soothed it with gentle touches, his heart pounding from the misery that radiated from the other—schism between man and dus: the very air ached with it.

"You are hurting it," Niun said. "Give way to it. Give it only a little."

"It and I have an accommodation. I do not push it and it does not push me. Only sometimes it comes too fast. It forgets where the line is."

"Dusei have no memories. There is only *now* with them."

"Fortunate animals," Duncan said hoarsely.

"Give way to it. You lose nothing."

Duncan shook his head. "I am not mri. And I cannot forget."

There was weariness in his voice; it trembled. For a moment there was again the man who had been long absent from them. Niun reached out, pressed his arm in a gesture he would have offered a brother of the Kel. "Duncan, I have tried to help you. All that I could do, I have tried."

Duncan closed his eyes, opened them again; his fingers at the dus' neck lifted in a gesture of surrender. "I think that, at least, is the truth."

"We do not lie," he said. "There are the dusei. We cannot."

"I can understand that." Duncan pressed his lips together, a white line, relaxed again, his hand still caressing the dus.

"I would not play at *shon'ai* with a man in your mood," Niun said, baiting him, searching after hidden things. They had not, in fact, played in some time.

The dus began slowly to give forth its pleasure sound, relaxed to Duncan's fingers as Duncan eased his arm about its fat-rolled neck; it sighed, oblivious to past grief, delighting in present love.

The human pressed his brow to that thick skull, then turned his face to look at Niun. His eyes bore a bruised look, like one long without rest. "It has no happier a life than mine," Duncan said. "I cannot let it have what it wants, and it cannot make me over into a mri."

Niun drew a deep breath, tried to keep images from his mind. "I might destroy it," he said, hushed and quickly. The human, in contact with the beast, flinched, soothed the dus with his hands. Niun understood; he felt soiled even in offering—but sometimes it was necessary, when a dus, losing its kel'en, could not be controlled. This one had never gained the kel'en it wished.

"No," Duncan said at last. "No."

He pushed the animal away, and it rose and ambled over to the corner. There was peace in the feeling of the beasts. It was better than it had been.

"I would be pleased," said Niun, "if you would send to the she'pan your apology."

Duncan sat quietly for a moment, arms on knees. At last he nodded, changed the gesture for a mri one. "When she needs me," he said, "I will come. Tell her so."

"I will tell her."

"Tell her I am sorry."

"I will tell her that too."

Duncan looked at him for a moment, and then gathered himself up and stood looking at the dus. He gave a low whistle to it; it whuffed in interest and heaved itself up and came, followed to the corner where the pallets were.

And for a long time the human sat and worked over the dus, grooming it and soothing it, even talking to it, which seemed to please the beast. The dus settled, slept. In time, the man did.

Three days later the siren sounded, and they left Nhequuy and its sun. The next world was also without life.

Chapter Fifteen

———◦◦◦———

DUNCAN TURNED from the screen that showed the stars and found his dus behind him—always, always the beast was with him, shadow, herald, partaker of every privacy of his life. He found no need to touch it. It sighed and settled against his back. He felt it content.

It was strange, when a pain ceased, that it could be gone some considerable time before it was missed.

And that when that pain was gone, it could not be accurately remembered.

Duncan had known in this place, in kel-hall, upon a certain instant, that he was no longer in pain: he had realized it, sitting here upon the floor; and he could remember the moment, the details, the place that the dus had been lying, the fact that Niun had been sitting exactly so, across the room—sewing, that day: odd occupation for a mri warrior, but Duncan had learned well enough that a man tended all his own necessities in the Kel—save food, that was taken in common.

Niun's face had been intent, the needle pursuing a steady rhythm. He had worked with skill, as Niun's slender hands knew so many skills. It would take years to learn the half of what Niun's native reflexes and the teaching of his masters had done for him.

Not an arrogant man, Niun: prideful, perhaps, but he never vaunted his abilities . . . save now and again when they practiced a passage of arms with the *yin'ein* that Duncan had made to match the beautiful old weapons that were Niun's. Then Niun was sometimes moved, perhaps from the sheer ennui of practicing with a man with whom he could not extend himself—to make a move so fast the eye could not follow it, so tiny and deft and subtle that Duncan hardly knew what had happened to him. Niun did such things, Duncan had noticed also, when he himself had almost settled into smugness in his practice with Niun. The mri subtly informed his student that he was still restraining himself.

Restraint.

It governed the kel'en's whole being.

And Niun's restraint made peace where there was none: extended to a human who provoked him, to dusei that at times grew restive and destructive in their confinement—extended even to Melein.

There was none of them, Duncan reflected with sudden grim humor, that wanted to disturb Niun, neither human, nor dusei, nor child-queen who relied on him.

It was Niun's peace that was on them.

The most efficient killers in all creation, Stavros had said of the mri.

He spoke of the Kel, of Niun's kind.

He had spoken before humankind even suspected the waste of stars that now surrounded them.

The record would be traced out, human ships tracking them to dead world after dead world; and there was no other conclusion that could occur to the Haveners manning those ships, but that they were tracing something monstrous to its source.

Duncan absently caressed the shoulder of his dus, thinking, as the same fearful thoughts had circled through his brain endlessly in the passing days—staring helplessly at Niun, whose imagination surely was sufficient to know what pursued them.

Yet there was no mention of this from Niun; and Melein, having asked her questions, asked nothing more; Niun went to her, but Duncan was not permitted, continuing in her disfavor.

The mri chose to ignore what pursued, to ask no further, to do nothing. Niun lived with him, slept beside him at night in apparent trust—and cultivated only the ancient skills of his kind, the weapons of ritual and duel, as if they could avail him at the end.

The *yin'ein,* ancient blades, against warships, against the likes of *Saber.*

Niun chose, advisedly.

An image came: night, and fire, and mri obstinacy. Duncan pushed it aside, and it came back again, recollection of mri stubbornness that would not surrender, that would not compromise, whose concept of *modern* was lapped in Darks and Betweens and the ways of tsi'mri who were only a moment in the experience of the People.

Modern weapons.

Duncan felt the taint of the word, the scorn implicit in the hal'ari, and hated the human in him that had been too blind to see.

The last battle of the People.

To meet it with modern weapons—if it came to that—that the People should come to a hopeless fight. . . .

Niun would not, then, plan to survive: the last mri would choose the things that made sense to his own logic, which was precisely what he was doing.

To seek his home.

To recover his ancient ways.

To be mri until the holocaust ended it.

It was all Niun could do, if he chose to think about it, save yield to tsi'mri. Duncan reckoned the depth of the mri's patience, that had borne with an outsider under such conditions—even Melein's, who endured Niun's tolerance of a tsi'mri, even that was considerable.

And Niun only practiced at duel with him, patiently, gently practiced, as if he could forget the nature of him.

The *yin'ein*. They were for Niun the only reasonable choice.

Duncan rested his arm on his knee and gnawed at his lip, felt the disturbance of the dus at his back and reached to settle it—guilty in his humanity, that troubled Niun. And yet the thought worried at him and would not let him go—that, human that he was, he could not do as Niun did.

That there were for him alternatives that Niun did not possess.

Perhaps, at the end, the mri would let him go.

Or expect him to lift arms against humankind. He tried to imagine it; and all that he could imagine in his hand was the service pistol that rested among his belongings—to deal large-scale death for his death: the inclination came on him. He could fight, cornered; he would wish to take a dozen of the lives, human or not, that would take his. But to take up the *yin'ein* . . . he was not mri enough.

There were means of fighting the mri would not use.

Human choices.

Slowly, slowly, shattered bits of what had been a SurTac began to sort themselves into order again.

"Niun," he said.

The mri was shaping a bit of metal into a thing that looked like an ornament. For several days he had been working at it, painstaking in his attention.

"*A?*" Niun answered.

"I have been thinking: we suffered one failure in instruments. If the she'pan would permit it, I would like to go back to controls, to test the instruments."

Niun stopped. A frown was on his face when he looked up. "I will ask the she'pan," he said.

"I would like," Duncan said, "to give her the benefit of what skills I do have."

"She will send if there is need."

"Niun, *ask her.*"

The frown deepened. The mri rested hands on his knees, his metalwork forgotten, then expelled a deep breath and gathered up his work again.

"I want peace with her," Duncan said. "Niun, I have done all that you have asked of me. I have tried to be one of you."

"Other things you have done," said Niun. "That is the problem."

"I am sorry for those things. I want them forgotten. Ask her to see me again, and I give you my word I will not offend against her. There is no peace on this ship without peace with her—and none with you."

For a moment Niun said nothing. Then he gave a long sigh. "She has waited for you to ask."

The mri still had power to surprise him. Duncan sat back in confusion, all his reckonings of them in disorder. "She will see me, then."

"Whenever you would decide to ask. Go and speak to her. The doors are not locked."

Duncan rested yet a moment, all impetus taken from him; and then he gathered himself to his feet and started for the door, the dus behind him.

"Duncan."

He turned.

"My brother of the Kel," said Niun softly, "in all regard

for you—remember that I am the she'pan's hand, and that should you err with her—I must not tolerate it."

There was, for the moment, a ward-impulse in the room: the dus backed and its ears lay down. "No," said Duncan. It stopped. And he drew the *av-tlen* from his belt, and would have laid aside all his weapons. "Hold these if you suspect any such thing of me." It was demeaning to surrender weapons; Duncan offered, knowing this, and the mri flinched visibly.

"No," Niun said.

Duncan slid the blade back into place, and left, the dus walking behind him. Niun did not follow: the sting of that last exchange perhaps forbade, and his suspicion would worry at him the while—Duncan reckoned it, that although Niun slept by him, though he let down his guard to him in weapons-practice, to teach him, Melein's safety was another matter: the kel'en was deeply, deeply uneasy.

To admit a tsi'mri to the she'pan's presence, armed: it surely went against the mri's instincts.

But the doors had been unlocked.

The doors had always been unlocked, Duncan supposed suddenly; he had never thought to try them. Melein herself had slept with unlocked doors, trusting him; and that shocked him deeply, that the mri could be in that regard so careless with him.

And not careless.

Prisons, locked doors, things sealed, depriving a man of weapons—all these things went against mri nature. He had known it from the beginning in dealing with them: no prisoners, no capture—and even in the shrine, the pan'en was only screened off, not locked away.

Even controls, even that had always been accessible to him, any time that he had decided to walk where he had been told not to go; he might have quietly gone forward, sealed the doors, and held the ship—could, at this moment.

He did not.

He went to the door that was Melein's, to that dim hall, painted with symbols, vacant of all but a chair and the mats for sitting. He entered it, his steps loud on the tiles.

"She'pan," he called, and stood and waited: stood, for it was the she'pan who offered or did not offer, to sit. The dus settled heavily next to him, resting on its hindquarters—finally sank down to lay its head on the tiles. A sigh gusted from it.

And suddenly a light step sounded behind him. Duncan turned, faced the ghost-like figure in the shadow, white-robed and silent. He was not veiled. He was not sure whether this was polite or not, and glanced down to show his respect.

"Why are you here?" she asked.

"To beg your pardon," he said.

She answered nothing for a moment, only stared at him as if she waited for something further.

"Niun said," he added, "that you were willing to see me."

Her lips tautened. "You still have a tsi'mri's manners."

Anger came on him; but the statement was the simple truth. He smothered it and averted his eyes a second time to the floor. "She'pan," he said softly, "I beg your pardon."

"I give it," she said. "Come, sit down."

The tone was suddenly gracious; it threw him off his balance, and for an instant he stared at her, who moved and took her chair, expecting him to settle at her feet.

"By your leave," he said, remembering Niun, "I ought to go back. I think Niun wanted to follow me. Let me go and bring him."

A frown creased Melein's smooth brow. "That would reproach him, kel Duncan, if you let him know why. No. Stay. If there is peace in the House, he will know it; and if not, he will know that. And do not call him by his name to me; he is first in the Kel."

"I am sorry," he said, and came and sat at her feet, while the dus came and cast itself down between them. The beast was uneasy. He soothed it with his hand.

"Why," asked Melein, "have you been driven to come to me?"

The question struck him with confusion—rude and abrupt, she was, and able to read him. He shrugged, tried to think of something at the edge of the truth, and could not. "She'pan, I am a resource you have. And I wish that you would make use of what I know—while there is time."

The membrane flashed across her eyes, and the dus lifted its head. She leaned forward and soothed the beast, her fingers gently moving on its velvet fur. "And what do you know, kel Duncan, that so suddenly troubles you?"

"That I can get you home alive." He laid his hand on the dus, fearless to do so, and looked into the she'pan's golden eyes. "*He* has taught me; is not managing ships a part of the skill of a kel'en? If he will learn, I will teach him; and if not—then I will take what care of the ship I can do myself. His skill is with the *yin'ein*, and mine never will approach his—but this I can do, this one thing. My gift to you, she'pan, and worth a great deal to you when you reach your home."

"Do you bargain?"

"No. There is no *if* in it. A gift, that is all."

Her fingers did not cease to stroke the dus' warm hide. Her eyes lifted again to his. "Are you *my* kel'en, kel Duncan?"

Breath failed him an instant. The hal'ari, the kel-law had begun to flow in his mind like blood in his veins: the question stood, yes or no, and there was no going back afterward.

"Yes," he said, and the word almost failed of sound.

Her slim fingers slipped to his, took his broad and human hand. "Will you not turn on us, as you turn on your own kind?"

The dus moved at his shock: he held it, soothed it with both his hands, and looked up after a moment at Melein's clear eyes.

"No," she judged, answering her own question, and how, or of what source he did not know. Her sureness disturbed him.

"I have touched a human," she said, "and I did not, just then."

It chilled. He held to the dus, drawing on its warmth, and stared at her.

"What do you seek to do?" she asked.

"Give me access to controls. Let me maintain the machinery, do what is needful. We went wrong once. We cannot risk it again."

He expected refusal, expected long days, months of argument before he could win that of her.

But controls, he thought, had never been locked. And Melein's amber eyes lowered, by that silent gesture giving permission. She lifted her hand toward the door.

He hesitated, then gathered himself to his feet, made an awkward gesture of courtesy to her, and went.

She followed. He heard her soft footfalls behind the dus. And when he settled at the console in the brightly lit control room, she stood at his shoulder and watched: he could see

her white-robed reflection in the screens that showed the star-
fields.

He began running the checks he desired, dismissing Melein's presence from his concerns. He had feared, since last
he was dismissed from controls, that the ship was not capable
of running so long and hard a voyage under total automatic;
but to his relief everything checked out clean, system after
system, nothing failed, no hairbreadth errors that could ruin
them, losing them forever in this chartless space.

"It is good," he told Melein.

"You feared something in particular?"

"Only neglect," he said, "she'pan."

She stood beside him, occasionally seeming to watch the
reflection of his face as he glanced sometimes to that of hers.
He was content to be where he was, doing what his hands
well remembered: he ran through things that he had already
done, only to have the extra time, until she grew weary of
standing and departed his shoulder to sit at the second man's
post across the console.

Lonely, perhaps, interested in what he did: he recalled that
she was not ignorant of such machinery, only of that human-
made, and he dared not try too much in her presence. She
surely knew that he was repeating operations.

He took the chance.

Elapsed time, he asked of the records-storage.

It flashed back refusal. *No record.*

Other details he asked. *No record. No record,* it answered.

Something cold and hard swelled in his throat. Carefully
he checked the status of the navigational tapes, whether re-
trace was available, to bring him home again.

Classified, the screen flashed at him.

He stopped, mindful of the auto-destruct linked into the
tape mechanism. Suspicion crept horridly through his recol-
lections.

We want nothing coming home with you by accident.

Stavros' words.

Sweat trickled down his side. He felt it prickling on his
face, wiped the edge of his hand across his mouth and tried
to disguise the gesture. Melein still sat beside him.

The dus came nearer, moved between them, close to the
delicate instruments. "Get out of there," Duncan wished it. It
only lay down.

"Kel'en," said Melein, "what do you see that troubles you?"

He moistened his lips, shifted his eyes to her. "She'pan—we have found no life . . . I have lost count of the worlds, and we have found no life. What makes you think that your homeworld will be different?"

Her face became unreadable. "Do you find reason there, kel'en, to think we shall not?"

"I have found reason here . . . to believe that this ship is locked against me. She'pan, when that tape runs to its end, it may have no navigational memory left."

Amber eyes flickered. She sat still with her hands folded in her lap. "Did you plan to leave?"

"We may not be able to run. We will have no other options, she'pan."

"We never did."

He drew in his breath, wiped at the moisture that had gone cold on his cheek, and let the breath go again. Her calm was unshakable, thoroughly rational: *Shon'ai* . . . the throw was cast, for them—by birth. It was like Niun with his weapons.

"She'pan," he said quietly, "you have named each world as we have passed. Do you know the number that we have yet to see?"

She nodded in the fashion of the People, a tilt of the head to the left. "Before we reach homeworld," she said, "Mlara and Sha, and Hlar and Sa'a-no-kli'i."

"Four," he said, stunned at the sudden knowledge of an end. "Have you told—?"

"I have told him." She leaned forward, her arms twined on her white-robed knees. "Kel Duncan, your ships will come. They are coming."

"Yes."

"You have chosen your service."

"Yes," he said. "With the People, she'pan." And when she still stared at him, troubled by his treachery: "On their side, she'pan, there are so many kel'ein one will not be missed. But on the side of the People, there is only one—twice that, with me. Humankind will not miss one kel'en."

Melein's eyes held to his, painfully intense. "Your mathematics is without reproach, kel Duncan."

"She'pan," he said softly, moved by the gratitude he realized in her.

She rose, and left.

Committed the ship to him.

He sat still a moment, finding everything that he had sought under his hands, and suddenly a burden on him that he had not thought to bear. Had he intended betrayal, he did not think he could commit it now; and to do to them again what he had done on Kesrith, even to save their lives—

That was not an act of love, but of selfishness . . . here, and hereafter. He knew them too well to believe it for their own good.

He scanned the banks of instruments, that hid their horrid secrets, programs locked from his tampering, things triggered perhaps from the moment he had violated orders and thrown them prematurely onto taped running.

Or perhaps—as SurTacs had been expended before—it was planned from the beginning, that *Fox* would not come home, save as a rider to *Saber*.

There was the pan'en, and the record in that; but under *Saber*'s firepower, *Fox* was nothing . . . and it was not impossible that the navigational computer would go down as the tape expired, crippling them.

He reached for the board again, plied the keys repeatedly, receiving over and over again *No Record* and *Classified*.

And at last he gave over trying, and pushed himself to his feet, reached absently for the dus that crowded wistfully against him, sensing his distress and trying to distract him from it.

Four worlds.

A day, or more than a month: the span between jumps was irregular.

The time seemed suddenly very short.

Chapter Sixteen

———•◉•———

MLARA AND Sha and Hlar and Sa'a-no-kli'i.

Niun watched them pass, lifeless as they were, with an excitement in his blood that the somber sights could not wholly kill.

They jumped again, and just after ship's noon there appeared a new star centered in the field.

"This is home," said Melein softly, when they gathered in the she'pan's hall to see it with her. "This is the Sun."

In the hal'ari, it was Na'i'in.

Niun looked upon it, a mere pinprick of light at the distance from which they entered the system, and agonized that it would be so long a journey yet. Na'i'in. The Sun.

And the World, that was Kutath.

"By your leave," Duncan murmured, "—I had better go to controls."

They all went, even the dusei, into the small control room.

And there was something eerie in the darkness of that section of the panels that had been most active. Duncan stood and looked at it a moment, then settled in at controls, called forth activity elsewhere, but not in that crippled section.

Niun left the she'pan's side to stand at the panel to Duncan's right: little enough he knew of the instruments, save only what Duncan had shown him—but he had knowledge enough to be sure there was something amiss.

"The navigational computer," Duncan said. "Gone."

"You can bring us in," Niun said without doubt.

Duncan nodded. His hands moved on the boards, and the

176

screens built patterns, built structures about a point that was Na'i'in.

"We are on course," he said. "We have no starflight navigation, that is all."

It was not of concern. Long after the she'pan had returned to her own hall, Niun still stayed by Duncan, sitting in the cushion across the console, watching the operations that Duncan undertook.

It was five days before Kutath itself took shape before them, third out from Na'i'in . . . Kutath. Duncan guided them, present at controls surely more than reason called for: he took his meals in this room, and entered kel-hall only to wash and to take a little sleep in night-cycle. Restlessly he would go back before the night was done, and Niun knew where to find him.

Nothing required his presence at controls.

There were no alarms, nothing.

It was, Niun began to reckon with growing despair, the same as the others. Melein surely made her own estimation of the lasting silence, and Duncan did, and none spoke it aloud.

No ships.

No reaction.

The sixth day there were the first clear images of the world, and Melein came to controls to look at them. Niun set his hand upon hers, silent offering.

It was a red world and lifeless.

Old. Very, very old.

Duncan cut the image off the screens. There was agony in his face when he looked at them both, as if he thought himself to blame. But Niun drew a deep breath and let it go, surrendering to what he had known all his life.

That they were, after all, the last-born.

Somewhere in the ship the dusei moaned, gathering in the grief that was sent them.

"The voyage of the People," said Melein, "has been very, very long. If we are the last, still we will go home. Take us there, Duncan."

"Yes," Duncan said simply, and bowed his head and turned to the boards so that he did not have to look on their faces. Niun found it difficult to breathe, a great tightness about his heart, as when he had seen the People die on

Kesrith; but it was an old grief, and already mourned. He stood still while Melein went her way back to her hall.

Then he went apart, unto himself, and sat down with his dus, and wept, as the Kel could not weep.

"Why should we be sorrowful?" asked Melein, when they had met again that evening, for their first common-meal in many days, and their last, before landing. "We always knew that we were the last. For a time we believed otherwise, and we were happier, but it is only the same truth that has always been. We should still be glad. We have come home. We have seen what was our beginning, and that is a fit ending."

This was something the human could not understand. He simply shook his head as he would do in pain, and his dus nosed at him, disconsolate.

But Niun inclined himself wholly to Melein's thoughts: they were true. There were far worse things than what lay before them: there was Kesrith; there were humans, and regul.

"Do not grieve for us," Niun said to Duncan, and touched his sleeve. "We are where we wish to be."

"I will get back to controls," Duncan said, and flung himself to his feet, veiled himself and left their company without asking permission or looking back. His dus trailed after him, radiating distress.

"He can do nothing there," said Melein with a shrug. "But it comforts him."

"Our Duncan," said Niun, "will not let go. He is obsessed with blame."

"For us?"

Niun shrugged, pressed his lips together, looked aside.

She put out her hand and touched his face, recalled his attention, regarding him sadly. "I have known that it was possible, that it might have been too long. Niun, there have been above eighty Darks, and in each more than one generation has passed; and there have been above eighty Betweens, and the most of them have lasted above a thousand years."

He attempted a deprecating laugh, a shake of his head: it did not come out as a laugh. "I can reckon that in distance—but not in years. Twenty years is long for a kel'en. I cannot reckon a thousand."

She bent and pressed her lips to his brow. "Niun, the accounting is no matter. It is beyond my reckoning too."

That night, and the night after, Niun slept sitting, his head against her chair. Melein did not ask it. He simply did not want to leave her. And when Duncan came from his lonely watch for what few hours of true sleep he sought, he curled up against his dus in the corner—here, and not in kel-hall. It was not a time that any of them wanted to be alone. The loneliness of Kutath itself was overwhelming.

On the eighth day Kutath swung beneath them, filling all the screen in the she'pan's hall—angry, arid, scarred with its age.

And Duncan came to the she'pan's presence, burst in like a gust of wind and swept off *mez* and *zaidhe* to show his face: it was aglow.

"Life!" he said. "The scan shows it. She'pan, Niun—your world is not dead."

For an instant neither of them moved.

And of a sudden Melein struck her hands together and thanked the several gods; and only then Niun dared to draw breath and hope.

Behind Duncan, Melein went to controls, and Niun followed after, with the dusei padding behind them and blowing great puffs of excitement. Melein settled on the arm of the cushion and Niun leaned beside her, the while Duncan tried to make clear to them what his search had found, showing them the screens and the figures and all the chattering flow of data that meant life.

Life of machines; and very, very scant, the evidence of growing things.

"It looks like Kesrith from space," said Duncan softly, and sent a chill over Niun's flesh, for often enough the old she'pan had called Kesrith the forge that would prepare the People . . . for all that would lie before them. "The dusei," said Duncan, "should fare well enough there."

"One moon," Niun read the screen, remembering with homesickness the two that had coursed the skies of Kesrith; remembering his hills, and the familiar places that he had hunted before humans came.

This world of their ancestors would hold its own secrets, its own graces and beauties, and its own dangers.

And humans—soon enough.

"Duncan," said Melein, "take us down."

Chapter Seventeen

———————◆◎◆———————

KUTATH.

Duncan inhaled the air that blew into the hatch, the first breath off the surface of the world, cold and thin, faintly scented. He looked beyond the hatch at the red and amber sands, at the ridge of distant, rounded mountains, at a sun sullen-hued and distorted in its sky.

And he did not go down. This was for the mri, to go first onto their native soil. He stood in the ship and watched them descend the ramp, Melein first, and Niun after her—children returned to their ancient mother. They looked about them, their eyes surely seeing things in a different way than his might, their senses finding something familiar in the touch of Kutath's gravity, the flavor of its air—something that must call to their blood and senses and say *this is home*.

Sad for them if it did not, if the People had indeed voyaged too long, and lost everything for which they had come. He did not think they had; he had seen the look in Niun's eyes when they beheld the world beyond the hatch.

He felt his own throat tight, his muscles trembling with the terrible chill of the world, and with anxiety. If he felt anything clearly, it was a sense of loss—and he did not know why. He had succeeded for them, had brought them home, and down safely, and yet there was a sadness on him.

It was not all he had done, that service for the People.

Across the system a beacon pulsed, a marker on the path incoming ships would use; and on Kutath, the ship itself now served as a beacon. Silent the pulse was, but it was going now . . . would go on so long as power remained in the ship— and that would be beyond their brief lifespans.

Friendship, friendship, the ship cried at the heavens, and did human ships care to inquire of that signal or the other, there was more.

He had not confessed this to Niun or Melein. He did not think they would approve any gesture toward tsi'mri, and therefore he did not ask their approval.

He saw the dusei go, whuffing and sniffing the air as they edged their turn-toed way down the ramp—rolling with fat from their long, well-fed inactivity on the ship, sleek and shining under the wan sun. They reached the sand and rolled in delight, shaking clouds of red powder from their velvet hides when they rose up again. The greater one towered up on his hind legs, came down, playing, puffing a cloud of dust at the mri, and Niun scolded him off.

The beasts went their own way then, circling out, exploring their new world. They would allow no danger to come to the mri without raising alarm about it, and their present manner was one of great ease. Unharmed by the wind of the ship, a clump of blue-green pipes grew nearby. The dusei destroyed it, munching the plants with evident relish. Their digestion could handle anything, even most poisons; there was no concern for that.

Where plants grew, there was surely water, be it ever so scant. Duncan looked on that sparse growth with satisfaction, with pride, for he had found them a place where life existed in this otherwise barren land, had put their little ship down within reach of water—

And close also to the power source that scan detected.

There was no reaction to their presence, none in their descent, none now. The ship's instruments still scanned the skies, ready to trip the sirens and warn them to cover, but the skies remained vacant . . . both desired and undesired, that hush that prevailed.

He felt the pleasure-feelings of the dusei, lotus-balm, and yielded.

Almost timidly he came down the ramp, feeling out of place and strange, and approached the mri silently, hoping that they would not take offense at his presence: well as he knew Niun, he felt him capable of that, toward a tsi'mri.

"She'pan," he heard Niun say softly, and she turned and noticed him, and reached out her hand to him. They put their arms about him as they would a brother, and Duncan felt an impulse to tears that a man who would be kel'en could not shed. He bowed his head for a moment, and felt their warmth near him. There was a healthy wind blowing, whipping at their robes. He put his arms about them too, feeling on the one side the fragility that was Melein and on the other the lean strength of Niun; and themselves alien, beast-warm, and savoring the chill that set him shivering.

The dusei roved the area more and more widely, emitting their hunting moans, that would frighten anything with ears to hear.

And they looked about them, and save for the ship's alien presence, there was nothing but the earth and sky: flat in one direction, and beyond that flatness at the sky's edge lay mountains, rounded and eroded by time; and in the other direction the land fell away into apricot haze misted with purples, showing a naked depth that drew at the eye and disturbed the senses—no mere valley, but an edge to the very world, a distance that extended to the horizon and blended into the sky; and it reached up arms of cliffs that were red and bright where they were nearest and faded into the ambiguous sky at the far horizon.

Duncan breathed an exclamation in his own tongue, forbidden, but the mri did not seem to notice. He had seen the chasm from above, had brought them down near it because it seemed the best place—easier to descend than to ascend, he had thought when choosing the highlands landing, but he had kept them far from the edge. From above it had seemed perilous enough; but here, themselves reduced to mortal perspective, it gaped into depths so great it faded into haze at the bottom, in terraces and slopes and shelves, eroded points and mounts . . . and distantly, apricot-silver, shone what might be a lake, a drying arm of what had been a sea.

A salt lake, it would surely be, and dead: minerals and salts would have gathered there for aeons, as they had in Kesrith's shallow, drying seas.

They stood still for some time, looking about them at the world, until even the mri began to shiver from the cold.

"We must find that source of power you spoke of," said Melein. "We must see if there are others."

"You are close," said Duncan, and lifted his arm in the direction he knew it to be. "I brought you down as near as I dared."

"Nothing responded to your attempts to contact."

"Nothing," Duncan said, and shivered.

"We must put on another layer of robes," said Niun. "We must have a sled packed with stores. We will range out so far as we can—shall we not, she'pan?—and see what there is to be seen."

"Yes," said Melein. "We shall see."

Duncan started to turn away, to do what would be necessary, and finding no better time he hesitated, pulled aside the veil he had assumed for warmth. "She'pan," he said. "It would be better—that I should stay with the ship."

"We will not come back," said Melein.

Duncan looked from one to the other of them, found pain in Niun's eyes, realized suddenly the reason of that sense of loss.

"It is necessary," Duncan said, "that I take the ship—to stand guard for you, she'pan. I will not leave this sun. I will stay. But it is possible that I may be able to stop them."

"The markers that you have left . . . Are they for that?"

Shock coursed through him, the realization that Melein had not been deceived.

"Yes," he said, hoarse. "To let them know that here are friends. And it may be that they will listen."

"Then you will not take the ship," she said. "What message you have left is enough. If they will not regard that, then there is nothing further to be said. The ship carries no weapons."

"I could talk with them."

"They would take you back," she said.

It was truth. He stared at her, chilled to the bone by the wind that rocked at them.

"You could not fight," she said, and looked about at the wide horizon, lifted her arm toward it. "If they would seek us out in all of this, then they would not listen to you; and if they would not, then that is well. Come with us, kel Duncan."

"She'pan," he said softly, accepting.

And he turned and ascended the ramp.

There were supplies to find: Niun named what was needed, and together they bolted aluminum tubing into what passed very well for a sled. They loaded it into the cargo lift, and secured on it what stores Niun chose: water containers, food, and the light mats that were for sleeping; aluminum rods for shelter, and thermal sheets—tsi'mri luxury that they were, yet even Niun found the cold outside persuasive.

They chose spare clothing, and a change of boots; and wore a second *siga* over the first.

And last and most important of all they visited the shrine of the pan'en, and Niun gathered the ovoid reverently into his arms and bore it down to the sled, settling it into the place that was prepared for it.

"Take us down," Melein said.

Duncan pressed the switch and the cargo lift settled slowly groundward, to let them step off onto the red sands.

It was already late afternoon.

Behind them, the cargo lift ascended, crashed into place again with a sound alien in all this desert, and there was no sound after but the wind. The mri began to walk, never looking back; but once, twice, a third time, Duncan could not bear it, and glanced over his shoulder. The ship's vast bulk dwindled behind them. It assumed a strange, frozen quality as it diminished, sheened in the apricot light, blending with the land: no light, no motion, no sound.

Then a rise of the land came between and it passed from view. Duncan felt a sudden pang of desolation, felt the touch of the mri garments, that had become natural to him, felt the keen cold of the wind, that he had desired, and was still conscious that he was alone. They walked toward the sun— toward the source of activity that the instruments had detected, and the thought occurred to him that did they find others, his companions would be hard put to account for his presence with them.

That there could come a time when his presence would prove more than inconvenient for Niun and Melein.

It was a bad way to end, alone, and different.

It struck him that in his madness he had changed places with those he pitied, and sorriest of all, he did not believe that Niun would willingly desert him.

Na'i'in set, providing them a ruddy twilight that flung the dying sea into hazy limbo, a great and terrifying chasm on their left, with spires upthrust through the haze as if they had no foundation. They rested in the beginning of that sunset, double-robed against the chill and still warm from walking, and shared a meal together. The dusei, that they had thought would have come at the scent of food on the wind, did not appear. Niun looked often during that rest, scanning their backtrail, and Duncan looked also, and fretted after the missing beasts.

"They are of a world no less hard," Niun said finally, "and they are likely ranging out in search of their own meal."

But he frowned and still watched the horizon.

And a strange thing began to happen as the sun declined. Through the gentle haze in the air, mountains leaped into being that had not been visible before, and the land grew and extended before them, developing new limits with the sun behind the hills.

On the shores of the dying sea rose towers and slender spires, only a shade darker than the apricot sky.

"Ah!" breathed Melein, rising; and they two rose up and stood gazing at that horizon, at that mirage-like city that hung before them. It remained distinct only for a few moments, and then faded into shadow as the rim of Na'i'in slipped beneath the horizon and brought them dusk.

"That was surely what the instruments sensed," said Duncan.

"Something is alive there."

"Perhaps," said Niun. Surely he yearned to believe so, but he evinced no hope, no anxiousness. He accepted the worst first: he had constantly done so; it seemed to keep the mri sane, in a history that held little but destructions.

Melein settled again to her mat on the sand, and locked her arms about her knees and said nothing at all.

"It could be very far," Duncan said.

"If it is the source of what you scanned?" Niun asked.

Duncan shrugged. "A day or so."

Niun frowned, slipped the *mez* lower to expose most of his face. "Tell me truth: are you able to make such a walk?"

Duncan nodded, mri-fashion. "The air is thin, but not beyond my limits. Mostly the cold troubles me."

"Wrap yourself. I think that we will rest in this place tonight."

"Niun, I will not be a burden on you."

Niun considered this, nodded finally. "Mri are not bearers of burdens," he said, which Duncan took for kel humor, and the precise truth. He grinned, and Niun did likewise, a sudden and startling gesture, quickly gone.

The veils were replaced. Duncan settled to rest in a thermal sheet with rather more peace at heart than he knew was rational under the circumstances. In the chill air, the blanket and the robes together made a comfortably warm rest, deliciously so. Overhead, the stars, strangely few in a clear sky, observed no familiar patterns. He made up his own, a triangle, a serpent, and a man with a great dus at his heels. The effort exhausted his fading mind, and he slept, to wake with Niun shaking his shoulder and advising him he must keep his turn at watch: the dusei had not yet returned.

He sat wrapped in warmth the remaining part of the night, gazing at the horizon that was made strange by the growth of pipes atop the plainsward ridge, watching in solitude the rise of Na'i'in over their backtrail, a heart-filling beauty.

It was more than a fair trade, he thought.

As the light grew, the mri began to stir; they took a morning meal, leisurely in their preparations, content to say little and to gaze often about them.

And on the rising wind came a strange, distant note that made them stop in the attitudes of the instant, and listen; and then Niun and Melein laughed aloud, relieved.

The dusei were a-hunt, and nearby.

They packed up, and loaded the sled: Duncan drew it. Niun, kel'anth, senior of the Kel, could not take such work while there was another to do it; this had long been the order of things, and Duncan assumed it without question. But the mri watched him, and at the first rise they approached, Niun silently set his hand on the rope and disengaged him from it, looping it across his own shoulder.

It was not hard work for the mri, for the land was relatively flat and the powdery red sand glided easily under the metal runners. The chill that made their breaths hang in frosty puffs in the dawn grew less and less, until by midmorning both Niun and Melein shed their extra robes and walked in apparent comfort.

During a rest stop, one of the dusei appeared on the horizon, stood for a time, and the other joined it. Ever and again the beasts put in an appearance and as quickly vanished; they had been gone some time in this last absence. Duncan willed his back, concerned for it and distressed at its irrational behavior, but it came only halfway and stopped. It looked different; he would not have recognized it, but that there were only two on all Kutath, and the larger one was still hanging back at the crest of the slope. Both looked different.

Leaner. The sleek look was gone, overnight.

The dus swung about suddenly and joined its partner on the ridge. Both went over that low rolling of the land; Duncan watched to see them reappear going away, and blinked, for it seemed impossible that something so large could vanish so thoroughly in so flat a land.

"What is the matter with them?" he asked of Niun; the mri shrugged and resumed his course behind Melein, meaning, Duncan supposed, that Niun did not know.

And soon after, as their course brought them near some of the blue-green pipe, Niun cut a bit of it with his *av-tlen* and watched it fill with water in the uncut portion.

"I would not sample that," Duncan said uneasily.

But the mri took a little into his mouth, a very little, and spat it out again in a moment. "Not so bad," he said. "Sweet. Possibly the pulp is edible. We shall see if I sicken from it. The dusei did not think so."

This was a mystery still, that there could be communication of such precise nature between dus and man; but Duncan remembered the feeling they had had in the first discovery of the plants—an intense pleasure.

Niun did not sicken. After midday he sampled a bit more, and by evening pronounced it acceptable. Duncan tasted, and it was sweet like sugared fruit, and pleasant and cold. Melein took some last of all, after camp was made and after it was clear that neither mri nor human had taken harm of it.

The sun slipped to the rim of the chasm and shredded into ribbons, lingering for a last moment. Their city returned amid the haze.

It was large; it was firmly grounded on the earth, and no floating mirage. The towers were distinctly touched by the light before it vanished.

"It is written in the pan'en," Melein said softly, "that there was a city of towers—yellow-towered Ar-ehon. Other cities are named there: Zohain, Tho'e'i-shai and Le'a'haen. The sea was Sha'it, and the plains had their names, too."

There was the wind, and the whisper of the sand grains moving. It was all that moved, save themselves, who came as strangers, and one of them strange indeed.

But Melein named them names, and Kutath acquired substance about them, terrible as it was in its desolation. Niun and Melein talked together, laughed somewhat in all that stillness, but the stillness settled into the bones, and stopped the breath, and Duncan found difficulty in moving for a moment until Niun touched his wrist and asked him a question that he must, in embarrassment, beg the mri to repeat.

"Duncan?" Niun asked then, sensing the disturbance in him.

"It is nothing," Duncan said, and wished for the dus back, to no avail. He gazed beyond the mri into the darkening chasm of the dying sea, and wondered that they could laugh in such a place.

And that Melein in her mind saw the vast waters that had lapped and surged in that nakedness: that more than anything else thrust home to him the span of time that these two mri had crossed.

Niun pressed his arm and withdrew, wrapped himself in his blanket and lay down to sleep, as Melein likewise settled for the night.

Duncan took the watch, wrapped in his thermal sheet and warm in the air that frosted his breath. The moon was aloft, gibbous. A wisp of high clouds appeared in the north, not enough to obscure the stars.

He felt the presence of the dus once. It did not come close, but it was there, somewhere near them, reassurance.

Chapter Eighteen

———◦❂◦———

SHARN, TREMBLING with weakness, pressed the button that brought the food dispenser within reach. A slight inclination of her body brought her mouth against it, and for a time she was content to drink and to let the warmth flow into her belly. The tube already increased the flow of nutrient into her veins, but the long food deprivation had psychological effects that no tube-feeding could diminish.

About her, on the bridge of *Shirug,* a double hand of younglings slept, still deep in the hibernation in which they had spent major portions of the long voyage. Only Suth and a Geleg youngling named Melek had remained awake throughout, save for the brief sleeps into which jump cast them. Suth was fully awake already, and made haste to approach Sharn, dutiful in concern for the elder to whom it belonged, bai Hulagh's lending.

"May I serve?" Suth asked hoarsely. Fever-brightness glittered in Suth's eyes. The bony plating of his cheeks was white-edged and cloudy, an unhealthful sign. Sharn saw the suffering of the youngling, who had endured so long a voyage fully awake, and in a rare courtesy, offered Suth the same dispenser which she was using. Suth flushed dark in pleasure and took it hungrily, consumed food in great noisy gulps that surely brought strength to his tottering limbs—then returned it to her, worship in his eyes.

"Awaken the others," she bade Suth then, and the youngling moved at once to obey.

Mission tape stood at zero.

They had arrived.

A quick look at scan showed the human ship riding close

at hand, but the humans would hardly be organized yet. Often during the voyage Sharn had awakened for consultation with Suth, and each time she had known the humans slower than regul in coming to focus after jump: drugs; they had not the biological advantage of hibernation. Some few were operating, but they were still hazed. This was known; the mri, who needed neither hibernation nor drugs, had always been able to take advantage of it.

And about them lay the mri home system.

That thought sent chills through Sharn's blood and set her two hearts pumping almost out of time. From her remote console, she called up new plottings, activated her instruments, and sent the ship easing away from the human escort while they were still dazed. Automatic challenge sounded on the instruments, a human computer advising her that she was breaking pattern. She ignored it and increased speed in real space.

She was bound for the inner planets. Behind her, humans stirred to wakefulness, and sent her furious demands to return. She ignored them. She was ally, not subject, and felt no obligation to their commands. About her, the younglings stirred to life again under the ministrations of the skillful youngling provided her by the bai—a measure of his esteem, this lending of his personal attendant: Sharn reckoned dizzyingly of her own possible favor, as well as her own present dangers.

"We will serve as probe," she sent the angered humans at last, deigning to reply. "It is needful, human allies, that we quickly learn what manner of armed threat we face, and *Shirug* has sufficient mobility to evade."

It was not the regul habit to go first.

But regul interests were at stake. Dead world after dead world: the incredible record of devastation enforced what decisions had been made on Kesrith. Doch-survival was personal survival, and more than that . . . incredible in itself . . . there was consciousness of threat against the regul species, that no regul had ever had to reckon.

Behind her, visible on the screens, the human ship seemed to fragment. *Saber* shed her riders, the little in-system fighter *Santiago* and the harmless probe *Flower*. Neither warships nor probe had the star-capable flexibility of *Shirug*, medium-sized and heavily armed, capable of evading directly out of the system and back again, capable of near-world maneuvers which would prove disaster for vast and fragile *Saber*, that was all shielding and firepower.

The humans were not happy. *Saber* gathered speed and her riders stayed with her. It was not pursuit. Sharn was nervous for a time, and snapped pettishly at her recovering younglings, but she determined at last that the humans were not going to take measures against her, not with all of them in reach of the mri. Their threats, had they issued them, would have made no difference. Sharn had her orders from Hulagh, and while she distrusted the Alagn elder's sometimes youngling-impulsive decisiveness, she also trusted his knowledge and experience, which was a hundred twelve years longer than hers.

In particular, Hulagh knew humans, and evidently had confidence that the peace which was in force would not be breached, not even if regul pressed it hard. This was a distasteful course. Regul were not fighters; their aggressiveness was verbal and theoretical. Sharn would have felt far more secure had she a mri aboard to handle such irrational processes as evasion and combat. Random action was something at which mri excelled. But of course they were facing mri, and the unaccustomed prospect of fighting against mri disturbed her to the depth.

Destroy.

Destroy and leave the humans to mop up the untidiness. Regul knew how to use the lesser races. Regul decided; the lesser species simply coped with the situation . . . and Hulagh in his experience found that the humans would do precisely that.

A beacon-pulse came faintly: hearts pounding, Sharn adjusted the pickup and amplified.

Friendship, it said. *Friendship*.

In human language.

Treachery.

Just such a thing had Hulagh feared, that the mri, who had left regul employ, would hire again. There was a human named Duncan, a contact with the mri, who worked to that end.

Sharn sighted on the source of the signal, fired. It ceased.

Human voices chattered at her in a few moments, seeking to know why she had fired. They had not, then, picked up the signal.

"Debris," Sharn answered. Regul did not lie; neither did they always tell the truth.

The answer was, perhaps, accepted. There was no comment.

Shirug's lead widened. It was possible she had the advantage of speed. Possibly the human craft were content to let her probe the inner system defenses, taking her at her word, reasoning no further into it. She doubted that. She had confidence rather in *Shirug's* speed: strike-and-run, that was the ship's build—*Saber's* was that of a carrier, stand-and-fight. Doubtless the insystem fighter, *Santiago,* was the speed in the combination, and it was no threat to *Shirug. Flower* was not even considerable in that reckoning.

Sharn dismissed concern for them: Hulagh's information was accurate as it had been consistently accurate. *Shirug,* stripped of riders according to their operating agreement, still had the advantage in everything but shielding and firepower.

She gave whole attention to that matter and allotted the chatter of humans to Suth's attention thereafter. There was the matter of locating the world itself, of reaching it first.

Destroy, and leave the humans to cope with what followed.

Chapter Nineteen

———◆———

IT WAS painful to stop, with the city in view, so close, so tantalizingly close—but the night was on them, and Niun saw that Duncan was laboring: his breath came audibly now. And at last Melein paused, and with a sliding glance toward Duncan that was for Niun alone, signaled her intent to halt.

"Best we rest here the night," she said.

Duncan accepted the decision without so much as a glance, and they spread the mats for sitting on the cold sand and watched the sun go down. Its rays tinted the city spires against the hills.

"I am sorry," Duncan said suddenly.

Niun looked at him; Duncan remained veiled, not out of reticence, he thought, but that the air hurt him less that way. He felt the mood behind that veil, an apartness that was itself a wound.

"*Sov-kela,*" Niun hailed him softly, kel-brother, the gentlest word of affection but true brother. "Come sit close to us. It is cold."

It was less cold for them, but Duncan came, and seemed cheered by it, and perhaps more comfortable, for his body heat was less than theirs. They two leaned together, back to back, lacking any other rest. Even Melein finally deigned to use Niun's knee for her back. They said nothing, only gazed at the city that was sunk in dark now, and at the stars, fewer than those in skies he had known . . . so that he wondered if they lay at the very rim of the galaxy, first-born perhaps, as Duncan's folk came from inward.

A long, long journey, that of the People inward. He almost wished that this trek last forever, that they might forever

walk toward that city, still with hope, and not know what
truth lay there.

And yet Duncan had claimed to have detected power use
in that place.

Niun bit at his lip and shifted his weight, so that everyone
shifted uncomfortably, and was aware, subtly, of that which
had suddenly disturbed him.

Dus-presence.

"They are back," he said softly. "Yes," said Duncan after a
moment.

Sand scuffed. There was a whuffing sound. Eventually the
beasts appeared, heads lowered, absent-mindedly looking this
way and that as if at this last moment they could not recall
what they were doing there.

And this time they did not shy off, but came within reach.
Melein moved aside and Niun and Duncan accepted the
beasts that sought them.

Pleasure thoughts. Niun caressed the massive head that
thrust at his ribs and ran his hand over a body gone rough-
coated and thin, every rib pronounced.

"It is changed," Duncan exclaimed. "Niun, both of them
are thinner. Could they have had young?"

"No one has ever decided whether a dus is he or she."
Niun fretted at the change in them—was nettled, too, that
Duncan should seize what thought he had half-shaped,
Duncan, who was new to the beasts. "Some have said they
are both. But the People have never seen this change in them.
We have never," he added truthfully, "seen young dusei."

"It is possible," said Melein, "that there are no young
dusei, not as we know young. Nothing survives where they
come from that is born helpless."

Niun stood up and looked all about the moonlit land, but
dusei could well conceal themselves, and if there were young
thereabouts, he could not find them. But when he sat down
again, the head of his dus in his lap, he had still a feeling of
unease about the beast.

"It is dangerous," said Duncan, "to loose a new species on
a world, particularly one so fragile as this."

Duncan spoke. Niun had a thought, and for love, forbore
to say it.

And suddenly Duncan bowed his head, and there was discomfort in the dus-feelings.

"This is so," said Melein gently, "but we should feel lonely without them."

Duncan looked at her in silence, and finally put his arms about his beast's neck, and bowed his head and rested. Niun made place for Melein between them, and they slept, all slept for the first time since the ship, for the dusei were with them to guard them, and they had the body warmth of the beasts for their comfort.

Dusei multiplied, begat other dusei, that were born adult and filled the world until all Kutath belonged to them, and they filled the streets of the dead cities and had no need of mri.

Niun wakened, disturbed at once by the dus thoughts that edged upon the nightmare, aware of sweat cold on his face, of the others likewise disturbed . . . perplexed, perhaps, what had wakened them. Duncan looked round at the hills, as if some night wanderer might have come nigh them.

"It is nothing," Niun said.

He did not admit to the dream; the fright was still with him. He had never in his life felt exposed to the dusei, only sharing. Human presence: it was something that Duncan's presence had fostered, suspicion, where none had existed.

Dusei, he reminded himself, *have no memories.* For these two dusei, Kesrith no longer existed. They would never recall it until they saw it again, and that would be never. Persons and places: that was all that stayed in their thick skulls . . . and for them now there was only Kutath. They were native, by that token, one with the land, sooner than they.

Niun closed his eyes again, shamed by the dream that he was sure at least Melein suspected, though she might falsely blame it on Duncan, and feel herself fouled to have shared a human's night fears, dus-borne. The beast sent comfort now. Niun took it, and relaxed into that warmth, denying the fear.

The dus would not in any wise remember.

They made no great haste on the morrow: they knew Duncan's limit in the thin air, and would not press him harder.

And they were cautious; they followed the rolls of the land in their approach, and, dus-wise, appeared no plainer to the city than they must.

But the nearer they came, the less useful such precaution seemed.

Old, old. Niun saw clearly what he had suspected: spires in ruins, unrepaired, the sordidness of decay about the whole place. None of them spoke of it; it was not a thing that they wanted to admit.

At the last they abandoned caution. The wind that had tugged at them gently for days suddenly swelled, kicking up sand in a veil that itself was enough to screen them, and the force of it exhausted them. The dusei went with nostrils pressed close and heads lowered, snorting now and again and doubtless questioning the sanity of them that insisted on moving. Niun's eyes burned despite the protection of the membrane, and he lowered the visor of the *zaidhe* as Duncan had done from the first that the sand had begun to blow; Melein lowered the gauzy inner veil of her headcloth, the *sarahe*, that covered all her face and made of her a featureless figure of white, as they were of black.

Under other circumstances, prudence would have driven them to shelter: there were places that offered it; but they kept walking, slowly, and took turn and turn about with the stubborn sled.

Sand flowed in rivers through the streets of the city. They went like ghosts into the ruins, and their tracks vanished behind them as they walked. Spires towered above them, indistinct beyond rusty streamers of dust, save where outlined by the sun that pierced the murk; and the wind howled with a demon-voice down the narrow ways, rattling sand against their visors.

Spires and cylinders spanned by arches, squarish cylinders looming against the sand-veiled sun . . . no such buildings had stood in Niun's memory, anywhere. He gaze round at them and found nothing familiar, nothing that said to him, *here dwelled the People.* Fear settled over him, a deep depression of soul.

For a time they had to rest, sheltered in the shell of a broken spire, oppressed by the noise of the wind outside. Duncan coughed, a shallow, tired sound, that ceased finally when he was persuaded to take a little of their water; and he doubled the veil over his face, which did for him what the gods in their wisdom had done for the mri, helping him breathe in the fine dust.

But of the city, of what they saw, none of them spoke.

They rested, and when they could, they set out into the storm again, Duncan taking his own turn at the sled, that by turns hissed over sand and grated over stone: burden that it was, they would not leave what it bore. There was a question of it.

Melein led them, tending toward the center of the city, that was the direction that Niun himself would have chosen: to the heart of the maze of streets, for always in the center were the sacred places, the shrines, and always to the right of center stood the *e'ed su-shepani*, the she'pan's tower access. In any mri construction in all creation a mri knew his way: so it had been, surely, when there had been cities.

The dusei vanished again. Niun looked about and they were gone, though he could still feel their touch. Duncan turned a blind, black-masked face in the same direction, then faced again the way that Melein led and flung his weight against the ropes. The squeal of runners on naked stone shrilled above the roar of the wind, diminished as they went on sand again.

And the spires thinned, and they entered a great square.

There stood the edun, the House that they had sought . . . slanted walls, four towers with a common base: the House that they had known had been of earth, squat and rough . . . but this was of saffron stone, veiled with the sand-haze, and arches joined its upper portions, an awesome mass, making of all his memories something crude and small . . . the song, of which his age was the echo.

"Gods," Niun breathed, to know what the People had once been capable of creating.

Here would be the Shrine, if one existed; here would be the heart of the People, if any lived. "Come," Melein urged them.

With difficulty they began that ascent to its doors: Duncan labored with the sled, and Niun lent a hand to the rope and helped him. The doors were open before them: Melein's white figure entered the dark first, and Niun deserted Duncan, alarmed at her rashness.

The dark inside held no threat; it was quieter there, and the clouds of sand and dust did not pursue them far inside. In that dim light from the open door, Melein folded back her veil and settled it over her mane; Niun lifted his visor and went back to help Duncan, who had gained the doorway: the squeal of the sled's runners sounded briefly as they drew it inside. The sound echoed off shadowed walls and vaulted ceiling.

"Guard your eyes," Melein said.

Niun turned, saw her reach for a panel at the doorway: light blazed, cold and sudden. The membrane's reaction was instantaneous, and even through the hazing Niun saw black traceries on the walls that soared over them: writings, like and unlike what Melein had made, stark and angular and powerful. An exclamation broke from Melein's own lips, awe at what she had uncovered.

"The hall floors are clean," Duncan remarked strangely, wiping dusty tears from his face, leaving smears behind. Niun looked down the corridors that radiated out from this hall, and saw that the dust stopped at the margin of this room: the way beyond lay clean and polished. A prickling stirred the nape of Niun's neck, like dus-sense. The place should have filled him with hope. It was rather apprehension, a consciousness of being alien in this hall. He wondered where the dusei were, why they had gone, and wished the beasts beside them now.

"Come," said Melein. She spoke in a hushed tone, and still her voice echoed. "Bring the pan'en. You will have to carry it."

They unbound it from the sled, and Niun gave it carefully into Duncan's arms—one burden that he would have been honored to bear, but it came to him that his place was to defend it, and he could not do that with his arms hindered. "Can you bear it, sov-kela?" he asked, for it was heavy and strangely balanced, and Duncan breathed audibly: but Duncan tilted his head mri-wise, avowing he could, and they went soft-footed after Melein, into the lighted and polished halls.

The shrine of the House must lie between kel-access and sen-. The Kel, the guardians of the door, the Face that was Turned Outward, always came first; then the shrine, the Holy; and then the sen-access, the tower of the Mind of the People, the Face that was Turned Inward, the Veilless. Such a shrine there was indeed, a small, shadowed room, where the lamps were cold and the glass of the vessels had gone irridescent with age.

"Ai," Melein grieved, and touched the corroded bronze of the screen of the Pana. Niun averted his eyes, for he saw only dark beyond, nothing remaining in the Holy.

They retreated quickly from that place, gathered up Duncan, who waited at the door, shy of entering there: and yet by his troubled look Niun thought he understood: that had there been any of the People here, the House shrine would have held fire. Niun touched the chill surface of the pan'en as they walked, reaffirmation, a cleansing after the desolation in the shrine.

Yet there were the lights, the cold, clean light; their steps echoed on immaculate tiles, though dust lay thick everywhere outside. The place lived. It drew power from some source. Melein paused at yet another panel, and light came to other hallways . . . the recess of the sen-tower, and on the right, that which had been the tower of some long-dead she'pan.

And most bitter of all, the access to the kath-tower, that mocked them with its emptiness.

"There could be defenses," Duncan said.

"That is so," said Melein.

But she turned then and began to climb the ramp of the sen-tower, where kel'ein might not follow. Niun stood helpless, anxious until she paused and nodded a summons to him, permission to trespass.

Duncan came after him, bearing the pan'en, hard-breathing; and slowly they ascended the curving ramp, past blockish markings that were like the signs of the old edun, but machine-precise and strange.

More lights: the final access of sen-hall gave way before them, and they entered behind Melein into a vast chamber that echoed to their steps. It was naked. There were no carpets, no cushions, nothing save a corroded brass dinner service that sat on a saffron stone shelf. It looked as if a touch would destroy it: corrosion made lacery of it.

But there was no trace of dust, nothing, save on that shelf, where it lay thick as one would expect for such age.

Melein continued on, through farther doorways, into territory that was surely familiar to one six years a sen'e'en; and again she paused to bid them stay with her, to see things that had been eternally forbidden the Kel. Perhaps, Niun thought sadly, it no longer mattered.

Lights flared to her touch. Machinery lay before them, a vast room of machinery—bank upon bank: like the shrine at Sil'athen it was, but far larger. Niun delayed, awestruck, then committed himself unbidden to stay at her back. She did not forbid, and Duncan followed.

Computers, monitoring boards: some portions of the assemblage he compared to the boards of the ship; and some he could not at all recognize. The walls were stark white, with five symbols blazoned above the center of the panels, tall as a man's widest reach. In gleaming, incorruptible metal they were shaped, like the metal of the pan'en that they bore.

"*An-ehon*," Melein said aloud, and the sound rang like a thunderclap into that long silence.

The machinery blazed to life, activated with a suddenness that made Niun flinch in spite of himself, and he heard the beginnings of an outcry from Duncan, one immediately stifled. The human stood beside him, knelt to set the pan'en down, and rose again, hand on his pistol.

"I am receiving," said a deep and soulless voice. "Proceed."

By the name of the city Melein had called it: Niun's skin prickled, first at the realization that he had seen a symbol and heard it named, a forbidden thing . . . and then that such a creation had answered them. He saw Melein herself take a step back, her hand at her heart.

"*An-ehon*," she addressed the machine, and the very floor seemed to pulse in time with the throb of the lights. It was indeed the city that spoke to them, and it had used the hal'ari, the High Language, that was echoed unchanged throughout all of mri time. "An-ehon, where are your people?"

A brighter flurry of lights ran the boards.

"Unknown," the machine pronounced at last.

Melein drew a deep breath—stood still for several moments in which Niun did not dare to move. "An-ehon," she said then, "we are your people. We have returned. We are descended from the People of An-ehon and from Zohain and Tho'ei'i-shai and Le'a'haen. Do you know these names?"

There was again a flurry of lights and sounds, extreme agitation in the machine. Niun took a step forward, put a cautioning hand toward Melein, but she stood firmly, disregarding him. Bank after bank in the farthest reaches of the hall flared to life: section after section illumined itself.

"We are present," said another voice. "I am Zohain."

"State your name, visitor," said An-ehon's deeper voice. "Please state your names. I see one who is not of the People. Please state your authority to invoke us, visitor."

"I am Melein s'Intel Zain-Abrin, she'pan of the People that went out from Kutath."

The lights pulsed, in increasing unison. "I am An-ehon. I am at the orders of the she'pan of the People. Zohain and Tho'e'i-shai and Le'a'haen are speaking through me. I perceive others. I perceive one of the not-People."

"They are here with my permission."

The lights pulsed, all in unison now. "May An-ehon ask permission to ask?" the machine began, the ritual courtesy of one who would question a she'pan; and the source of it sent cold over Niun's skin.

"Ask."

"What is this person of the not-People? Shall we accept it, she'pan?"

"Accept him. He is Duncan-without-a-Mother. He comes from the Dark. This, of the People, is Niun s'Intel Zain-Abrin, kel'anth of my Kel; this other is a shadow-who-sits-at-our-door."

"Other shadows have entered the city with you."

"The dusei are likewise shadows in our house."

"There was a ship which we permitted to land."

"It brought us."

"There is a signal which it gives, not in the language of the People."

"An-ehon, let it continue."

"She'pan," it responded.

"There are none of the People in your limits?"

"No."

"Do any remain, An-ehon?"

"Rephrase."

"Do any others of the People survive, An-ehon?"

"Yes, she'pan. Many live."

The answer struck; it went uncomprehended for several heartbeats, for Niun had waited for *no*. Yes. Yes, many, *many, MANY!*

"She'pan," Niun exclaimed, and tears stung his eyes. He stood still, nonetheless, and breathed deeply to drive the weakness from him, felt Duncan's hand on his shoulder, offering whatever moved the human, and after a moment he was aware of that, too. Gladness, he thought; Duncan was glad for them. He was touched by this, and at the same time annoyed by the human contact.

Human.

Before he had heard An-ehon speak, he had had no resentment for Duncan's humanity; before he had known that there were others, he had not felt the difference in them so keenly.

Shame touched him, that he should go before others of the People, drawing this with them—self-interested shame and dishonorable, and hurtful. Perhaps Duncan even sensed it. Niun lifted his arm, set it likewise on Duncan's shoulder, pressed with his fingers.

"Sov-kela," he said in a low voice.

The human did not speak. Perhaps he likewise found nothing to say.

"An-ehon," Melein addressed the machine, "where are they now?"

A graphic flashed to a central screen: dots flashed.

Ten, twenty sites. The globe shaped, turned in the viewer, and there were others.

"There were no power readings for those sites," Duncan murmured. Niun tightened his hand, warning him to silence.

Melein turned to them, hands open in dismissal. "Go. Wait below."

Perhaps it was because of Duncan; more likely it was that here began sen-matters that the Kel had no business to overhear.

The People survived.

Melein would guide them: the thought came suddenly that he would have need of all the skill that his masters had taught him—that first in finding the People, it would be necessary to kill: and this was a bitterness more than such killing ever had been.

"Come," he said to Duncan. He bent to take the pan'en into his own arms, trusting their safety now to the city, that obeyed Melein.

"No," Melein said. "Leave it."

He did so, brought Duncan out and down again, where they had left their other belongings; and there they prepared to wait.

Night came on them. From sen-tower there was no stir; Niun sat and fretted at Melein's long silence, and Duncan did not venture conversation with him. Once, restless, he left the human to watch and climbed up to kel-hall: there was only emptiness there, vaster by far than the earth-walled kel-hall he had known. There were pictures, maps, painted there, age-faded, showing a world that had ceased to be, and the sight depressed him.

He left the place, anxious for Duncan, alone in main hall, and started down the winding ramp. A chittering, mechanical thing darted behind him . . . he whirled and caught at his pistol, but it was only an automaton, a cleaner such as regul had employed. It answered what kept the place clean, or what did repairs to keep the ancient machinery running.

He shrugged, half a shiver, and descended to Duncan—startled the human, who settled back again, distressed and relieved at once.

"I wish the dusei would come back," Duncan said.

"Yes," Niun agreed. They were limited without the animals. They dared not leave the outer door unguarded. He looked in that direction, where there was only night, and then began to search through their packs. "I am going to take the she'pan up some food. I do not think we will be moving tonight. And mind, there are some small machines about. I think they are harmless. Do not damage one."

"It comes to me," Duncan said softly, "that An-ehon could be dangerous if it chose to be."

"It comes to me too."

"It said . . . that it *permitted* the ship to land. That means it could have prevented it."

Niun drew a slow breath and let it go, gathered up the packet of food and a flask, the while Duncan's words nagged at him. The human had learned well how to keep his thoughts from his face; he could no longer read him with absolute success. The implications disturbed him; it was not the landing of their own ship that Duncan was thinking of.

Others.

The humans that would come.

Such a thought Duncan offered to him.

He rose and went without looking back, climbed the way to sen-hall, thoughts of treachery moiling in him: and not treachery, if Duncan were Melein's.

What *was* the man?

He entered cautiously into the outer hall of the Sen, called out aloud, for the door was left open; he could hear the voice of the machine, drowning his words, perhaps.

But Melein came. Her eyes were shadowed and held a dazed look. Her weariness frightened him.

"I have brought you food," he said.

She gathered the offering into her hands. "Thank you," she said, and turned away, walked slowly back into that room. He lingered, and saw what he ought not, the pan'en open, and filled with leaves of gold . . . saw the pulse of lights welcome Melein, mortal flesh conversing with machines that were cities. She stood, and light bathed her white-robed figure until it blazed blue-white like a star. The packet of food tumbled from her loose hand, rolled. The flask slipped from the other and struck the floor without a sound. She did not seem to notice.

"Melein!" he cried, and started forward.

She turned, held out her hands, forbidding, panic on her face. Blue light broke across his vision: he flung himself back, crashed to the floor, half dazed.

Voices echoed, and one was Melein's. He gathered himself to one knee as she reached him, touched him: he gained his feet, though his heart still hammered from the shock that had passed through him.

"He is well?" asked the voice of An-ehon. "He is well?"

"Yes," Melein said.

"Come away," Niun urged her. "Come away; leave this thing, at least until the morning. What is time to this machine? Come away from it, and rest."

"I shall eat and rest here," she said. Her hands caressed his arm, withdrew as she stepped back from him, retreating into the room with the machine. "Do not try to come here."

"I fear this thing."

"It should be feared," she lingered to say, and her eyes held ineffable weariness. "We are not alone. We are not alone, Niun. We will find the People. Look at yourself, she'pan's-kel'en."

"Where shall we find them, and when, she'pan? Does it know?"

"There have been wars. The seas have dried; the People have diminished and fought among themselves; cities are abandoned for want of water. Only machines remain here: An-ehon says that it teaches the she'panei that come here, to learn of it. Go away. I do not know it all. And I must. It learns of me too; it will share the knowledge with all the Cities of the People, and perhaps, with that One it calls the Living City. I do not know, I cannot grasp what the connection is among the cities. But I hold An-ehon. It listens to me. And by it I will hold Kutath."

"I am," he said, dazed by the temerity of such a vision, "the she'pan's Hand."

"Look to Duncan."

"Yes," he said; and accepted her gesture of dismissal and left, still feeling in his bones the ache that the machine's weapon had left; dazed he was still, and much that she had said wandered his mind without a tether to hold it . . . only that Melein meant to fight, and that therefore she would need him.

A'ani. Challenge. She'panei did not share: the she'pan served by the most skillful kel'en, survived.

Melein prepared herself.

He returned in silence to the hall below, curled up in the corner, massaging his aching arms and reckoning in troubled thoughts that there was killing to be done.

"Is she all right?" Duncan intruded into his silence, unwelcome.

"She will not leave. She is talking to it, with *them.* She speaks of wars, kel Duncan."

"Is that remarkable for the People?"

Niun looked at him, prepared to be angry, and realized that it was a failure of words. "Wars. Mri wars. Wars-with-distance-weapons." He resorted to the forbidden mu'ara, and Duncan seemed then to understand him, and fell quickly silent.

"Would that the dusei would come," Niun declared suddenly, wrenching his thoughts from such prospects; and in his restlessness he went to the door and ventured to call to them, that lilting call that sometimes, only sometimes, could summon them.

It did not work this time. There was no answer this night, nor the next.

But on the third, while Melein remained shut in sen-tower, and they fretted in their isolation below, there came a familiar breathing and rattle of claws on the steps outside, and that peculiar pressure at the senses that heralded the dusei.

It was the first night that they two dared sleep soundly, warm next their beasts and sure that they would be warned if danger came on them.

It was Melein that came; a clap of her hands startled them

and the beasts together, wakened them in dismay that she, though one of them, had found them sleeping.

"Come," she said; and when they had both gained their feet and stood ready to do her bidding: "The People are near. An-ehon has lit a beacon for them. They are coming."

Chapter Twenty

———◆◉◆———

THE STORM days past had left banks of sand heaped in the city, high dunes that made unreal shapes in the light that whipped about the square.

Duncan looked back at the source, a beacon from the edun's crest that flashed powerfully in the still-dark sky, a summons to any that might be within sight of the city.

And the People would come to that summoning.

They took nothing with them: the pan'en, the sled, everything they owned was left in the edun. If they fared well, they would return; if not, they had no further need. There was, he suspected, though Niun had not spoken overmuch of their chances, no question of flight, whatever happened.

The dusei were disturbed, the more so as they neared the city's limits. Niun scattered them with a sharp command; it was not a situation for dus-feelings. The beasts left them, and vanished quickly into the dark and the ruins.

"Should I not go also?" Duncan asked.

The mri both looked at him. "No," said Niun. "No," Melein echoed, as if such an offering offended them.

And in the dawning, on the sand ridge facing the city, appeared a line of black.

Kel'ein.

The Face that is Turned Outward.

"*Shon'ai*," Niun said softly. *Shon'ai sa'jiran*, the mot ran. The cast is made: no recalling it. "She'pan, will you wait, or will you come?"

"I will walk with you . . . lest there be some over-anxious kel'en on the other side. There are still she'panei. We will see if there is still respect for law."

207

And in the first light of Na'i'in, the black line advanced, a single column. They walked to meet it, the three of them, and there were no words.

The column stopped, and a pair of kel'ein detached themselves and came forward.

Melein stopped. "Come," Niun said to Duncan.

They walked without her. "Keep silent," Niun said, "and keep to my left flank."

And at speaking-distance, only barely, the strange kel'ein stopped; and hailed them. It was a mu'ara, and not a word of it could Duncan understand, but only *she'pan*.

"Among the People," Niun shouted them back, "is the hal'ari forgotten?"

The two strangers came forward still further, and paused: Duncan felt their eyes on him, on what of his face was not veiled. They knew something amiss; he felt it in that too-close scrutiny.

"What do you bring?" the elder asked Niun, and it was the hal'ari. "What is this, kel'en?"

Niun said nothing.

The stranger's eyes went beyond Niun, distant, and came back again. "Here is Sochil's land. Whatever you are, advise your she'pan so, and seek her grace to go away. We do not want this meeting."

"A ship has touched your lands," Niun said.

There was silence from the other side. They knew, and were perturbed: it did not need dusei to feel that in the air.

"We are of Melein s'Intel," said Niun.

"I am Hlil s'Sochil," said the younger, slipping hand into belt in a threatening posture. "And you, stranger?"

"I am daithon Niun s'Intel Zain-Abrin, kel'anth of the Kel of Melein."

Hlil at once adopted a quieter posture, made a slight gesture of respect. He and his elder companion were clad in coarse, faded black; but they were adorned with many *j'tai*, honors that glittered and winked in the cold sun—and the weapons they bore were the *yin'ein*, worn and businesslike.

"I am Merai s'Elil Kov-Nelan," said the elder. "Daithon and kel'anth of Kel of Edun An-ehon. What shall we say to our she'pan, kel'anth?"

"Say that it is challenge."

There was a moment's silence. Merai's eyes went to Duncan, worrying at a presence that did not belong; worry-

ing, Duncan thought, at questions that he would ask if he
could. They knew of the ship; and Merai's amber eyes were
filled with apprehension.

But suddenly Merai inclined his head and walked off, he
and Hlil together.

"They sense something wrong in me," Duncan said.

"Their she'pan will come. It is a question for her now.
Stand still; fold your hands behind you. Do nothing you are
not bidden to do."

So they stood, with the wind fluttering gently at their robes
and blowing a fine sifting off the surface of sand. A tread disturbed the silence after a time; Melein joined them.

"Her name is Sochil," Niun said without looking about
her. "We have advised her kel'anth of your intentions."

She said nothing, but waited.

And in utter silence the People came, the kel'ein first, ranging themselves in a circle about them, rank upon rank, so
that had they intended flight there was no retreat. Duncan
stood stone-still as his companions, as did the hostile Kel, and
felt the stares that were fixed on him, on them all, for surely
there was strangeness even in Niun and Melein, the fineness
of their clothing, the *zahen'ein* that they bore with the
yin'ein, the different style of the *zaidhe*, with its dark plastic
visor and careful folding, while their own were mere squares
and twists of cloth, and their veils were twisted into the head-
cloths, and not fastened to the metal band that theirs had.
Hems were ragged, sleeves frayed. Their weapon hilts were in
bone and lacquered fiber, while those of Niun were of brass
and gold and *cho*-silk wrappings: Duncan thought even his
own finer than those these strangers bore.

A figure of awe among them, Niun: Duncan did not know
the name that Niun had called himself—*daithon* was like a
word for son, but different; but he reckoned suddenly that the
kinsman of a she'pan ranked nigh the she'pan herself.

And himself, Duncan-without-a-Mother. He began to wonder what would become of himself—and what this talk was
of challenge. He had no skill. He could not take up the
yin'ein against the likes of these. He did not know what Niun
expected him to do.

Do nothing you are not bidden to do. He knew the mri
well enough to believe Niun literally. There were lives in the
balance.

Gold robes appeared beyond the black. There stood the

Sen, the scholars of the People; and they came veilless, old and young, male and female, lacking the *seta'al* for the most part, though some few bore them, the blue kel-scars. The Sen posed themselves among the Kel, arms folded, waiting.

But when Melein stepped forward, the sen'ein veiled, and turned aside. And through their midst came an old, white-robed woman.

Sochil, she'pan. Her robes were black-bordered, while Melein's were entirely white. She bore no *seta'al*, though Melein did. She came forward and stopped, facing Melein.

"I am Sochil, she'pan of the ja'anom mri. You are out of your proper territory, she'pan."

"This city," said Melein, "is the city of my ancestors. It is mine."

"Go away from my lands. Go unharmed. This is neutral ground. No one can claim An-ehon. There can be no challenge here."

"I am Melein, she'pan of all the People; and I have come home, Sochil."

Sochil's lips trembled. Her face was seamed with the sun and the weather. Her eyes searched Melein, and the tremor persisted. "You are mad. She'pan of the People? You are more than mad. How many of us will you kill?"

"The People went out from the World; and I am she'pan of all that went out and all that have returned, and of all the cities that sent us. I challenge, Sochil."

Sochil's eyes flickered as the membrane went across them, and her hands went up in a warding gesture. "Cursed be you," she cried, and veiled, and retreated among her Sen.

"You are challenged," Melein said in a loud voice. "Either yield me your children, she'pan of the ja'anom mri, or I will take them."

The she'pan withdrew without answering, and her Kel formed a wall protecting her. None moved. None spoke. A misery crept into taut muscles. The side of the body turned to the wind grew chill and then numb.

And came kel'anth Merai, and two kel'ein, one male, one female.

"She'pan," said Merai, making a gesture of respect before Melein. "I am kel'anth Merai s'Elil Kov-Nelan. The she'pan offers you two kel'ein."

Melein set her arms in an attitude of shock and scorn. "Will she bargain? Then let her give me half her people."

The kel'anth's face betrayed nothing; but the young kel'ein at his side looked dismayed. "I will tell her," the kel'anth said, and tore himself away and retreated into the black ranks that protected Sochil.

"She will not accept," Melein predicted, a whisper to Niun, almost lost in the wind.

It was a long wait. At last the kel'ein gave way, and Sochil herself returned. She was veiled, and she stood with her hands tucked into the wide sleeves of her robes.

"Go away," Sochil said softly then. "I ask you go away and let my children be. What have you to do with them?"

"I see them houseless, she'pan. I will give them a house."

There was a pause. At last Sochil swept her arm at the land. "I see you destitute, fine she'pan with your elegant robes. I see you with no land, no Kel, no Kath, no Sen. Two kel'ein, and nothing more. But you will take my children and give them a house."

"I shall."

"This," said Sochil, stabbing a gesture at Duncan, "is *this* called of the People where you have been? Is this the reward of my Kel when it defeats your kel'anth? What is this that you bring to us, dressed in a kel'en's robes? Let us see its face."

Niun's hand went to his belt, warning.

"You demean yourself," Melein said. "And all this is without point, she'pan. I have told you what I want and what I will do. I will settle your people in a house, either half or all, as you will. And I will go and take clan after clan, until I have all. I am she'pan of the People, and I will have your children, half now, all later. But if you will give half, I will take them and withdraw challenge."

"It cannot be done. The high plains cities have no water. Stranger-she'pan, you are mad. You do not understand. We cannot build; we cannot take the elee way. We are enough for the land, and it for us. You will kill us."

"Ask An-ehon that was your teacher, Sochil, and learn that it is possible."

"You dream. Daughter of my ancestors, you dream."

"No," said Melein. "Mother of the ja'anom, you are a bad dream that the People have dreamed, and I will make a house for your children."

"You will kill them. I will not let you have them."

"Will you divide, she'pan, or will you challenge?"

There were tears in Sochil's eyes, that ran down and dampened her veil. She looked on Niun fearfully, and on Melein again. "He is very young. You are both very young, and in strange company. The gods know that you do not know what you are doing. How can I divide my children?—She'pan, they are terrified of you."

"Answer."

Sochil's head went back. Her glistening eyes nictitated and shed their tears, and she turned her back and stalked off.

Her people stood silent. They might have done something, Duncan thought, might have shown her support. But Melein would claim them; they would remain Sochil's only if Sochil would return challenge.

Sochil stopped in her retreat, among the ranks of her Kel, turned suddenly. "*A'ani!*" she cried. It was challenge.

Melein turned to Niun, and carefully he shed the belt of the *zahen'ein,* handed the modern weapons to Duncan; then with a bow to Melein, he turned and walked forward.

Likewise did Merai s'Elil.

Duncan stood still, the belt a weight in his hands. Melein laid her hand on his sleeve. "Kel Duncan: you understand . . . you must not interfere."

And she veiled herself and walked away through the enemy kel'ein, and likewise did Sochil, in her wake. The wall of kel'ein reformed behind them.

There was silence, save for the whistling of the wind.

In the center of the circle and Niun and Merai took up their positions, facing one another at fencers' distance and a half. Each gathered a handful of sand and cast it on the wind.

Then the *av'ein-kel,* the great-swords, whispered from sheaths.

A pass, in which they exchanged position; the blades flashed, rang lightly against each other, rested. A second pass: and kel Merai stopped, and seemed simply to forget where he was; and fell. The blade had not seemed to touch him.

But darkness spread over the sand beneath him.

Niun bent and gathered dust on his fingers, and smeared it across his brow . . . began, as if there were nothing else in the world, as if there were no watching ring of strangers, to cleanse his blade with a second handful of sand.

Then he straightened, sheathed the *av-kel*, stood still.

For a time there was only the flutter of robes in the wind. Then came a wail from the People beyond the ranks of the Kel.

Duncan stood still, lost; he saw, he heard, he watched the shifting of ranks: Niun also left him. He was forgotten in the confusion.

Men bore away the dead kel'anth, quietly, toward the desert. Soon enough came kel'ein bearing a bundle wrapped in white, and that shook Duncan's confidence: Sochil, he thought, hoping that he was right. How she had died, by whose hand, he had no means to tell. Many kel'ein attended that corpse away. Others spread black tents and made a camp.

And the wan sun sank, and the wind grew cold; Duncan stood, in twilight, at the camp's edge, and watched the return of the burial parties . . . sank down to sit finally, for his legs grew numb and he had no more strength to stand in the cold and the wind.

There was a breathing near him: soft-footed, the dusei, when they chose to be. He felt them, and they came and nosed at him, identifying him. One ventured away; he called it back, Niun's dus. It came and settled uneasily with him. He was glad of their presence, less lonely with them, less afraid.

And after full dark he saw a tall shadow come out of the camp, and saw the gleam of moonlight on bronze-hilted weapons and on the *zaidhe's* visor, and knew Niun even at great distance.

He rose. Niun beckoned, and he came, the dusei padding behind him.

There was no explanation, nothing. The dusei caught Niun's mood, that was still tense. They walked, they and the beasts, into the midst of the strange camp, into the largest of the tents.

Black-robes filled it, heads and bodies alike swathed in kel-cloth, veiled and expressionless; at one side was a small cluster of the eldest gold-robes, unveiled, and one ancient blue-robe, that sudden surmise told Duncan would be the kath'anth, senior of the Kath.

And one white, veilless figure seated at the end, that was Melein.

Golden skins, golden, membraned eyes, all alike—and only the beasts and himself were alien. Duncan walked the aisle Niun and the beasts made toward Melein, his heart beating in a lost, forlorn terror, for the dusei gathered the tension they felt and cast it back to him, and he forbade it to swell to rage: no enemies these, not now.

Nor friendly to him.

The dusei came to Melein's hand before they turned, as Niun took his place by her side and Duncan took the shadowed place behind her; the beasts began to pace back and forth, back and forth, eyeing the crowd with hostility scarcely contained.

"Yai!" Niun forbade them. The little one half-reared and came down again slowly, no play this time. The company did not flinch, but waves of fear were intense in their midst. The dusei snorted and came and settled between Niun and Duncan.

Hlil s'Sochil, in the front rank of the Kel, rose and unveiled; so did others. Hlil came bringing a handful of small gold objects, offered them into Niun's hands, and Niun unveiled and took them, bowed; there was an easier feeling in the company then.

J'tai. Honor medals—Merai's. Duncan listened, watched, as there came two kel'e'ein, a woman of years and another younger: to each Niun surrendered one of the *j'tai*—kinswomen of Merai, they were, proud and fierce: they touched Niun's hands, and bowed, and walked away, to settle again among their comrades.

More veils were put aside, all the Kel, eventually, yielding their faces to the sight of the Mother that had taken them.

Duncan kept his own, ashamed of his strangeness in this company, and hating his shame for it.

Kel'ein came, nine of them, old and young, to press the hand of Melein to their brows and give their names: Husbands, they proclaimed themselves, of Sochil.

"I accept you," Melein said, after all had done; and then she rose and touched Niun's arm. "This is born of a birth with me, and he is the she'pan's kel'en, and kel'anth over my Kel. Will any challenge?"

There was an inclining of heads, and no challenge.

And to Duncan's dismay, Melein took his hand, bringing him forward.

"There are no veils, Duncan," she whispered.

He dropped his, and even kel-discipline could not prevent the looks of shock.

"This is kel Duncan, Duncan-without-a-Mother. He is a friend of the People. That is my word. None will touch him."

Again heads inclined, less readily. Released, Duncan retreated into the shadows again and stood next the dusei. Challenge: if it came, Niun must answer it, would answer it. He was not competent for his own defense among them, Duncan-without-a-Mother, the man with no beginnings.

"And listen to me now," Melein said softly, settling again to her chair, the only furniture in the tent. "Listen and I will open a Dark to the understanding of my companions; tell me where you remember. These are the things that I know:

"That from this world came mri and elee and surai and kalath, and in the passing of years, the elee took the surai and kalath, and the mri lived in the shadow of the elee . . .

"That since An-ehon has stood, mri and elee knew the same cities, and shared . . .

"That the elee built and the mri defended.

"That as the sun faded and wealth declined, the ships went out. They were slow, those ships, but with them the mri took worlds. There was wealth . . .

"And war. *Zahen'ein* wars. Strangers' wars."

"This is so," said the Sen, and the Kel and the kath'anth murmured in astonishment.

"We would have made the folk of Kutath masters. The elee rejected us. Some mri rejected us. We continued the war. Whether we won or not, I do not know. Some of us stayed and some of us parted this world. Slow ships, and ages. Sometimes we fought. We took service with strangers eighty and more times. What we have seen in our returning . . . the track of People that went out, ja-anom, is desolation.

"We came home. We thought that we were the last, and we are not. Eighty-three Darks. Eighty-three. We are all that survive, of all the millions that went out."

"Ai," the People murmured, and eyes mirrored struggle to understand.

The eldest sen'en arose then, a man bent with age. "We have known Darks. That into which you went was one. That in which we remained was another. Tsi'mri came. We did not fall to them, and they did not come back. We had strength then, but it faded. No tsi'mri came again. And the cities died, and in the last years even the elee fought, elee against elee. It was a burden-bearer's war, and wasteful. We had a she'pan then named Gar'ai. She led us out into the mountains, where the elee could not live. Even then some of the People denied her Sight and would not come, and stayed in the elee cities, and died, fighting for bearers-of-burdens. Now the elee are fading, and we are strong. That is because we cannot be held in the hand. We are the land's wind, she'pan; we go and we come and the land is enough for us. We ask you, do not lead us back. There is no water enough for cities. The land will not bear it. We will perish if we leave it."

Melein was silent for a long moment, then swept a glance about the assembly. "From a land like this came we. We do not fold our hands and wait to die. That is not what the she'pan of my birth taught."

The words stung like a blow. Kel'ein straightened, and the sen'anth looked confused, and the kath'anth sat twisting her hands in her lap.

"Tsi'mri are following us," Melein said. "Armed."

The dusei surged to their feet. Duncan moved for them flung his arms about them both, whispering to them.

"What have you brought us?" cried the sen'anth.

"A thing that must be faced," Melein snapped, and bodies froze in the attitudes that they then occupied. "We are mri! We were attacked and challenged, and will this remnant deny that you are also mri, and that I am she'pan of this edun, and of all the People?"

"Kel'anth," breathed an old kel'en, "ask permission to ask . . . who, and when, and with what arms."

"I answer," said Niun. "The People have another chance. Another life. *Life* is coming across this desert of dead worlds. We have it in our wake, and it can be seized!"

Duncan heard, and clenched his fists the tighter on the dusei's loose skin, close to shivering in the fever-warmth of the tent. They had forgotten him. Their eyes were on Niun, on the stranger-kel'anth, on a she'pan that promised and threatened them.

Hope.

It glittered in the golden eyes of the black-robed Kel, ventured timidly into the calculating faces of the Sen. Only the old kath'en looked afraid.

"An-ehon has given me its records," Melein said. "I have poured into An-ehon and into all the cities linked with him the sum of all that the People have gathered in our wander-

ings. We are armed, my children. We are armed. We were
the last, my kel'anth and I. No more. No more. A last time
the Kel goes out, and this time we are not for hire. This time
we take no pay. This time is for ourselves."

"Ai-e!" cried one of the Kel, a shout that stirred the others
and tightened on Duncan's heart. Dus-feelings washed about
him, confused, threatening for his sake, stirred for Niun's.

Kel'ein came to their feet with a deafening shout, and the
sen'ein folded their arms and stood too, stern eyes gleaming
with calculation; and lastly the kath'anth rose, and tears
flowed on her face.

Tears for the children, Duncan thought, and something
welled up in his throat too.

"Strike the tents," Melein shouted. "We will rest a time in
the city, recover what we have left there, ask questions of
each other. Strike the tents."

The tent began to clear, rapidly; there were shouts in the
mu'ara of the ja'anom, orders conveyed.

And Niun stood watching their backs, and when Melein
had walked out into the night, Duncan rose and followed
with him, the dusei padding after.

Melein went apart from them, among the Sen. It was not a
place for kel'ein. Duncan stood shivering in the chill wind
and at last Niun drew him over to a clear space where they
could watch the tents come down, where they could breathe
easily.

The dusei crowded close to them, disturbed.

"Do not worry for yourself," Niun said to him suddenly.

"I do not."

"The killing," said Niun, "was bitter."

And he settled on the sand where they stood, with a mri's
disregard for furniture. Duncan knelt down beside him,
watched as Niun drew from his robes a folded cloth that held
the *j'tai* that he had received of Merai's death, watched as
Niun began to knot them to the belt that should hold them,
so that their cords let them hang freely in his robes.

Complicated knots. Mri knots. Niun's slender fingers wove
designs he had not yet mastered, meanings he had not yet
learned, intricacies for intricacy's sake.

He tried to think only of that, to shut from his mind what
he had seen in the tent, the shout that still echoed in his ears,
hundreds of voices lifted, and himself the enemy.

About them appeared blue-robes, striking the tent of assem-

bly, the oldest boys and girls taking the poles down, bearing
the brunt of the work, and the women and middle-years children aiding. Only the littlest children in their mothers' arms
sometimes raised a whimper in all the confusion, and the
little ones that could walk finally slipped discipline and began
a game of tag among their busy elders, uncomprehending
what changes had turned their world upside down.

"The Face that Smiles," said Niun of them. "Ah, Duncan,
it is good to see."

A cold closed about Duncan, a foreboding heavy as the
she'pan's alleged Sight . . . the children's voices in the dark
as the tent came down, laughter . . .

The towers that had fallen on Kesrith . . .

"Let me go back," Duncan said suddenly. "Niun, ask the
she'pan. Now, tonight, let me go back to the ship."

The mri turned, looked at him, a piercing and wondering
look. "Fear of us?"

"*For* you. For them."

"You left your markers. The she'pan has already said that
it was enough. She gave you her word on the matter. If you
go back, they will take you back, and we will not permit
that."

"Am I a prisoner?"

Niun's eyes nictitated. "You are kel'en of this Kel, and we
will not give you away. Do you wish to go back?"

For a moment Duncan could not answer. The children
shouted, laughed aloud, and he winced at the sound. "I am of
this Kel," he said at last. "And I could serve it best there."

"That is for the she'pan to decide, and she has already decided. If she wishes to send you, she will send."

"Better that. I am not wanted here. And I could be of use
there."

"I would die a death myself if harm came to you. Stay
close by me. No kel'en that has won the *seta'al* would challenge you, but the unscarred might . . . and no unscarred
will trespass with me. Put such thoughts out of your mind.
Your place is here, not there."

"It is not because I would run from them that I ask. It is
because of what I hear. Because you have not learned of all
that you have seen. Dead worlds, Niun."

"Sov-kela," said Niun, and his voice was edged, "have
care."

"You are preparing to fight."

"We are mri."

The beast beside him stirred. Duncan held to it, his blood pounding in his ears. "The survival of the species."

"Yes," said Niun.

"For that, you would—do what, Niun?"

"Everything."

There was long silence.

"Will you," asked Niun, "seek to go back to them?"

"I am at the she'pan's orders," he said at last. "With my own kind, I can be damned no more than I am. Only listen to me sometimes. Is it revenge you want?"

The mri's nostrils flared, rapid breathing, and his hands moved over the dus' velvet skin, long-fingered and oddly graceful. "Species survival. To gather the People. To have our homeworld. To be mri."

He was answered. The human in him would not understand it; but kel-law did . . . to be the sum of all things the mri had ever been, and that meant to be bound by nothing.

No agreements, no conditions, no promises.

And if it pleased the mri to strike, they would strike, for mri reasons.

Peace was four words in the hal'ari. There was *ai'a*, that was self-peace, being right with one's place; and *an'edi*, that was house-peace, that rested on the she'pan; and there was *kuta'i*, that was the tranquillity of nature; and there was *sa'ahan*, that was the tranquillity of strength.

Treaty-peace was a mu'ara word, and the mu'ara lay in the past, with the regul, that had broken it.

Melein had killed for power, would kill, repeatedly, to unite the People.

Would take the elee, their former allies.

Would take Kutath.

We will have ships, he could hear her saying in her heart.

And they knew the way, to Arain, to human and regul space.

It was not revenge they sought, nothing so human, but peace—*sa'ahan*-peace, that could only exist in a mri universe.

No compromise.

"Come," said Niun. "They are almost done. We will be moving now."

THE FADING SUN: SHON'JIR

...soon shut away, the hall was still, the People were
...ways
...enpassed hall.

Chapter Twenty-One

———•◉•———

THE HOUSE murmured with voices, adults' and children's. The
People stared about them, curious at this place that only
sen'ein had seen for so many hundreds of years . . . mar-
veling at the lights, the powers of it—and, mri-fashion, un-
amazed by them. The forces were there; they were to be used.
Many things were not for Kath or Kel to understand, but to
use, with permission.

And the Shrine held light again: lights were lit by Melein's
own hands, and the pan'en was brought and set there behind
the corroded screens, to be moved when they moved, to be
reverenced by the House while they stayed. There were chants
spoken, the Shon'jir of the mri that had gone out from
Kutath; and the An'jir of the mri that stayed on homeworld.

> *We are they that went not out:*
> *landwalkers, sky-watchers;*
> *We are they that went not out:*
> *world-holders, faith-keepers;*
> *We are they that went not out:*
> *and beautiful our morning;*
> *We are they that went not out:*
> *and beautiful our night.*

The rhythmic words haunted the air: the long night,
Duncan thought, standing at Niun's side . . . a folk that had
waited their end on dying Kutath.

Until Melein.

220

The songs sank away; the hall was still; the People went their ways.

There was kel-hall.

A long spiral up, a shadowed hall thrown into sudden light . . . the Kel spread carpets that had been the floors of their tents, still sandy: the cleaners skittered about in the outer hall, but stayed from their presence.

The Kel settled, made a circle. There was time for curiosity, then, in the privacy of the hall. Eyes wandered over Niun, over the dusei, over Duncan most of all.

"He will be welcomed," Niun said suddenly and harshly, answering unspoken thoughts.

There were frowns, but no words. Duncan swept a glance about the circle, meeting golden eyes that locked with his and did not flinch—without love, without trust, but without, he thought, outright hate. One by one he met such stares, let them look their fill; and he would have taken off the *zaidhe* too, and let them see the rest of his alienness; but to do so was demeaning, and insulting if offered in anger, a reproach to them. They could not ask it; it was the depth of insult.

A cup was passed, to Niun first, and to Duncan: water, of the blue pipe, in a brass cup. Duncan wet his lips with it, and passed it to Hlil, who was next. Hlil hesitated just the barest instant, as he might if he were expected to drink after the dusei; and then the kel'en touched his lips to it and passed it on.

One after the other drank in peace, even the kel'e'ein, the two kinswomen of Merai. There were no refusals.

Then Niun laid his longsword in Duncan's lap, and in curious and elaborate ceremony, all kel'ein likewise drew, and the *av'ein-kel*, Duncan's as well, passed from man and woman about the circle until each held his own again.

Then each spoke his name in full, one after the other. Some had names of both parents; some had only Sochil's; and Duncan, glancing down, gave his, Duncan-without-a-Mother, feeling curiously lost among these folk who knew what they were.

"The kel-ritual," said Niun when that had been done, "is still the same."

It pleased them, perhaps, to know that this was true; there was gestured agreement.

"You will teach us," said Niun, "the mu'ara of home-world."

"Aye," said Hlil readily.

There was a long silence.

"One part of the ritual that I know," said Niun, "I do not hear."

Hlil bit his lip . . . a man of scars more than the *seta'al*, Hlil s'Sochil, rough-faced for a mri, who were slender and fine-boned. "Our Kath—our Kath is frightened of this—" Hlil stopped short of *tsi'mri*, and glanced full at Duncan.

"Do you," Niun asked in a hard voice, "wish to make a formal statement of this?"

"We are concerned," Hlil said, glancing down.

"We."

"Kel'anth," said Hlil, scarcely audible, "it is your right, and his."

"No," Duncan said softly, but Niun affected not to hear; Niun looked about him, waiting.

"The Kath will make you welcome," said one of the old kel'e'ein.

"The Kath will make you welcome," others echoed then, and last of all, Hlil.

"So," said Niun, and arose—waited for Duncan, while others stayed seated, and Duncan sought any other point but the eyes that stared at them.

The dusei would have come. Niun forbade.

And the two of them went alone from kel-hall, and down the ramp. It was late, in the last part of the night. Duncan felt cold, and dreaded the meeting to which they went: the Kath, the women and the children of the House, and—perhaps, he hoped, only ceremony, only ritual, in which he could remain silent and unnoticed.

They ascended kath-tower; the kath'anth met them at the door. Silently she led them within, where exhausted children sprawled on their mats and carpets, and some few of the older ones, male and female, sleepless in the excitement of the night, stared at them from the shadows.

They came to a door in a narrow hall: "Go in," the kath'anth said to Duncan; he did, and found it spread with carpets, and nothing more. The door closed; Niun and the kath'anth had left him there, in that dim chamber, lit with an oil lamp.

He settled then, in a corner, apprehensive at the first, and conscious finally that he was cold and sleepy, and that perhaps the kath'ein would abhor him and would not come at

all. It was a bitter thought; but it was better than the trouble
that he foresaw. He wished only to be let alone, and perhaps
to sleep the night out, and not to be questioned after.

And the door opened.

A blue-robe stepped inside, bearing a small tray of food
and drink; the door closed without her effort, and she
brought the offering—knelt down to set it before him, and
the cups rattled loudly on the tray. She wore no veil, not
even on her mane; she was of about his years, and from what
he could see of her downcast face in the lamplight, she was
lovely.

Tears rolled down her cheeks, forced by a blink.

"Were you made to come?" he asked.

"No, kel'en." She lifted her face, and gentle as it was, there
was stubborn pride in it. "It is my time, and I did not decline
it."

He thought of it, of trying to deal with her, and the
coldness stayed in him. "It would be bitter. Would it offend
the Kath if we only sat and talked?"

Golden eyes wandered his face, through a sheen of tears.
The membrane flashed, clearing them.

"Would it offend?" he asked again.

Pride. Mri honor. He saw the war in her eyes, suspecting
offense, suspecting kindness. He had seen that wariness often
enough in Niun's eyes.

"No," she agreed, smoothing her skirts; and after a moment she tilted her head and firmed her chin. "My son will
call you father, all the same."

"I do not understand."

She looked puzzled, as much as he. "I mean that I shall
not make it public what you wish. My son's name is Ka'aros,
and he has five years. It is a courtesy, do you not understand?"

"Are we—permanent?"

She laughed outright despite herself, and her laugh was
gentle and the sudden touch of her hand on his was pleasant.
"Kel'en, kel'en . . . no. My son has twenty-three fathers."
Her face grew sober again, and wistfully so. "I shall make
you comfortable at least. Will you sleep, kel'en?"

He nodded mri-fashion, bewildered and weary and finding
this offer the least burdensome. Her gentle fingers eased the
zaidhe from him, and she stared in shock at the manner of
his hair that, although he had let it grow shoulder-length,

mri-fashion, was not the coarse bronze mane of her kind. She touched it, unbound by the formalities of kel-caste, tugged a lock between her fingers, discovered the shape of his ears and was amazed by that.

And from the covered wooden dish on her tray she took a fragrant damp cloth, and carefully, carefully bathed his face and hands—it was easement for the sandburns and the sunburn; and he loosed his robes at her insistence, and lay down, her knees for his pillow. She spread his robes over him and softly caressed his brow, so that he felt distant from all the world, and it was very easy to let go.

He did not wish to: treacheries occurred to him, murder—he strove to stay awake, not to show his distrust, but all the same, not to slip beyond awareness what passed.

But he did drift for a moment, and wakened in her arms, safe. He caressed her cradling arm, slowly, sleepily, until he looked into her golden eyes and remembered that he had promised not to touch her.

He took his hand away.

She bent and touched her lips to his brow, and this disturbed him.

"If I came back another night," he said, for the time was short, and there suddenly seemed a thousand things he wished to know of the Kath—of this kath'en, who was gracious to a tsi'mri, "if I came back again, could I ask for you?"

"Any kel'en may ask."

"May *I* ask?"

She understood then, and looked embarrassed, and distressed—and he understood, and forced a smile.

"I shall not ask," he said.

"It would be shameless of me to say that you might."

Then he was utterly confused, and lay staring up at her.

A soft, lilting call rang out somewhere in kath-hall.

"It is morning," she said, and began to seek to leave. She arose when he sat up, and started for the door.

"I do not know your name," he said, getting to his feet— human courtesy.

"Kel'en, it is Sa'er."

And she performed a graceful gesture of respect and left him.

He regretted, then, that he had declined . . . regretted, with a curious sense of anticipation . . . that perhaps, on some other night, things would be different.

Sa'er: it was like the word for morning. It was appropriate.

His thoughts wrenched back to Elag/Haven, to rough and careless times, and next Sa'er, the memory was ugly.

One did not, he knew in all the principles of kel-law, hurt a kath'en, either child or woman. There was in him a deep certainty that he had done in this meeting what was right to do.

And there was in him increasing belief that she would not, as she had said, breach confidence; would not make little of him with others; would not come next time with tears, but with a smile for him.

Cheerful in that thought, he settled to the carpets and put his boots on, gathered his robes about him, and his belts and weapons, that he had put aside: rising, he put them to rights; and put on the *zaidhe*, that was more essential to modesty than the robes; but the *mez* he flung across his throat and over his shoulder.

Then he went out into the hall, and flushed hot with sudden embarrassment, for there was Niun, at the same moment, and he hoped that kel reticence would prevent questions.

The mri, he thought, looked well-content.

"Was it well with you?" Niun asked.

He nodded.

"Come," said Niun. "There is a courtesy to be done."

Kath-hall looked different under day-phase lighting. The mats were cleared away, and the children scurried about madly at their coming, ran each to a kath'en, and with amazing swiftness a line formed, guiding them to the door.

First was the kath'anth, who stood alone, and took Niun's hands together and smiled at him. "Tell the Kel that we do not understand the machines in this place, but there will be dinner."

"Perhaps I could assist with the machines," Duncan suggested when the kath'anth took his hands in turn; and the kath'anth laughed, and so did Niun, and all the kath'ein that heard.

"He or I might," Niun said, covering his embarrassment with grace. "We have many skills, he and I."

"If the Kel would deign," said the kath'anth.

"Send when we are needed," said Niun.

And they passed from her to the line of kath'ein; Niun went first and gravely took the hands of a certain kath'en, bowed to her and took the hands of her little daughter and performed the same ritual.

Duncan understood then, and went to Sa'er, and did the same; and took the hand of her son as the boy offered his, wrist to wrist as men touched.

"He is kel Duncan," said Sa'er to her son, and to Duncan: "He is Ka'aros."

The child stared, wide-eyed with a child's honesty, and did not return Duncan's shy smile. Sa'er nudged the boy. "Sir," he said, and the membrane flicked across his eyes. He did not yet have the adult's mane: his was short and revealed his ears, that were tipped with a little curl of transparent down.

"Good day," said Sa'er, and smiled at him.

"Good day," he wished her; and joined Niun, who waited at the door. Silence reigned in the hall. They left, and then he heard a murmuring of voices after them, knowing that questions were being asked.

"I liked her," he confessed to Niun. And then further confession: "We did nothing."

Niun shrugged, and put on his veil. "It is important that a man have good report of the Kath. The kath'en was more than gracious in the parting. Had you offended her, she would have made that known, and that would have hurt you sorely in the House."

"I was surprised that you took me there."

"I had no choice. It is always done. I could not bring you into the Kel like a kel'e'en, without this night."

Duncan tucked in his own veil, and breathed easier to know himself well-acquitted. "Doubtless you were worried."

"You are kel'en; you have learned to think as we think. I am not surprised that you chose a resting-night. It was wise, And," he added, "if you send the kath'en the *ka'islai*, and she does not return them, then you must go and fetch them."

"Is that how it is done?"

Niun laughed, a soft breath. "So I have heard. I myself am naïve in such matters."

They came to main hall, and Duncan went behind Niun as he paid his morning respects at the shrine; he stood silently there, thinking strangely of a place in his childhood, sensing in another part of his thoughts a dus that was fretting and impatient, confined in kel-hall.

And of a sudden came the machine-voice, An-ehon, deep and thundering through all the halls, through stone and flesh:

Alarm . . . alarm . . . ALARM.

He froze, dazed, as Niun thrust past him. "Stay here!"
Niun shouted at him, and rushed for sen-hall access, where a
kel'en had no business to be. Duncan stopped in mid-step—
cast about left and right, saw other kel'ein rushing down from
kel-tower; and there were kath'ein; and Melein herself,
descending from the tower of the she'pan, seeking sen-access
at a near-run amid the frightened questions that were thrown
at her.

"Let me come!" Duncan cried at her, overtaking her, and
she did not forbid him. He followed her up, up into sen-hall,
where alarmed sen'ein boiled about like disturbed insects,
gold about Niun's black, who stood before An-ehon's flickering lights—who questioned it, and obtained screens lighted
with pictures the rudest kel'en could understand: the desert,
and a dying glow in a rising cloud on the far horizon.

The ship.

Melein thrust her way through the sen'ein, that crowded
from her path, and the while she laid hands on the panels her
eyes were for the screens. Duncan tried to follow her, but the
sen'ein caught at him, thrust out their hands in his path, forbidding.

"Strike was made from orbit," An-ehon droned, the while
the mad alarm dinned from another channel.

"Strike back," Melein ordered.

"*No!*" Duncan shouted at her. But An-ehon's flicker-swift
reaction showed a line of retaliation plotted, intersecting orbit.

Lines flashed rapidly, perspectives shifting.

"Unsuccessful," An-ehon droned.

And the panels all flared, and the air filled with sound that
began too deep to hear and finished like thunder. The floor,
the very foundations shook.

"Attack has been returned," said An-ehon. "Shields have
held."

"Stop it," Duncan shouted, pushed sen'ein brutally aside
and broke through to Melein, stopped when Niun himself
thrust a hand in his way. "Listen to me. That will be a class-
one warship up there. You cannot beat it from earthside. We
have no ship now, no way out—do not answer fire. They can
make a cinder of this world. Let me call them, let me contact
them, she'pan."

Melein's eyes were terrible as they met his: suspicion, anger . . . in that moment he was alien, and close to the edge of her rage.

The thunder came again. The mri held their sensitive ears, and Melein shouted another order for attack.

"Target is passing out of range," An-ehon said when the noise had faded. "Soon coming up over Zohain. Zohain will attack."

"You cannot fight it," Duncan shouted at them, and seized Niun's arm, received from the mri a look that matched Melein's. "Niun, make her see. Your shielding will not go on holding. Let me call them."

"You see what good your signal from the ship did," said Niun. "That is their answer to your signal of friendship. That is their word on it."

"Zohain has fallen," said An-ehon. "Shields did not hold. I am receiving alarm from Le'a'haen . . . There is another attack approaching this zone. Alarm . . . alarm . . . ALARM . . . ALARM. . . ."

"Get your people out!" Duncan shouted at them.

Terror was written in the eyes of Melein and Niun, nightmare repeated: the floor shook. There was a rumbling crash outside the edun.

"Go!" Melein cried. "The hills, seek the hills!"

But she did not, nor Niun, while the Sen broke for the door, for outside, abandoning possessions, everything. Even over the sounds of An-ehon cries could be heard elsewhere in the edun.

"Get out, get out—both of you," Duncan pleaded. "Wait for a break in the attack and get out of here. Let me try with the machine."

Melein turned to Niun, ignoring him. "Kel'anth, lead your people." And before Niun could move, she looked up at the banks that were An-ehon. "Continue to fight. Destroy the invaders."

"This city is holding," droned the machine. "Outer structures may be drained of shielding to protect the edun complex. When this city falls, there are others. We are coordinating defenses. We are under multiple attack. We advise immediate evacuation. We advise the she'pan to secure her person. Preservation of her person is of overriding importance."

"I am leaving," Melein said; and to Duncan, for Niun had gone: "Come. Haste."

He thrust past her, to the console. "An-ehon," he said, "give me communication—"

"Do not permit it!" Melein shouted, and the machine struck, a force that lit the air and hurled him numb and cold against the floor.

He saw her robes pass him, and she was running, running, down the center of sen-hall, with the floor shuddering under renewed attack . . . it shook beneath him, and he tried repeatedly to gather his numbed limbs under him.

The floor bucked.

"Alarm . . . ALARM . . . ALARMLLL . . ." cried An-ehon.

He rolled his head, dragged a shoulder over, saw areas of the banks going dark.

And the floor shook again, and the lights began dimming.

There was a time of quiet.

He found it possible finally to move his legs, arms, to drag himself up, and he staggered through littered sen-hall into the winding corridor down to main hall. A great shadow met him there, his dus, that almost threw him off his feet in the pressure of its body: he used it then, leaning on it, and staggered past the litter that confused the hall, and out into the light, the open city—there began to see the dead, old sen'ein, children of the Kath—a kel'en, crushed by a toppling wall.

He found Sa'er, a huddled shape in blue at the bottom of the ramp, a golden hand clenched about a stone, a face open-eyed and dusty with the sand of Kutath.

"Ka'aros!" he called with all the strength in him, remembering her son, and there was no answer.

The People's trail was marked with dead, the old, the fragile, the young: all that was gentle, he thought, everything.

He heard a sound of thunder, looked up and saw a flash, a mote of light. Something operating in-atmosphere. He expected, even while he ran with all the speed that was in him, the white flash that would kill him, as he left the protective zone.

But it went over the horizon. The sound died.

Beyond the city, beyond the pitiful ruin, there stretched a line of figures, alive and moving. He made haste to follow, desperate, exhausted. The dus moved with him, blood-feelings stirred in it, that caught up his rage and fear and cast it back amplified.

He overtook the last of the column finally, his throat dry, his lungs wracked with coughing. Blood poured from his nose and tasted salt-coppery in his mouth.

"The kel'anth?" he asked. A narrow-eyed kel'e'en pointed toward the head of the column. "The she'pan?" he asked again. "Is she well?"

"Yes," one said, as if to answer him at all were contamination.

He kept moving at more than their pace, seeking the column's head, passed kel'ein that carried kath-children, and kath'ein that carried infants, and kel'ein that supported old ones of any caste, though few enough of the old were left them.

They went toward the mountains, that promised concealment, as they were pitifully exposed on this bare, naked sand. He saw the line extended over the roll of the land, and it seemed yet impossibly far, beyond his strength at the pace he tried. He paused, cut a bit of pipe that was left as a stub from someone else's cutting, a prize that was seen by others too, and he offered them of his, but none would deign to touch it. Leaving the rest to them, he sucked the water from a sliver and managed simply to keep his feet under him and to stay with the middle of the column—outside it, for he felt their hatred, the looks that the Sen cast him.

He had betrayed himself before the Sen; they knew, they had seen the nature of him, and whence he was they guessed . . . if not what. They could not know the reason that they were attacked, but that they were mri, and that the tsi'mri invaded, and they were dying at such hands as his.

No attack came on them. He was not amazed by it, for there was little inclination for a large orbiting craft to waste its energies on so small a target as they made. But the city came under periodic fire. They could look back and see it, the shields flaring rainbow colors under the rainless sun, and the whole of the city settling into increasing ruin. The city that had stood dreamlike against the setting sun itself glowed and died like embers, and the towers were down, and ugliness settled over it.

"A-ei," mourned an old kath'en. "A-ei."

And the children wept fretfully, and were hushed.

The Sen shook their heads, and there were tears on the faces of the old ones.

From the Kel there were no tears, only looks that burned, that raged. Duncan turned his face from them, and kept moving at such times as the column rested, until at last he had sight of Melein's white robes, and he knew the tall kel'en by her, with the dus.

They were well; that was enough to know, to take from him some of the anguish. He kept them in sight for the rest of that day, and when they at last paused at evenfall, he came to them.

Niun knew his presence. The dus went first, and Niun turned, looking for his approach.

Duncan settled quietly near them.

"You are all right?" Niun asked him.

He nodded.

Melein turned her face from him. "Doubtless," she said finally, "your wish was good, Duncan; I believe that. But it was useless."

"She'pan," he murmured with a gesture of reverence, grateful even for that; he forbore to argue with her: among so many dead, argument had no place.

Niun offered him a bit of pipe. He showed his, and declined, and with his *av-tlen*, cut off a bit of it that was sickly sweet in his mouth. There was a knot at his stomach that would not go away.

A cry went up from the Kel. Hands pointed. What looked like a shooting star went over, and descended toward the horizon.

"Landing," Duncan murmured, "near where the ship was. There will be a search now."

"Let them come into the mountains looking," said Niun.

Duncan put a hand to his stomach, and coughed, and wiped his eyes of the pain-tears. He found himself shaking.

He also knew what had to be done.

He rested. In time he made excuse, a modest sort of shrug that denoted a man on private business, and rose and moved away from the column; the dus followed him. He was afraid. He tried to keep that feeling down, for the dus could transmit that. He saw the desert before him, and felt the weakness of his own limbs, and the terror came close to overwhelming him, but he had no other options.

The dus suddenly sent a ward-impulse, turned.

He looked back, saw the other dus.

There was a black shadow a distance to the side of it. Duncan froze, remembering that Niun, like him, had a gun.

Niun walked across the sand toward him, a black shape in the dark. The wind fluttered at his robes, the moon winked on the brass of the *yin'ein* and the plastic of the visor, and on the *j'tai* that he had gained. The great dus walked at his side, turn-toed, head down.

"Yai," Duncan cautioned his, made it sit beside him.

Niun stopped at talking distance, set hand in belt, a warning. "You have strayed the column widely, sov-kela."

Duncan nodded over his shoulder, toward the horizon. "Let me go."

"To rejoin them?"

"I still serve the she'pan."

Niun looked at him long and closely, and finally dropped his veil. Duncan did the same, wiped at the blood that began to dry on his lips.

"What will you do?" Niun asked.

"Make them listen."

Niun made a gesture that spoke of hopelessness. "It has already failed. You throw yourself away."

"Take the People to safety. Let me try this. Trust me in this, Niun."

"We will not surrender."

"I know that. I will tell them so."

Niun looked down. His slender fingers worked at one of the several belts. He freed one of the *j'tai*, came toward Duncan, stood and patiently knotted the thong in a complicated knot.

Duncan looked at it when he had done, found a strange and delicate leaf, one of the three *j'tai* that Niun had had from Kesrith.

"It was given me by one of my masters, a man named Palazi, who had it from a world named Guragen. Trees grew there. For luck, he said. Good-bye, Duncan."

He gave his hand.

Duncan gave his. "Good-bye, Niun."

And the mri turned from him, and walked away, the one dus following.

Duncan watched him meet the shadow, and vanish, and

himself turned and started on the course that he had plotted, the sand and rocks distorted in his vision for a time. He resumed the veil, grateful for the warmth of the beast that walked beside him.

Chapter Twenty-Two

───◆◈◆───

BEAST MIND, beast sense. It protected. Duncan inhaled the cold air carefully and staggered as he came down the gentle rise—an ankle almost twisted: death in the flats. He took his warning from that and rested, leaned against the dus as he settled to the cold sands and let the fatigue flow from his joints. A little of the blue-green pipe remained in his belt-pouch. He drew his *av-tlen* and cut a bit of it, chewed at it and felt its healing sweetness ease his throat.

It was madness to have tried it, he had to realize in the burning days, madness to have imagined that he could make the wreckage in time, that they would have stayed where there was no life.

But there was no choice. He was nothing among the People, but a problem that Niun did not need, an issue over which he might have to kill; a problem to Melein, who must explain him.

He served the she'pan.

There was no question of this in him now: if he walked and found nothing, still it only proved that his own efforts were worth nothing, as those of An-ehon had been nothing, and the burden passed: the she'pan had other kel'ein.

He gathered himself and began to walk again, staggered as the dus suddenly lurched against him with a snarl. He blinked in dull amazement as a cloud of sand puffed up from the side of a rock and something ran beneath the sand, not like a burrower's fluttering broad mantle, but something lithe and narrow that—like the burrower—dug a small pit, a funnel of sand.

"Yai," he called hoarsely, restraining the dus, that would

have gone for it and dug it into the light with its long venomed claws. Whatever was there, he did not know the size of
it, or its dangers. He caught the hunt-sense from the dus, put
it down with his own will, and they skirted the area, climbed
up the near ridge. When he looked down, he saw all the area
dotted with such small pits. There was regularity about them,
like points on concentric circles. They formed a configuration
wide enough to embrace a dus.

"Come," he wished the beast, and they moved, the dus giving small, dissatisfied whuffs, still desiring to go back.

But of other presence there had been no sign. There
was the cold and the wind and the streaming light of Na'i'in;
there was the track of their own passing swiftly obliterated by
the wind, and once, only once, a tall black figure on a dune-
crest.

One of the kel'ein, an outrunner of the People, another
band, perhaps, insolently letting himself be seen. Duncan had
felt exposed at that, felt his lack of skill with the *yin'ein* . . .
the unknown under the sand did not frighten him half so
much as the thought of encounter with others.

—Of encountering a she'pan other than Melein. It was, he
thought, a mri sort of fear—a hesitance to break out of that
familiarity which was Melein's law. With that fear, with mri
canniness, he kept to the low places, the sides, the conceal-
ments available in the land, and his eyes, dimmed by his lowered visor, carefully scanned the naked horizons when he
must again venture across the flat.

The great rift of the lost sea came into view at noontime.
He looked away into that hazy depth where sand ribboned off
into the chasm in wind-driven falls, and lost his sense of
height and depth in such dimensions. But scanning the horizon, he knew where he was, that was not far from the place
he sought.

He kept moving, and by now the lack of solid food had his
stomach knotting. The ache in his side was a constant
presence, and that in his chest beat in time with the ebb and
flow of his life.

Dus.

He felt it, and looked up as if someone had called his
name. *Niun?* he wondered, looking about him, and yet did
not believe it. Niun was with the People; he would not have
deserted Melein, or those in his charge. There were the Kath

and the Sen, that could not make such a trek as he had made, kel'en and unencumbered.

Yet the dus-feeling was there.

Left. Right. He scanned those horizons, stroked the velvet rolls of flesh on the neck of his own beast, sent question to its mind. Ward-impulse went out from it.

No illusion, then.

With his nape hairs prickling he kept moving, constantly aware of that weight against his senses.

Brother-presence.

Dus-brother.

The dus beside him began to sing a song of contentment, of harmony, that stole the pain and stole his senses, until he realized that he had walked far and no longer knew the way he walked.

No, he projected at it, *no, no, no*. He thought of the ship, thought of it again and again, and desired, urged toward it.

Affirmation.

And threat.

Darkness came then, sudden and soft and deep, and full of menace, claws that tore and fangs that bit and over it all a presence that would not let him go. He came to awareness again still walking, shivering periodically in the dry, cold wind. His hands and arms were sandburned and bloody, so that he knew that he had fallen hard at some time and not known.

Ship, he thought at the beast.

Hostile senses surrounded him. He cried out at the dark and it thrust itself across his path, stopping him. He stood shuddering as it rubbed round his legs, vast, heavy creature that circled him and wove a pattern of steps.

Others came, two, five, six dusei, a third the size of the one that wove him protection. He shuddered in horror as they came near and surrounded him, as one after another they reared up man-tall and came down again, making the sand fly in clouds.

There was a storm-feeling in the air, a sense charged and heavy with menace.

Storm-friends, the mri called them, the great brothers of the cold wind.

And none such had been known on arid Kutath, no such monsters had this world known.

They have come here of their own purpose, Duncan

thought suddenly, cold, and frightened. He remembered them entering the ship, remembered them, whose hearts he had never reached, living with them on the long voyage.

A refuge from humans, from regul. They had fled their world. They chose a new one, the escape that had lain open for them, that he had provided.

Closer they came, and his dus radiated darkness. Bodies touched, and a numbing pulse filled the air, rumbling like a windsound or like earthquake. They circled, all circled, touching. Duncan flung himself to his knees and put his arms about the neck of his beast, stopping it, feeling the nose of a stranger-dus at the nape of his neck, smelling the hot breath of the beast, heat that wrapped and stifled him.

Ship, he remembered to think at them, and cast the disaster of An-ehon with his mind, the towers of Kesrith falling. Pleasure came back, appalling him.

No! he cried, silently and aloud. They fled back from him.

He cast them images of waterless waste, of a sun dying, of dusei wasting in desolation.

Their anger flooded at him, and his own beast shuddered, and drew back. It fled, and he could not hold it.

He was alone, desolate and blind. Suddenly he did not know direction or world-sense. His senses were clear, ice-clear, and yet he was cut off and without that inner direction that he had known so long.

"Come back," he cried at the dus that lingered.

He cast it edun-pictures, of water flowing, of Kesrith's storms, and ships coming and going. Whether it received on this level he did not know. He cast it desire, desperate desire, and the image of the ship.

There was a touch, tentative, not the warding impulse.

"Come," he called it aloud, held out his hands to it. He cast it fellowship, mri-wise—together, man and dus.

Life, he cast it.

There was hesitance. The warding impulse lashed fear across his senses, and he would not accept it. *Life*, he insisted.

It came. All about him he felt warding impulse, strong and full of terrors, such that the sweat broke out on him and dried at once in the wind. But his dus was there. It began to walk with him, warding with all its might.

Traitor to its kind. Traitor human and traitor dus. He had

corrupted it, and it served him, went with him, began to be as he was.

Fear cast darkness about them and the afternoon sun seemed dimmer for a time; and then the others were gone, and there appeared finally black dots along a distant ridge, watching.

Children of Kutath, these dusei, flesh of the flesh that had come from Kesrith, and partaking not at all of it.

Only the old one remembered—not events, but person, remembered him, and stayed.

By late afternoon the wind began rising, little gusts at first that skirled the sand off the dune crests and swept out in great streamers over the dead sea chasm. Then came the flurries of sand that rode on battering force, that made walking difficult, that rattled off the protective visor and made Duncan again wrap the *mez* doubled about his face. The dus itself walked half-blind, tear-trails running down its face. It moaned plaintively, and in sudden temper reared up, shook itself, blew dust and settled again to walk against the wind.

The others appeared from time to time, walking the ridges, keeping their pace. They appeared as dark shadows in the curtain of sand that rode the wind, materialized as now a head and now less, or a retreating flank. What they sent was still hostile, and full of blood.

Duncan's beast growled and shook its head, and they kept moving, though it seemed by now his limbs were hung with lead and his muscles laced with fire. He coughed, and blood came, and he became conscious of the weight of the weapons that he bore, weapons that were useless where he was bound, and more useless still were he dead, but he would not give them up. He clenched in one hand the sole *j'tal* he wore, and remembered the man that had given it, and would not be less.

Su-she'pani kel'en. The she'pan's kel'en.

Pain lanced up his leg. He fell, cast down by the treacherous turn of stone, carefully gathered himself up again and leaned on the dus. The leg was not injured. He tried to suck at the wound the stone had made on his hand, but his mouth was dry and he could not. There was no pipe hereabouts. He hoarded what moisture he had and chose not to use the little supply that remained to him, not yet.

And one of the lesser dusei came close to him, reared up

so that his own interposed its body. There was a whuffing of great lungs, and the lesser backed off.

Ship, he thought suddenly, and for no reason.

Desire.

There was no warding impulse from the stranger. He felt only direction, sensed presence.

He called to his dus, softly, from a throat that had almost forgotten sound, and went, felt a presence at his left side, a warm breathing on the hand that hung beside him.

Doubly attended now he went. Another was with them, thought of destination, desired what they desired.

Men.

Shapes wandered his subconscious. Memory, no. Some elsewhere saw, cast vision, guided him. He knew this.

Shapes obscured in sand, a half-dome. Jaws closed on his hand, gently, gently . . . he realized that he was down, and that the dus urged him. He gathered himself up again and started moving, staggered as his boot hit something buried and something whipped at the leather, but it did not penetrate, and whipped sinuously away in the amber murk. Dus-feelings raged at it, and ignored it thereafter, preferring his company.

Night was on them, storm-night and world-night, friendly to them, hiding them. He knew the ship near, stumbled on pieces of it, bits of wreckage, bits of heat-fused sand, before its alien hulk took shape in the ribbons of sand, and he saw the havoc that had been made there.

And a half-dome, squat half-ovoid on stilts, the red wink of lights beaconing through the murk.

Dusei ringed him, all of them; fear-desire-fear, they sent.

"Yai!" he cried at them, voice lost in the wind. But his stayed, plodded its turn-toed way beside him as he walked toward that place, that alien shape on Kutath's dead seashore.

He knew it as he came near, vast and blind as it was, knew the patterning of its lights—

And for an instant he did not know how to name it.

Flower.

The word for it came back, a shifting from reality to reality.

"*Flower*," he hailed it, a cracked and unrecognizable voice in the living wind. "*Flower*—open your hatch."

But nothing responded. He gathered up a fist-sized stone

and threw it against the hull, and another, and nothing answered. The storm grew, and he knew that he had soon to seek shelter.

And then he saw the sweep of a scanner eye, and light followed it, fixing him and the dus together in its beam. The beast shied and protested. He flung his arm up to shield his visored eyes, and stood still, mind flung back to another night when he had stood with this dus in the lights, before guns.

There was long silence.

"*Flower!*" he cried.

The lights stayed fixed. He stood swaying in the gusts of wind, and held one hand firm against the dus' back so that the beast would stand.

Suddenly the hatch parted and the ramp shot down, invitation.

He walked toward it, set foot on the ringing metal, and the dus stayed beside him. He lifted his hands, lest they mistake, and moved slowly.

"Boz," he said.

It was strange to see her, the gray suddenly more pronounced in her hair, reminding him of time that had passed. He was conscious of the guns that surrounded him, of men that held rifles trained on him and on the dus. He took off the *mez* and *zaidhe*, so that they might know him. He smoothed his hair, that he had let grow: there was the stubble of beard on his face, that no mri would have. He felt naked before them, before Boaz and Luiz. He looked at their faces, saw dismay mirrored in their eyes.

"We've contacted *Saber*," Luiz said. "They want to see you."

He saw the hardness in their looks: he had run, taken the enemy side; this, not even Boaz was prepared to understand.

And they had seen the mri track, the desert of stars.

"I will go," he said.

"Put off the weapons," said Liuz, "and put the dus outside."

"No," he said quietly. "You would have to take those, and the beast stays with me."

It was clear that there were men prepared to move on him. He stood quietly, felt the dus' ward impulse, and the fear that was thick in the room.

"There are arguments you could make in your defense,"

Boaz said. "None of them are worth anything if you make trouble now. Sten, what side are you playing?"

He thought a moment. Human language came with difficulty, a strange, déjà-vu reference in which he knew how to function, but distantly, distantly. There were ideas that refused clear shaping. "I won't draw my weapons unless I'm touched," he said. "Let *Saber* decide. Take me there. *Peace*." He found the word he had lost for a time. "It's peace I bring if they'll have it."

"We'll consult," said Luiz.

"We can lift and consult later. Time is short."

Boaz nodded slowly. Luiz looked at her and agreed. Orders were passed with gestures, and a man left.

"Where are the others?" Luiz asked.

Duncan did not answer. Slowly, carefully, lest they misinterpret any move, he began to resume the *zaidhe*, which made him more comfortable. And while Luiz and Boaz consulted together, he put back the veil, and adjusted it to the formal position. The dus stood beside him, and the men with guns remained in their places.

But elsewhere in the ship came the sound of machinery at work—preparation for lift, he thought, and panic assailed him. He was a prisoner; they had him back, and doors had closed that he could not pass.

Warning lights began to flash in the overhead. He looked about apprehensively as another three regulars came into the compartment, rifles leveled at him, and Luiz left.

"Sit down," Boaz advised him. "Sit down over there and steady that beast for lift. Will it stay put?"

"Yes." He retreated to the cushioned bench and settled there, leaned forward to keep his hand on the dus that sat at his feet.

Boaz delayed, looking down at him: blonde, plump Boaz, who had grown thinner and grayer, whose face had acquired frown lines—wondering now, he thought, and not understanding.

"You speak with an accent," she said.

He shrugged. Perhaps it was true.

The warning siren sounded. They were approaching lift. Boaz went to the opposite side of the room, to the bench there; the regulars with their guns clustered there, weapons carefully across laps. The dus lay down at Duncan's feet, as the stress began, flattening itself to bear it.

The lift was hard, reckless. Duncan felt sweat breaking from him and his head spinning as they lofted. The dus sent fear . . . afraid, Duncan thought, of these men with guns. The fear turned his hands cold, and yet the heat of the compartment was stifling.

It was long before they broke from the force of lift, before new orientation took over and it was possible to move again. Duncan sat still, not willing to provoke them by attempting to rise. He desired nothing of them. Boaz sat still and stared at him.

"Stavros did this to you," she said finally, with a look of pity.

Again he shrugged, and kept his eyes unfixed and elsewhere, lost in waiting.

"Sten," she said.

He looked at her, distressed, knowing that she wanted response of him, and it was not there. "He is dead," he said finally, to make her understand.

There was pain in her eyes: comprehension, perhaps.

"I feel no bitterness," he said, "Boz."

She bit at her lips and sat white-faced, staring at him.

Luiz called; there was an exchange not audible to him, and the regulars stood by with lowered guns, kept them constantly trained on him. He sat and stroked the dus and soothed it.

The guards sweated visibly. To confront a disturbed dus took something from a man. They were steady. There was no panic. Boaz sat and mopped at her face.

"We're some little time from rendezvous," she said. "Do you want some water or something to eat?"

It was the first offering of such. A slight hesitation still occurred to him, consciousness that there was obligation involved, had they been mri.

Here too, obligation.

"If it is set before me," he said, "free, I will take it."

It was. Boaz ordered, and a guard set a paper cup of water within reach on the bench, and a sandwich wrapped in plastics. He took the water, held it under the *mez* to sip at it slowly. It was ice-cold and strange after days on the desert water: antiseptic.

Likewise he tore off bits of the sandwich with his fingers and ate, without removing his veil. He would not give his face for their curiosity. He had no strength to sit and trade hate with them, and the veil saved questions. His hands shook, all the same. He tried to prevent it, but it was weakness: he had been too long without more than the pipe for nourishment. His stomach rebelled at more than a few bites. He wrapped the remainder in the plastic again and tucked it into his belt-pouch, saving it against need.

And he folded his hands and waited. He was tired, inexpressibly tired. In the long monotony of approach he wished to sleep, and did so, eyes shut, hands folded, knowing that the dus watched balefully those others that occupied the compartment, watching him.

Boaz came and went. Luiz came and offered—a sincere offer, Duncan reckoned—to give him treatment for the cough that sometimes wracked him.

"No," he said softly. "Thank you, no."

The answer silenced Luiz, as he had silenced Boaz. He was relieved to be let alone, and breathed quietly. He stared at the man in command of the regulars—knew that one's mind without the help of the dus, the cool mistrust, the almost-hate that would let the human kill. Dead eyes, unlike the liveliness of the mri among brothers: Havener, who had seen evils in plenty. There was a burn scar on one cheek, that the man had not had repaired. A line man, by that, no rear-lines officer. He had respect for this one.

And the man, perhaps, estimated him. Eyes locked, clashed. *Renegade*, that was the thought that went visibly through the man's gaze; it wondered, but it did not forgive. Such a man Ducan well understood.

This man he would kill first if they laid hands on him. The dus would care for the others.

Let them not touch me, he thought then, over and over, for he remembered why he had come, and what was hazarded on his life; but still outwardly he kept that quiet that he had maintained, hands folded, eyes unfocused, sometimes closed. There was need for the moment only of rest.

At last came maneuvering for dock, and the gentle collision. Neither Boaz nor Luiz had been there for some time ... consulting, doubtless, with higher authority.

And Luiz nodded toward the door.

"You will have to leave your weapons," Luiz said. "That is the simplest way; otherwise they'll force it, and we'd rather not have that."

Duncan rose, weighed the situation, finally loosed the belt of the *yin'ein* and the lesser one of the *zahen'ein*, turned and laid them on the bench he had quitted.

"Boz," he said, "you bring them for me. I will be needing them."

She moved to gather them up, did so carefully.

"And the dus stays," Luiz said.

"That is wise," he said; he had not wanted the beast thrown into the stress of things to come. "It will stay here. Have you made all your conditions?"

Luiz nodded, and the guards took positions to escort him out. He felt strangely light without his weapons. He paused, looked at the dus, spoke to it, and it moaned and settled unhappily, head on paws. He looked back at Boaz. "I would not let anyone try to touch him if I were you," he said.

And he went with the guard.

Saber's polished metal corridors rang with the sound of doors sealing and unsealing. Duncan waited as another detachment of regulars arranged itself to take charge of him.

And little as he had given notice to these professionals, he gave it to the freckled man that commanded the group from *Saber*.

"Galey," he said.

The regular looked at him, tried to stiffen his back, turned it into a shrug. "I got this because I knew you. Sir, come along. The admiral will see you. Let's keep this quiet, all right?"

"I came here to see him," Duncan said. Galey looked relieved.

"You all right? You walked in, they said. You're coming in of your own accord?"

Duncan nodded, mri-wise. "Yes," he amended. "Of my choice."

"I have to search you."

Duncan considered it, considered Galey, who had no choice, and nodded consent, stood with his arms wide while Galey performed the cursory search himself. When Galey was done, he rearranged his robes and stood still.

"I've got a uniform might fit," Galey said.

"No."

Galey looked taken aback at that. He nodded at the others.

They started to move, and Duncan went beside Galey, but there were rifles before and rifles at his back.

A taint was in the air, an old and familiar smell, dank and musky. *Humanity,* Duncan thought; but there was an edge of it he had not noticed on the other ship.

Regul.

Duncan stopped. A rifle prodded his back. He drew a full breath of the tainted air and started walking again, keeping with Galey.

The office door was open; he turned where he knew he must, and Galey went with him into the office, into the admiral's presence.

Koch occupied the desk chair.

And beside him was a regul, sled-bound. Duncan looked into that bony countenance with his heart slamming against his ribs: the feeling was reciprocated. The regul's nostrils snapped shut.

"Ally, sir?" Duncan asked of Koch, before he had been invited to speak, before anyone had spoken.

"Sharn Alagn-ni." The admiral's eyes were dark and narrow as the regul's. His white, close-shaven head was balder than it had been, his face thinner and harder. "Sit down, Sur-Tac."

Duncan sat, on the chair at the corner of the desk, leaned back and stared from Koch to the regul. "Am I going to have to give my report in front of a stranger?"

"An ally. This is a joint command."

Pieces sorted into order. "An ally," Duncan said, looking full at Sharn, "who tried to kill us and who destroyed my ship."

The regul hissed. "Bai Koch, this is a mri. This is nothing of yours. It speaks for its own purposes, this youngling-with-out-a-nest. We have seen the way these mri have passed, the places without life. We have seen their work. This impressionable youngling has been impressed by them, and it is theirs."

"I left beacons," Duncan said, looking at Koch, "to explain. Did you read them? Did anyone listen to my messages before you started firing—or did someone get to them first?"

Koch's eyes flickered, no more than that. Darker color came to Sharn's rough skin.

"I told you in those messages that the mri were inclined to friendship. That we reached agreement."

Sharn hissed suddenly: the color fled. "Treachery."

"In both our houses," Duncan said. "Bai Sharn, I was sent to approach the mri—as you were surely sent to stop me. We may be the only ones in this room who really understand each other."

"You are doing yourself no good," said Koch.

Duncan shrugged. "Am I right about the beacons? Was it Sharn who chose to move against the cities?"

"We were fired on," Koch said.

"From my ship? Was it not the regul that came in first?"

Koch was silent.

"You have done murder," Duncan said. "The mri would have chosen to talk; but you let the regul come in ahead of you. Defenses have been triggered. The mri no longer have control of them. You are fighting against machines. And when you stop, they will stop. If you go on, you will wipe out a planet."

"That might be the safest course."

Duncan retreated to a distant cold place within himself, continued to stare at the admiral. "*Flower* witnesses what you do. What you do here will be told; and it will change human-kind. Perhaps you don't understand that, but it will change you if you do this. You will put the finishing touch on the desert of stars that you have traveled. You will be the monsters."

"Nonsense."

"You know what I mean. *Flower* is your conscience. Stavros—whoever sent them—did right. There will be witnesses. The lieutenant here—others in your crew—they will be witnesses. You are warring against a dying people, killing an ancient, ancient world." His eyes wandered to Sharn, who sat with nose-slits completely closed. "And you likewise. Bai Sharn, do you think that you want humanity without the mri? Think on checks and balances. Look at your present allies. Either without the other is dangerous to regul. Do not think that humankind loves you. Look at me, bai Sharn."

The bai's nostrils fluttered rapidly. "Kill this youngling. Be rid of it and its counsels, bai Koch. It is poisonous."

Duncan looked back to Koch, to the cold and level stare that refused to be ruffled by him or by Sharn, and of a sudden, thinking of humans again, he knew this one too:

Havener, full of hate. A mri could not hold such opinions as ran in Koch: a mri had allegiance to a she'pan, and a she'pan considered for the ages.

"You want to kill them," he said to Koch. "And you are thinking perhaps that you will hold me here as a source of information. I will tell you what I know. But I would prefer to tell you without the presence of the bai."

He had set Koch at disadvantage. Koch had to dismiss Sharn or keep her, and either was a decision.

"Do your explaining to the security chief," Koch said. "The report will reach me."

"I will say nothing to them," Duncan said.

Koch sat and stared at him, and perhaps believed him. Red flooded his face and stayed there; a vein beat at his temple. "What is it you have to say, then?"

"First, that when I am done, I am leaving. I have left the Service. I am second to the kel'anth of the mri. If you hold me, that is your choice, but I am no longer under orders of Stavros or of your service."

"You are a deserter."

Duncan released a gentle breath. "I was set aboard a mri ship to learn them. I was thrown away. The she'pan gathered me up again."

Koch was silent a long time. Finally he opened his desk, drew out a sheet of paper, slid it across the desk. Duncan reached for it, finding the blockish print strange to his eyes.

Code numbers. One was his. *Credentials, special liaison Sten X Duncan: detached from Service 9/4/21 mission code Prober. Authorization code Phoenix, limitations encoded file SS-DS-34. By my authority, this date, George T. Stavros, governor, Kesrith Zone.*

Duncan looked up.

"Your authorizations," said Koch, "are for mediation—at my discretion. Your defection was anticipated."

Duncan folded the paper, carefully, put it into his belt, and all the while rage was building in him. He smothered the impulses. *If I can make you angry,* Niun had said once, *I have passed your guard again. I have given you something to think about besides the Game.*

He looked at Sharn, whose nostrils trembled, whose bony lips were clamped shut.

"If there is no further firing," said Koch, "we will cease fire."

"That relieves my mind," Duncan said from that same cold distance.

"And we will land, and establish that things are permanently settled."

"I will arrange cease-fire. Set me on-world again."

"Do not," said Sharn. "The bai will take a harsh view of any accommodation with these creatures."

"Do you," Duncan asked cynically, "fear a mri's memory?"

Sharn's nostrils snapped shut and color came and went in her skin. Her fingers moved on her console, rapidly, and still she stared at them both.

"Mri can adapt to non-mri," Duncan said. "I am living proof that it is possible."

Koch's dark eyes wandered over him. "Drop the veil, Sur-Tac."

Duncan did so, stared at the man naked-faced.

"You do not find it easy," Koch said.

"I have not passed far enough that you can't deal with me. I am what Stavros, perhaps, intended. I am useful to you. I can get a she'pan of the People to talk, and that is more than you could win by any other means."

"You can spare a day. Firing has stopped, while we maintain our distance. You will debrief."

"Yes. I will talk to Boaz."

"She is not qualified."

"More than your security people, she is qualified. Her work makes her qualified. I will talk to her. She can understand what I say. They wouldn't. They would try to interpret."

"One of the security personnel will be there. He will suggest questions."

"I will answer what I think proper. I will not help you locate the mri."

"You know, then, where their headquarters are."

Duncan smiled. "Rock and sand, dune and flats. That is where you will have to find them. Nothing else will you get from me."

"We will find you again when we want you."

"I will be easy to find. Just send *Flower* to the same landing site and wait. I will come, eventually."

Koch gnawed at his lip. "You can deliver a settlement in this?"

"Yes."

"I distrust your confidence."

"They will listen to me. I speak to them in their own language."

"Doubtless you do. Go do your talking to Boaz."

"I want a shuttlecraft ready."

Koch frowned.

"I will need it," Duncan said. "Or arrange me transport your own way. I would advise sending me back relatively quickly. The mri will not be easy to find. It may take some time."

Koch swore softly. "Boaz can have ten hours of you. Go on. Dismissed."

Duncan veiled himself and rose, folded his arms and made the slight inclination of the head that was respect.

And among the guard that had remained at the door, he started out.

A squat shadow was there. He hurled himself back. A regul hand closed on his arm with crushing strength. The regul shrilled at him, and he twisted in that grip; a blade burned his ribs, passing across them.

Security moved. Human bodies interceded, and the regul lost balance, went down, dragging Duncan with him. Galey's boot slammed down repeatedly on the regul's wrist, trying to shake the knife loose.

Duncan wrenched over, ripped a pistol from its owner's holster and turned. Men reached for him, hurled themselves for him.

Sharn.

The regul's dark eyes showed white round the edges, terror. Duncan fired, went loose as the guard's seized him, let them have the pistol easily.

He had removed the People's enemy. The others, the younglings, were nothing. He drew a deep breath as the guards set him on his feet, and regarded the collapsed bulk in the sled with a sober regret.

And Koch was on his feet, red-faced, nostrils white-edged.

"I serve the she'pan of the People," Duncan said quietly, refusing to struggle in the hands that held him. "I have done an execution. Now do yours or let me go and serve both our interests. The regul know what I am. They will not be surprised. You know this. I can give you that peace with Kutath now."

In the corner the regul youngling, released, disarmed, crept to the side of the sled. A curious bubbling sound came from it, regul grief. Dark eyes stared up at Duncan. He ignored it.

"Go," said Koch. The anger on his face had somewhat subsided. There was a curious calculation in his eyes. He looked at the guard, at Galey. "He will go with you. Don't set hands on him."

Duncan shook his arms free, adjusted his robes, walked from the room, passing through a confused knot of regul younglings that gathered outside. One, more adult than youngling, stared at him with nostrils flaring and shutting in extreme agitation, darted behind another as he passed.

Quietly, without a glance at the humans who lined the corridor to stare, Duncan passed back to *Flower*.

"What are you going to do now?" Boaz asked after long silence.

Duncan looked at the tape. Boaz turned it off. He sat cross-legged on the large chair, elbows on knees, not choosing the floor in deference to Boaz.

"What I said. Absolutely what I said."

"Reason with mri?"

"You yourself don't think it's possible."

"You're the expert," she said. "Tell me."

"It's possible, Boz. It's possible. On mri terms."

"After murder."

He blinked slowly. He was veiled. He was not comfortable among them, even here, even in conditions of hospitality. "I did what had to be done. No other could have done it."

"Revenge?"

"Practicality."

"They do not hold resentment toward the regul, you say."

"They have forgotten the regul. It is a Dark ago. I have wiped the present slate clean. It is over, Boz. Clean."

"And your hands?"

"No regret."

She was silent a time, and whatever she would have said, she did not say. It was like a veil upon her eyes, that sudden distance in them. "Yes. I imagine there is not."

"There was a woman whom the regul caused to be killed. She was not the only one."

"I am glad there is that much left in you."

"It was not for her that I killed the regul."

Boz went silent on him again. There was less and less that remained possible to say.

"I will remember the other Sten Duncan," she said at last.

"He is the only one you will understand."

She rose, gathered up his weapons from the counter, gave them back to him. "Galey is going to fly you down. He asked to. I think he has delusions that he knows you. The dus is shut in the hatch-way."

"Yes." He knew where the dus was. It knew his presence too, and remained calm. He buckled on the weapons, familiar weight, touched the *j'tal* that was his, straightening the belts. "I'd like to be away now."

"It's arranged. There's a signal beacon provided in a kit they want you to carry. They want you to use it when you can provide them a meeting."

"I will need awhile." He walked to the door, stopped, and thought of unveiling, of giving that one gesture to what had been a friend.

He did not feel it welcome.

He went out among the guards that waited, and did not look back.

And with the dus beside him he descended to the shuttle bay, accepted from security the kit that they provided; he left the guards there and walked the ramp to the ship, the first moment that he had been free of them.

He entered and went through to controls, where Galey waited.

Brave man, Galey. Duncan looked at him critically as the man rose to meet him, giving place to the dus that crowded between. *Afraid:* he felt that in the dus-feelings; but something else had driven Galey to be present despite that.

Loyalty?

He did not know to what, or why, or how he could have stirred that in a man he hardly knew . . . only that they two had walked Sil'athen—that this man, too, had known the outback of Kesrith, as few of his kind had seen it.

He gave his hand to Galey, human-fashion, and Galey's hand was damp.

"Got some idea where you want to go?"

"Let me out by the ship, at *Flower*'s recent landing site. I'll manage."

"Sir," Galey said.

He settled into his place at controls; Duncan took the seat beside him, buckled in while the dus wedged itself in firmly, anchoring itself: spacewise, the beast.

Lights flared. Duncan watched Galey's intent face, green-dyed in the light of the instruments. The port opened and the shuttle flung itself outward, toward the world.

"High polar," Duncan advised. "Defenses are still active."

"We know the route," said Galey. "We've used it."

And thereafter was little to say. The ground rushed up at them, became mountains and dunes over which the shuttle flew with decreasing speed.

There was the sea chasm, their guide home. The dus, feeling braver now, stood up and braced itself on four legs. Duncan soothed it with his fingers, and it began to rumble its pleasure sound, picking up that which was in his mind.

The shuttle settled, touched, rested. The hatch opened.

The cold, thin air of Kutath came to him. He freed himself of the harness and stood up, took his hand from the dus as he gathered up his kit and walked back to the hatch. He heard Galey rise behind him, paused and looked back at him.

"You're all right?" Galey asked strangely.

"Yes." He took about his face the extra lap of the veil that made the change in air more bearable, and gazed again at the wilderness that lay beyond the hatch. He started forward, down the ramp, and the dus padded at his heels, down to the sand, that had the comfortable feeling of reality after the world above.

Home.

He set his face toward the sea chasm, a false direction first. He would take the true one when light faded, when he was sure that there were none to watch him. He would bury the kit in the rocks there against future need, not trusting to bring any human gift among the mri; his weapons also he would strip and examine, distrusting what had been out of his hands among them. They would not trace him.

The she'pan's service. The wild, fresh land. He inhaled the wind, and only when he had come a considerable distance did it begin to worry at him that he had not heard the shuttle lift.

He looked back and saw a small figure standing in the hatchway, watching him.

He turned and kept walking, and finally heard it go.

It passed over. He looked up, saw the shuttle bend a turn as if in salute, and depart.

DAW

C.J. CHERRYH
THE ALLIANCE-UNION UNIVERSE

The Company Wars

☐ DOWNBELOW STATION   (UE2431—$4.50)

The Era of Rapprochement

☐ SERPENT'S REACH   (UE2088—$3.50)
☐ FORTY THOUSAND IN GEHENNA   (UE2429—$4.50)
☐ MERCHANTER'S LUCK   (UE2139—$3.50)

The Chanur Novels

☐ THE PRIDE OF CHANUR   (UE2292—$3.95)
☐ CHANUR'S VENTURE   (UE2293—$3.95)
☐ THE KIF STRIKE BACK   (UE2184—$3.95)
☐ CHANUR'S HOMECOMING   (UE2177—$3.95)

The Mri Wars

☐ THE FADED SUN: KESRITH   (UE2449—$4.50)
☐ THE FADED SUN: SHON'JIR   (UE2448—$4.50)
☐ THE FADED SUN: KUTATH   (UE2133—$4.50)

Merovingen Nights (Mri Wars Period)

☐ ANGEL WITH THE SWORD   (UE2143—$3.50)

Merovingen Nights—Anthologies

☐ FESTIVAL MOON (#1)   (UE2192—$3.50)
☐ FEVER SEASON (#2)   (UE2224—$3.50)
☐ TROUBLED WATERS (#3)   (UE2271—$3.50)
☐ SMUGGLER'S GOLD (#4)   (UE2299—$3.50)
☐ DIVINE RIGHT (#5)   (UE2380—$3.95)
☐ FLOOD TIDE (#6)   (UE2452—$4.50)

The Age of Exploration

☐ CUCKOO'S EGG   (UE2371—$4.50)
☐ VOYAGER IN NIGHT   (UE2107—$2.95)
☐ PORT ETERNITY   (UE2206—$2.95)

The Hanan Rebellion

☐ BROTHERS OF EARTH   (UE2290—$3.95)
☐ HUNTER OF WORLDS   (UE2217—$2.95)